PULSE

Sequel to Collide Volume 1

Gail McHugh

Visit my website at
http://www.facebook.com/AuthorGailMcHugh?ref=hl

Dedicated to women out there who have yet to find their voice, strength and courage. Never let them strip you of what you were born with. Take it back.

CHAPTER ONE

A Missed Last Encounter

Emily leaned her head against the taxi window, watching the city lights of Manhattan with tear-soaked eyes. In a blur, the look on Gavin's face as he walked away from her a few hours before rushed through her mind. The closer she got to his building, and the further away she got from her past with Dillon, the more she felt as though her sanity and heart were hanging by a delicate thread. She shifted restlessly and her gaze fell on the glowing green light of the digital clock. It was nearly one o'clock in the morning. A glimmer of hope flooded her body, and she squeezed her eyes shut, praying Gavin would take her back. As the taxi pulled up in front of his high-rise, she reached in her purse and pulled out a wad of cash. After handing the unknown amount to the driver, she swung open the door and stepped onto the sidewalk.

"Hey!" the Middle Eastern driver called. "You have to close the door, lady!"

Emily heard his words but paid him no mind. Her fumbling feet pushed her forward, kept her moving toward what she hoped would be a new start. A new future with the man she knew she couldn't live without. She pulled open the door and crossed the lobby. Sweat clung like decay across her flesh. With a trembling hand, she pressed the button for the elevator. Her nerves skyrocketed with love and anxiety. Once the elevator doors opened, she stepped inside and leaned against the wall, physically and mentally exhausted. As she tried to stop shaking, tears steadily fell. Unsure of Gavin's reaction, Emily struggled to pull in a decent breath.

She tried to tamp down the wicked emotions curling through her. The doors opened to what would either be a new beginning... or an end. Feet glued to the ground, she stood frozen for a moment, her eyes trained on the wall across the hallway. Vaguely aware of the elevator doors gliding closed, she became dizzy as she lifted her hand to hold it open. Slowly, she stepped out. Her vision tunneled as she turned toward Gavin's penthouse, and her mind spun out of control with every possible scenario. She strained to focus on his words from earlier, allowing her fear to wane as her feet led her closer. Her pace quickened with every step.

Once she reached his unit, her fears returned with a vengeance, anchoring heavy in her chest. With trepidation, she knocked on his door, each knock mimicking the fierce pounding of her heart. She wiped away tears as her body trembled from head to toe. The minutes ticked by with no answer, and she knocked again, harder.

"Please answer." She chanted the silent prayer while ringing his doorbell.

With tears trickling down her cheeks, she stared at the peephole, envisioning him staring back. The thought of him watching her stung and cut a path through her heart.

"Please," she cried, ringing the doorbell again. "God, Gavin, please. I love you. I'm so sorry."

Nothing.

Hands still shaking, she reached in her purse and pulled out her cell phone. She dialed Gavin's number. Eyes locked on his door, she listened to it ring over and over again.

"You've reached Gavin Blake. You know what to do."

Emily's heart clenched, tightened, and dropped into the pit in her stomach when she heard his voice. That sweet voice would forever haunt her if he didn't take her back. That sweet, pleading voice that had begged her to believe him. She hung up, dialed again, and listened once more. She didn't speak. She couldn't. Her frantic breathing would be the only message he would receive.

Words… she had none.

Emily pressed a hand to her mouth as the realization he wasn't forgiving her set in. For a few painful moments, she was silent. Then grief erupted in her chest. A torrent of tears flew down her cheeks. Her cries echoed throughout the hallway. She retreated and felt her back hit the wall. She stared at his door, the vivid memory of his face ingrained in her head. Searing pain surged and twisted in her gut as she slowly made her way into the elevator, her heart plummeting with its descent.

Shoulders slumped and spirit broken, Emily unlocked the door to her apartment. A small light above the stove cast a faint glow across the living room. Quieting her footsteps, so as not to wake Olivia, Emily made her way into her bedroom. Still shaking, a cloak of sadness enveloped her as she padded into her bathroom.

She flipped on the light and stared at her reflection. The green eyes, once vivid with hope, held no semblance of life. She ran her fingers over her cheeks, muddied with mascara. Her face looked pale. Even worse, her heart was stricken with loss. She flattened her palms against the cool marble surface of the sink, hung her head, and wept, gulping for air as pain so deep blanketed her soul. Regret in the most brutal form tightened like an unforgiving noose around her neck.

She tried to calm down by turning on the hot water and splashing her face. After reaching for a towel, she dried herself and shut off the light. Fatigue slowed her feet as she made her way to her bed, and she curled up on her side. Exhausted, she sank into the mattress, attempting to gain a few hours of sleep. But that wouldn't come.

No.

As seconds, minutes, and hours ticked by, Gavin's pained face and confused blue eyes invaded Emily's conscience. She drew in a shaky breath, rolled onto her back, and stared at the ceiling. Over the next few hours, swells of gut-wrenching pain rippled across her heart. She'd let him slip through her fingers.

Trying to ignore the ear-piercing sound of Blake Industries' private jet's engines firing up, Gavin wondered if Emily would remember things he'd never forget. Wondered how this was truly the end. He'd lost her. In less than seven hours, she would be Dillon's for good.

He tugged his suitcase from the back of Colton's Jeep, his heart sinking further into his stomach as he peered into the clear, cold night sky. Colton stepped onto the tarmac, his expression no more at ease than it'd been when Gavin came to him.

"You don't have to do this, little man," Colton yelled, tufts of his dark hair whipping around in the engines' fury. "Bouncing out of the city in the middle of the night won't bring her back."

Gavin wasn't sure if leaving would erase the mark Emily had seared into his soul. He also wasn't sure if he'd ever be free from the ache of needing her. The only emotion he truly fucking owned… he knew he had to get out of New York. Get the fuck out, and get far away from the ghost of Emily that would no doubt haunt him.

"I told you, I need to get off the grid for a while, Colton," Gavin argued, roughing a hand over his face. "I can't be here. Just take care of switching our stocks out of Dillon's hands."

Colton released a weighty breath and nodded. "I'll take care of it first thing Monday morning." He clapped Gavin's shoulder, his eyes softening. "You have to be good with all of this when you get back. Promise me you'll put Emily to rest while you're down there."

Gavin's chest palpitated at the sound of her name. "Yeah," he replied, his voice grave. "I'll try."

After a few moments of staring at one another, Gavin climbed the stairs to the jet. Turning, he watched his brother drive off the property of the small, private airport. Mind-fucked and in the deepest turmoil of his life, Gavin dug into the pocket of his jeans and pulled out his cell phone. Without looking at it, he tossed it onto the runway. It shattered when it hit the ground. Off the grid meant off the grid. No contact with anyone. No one trying to pull him from his pain, and no one trying to convince him his actions were destructive. After handing his bags to the flight attendant, the pilot came out to greet him.

"Good evening, Mr. Blake." The pilot firmly shook Gavin's hand. His gray hair spilled over his forehead. "Everything you've requested has been prepared, and we should arrive in Playa del Carmen in just over four hours, sir."

Gavin gave a weak nod and headed into his private cabin. He closed the door, and his eyes immediately landed on a bottle of bourbon screaming his name on the minibar. He gazed at it with contempt. Darkness seeped in around him. He peeled off his coat and tossed it onto the bed. Trying to stave off the evil angel invading his thoughts, he strode across the small space and reached for the mind-numbing amber liquid. Deciding to forgo a glass, he twisted off the cap and brought the bottle to his lips. The alcohol burned down his throat, offering up not an ounce of reprieve from his pain.

It was then Gavin knew there would never be a time in his life he wouldn't be aware of Emily's absence. Drunk or sober, she would riddle his heart and soul until the day he died. He loved her. Breathed her in as if she were the air around him... the air he would be deprived of forever. He placed the bottle down, ran an exhausted hand through his hair, and attempted to cast visions of Emily's beautiful eyes staring back at him from his memory. He walked over to the window, peering out at the city below, and knew it didn't work. Nothing would. Neither soaking his pain in alcohol nor running from her could mend what he was feeling.

She was gone. As the twinkling lights faded with the jet's climbing altitude, Gavin's heart continued to mourn the woman he'd lost while his mind wondered how long he would be at her funeral.

With the morning light sucking the last of the stars from the sky, and without a minute of sleep claimed, Emily sat up and made her way into the kitchen. Nausea filled her stomach. She reached for the refrigerator door, pulled it open, and grabbed a bottle of water. She sank into a seat at the table as Olivia rounded the corner.

"Hmm, I see Douchenugget dropped you off early this morning," Olivia clipped, giving Emily a quick once-over. She walked over to one of the cabinets and tugged it open. "How nice of him to allow his bride to actually get ready on her wedding day at *her* place."

"Olivia, I'm—"

"Before you defend Dillmonster, or your delusional thoughts, Emily, I want you to know how upset Gavin was last night." Olivia slammed the cabinet closed. "I've never seen him so hurt."

Emily closed her stinging eyes, her heart constricting at the thought of the pain she'd caused Gavin. She shook her head. "Olivia, please. I'm not—"

"I know, Emily. You're not in the mood to talk about this," she huffed, yanking open another cabinet. "Or let me guess, you're not delusional thinking you should marry Dillon because you don't believe Gavin?"

"Olivia," Emily let out, rising. "You're not listening to me. I'm not—"

Olivia whipped around, her brown eyes narrowed. "I fucking hate saying this, Em, but I can't be a part of this today. You love Gavin, and Gavin loves you. Done deal. I believe Gavin, and even if you don't, you're forcing me to choose." She placed one hand on her hip and rushed the other through her thick blonde hair. "I'm sorry, but I'm not going to the wedding today."

"Good, because neither am I," Emily whispered, sitting back down. "I'm not marrying Dillon."

Eyes wide with shock, a smile split Olivia's face. "You're not?" she gasped, rushing to Emily's side.

Emily shook her head as a fresh round of tears seeped from her eyes.

Olivia kneeled beside her and wrapped her arms around Emily's waist. Her words tumbled out against Emily's stomach. "Oh my God, oh my God. You're so not on my shit list anymore. I fucking love you to death right now!"

"I hurt Gavin." Emily nearly choked over her words. "I wanted to believe him, and part of me did I guess, but I was afraid, and now it's too late."

Confusion peppered Olivia's expression as she stood, bringing Emily with her. She cupped Emily's cheeks. "It's not too late. As soon as you call him, he'll forget everything. Gavin loves you. He was pissed last night, but he would die for you. Believe me. That's all he kept saying."

Trembling, Emily sucked in an unsteady breath. "No. I went to his penthouse last night, and he didn't open his door." She backed away from Olivia and tucked herself into a seat at the table. "I called his phone a few times, and he didn't answer. He's done with me, and I deserve every bit of pain coming to me." Emily shook her head, her voice trailing off. "I can't believe I let this happen."

"He didn't have me take him home last night." Olivia dropped to her knees again and grabbed Emily's hands. "From the rehearsal dinner, he had me bring him by Colton's house. What happened sobered him up a little, but I'm pretty damn sure homeboy's still knocked out. Think about how tanked he was. It's only seven in the morning. He probably didn't hear his phone. I'll call him in a little while, but you need to try to calm down, okay?"

Emily slowly pulled her hands away and pressed the heels of her palms against her eyes. She reluctantly nodded, swallowing down some of the worry coursing through her mind. "Okay, I'll try to calm down."

A slow smile touched the edge of Olivia's mouth. "I'm proud of you, Emily."

"Proud of me?" she questioned, wiping her nose with the back of her hand. "For what? For hurting Gavin? His face, Olivia. I can't get his face out of my head."

Eyes softening, Olivia brushed her hand against Emily's jaw. "I'm proud of you for finally seeing you *deserve* a better life with a man who honestly loves and cares for you. Again, you may have temporarily hurt Gavin, but the two of you are going to be fine. You'll see."

Emily stared at Olivia and allowed a flutter of hope to settle through her limbs. She nodded, praying Olivia's statement would prove true.

"All right," Olivia said, standing and looking at her watch, "your *un*-wedding day is supposed take place in a little less than four hours. What do you need me to do, other than go get us some coffee because there's none here? You definitely look like you can use a cup, and I know I can, too." Olivia walked to the hall closet, pulled out her coat, and slipped it on. "Do you want me to call your sister?" She halted midstride. "Better yet, can I call your *ex*-future husband and tell him to fuck off?"

Emily rose and moved across the kitchen. She grabbed a paper towel and blew her nose. The thought of Dillon waking to find her gone sent chills up her spine. "He doesn't know yet."

Confusion pinched Olivia's forehead. "What do you mean? I thought—"

"I left after he fell asleep," Emily interrupted, rushing her hands over her face. "He has no idea. You're the only one who knows."

Olivia's jaw dropped open, her eyes wide. "Umm… okay. I could be wrong, but shouldn't the expectant groom know this?"

On a sigh, Emily walked past Olivia into her bedroom. She started rummaging through her dresser drawers. Other than Gavin, the only thing she craved was a long, hot shower. "Yes, Olivia. I need to clean myself up, and when I'm done, I'm going to call him."

Olivia leaned against the doorway, concern edging her eyes. "Can you at least wait until I get back from the coffee shop? I'll shoot Lisa and Michael a call to let them know what's going on, okay?"

Knowing Olivia was worried, Emily slid her drawer closed and gazed at her. "Yes. I'll wait." She walked over to Olivia, her eyes soft. "Thank you."

Olivia cupped Emily's chin, giving it a light shake. "You're welcome. Go ahead. Get in your shower, and I'll be back in a few."

Emily nodded and watched her leave. After the front door snapped shut, Emily couldn't help but feel dread scorching her stomach. Confronting Dillon, with or without Gavin by her side, wouldn't be easy. She sighed, trying to ignore its festering presence. She made her way into the bathroom, set her sweatpants and sweatshirt on the vanity, and turned on the water. As hot steam curled through the air, she stripped last night's clothing from her body and slipped into the shower. She reached for the bar of soap and slowly ran it across the aching flesh between her legs as visions of what she'd allowed Dillon to do to her invaded her thoughts. With her head hung low in shame, her drenched auburn hair formed a curtain over her face. Her every muscle felt bruised, but the soreness paled in comparison to her battered and beaten heart.

She sank further into the darkest recess of her mind, replaying what he'd done last night over and over. It was nothing short of a nightmare. It was then she realized the enormity of what she'd allowed him to get away with over the past year. The awareness of how she'd deceived herself into thinking he loved her, cared for her, for them, knocked the air from her. The overwhelming, deep-seeded obligation she'd felt toward him for the things he'd helped her with, was something she knew brought her to this very moment. Anger at herself swelled, bubbling low in her belly as she scrubbed faster, harder at her flesh, over her arms, face, and legs. She wanted to remove his very existence from her pores. She turned the water on hotter and cringed at the way she let him manipulate her every action.

Her every thought.

Crying, she sucked in a deep breath and tried to pull herself back together. Dillon was no more. They were no more. He was gone. Through her daze, Emily placed the soap down, rinsed her body of not only bubbles lathering her skin, but also the malicious venom he'd poured into her soul. She stepped from the shower, reached for a towel, and pulled it around herself. Standing before the mirror, she glanced at the woman she'd part ways with. Forever.

"Never again," she whispered. She shook her head, smoothed her hands over her cheeks, and pressed her eyes closed. "Never."

After taking a moment to reflect on the insanity the day promised to bring, Emily slipped into her clothing, dried her hair, and made her way back into her bedroom. She jerked to a halt when she heard her phone buzz, the sound alerting her there was a message waiting. Taking hold, sudden anxiety it was Dillon and possible hope it could be from Gavin rushed through her mind. Swallowing, she edged toward the nightstand and, with a trembling hand, reached for her phone.

Both her anxiety and hope evaporated upon seeing it was a voice mail from Lisa. Emily gave into the fatigue chasing her, sank onto her bed, and rested her head on a pillow. As she listened to her sister's concerned voice, Emily heard the front door creaking open. She sat up and took in the last few seconds of Lisa's message, notifying her that she and Michael were on their way.

"Liv?" Emily called as she slid her phone shut. She tossed it onto the bed, ran a palm over her face, and stood to make her way into the other room. "I hope you got something to eat while…"

She paused in the living room archway, her words trailing off. Startled, she froze, silent and alert, when she found Dillon casually leaning against the counter. His eyes traced over her as he sipped orange juice from a glass.

"When I woke up, you were gone, Emily." After setting down the glass, he sauntered over, a cocky smirk plastered on his face. "That excited to get back here and get all prettied up so you can marry me today, huh?" He brushed his fingers against her cheek. "I figured I'd stop by before I went to Trevor's to get ready."

"Get away from me, Dillon," she whispered, her voice shaky. She jerked away, trying to hide the fear rushing through her veins.

Dillon blinked, clearing the roughness from his throat. With narrowed eyes, his face filled with confusion. "*What?*" he asked, stepping closer and grabbing her upper arm.

Emily yanked it from his firm grasp, her shoulder slamming against a curio cabinet as she stumbled back. "You heard me. I said get the *fuck* away from me." Her words dropped from her mouth in a low hiss. "I'm done, Dillon. This"—she pointed between them—"is over. I'm *no* longer your willing victim."

Before she knew it, he had her pinned against the wall, one hand gripping her hair as the other clenched her chin. He ran his tongue across his bottom lip and studied her. "You did fuck him, didn't you?"

Though a small cry pressed from Emily's mouth from the pain searing her skull, her answer dripped out as a sneer. "*Yes*, I fucked him. *Yes*, I'm in love with him, and *no*, I'm not now, nor will I *ever* marry you." Even as fear doused Emily's limbs, a sense of relief and freedom took over, rooting somewhere deep inside.

For half a heartbeat, she closed her eyes, allowing visions of Gavin to seep into her thoughts, but a hard crack to her cheek from the back of

Dillon's hand sent her eyes wide open. The sting rippled across her flesh as she thrashed her fists against his chest in an attempt to break free.

With one hand still tangled in her hair, Dillon jostled her across the room like a worn out little toy. Landing on all fours against the wooden floor, Emily tried to stand, but Dillon grabbed her hair and forced her down.

"You sick fuck!" she screamed, curling her hands around his wrists as he hovered above her.

Dillon dropped to his knees and yanked her head back, forcing her to look into his eyes. "After everything I've done for you, you turn around and fuck him behind my back?" he snarled, fisting her hair tighter.

Pulse thudding and using every bit of her strength, Emily clawed and dug her nails into his skin as she tried to untangle his hands from her hair. "You've done nothing for me but break me down!" she cried. When he wouldn't release her, a jeering smile split her face. Tears slipped down her cheeks. "I wish I could've fucked him right in front of you!"

Eyes glacial, hollow, and darker than the night sky, Dillon struck her face again. Emily felt the skin above her brow rip open, pain needling over her flesh. A gasp tore past her lips as warm, thick blood trickled along her temple, snaking down her cheekbone.

Still gripping her hair, Dillon pulled her up and hauled her body against his chest. Daring to meet his eyes, Emily swallowed down fear coating her throat as Dillon pegged her with a look telling her this torture wasn't over. With a rush of anger and adrenaline slicking through her nerves, she clawed at his face, digging her thumb nails into his eyes. Tiny slivers of blood streaked across Dillon's lids as a howl of pain scraped from deep within his throat.

Somewhere above the twisted havoc raking hard in her mind, Emily registered the sound of the front door swinging open, followed by Lisa's screams. In a flurry of commotion, Michael rushed up behind Dillon, grabbing him under the arms. Michael's movements were frantic as he pulled Dillon from Emily. Both men stumbled, their limbs flailing in every direction. Michael landed on his back on the floor. Dillon fell on top of him. The loud thud echoed through the room. Michael tossed Dillon away, rolled to the side, and sprang to his feet.

With Lisa's arm curled tight around her shoulders, Emily shook uncontrollably, crying as she watched Dillon stagger up from the ground.

Michael lunged, swung his fist, and caught Dillon against his mouth. The blow split his lip. "I should've done this to you last night, asshole!" Michael spewed.

As Dillon righted himself, he stumbled forward, clenching Michael's collar. Before he could do anything, Michael's fist landed in a continuous assault against Dillon's face, knocking him clear to the floor.

A clatter of voices, including Olivia's, rang in Emily's ears as nausea churned in her stomach. She stood frozen, her cries dying in her mouth, as she watched her apartment fill with concerned neighbors and, within a few minutes, a couple of New York City police officers. After a quick explanation from Michael, one of the cops dragged Dillon to his feet and cuffed his hands behind his back.

"You're a fucking whore!" Dillon wheezed, spitting a mouthful of blood in Emily's direction. "Nothing but a fucking whore! I hope he fucks you and leaves you like all the rest, you cunt!"

Dillon's poisonous words pressed into Emily's head in a violent explosion. She felt as if she were a tiny particle of dust moving in slow motion in the middle of a roaring tornado. Though insanity whirled around her in a room filled with people, she didn't see anything… but

Gavin's face. Though one of the cops threatened to make Dillon's overnight stay a memorable one, she couldn't hear anything… but the thrumming of her broken heart. The only thing she could comprehend was the numbness flooding her veins.

She freed herself from her sister's hold and made her way toward Dillon, where he stood with a cocky smirk toying at his bloodied lip. Staring into the wicked soul of the man she'd loved for so long, the man she'd given all of herself to, and without a tear in her eye, she smacked him across the face. Unable to stop the pent up anguish from the months of hell she'd allowed him to put her through, pain erupted in her hands, down to their fragile bones, as she continued to beat her fists against his face and chest.

"You did this to me!" she screamed, struggling against one of the officers. The officer pulled Emily back as she glared at Dillon. "I loved you, and you became everything you said you never would! And you want to know something, Dillon?" she asked, her breathing a ragged mess. With the smirk falling from his face, Dillon peered over his shoulder as an officer escorted him out of the apartment. "If Gavin does leave me and never talks to me again, I deserve every second of misery I'll be in without him."

After Olivia knocked him in the head, Emily watched Dillon walk out of her life as quickly as he'd walked into it. She wrapped her arms around her stomach, thoughts of Gavin splintering through her heart as she fell to her knees. With her last bit of strength, Emily backed herself against the coffee table, dropped her face into her hands, and began to violently cry. Lisa sat beside her, pulled her into her lap, and cradled her head against her shoulder. As Lisa rocked her back and forth, Emily realized she'd saved herself from becoming another statistic.

Another silent voice.

Surprised she'd let it get so far, visions of her mother accepting the same brutal treatment from not only her father but countless other men flashed through her memory. The haunting images chilled Emily's bones.

"Shh, Emily," Lisa whispered, holding her tighter. "It's over now."

Olivia knelt beside them, her voice soft. "Are you okay?" She handed Emily an ice pack and opened a first aid kit. Taking out a bandage, Olivia tore it open and placed her hand under Emily's chin. After securing a piece of gauze with medical tape over the fresh wound above Emily's brow, Olivia frowned.

Eyes watery, Emily nodded. "Yeah, I'm all right."

The remaining officer walked over to Emily, his overly round physique making his uniform look ill-fitted. "Miss, I'm gonna need a statement from you. Paramedics should be here soon. They'll take you to the hospital if you think you need to be seen."

"No." Emily brought the icepack up to her swollen cheekbone. She flinched as it made contact with her skin. "I don't want to go to the hospital."

"That's fine," the officer replied, looking at a clipboard. "You can refuse treatment when they get here, but they still need to show up because it was a domestic violence call."

Michael sat on the ottoman, his expression piqued in question. "Emily, I think you should go get checked out."

"I agree," Lisa said, concern brimming in her eyes.

Emily rose, trying to rein in the discord fucking with her mind. She moved unsteadily across the living room to check if Gavin had called back. Lisa and Olivia scrambled to their feet and followed her into her room.

"Em," Olivia said. She lightly grabbed Emily's arm, confusion creasing her forehead. "Why don't you want to go?"

Emily turned away and pushed her hands through her hair. She reached for her phone, her heart dipping when she saw she didn't have any missed calls from Gavin. "I said no, Olivia. I don't need to go to the hospital." Tears gathered in her eyes as she slumped onto her bed. "I'm fine. I just need some aspirin and sleep."

Olivia's lips formed into a hard line. She looked over to Lisa, her expression showing equal worry.

Lisa crossed her arms and leaned against the doorway. "Emily, I swear, you can be so stubborn sometimes."

"I know," Emily whispered. "But really, I'm fine."

Olivia lifted her head and exhaled toward the ceiling. Bringing her attention back to Emily, she placed a hand on her hip. "You want to know the only reason why I'm *not* going to push this issue further with you, friend?"

Emily pressed her eyes closed and shook her head. "Why, Olivia?"

"Well, that would be because you gave Duckleberry-Finn a pretty decent beat-down before his ass was hauled outta here."

Emily lay back, rolled to her side, and hugged her knees to her chest. Normally, she would've found Olivia's comment somewhat funny. But not now. She couldn't. It was all she could do to muster a reply.

"Right," Emily said, sadness clouding her voice. She brought the ice pack up to her cheek. Eyes steeped in pain from her discomfort, she stared at Olivia. "I guess I did." Emily inhaled a deep breath, grabbed her blanket, and pulled it over her body. "When the paramedics get here, send them in. But right now, I just need to rest."

Though concern still showed on their faces, Olivia and Lisa nodded. Without another word, they walked out of the room.

Over the next half hour, Emily filled out the necessary paperwork from the officer and refused treatment when the paramedics eventually showed up. Once the room became quiet and her thoughts finally started to settle, her eyes came to rest on her phone. Picking it up, she stared at it, her face paling when she saw it was void of any messages from Gavin. Tears streamed freely down her cheeks.

Knowing she had to explain the hurt she'd inflicted upon him, she dialed his number. She chewed at the inside of her lip as she listened to it ring. When his voice mail picked up, she went to close her phone but stopped. Worry plagued her, and an ache for him, so deep, tightened in her chest.

"Gavin... I... It's Emily," she whispered, trying not to trip over the emotions climbing up her throat. "I don't expect you to talk to me ever again, but I need to say a few things." Taking a deep breath and exhaling slowly, she continued. "Dillon diminished my sense of feeling alive, Gavin. But you... you brought that back to me. When Gina opened the door that morning, I..." Emily paused, wiping away tears. "I was scared you took her back, but I should've let you explain and I didn't. I'm so sorry. I'm sorry that out of any girl in this world you could've fallen in love with, you chose me. I'm sorry I didn't believe you when I should've, and it was me who broke your heart. I love you, Gavin. I know you're the one who said you thought you loved me from the moment you saw me, but I know I loved you from the moment I saw you. Something inside me told me I was supposed to be with you, but I fought against it. So many things about you scared me at first, and then you showed me who you really are."

Unable to keep fighting the raw emotion weighing heavy on her heart, Emily broke out into hysterics. "Please forgive me for fighting *against* us, Gavin. Please forgive me for not fighting *for* us when I knew we were supposed to be together. Forgive me for being the weak mess I am. But more than anything... thank you for loving me. Thank you for your dimpled smile and your bottle caps. I'll never be able to look at one without thinking of you. Thank you for your stupid Yankees and your wiseass remarks. Thank you for wanting late night drives and sunset-watching with me. Thank you for wanting the good, the bad, and the in-between." Emily paused and shook her head, but before she could say another word, the voice mail cut her off, the long beep alerting her that her time was up.

"I'm just sorry the only thing you got from me was the bad," she whispered, staring at the ceiling as she clenched her phone to her chest.

CHAPTER TWO

Numb

In her twenty-four years of living, there were times when Emily would experience a numbness that would set in when she wanted to shut something out. She allowed her mind to let go of poison plaguing her life at certain points. These were times she welcomed it. Breathed it in like the sweet smell of roses. It was the type of numbness one could say 'cleansed her.' However, as she sat at the coffee bar in Bella Lucina, tracing and retracing numbers on her order pad, the numbness planting itself in her heart like a thick, summer weed, was something she'd never felt before. Something she didn't want to feel.

216 hours… of feeling dead.

12,960 minutes… of feeling lost.

777,600 seconds… of feeling completely numb.

Days upon days, her concentration, which seemed to be carefully knitted together by strands of hope, was fading. Lost. Even while she slept, her mind lingered on Gavin, her dreams dangerous because they reminded her he was gone. He became a beautiful vapor that disappeared into thin air, taking Emily's very existence with it. Left with broken thoughts she was sure couldn't be repaired, Emily was suffering knowing he had loved her when she least deserved it. No. This wasn't something she was prepared for, yet she knew she had to own every hour, minute, and every second of it.

"I brought table twelve another round of drinks for you," Fallon announced, sitting down next to Emily.

With her head downcast, still immersed in the amount of time that'd passed since Gavin left, Emily didn't answer.

"They also ordered a pasta primavera for the monkey that joined them." At that, Emily reluctantly brought her gaze up to Fallon's, her face filled with confusion. "Yeah. They found him on the side of the road. Apparently a circus ditched him," Fallon added, throwing her hair into a messy bun.

"Did you just say something about a monkey?" Emily questioned, her voice puzzled. "And when did you dye your hair blue?"

"Nope. I didn't mention a word about a monkey." Fallon quirked a brow, placed her elbows on the bar, and tucked her palms under her chin. "It's been blue for three days, and you've seen it already."

"Oh." Emily went back to tracing the numbers.

"What do you got there?" Before Emily could answer, Fallon swiped the order pad. "What are all of these numbers?"

"It's nothing." Emily yanked it back from Fallon's grasp.

Frowning, Fallon studied Emily's face, her expression thick with concern. "Country, I'm not trying to be dark or dismal, but that's not some kind of countdown to you killing yourself, right?"

Eyes wide in shock, Emily leaned back. "Jesus, Fallon, do you honestly think I would do that?"

"Just answer the question, Country. Is that some kind of countdown?"

Emily sighed and tapped the pad on the granite surface of the bar. "It's been nine days since he left, Fallon. Nine days since I completely destroyed him. I've called, and he hasn't answered."

"Right, but he hasn't answered anyone's calls." Fallon snaked her arm around Emily's shoulder. "Colton told Trevor the other day he hasn't even answered for him."

"I understand that, but Colton's not the reason he left. I am." Emily shook her head, trying hard to fight back tears. "He handed me his heart, and I threw it away. I made him leave his family, his friends… his entire life."

"Emily, first of all, you need to stop beating yourself up. Considering what you saw that morning, he's lucky you even believe him. I'm not saying you shouldn't, but let's be real. That was some pretty heavy shit. Second, he left because he thought you were marrying Dillon. Once he finds out you didn't, you know he'll come right back."

"He already knows I didn't marry Dillon," Emily whispered, her heart breaking all over again. "Olivia told me Colton left a message with his housekeeper. He let him know I didn't go through with it."

"Oh. I didn't know that," Fallon mumbled and looked away. She twirled a piece of her hair and brought her attention back to Emily. "Maybe he just needs more time?"

"I don't know what to think anymore." Emily rubbed her temples. "All I know is I'm lost without him."

Fallon frowned and twisted her body toward Emily. Before she could say anything, Trevor snuck up behind her and tickled her ribcage.

Eyes wide, Fallon jerked around. "Trevor!" she squeaked, garnering Antonio's unwanted attention. He glared at her from across the restaurant. Fallon bit her lip and mouthed, "Sorry." Antonio shook his head and resumed eating his lunch. "You asshole," Fallon whispered, pushing Trevor away.

Trevor chuckled and popped a kiss on top of Fallon's head. "Sorry. I forgot you were ticklish, Blue."

"Sure you did, jackass." Fallon grimaced and stood up. "What are you doing here so early? You know I'm not off for another two hours."

"I actually came to talk to Emily." Trevor looked at Emily, his smile guarded. "Are you off yet?"

"No, not yet." Emily rose, plucking her order pad from the bar. Drawing in a deep breath, she glanced at it and shoved it into her apron. "I have another half hour until my shift is over."

"Country, I can keep an eye on your tables while you talk to my *forgetful* boyfriend." After shooting Trevor a look, Fallon slung her arm over Emily's shoulder. "I'll take care of your side work, and I'll even make sure the monkey at table twelve gets dessert."

Trevor scratched his chin, his brows drawn together. "Monkey?"

"Yeah. A monkey." Fallon slapped Trevor's back and aimed a wink in Emily's direction. Trevor shrugged. "Go ahead. Talk to him, and I'll call you later."

"Are you sure?" Emily asked, pulling her hair out of its ponytail.

"Yep. I'll call you tonight." Fallon placed a chaste kiss on Trevor's cheek and walked away.

Trevor looked at Emily. "Want to go sit in a booth?"

"Sure." Emily untied her apron and made her way behind the bar. "Do you want something to drink?"

"No, I'm cool. Thanks."

After making herself a double espresso, she led Trevor to a booth tucked in the back of the restaurant. Emily slid into the seat and sipped the hot liquid. With sleep coming close to non-existent the past several days, she hoped the double shot of caffeine would shock her zombie-like system back to life.

Trevor gazed at Emily, his eyes shimmering with remorse. "First, I want to say I feel like an asshole about this whole thing with Dillon."

Emily shifted, taken aback from his sudden declaration. "Come on, Trevor, none of this is your fault."

"No, Emily, really. I need you to hear me out, all right?"

Reluctantly, Emily nodded.

"I'm sorry this is the first time I've come to see you since all this shit went down. Part of me wanted to show up the day it happened, but I couldn't. Over the past year, I watched, without saying a fucking word, as he tore you down." Trevor paused, his fingers nervously tugging at the white linen tablecloth. "I remember how vibrant you were when you two started dating, and piece by piece, he dismantled everything about you. Don't get me wrong, I think I knew things were starting to get bad, but I guess I didn't realize how bad."

Pausing again, Trevor leaned back and shook his head. "You know what? Fuck that. I need to claim responsibility here. I saw it. I saw it with my own eyes, and I should've stopped it. I could've stopped it. I had a goddamn argument with Gavin about him vilifying Dillon because he was falling in love with you." Trevor plowed both hands through his hair and let out a breath, his voice lowering to a whisper. "For fuck's sake, Gavin's been my best friend since we were kids, and I didn't take his side during any of this. I watched Dillon hit him at your rehearsal dinner and didn't do a fucking thing. Not a fucking thing."

"Trevor, please. You're not—"

"No, wait. Let me finish, Emily."

Once again, Emily nodded.

"Olivia and I were raised by a father who would've never talked to my mother the way Dillon talked to you." Trevor's gaze fell on Fallon, preparing a fresh urn of coffee behind the bar. "Damn, I love her, and I could never imagine anyone treating her the way Dillon treated you. End of story, I tucked my tail between my legs, and I can only hope you and Gavin can forgive me for being such a pussy. But what's done is done. All I can do now is try to make this right. I left Morgan and Buckingham. I didn't see the asshole when I cleared out my things, but I'm done with him and his bullshit. When I said I considered you my second sister, I meant it. A brother would never allow his sister to be treated that way." Trevor reached for Emily's hand. "I just need to know you forgive me."

With tears slipping from her eyes, Emily clenched Trevor's hand, her thoughts scattered. "I can't forgive you because I never blamed you or anyone else for this. I played the biggest part in allowing him to do this to me, so I don't want you feeling responsible."

"Well, I do feel responsible."

"No, Trevor. I let him to do this to me." Emily released Trevor's hand and pointed at her chest. "Me, not you."

"But after everything you saw growing up? Olivia told me your mom bounced from one asshole to the next. I'm thinking that has something to do with it. Me, I have no excuse."

As the memory of her mother's destructive relationships soured her mouth, Emily tore her attention from Trevor. Her gaze landed on a couple walking into the restaurant. Their laughter echoed as Fallon saw them to a table.

"Right, she did. But I should've known better than to follow in her footsteps…" Emily's voice trailed as she fought hard to regain her composure. She brought her eyes back to Trevor's.

"Well, you've taken the first step, Em, and I'm proud of you for pressing charges and getting an order of protection against him. With Gavin gone, you need to call me if the asshole tries to get in touch with you, okay?"

Emily brushed her fingertips along the healing wound above her brow. "I will. Thank you." She hesitated a moment and cleared her throat. "Can I ask you something?"

"Sure."

"You've called Gavin and left him messages, right?"

"Yeah." Trevor nodded.

Emily drew in a long breath, her hands twisting in her lap. "Please tell me you didn't let him know what Dillon did to me."

"No, I figured telling him in a message wasn't the right thing to do. But when he gets back, I plan on talking to him about it."

"Please, listen to me. I don't want him to know what happened. He'll… I don't know. Just please, can you not say anything to him?"

Trevor angled his head to the side, a current of confusion lacing his voice. "Are you asking me to hide it from him?"

A pang of apprehension pooled in Emily's stomach as she swallowed. "I am. He's been hurt enough through all of this, Trevor. If he knows about it, he'll go after Dillon."

"Why are you trying to protect Dillon?" Palpable shock sobered his features.

"God, Trevor, I'm not trying to protect *him*. I'm trying to protect Gavin. He's been gutted by all this. If he finds out, there's no way he wouldn't go after Dillon. God forbid he really hurts him and winds up in jail. Jesus, Dillon could hurt him. I wouldn't be able to live with myself. I've already caused Gavin enough bullshit." Looking at the table, Emily swiped away tears gathering in her eyes. "Please," she whispered, "just don't say anything."

Trevor ran a hand through his hair and down the back of his neck. "Look, I won't bring it up, but Gavin knows Dillon. He knows he wouldn't let you walk away easily. But I have to be honest, Em, if he asks if anything happened, I'm not gonna lie."

Emily pressed her fingers to her temples. "I'm sorry. I shouldn't ask you to lie for me."

Releasing a weighty breath, Trevor blinked a few times and pushed his glasses up the bridge of his nose. "Don't apologize. The whole thing's fucked up. Just promise me you'll tell him if you two work things out."

"Yeah. Sure," Emily scoffed. "He hasn't even returned my calls." Returning her gaze to the couple seated across the restaurant, she tried to ignore the heaviness in the pit of her stomach. "He's finished with me."

"I think his head's a little fucked up right now, but Gavin's in love with you. I'm pretty sure when he comes back and gets one look at you, he won't be able to resist." Trevor rose and placed his hand on her shoulder. "Let's just hope he doesn't stay away for the next six months."

Feeling as though Trevor ripped the only remaining piece of her heart from her chest, Emily tried to breathe. She stood and stared into his eyes, her voice trembling. "Do you honestly think he would stay away that long?"

"Em, I didn't mean it like that."

"No, you did. What would make you say that?"

Trevor chewed at the side of his lip and briefly looked away. He shrugged. "Gavin can implode when he wants to. I don't know how long he'll be gone."

As thick disorientation melted across her mind, Emily brought her hand to her mouth. "Oh my God. I can't... He can't." She started making her way toward the bar, her feet moving quicker than her body could comprehend. She reached underneath the counter for her purse, coat, and scarf, her heart rate taking off.

"Look, I shouldn't have said that." Trevor approached the bar, his expression full of regret. "He can come back tomorrow—"

"Or in six months," she breathed, walking past him.

As she reached for the door, her chest squeezed, tightening with panic. A shiver moved through her when she stepped out of the restaurant. With her mind speeding a mile a minute, Emily tossed on her jacket and scurried, almost running, through swarms of bodies clogging the sidewalk. Car horns, conversations, and sirens danced around her, but she couldn't hear any of it. She felt deaf to it all.

The only sound she heard was Gavin's voice whispering in her ear, Gavin's laugh humming through the air, and Gavin's heart lulling her to sleep. A rush of tears fell at the thought of him being gone that long. Nine days nearly sank her. She knew six months would kill her.

As the front of the Chrysler building came into her view, uncertainty about what she was about to do rippled across Emily's skin. But no matter how uncertain she was, she wasn't about to let it stop her. Before she knew it, she found herself entering the lobby. As soon as she did, she felt the air whoosh from her lungs.

Her eyes locked onto the back of a gentleman leaned up against the information desk. Her vision blurred with black hair and a muscular physique matching Gavin's. She came to a complete standstill as she watched him leisurely tuck his hand into the pocket of his pants and run the other through his hair the same way Gavin did. Trying to suck in nonexistent air, Emily slowly moved in his direction. Consciousness void of what her body was doing, she lifted a trembling hand and tapped his shoulder. Senses craving Gavin, Emily attempted to pull in the scent of his cologne before he turned around. When he did, she was met by unfamiliar eyes, an unfamiliar face, and an unfamiliar smile. Her racing heart plummeted to her feet.

"Can I help you?" the man asked.

Unable to move, speak, or think, Emily stared at the stranger. Hit by a sudden wave of nausea, she felt dizzy as she opened her mouth in an effort to say something. Nothing came out.

"Miss, are you okay?" With trepidation, the man placed his hands on Emily's arms. "You look like you're going to pass out."

Emily cleared her throat, shook her head, and backed away. "I'm… I'm so sorry. I thought…" She couldn't finish her sentence. Blinking once, Emily turned and squeezed into the crowded elevator, her compulsion to press on nearly irresistible.

A woman in a red twill business suit craned her head around. "Which floor do you need?" she asked tersely.

Emily tried to regain some sense of reality, establish a hint of mental balance as she looked at the woman. But it wouldn't come. "I'm not sure."

At this, the woman laughed and shrugged.

An older gentleman with a pleasant smile spoke up. "What's the name of the company you're looking for?"

"Blake Industries," Emily answered, lifting her hand to her forehead.

"I'm familiar with it, and the two *very* charismatic owners," the man clipped. He gestured with his head to the less-than-friendly, red twill business suit-wearing woman peering over her shoulder. "That's the 62nd floor. Be nice and press it for this young lady."

With every effort she could gather, Emily smiled at the man. He nodded and winked. As the elevator opened and closed on each floor,

Emily couldn't help but sink into the memory of her and Gavin standing in the exact same elevator the first time she met him. Though the small space was still half full with others, in that moment, it was just him and her.

"She's not my girlfriend if that's what you're wondering."

"And who's to say I was?"

"And who's to say you weren't?"

The memory faded when the gentleman nudged her arm, letting her know they'd reached the 62nd floor. She rejected her sudden impulse to leave the building. Nodding in thanks, Emily brushed past a few people and stepped from the elevator. Once in the reception area, her gaze swept over a sand-blasted glass wall showcasing the name 'Blake Industries.' She swallowed and made her way to the receptionist seated behind a tall, crescent-shaped mahogany desk.

The dark-haired woman looked up from a computer screen, her smile warm and welcoming. "Can I help you?"

Emily nodded, somehow managing a smile. "Yes. I need to speak with Colton Blake."

"I apologize, but Mr. Blake's in a meeting right now. If you like, you can take a seat and wait for him. He shouldn't be more than another ten minutes." She gestured toward a seating area adjacent to a dozen or so cubicles. "Can I have your name, please?"

"Emily Cooper."

"I'll let him know you're waiting, Miss Cooper." The woman gave her another smile.

"Thank you." Emily went to turn around, but before she could, her attention shifted to an opening office door. Her nerves skyrocketed when she saw Colton stroll out, his deep, hearty chuckle hanging in the air as he shook hands with a man who'd exited the office with him. Emily felt ill when Colton's eyes latched on hers.

His jovial demeanor shifted almost immediately, his expression clear of any emotion. Staring at her, his mouth parted slightly as his eyes flitted between her and his business associate. Emily tensed and watched him rake a hand through his hair as he attempted to regain the friendly smile he was wearing just seconds before. Tugging anxiously at the hem of her white, button-down work shirt, Emily waited as he showed the man to the elevators. His gaze fell on hers once more before bidding the client a farewell.

"We'll catch up next week, Tom," Colton said, pressing the button for the elevator. "Tell Ellie I said hello and my mother should be calling her soon for brunch."

"Will do," the man answered with a clipped nod. He disappeared into the elevator when it opened.

"Mr. Blake," the secretary chimed, "you have a Miss Cooper here to see you."

"I see. Thank you, Natalie." Turning to face Emily, Colton dipped his head in greeting. "Emily."

"Hello, Colton."

"What are you doing here?" he asked, his tone noticeably guarded.

Emily shifted nervously, staring into his scrutinizing green eyes. She swallowed. "I have to speak with you."

"That's obvious."

"Then why did you ask?" She tilted her head in question.

Colton lifted a brow, a smirk tipping one corner of his mouth. "Let's go talk."

Following him, Emily tried to ward off the anxious nausea simmering in her stomach. Once in his office, Colton closed the door and shrugged out of his suit jacket. Without a word, he gestured to a chair in front of his desk. After shedding her coat and scarf, Emily took a seat as her thoughts contended with a powerful urge to leave. But she wouldn't. She knew she had to keep the reason she was there in her forethoughts. Casting a furtive glance in Colton's direction, she watched him hang his jacket in a closet, make his way over to his desk, and lounge into a seat across from her.

Colton cleared his throat, his eyes penetrating. "You hurt him, Emily."

Longing rolled through Emily's already aching heart, but somehow, hearing those words from Gavin's brother intensified it, thickened the feeling beyond any measure. "I know I did. I know that better than anyone. " Emily struggled to keep her voice from cracking. "But I love him, and I have to make this right. Olivia told me you said he's not in the country. I need you to tell me where he is, Colton."

Leaning back, a condescending snort slipped through his nose. "You love him? How come I find that hard to believe?" Emily reared back, shocked, but Colton continued. "And how do you plan on making things right with him? Even if I tell you where he is, who's to say he'll take you back? You didn't see what he looked like when he showed up at my house that night. The look in his eyes. The hurt on his face." Colton leisurely shrugged, smugness clinging to his voice. "That's right, how could you? You were too busy enjoying your rehearsal dinner."

Heavy tension fell over the room, its presence nearly depleting the oxygen in Emily's lungs. His insinuation slapped her hard across the face. No longer able to control her emotions, she blinked as tears slipped from her eyes. "I paid that night in more ways than one. I tortured myself in more ways than anyone will *ever* know."

The sour truth tumbled from her mouth as her mind replayed the self-inflicted pain she'd allowed from Dillon as punishment for her actions and indecision. As much as she loved Gavin, she refused to subject herself to Colton's accusations of her enjoying anything from that hideous evening. Fumbling out of her chair, she brought her hand to her chest. "You have no idea how much I love your brother. I can't breathe without him. I haven't slept. I've barely eaten. No, I didn't believe him at first. I couldn't. I opened the door that morning to his past when I thought I was his future. It killed me. My instincts told me to run, and so I did, and now we're both suffering for it."

Cupping her hand over her mouth, Emily looked down to the ground, her heart throbbing. She slowly brought her attention back to Colton, her frantic green eyes begging. "I don't know if he'll take me back, and I don't expect him to. I don't know if he'll even look at me, because I can barely look at myself. What I do know is I need to see him. I need to tell him how sorry I am. Even if it means putting myself out there without knowing any of those things, I have to do it." Emily drew in a gulp of air, her eyes narrowing. "But don't you *dare* tell me I don't love him because you're wrong."

Eyes no longer smug, understanding and compassion filled Colton's features. Rising, he grabbed a pen and a sticky note. After scribbling something onto it, he rounded the corner of his desk and handed her the tiny piece of paper. "Here's the address to his house and a beachside bar you'll probably find him hanging out at." Colton dug into his pants pocket and pulled out his wallet. After thumbing through some cash, a smile pulled at the edge of his mouth. "Though I wasn't *too* fond of you earlier, I'm not going to let you foot the bill to go down there for the little wiseass." Colton reached for Emily's hand and tucked the money into it. "It's not my style."

Looking at the cash, Emily sniffled. She shook her head. "I can't take this. It's enough you're letting me know where he is." She attempted to give it back.

"I insist." He lightly pushed her hand away. "Besides, it's only a few hundred bucks. I'll charter the jet to bring you down there, and I'll make sure everything else is taken care of, including your hotel." Colton cleared his throat and shoved his hands into his pockets. "Though I hope otherwise, we need to go with the assumption that… well, he might not be thrilled with you showing up."

Emily swallowed tightly and nodded. As she gathered her belongings, she tried to push that haunting fact from her thoughts, but she knew making a move like this was something she might have to face. After slipping on her coat, she stared at Colton for a moment. "Have you heard from him at all?"

"No." Colton shook his head. "Not yet."

Fear scissored through her stomach. "How do you know he made it down there? Something could've happened to him."

"Believe me, I know my brother. Nothing's happened to him." Assurance spun through his tone as he walked Emily to the door. "He's the only one who'll do harm to himself."

With her mouth parting and worry lines cinching her brows, Emily's eyes widened. "You don't think he'd—"

"No. No," Colton interrupted, a grin twisting his lips. "That came across the wrong way. Forget what I said." The tension in Emily's shoulders scattered like leaves in the wind. With his voice low, his grin fell away. "I apologize for my crudeness. He's my kid brother, and even though he's a diehard Yankees fan, which I loathe because I'm a diehard Mets fan, I kind of dig him."

"I kind of dig him, too," Emily whispered, staring at her feet. She brought her gaze back to Colton's eyes, traces of Gavin lingering in them. "I really do."

"I know, but you don't have to convince me. You have to get down there and prove it to him. I'll have my assistant call you with the information you'll need."

Emily hugged her purse to her chest, her eyes swimming with gratitude. "Thank you, Colton."

Colton nodded and pulled open the door.

Making her way out, tears trickled down Emily's cheeks. As she stood once again in the elevator where it'd all started, a mixture of relief and fear flooded Emily's body. A dangerous storm ricocheted through her nerves, escalating her heart rate. Still, though doubt about showing up unannounced in an attempt to salvage any relationship with Gavin strained through her muscles, Emily knew she couldn't add any more numbers to the growing seconds passing, keeping them apart.

Tick-tock...

CHAPTER THREE

Distance

The setting Caribbean sun cast low shadows against mosaic tiles lining a small outdoor bar on the beach. Sitting on the southernmost tip of 5th Avenue, Gavin knew the place well and frequented it each time he visited the area. Smoke lazily wended up from a fiery grill, the drifting aroma of shrimp tacos and tamales filled the air. With warm winds kicking up, Gavin's broken heart raced in rhythm with the waves crashing against the sand as he took in the sights and sounds around him.

Steel drums playing down the beach hummed through his ears as vacationers finished up a game of volleyball on the hot sand. Women with bodies to die for slapped layer upon layer of suntan lotion across their surgically-enhanced breasts. A toddler skipped into the turquoise water, and his father ran after him. Eventually picking him up, he spun the child around. The little boy let out a gut-belly laugh, his head undoubtedly dizzy. The corners of Gavin's mouth turned up a small smile while he watched them play. The man scurried out of the water, his son tucked tightly under his arm, and set the little boy on the sand next to his mother, abruptly interrupting her few peaceful moments.

Gavin couldn't help but feel a deep pang of longing as he watched the middle-aged man crouch down next to his wife. A grin on his face, he pulled his fair-skinned love into his arms and planted a kiss onto her lips. With adrenaline-spiked clarity, the memory of embracing Emily rushed through Gavin's thoughts. Reaching for his bourbon on the rocks, rocks melted from the heat, he forced his gaze away from the couple.

"Señor Blake." Gavin lifted his eyes and saw one of the cabana boys he'd come to know well over the years approaching with another bourbon. Placing the drink down in front of Gavin, Miguel wiggled his brows. "This, señor, is from the beautiful señorita." He craned his head toward a woman seated alone at the bar.

Gavin stole a sideways glance in her direction. Crossing her long legs under a short, silk sundress, the woman aimed a coy smile at Gavin and sipped her piña colada. Her lips lingered on the straw as she gazed at him intently.

Gavin simply nodded to thank her. He returned his attention to the young Mexican worker, fished his wallet from his back pocket, and handed the man a tip. "Thank you, Miguel. Go ahead and get her another round on me." Leaning back, he draped his arm across the chair next to him. "How's Maria and the little one doing?"

"Oh, they're doing wonderful, Señor Blake," he answered, the joy in his voice reaching his eyes. "We trying to teach him to play football." The young man smiled and swiped Gavin's empty glass from the table. "Well, you Americans call it soccer. We hope to see him play for… what do you call it? The Olympia?"

Gavin let out a light chuckle. "The Olympics."

Smiling, Miguel tossed a dishrag over his shoulder. "Yes. The Olympics. Then, he make me and my family have as much dinero as you one day. Much happiness comes with that. Si?"

Gavin picked up his new glass and swirled the liquid, the fresh ice clinking against the sides. He cast a weary smile at Miguel, his tone void of any emotion as visions of Emily plowed through his senses. "Right. Money brings much happiness, Miguel."

Miguel grinned and turned away, leaving demons of despair to torture Gavin. Buried just beneath the surface, a nearly insufferable pain latched onto his heart. Unwelcomed, flashes of Emily's auburn hair tickling his face ran rampant through his mind. No longer in his grasp, the thought sucked the last vestiges of feeling from Gavin's soul. As the mix of emotions ebbed with every unsteady breath he took, his pain gave way to anger. But try as he might, Gavin couldn't escape her. Need for her tensed every muscle in his body as memories of them together clouded his thoughts, tripping and tumbling over each other.

With a wall of unease settling around him, Gavin lifted his head. His gaze caught the attention of the woman who'd sent him a drink. Her features were pleasant enough. Rich, wavy, shoulder-length red hair fell easily over the straps of her sundress. Gavin flicked his eyes across her slender physique as she stared at him, a timid grin taking over her mouth. Though he didn't consider her a woman who would stick out in a crowd, her eyes and smile lit up her face, and Gavin found it hard to look away. He watched as she gracefully slid from the barstool.

She grabbed her drink, a clutch, and started making her way toward him. Eyes locked on hers, Gavin swallowed and listened to her heeled sandals clicking against the wooden deck. Before she closed their distance, the woman came to a stop. She tilted her head and studied his face as if asking if it was okay to join him. Gavin found her trepidation appealing. With a reluctant nod, he motioned to the seat across from him.

Smiling, she continued her pursuit and stepped down from the deck onto the patio lining the beach. As she pulled out a chair, she placed her drink and clutch onto the table, her hair blowing across her face with the warm breeze. When she brought her hand up to tuck the strands behind her ear, Gavin noticed her green eyes, their shade hauntingly familiar. Emotions swept over him as his mind desperately fought against thoughts of Emily.

"I can spot a man with a broken heart from a mile way," the woman purred, sinking into the seat. She crossed her legs and took a long sip from her frozen beverage. She subtly leaned across the table. A seductive smile tipped the corner of her glossed lips, her gaze falling from Gavin's face to his chest. After roaming over his upper body, she brought her eyes back to his. "What can I do to remedy this problem for you, Mr....?"

Gavin leaned back and shook his head. "Not as shy as you appear," he mumbled, reaching for his drink. "They do say looks can be deceiving. But it's all good. I'm not as shy as I may appear." Gavin chugged the rest of his drink, set his glass on the table, and flicked it with his thumb and middle finger. Its condensation allowed it to slide smoothly across the glass top, clinking against an ashtray. He rested his elbows on the table, smirked, and tented his fingers under his chin. "You want to remedy my problem? I'm intrigued, Miss...?"

The unnamed woman bit her lip and mimicked his pose. "One: I'm very happy you're intrigued. That was my sole purpose in coming over here. I enjoy it when a man finds me intriguing. Two: No, I'm not as shy as I appear, honey. Far from it. Three: I never said you looked shy. Nothing about you screams shy, and for me, that's a good thing." She uncrossed her legs, slipped her heel off her right foot, and reached down to massage it. With the tilt of his head, Gavin watched soberly as she slowly ran her blood red nails from the bottom of her foot up to her calf. Repositioning herself in her chair, she tucked her shoeless foot under her ass and smiled. "Four: Yes, I'd like to remedy your problem in whatever way you see fit. I'm going through a tough time myself, so it'll benefit us both. And, five: You never gave me your name, so why should I give you mine? It's apparent I'm slightly older than you, so you really should respect your elders. Wouldn't you agree, Mr....?"

Without moving, a grin pulled at the side of Gavin's mouth. "Gavin Blake."

"Ahh, well then, Mr. Blake, whose heart has clearly been hurt, it's very nice to meet you. I'm Miss Layton, but you can call me Jessica." Staring into his eyes, she reached across the table, offering Gavin her hand. He took it and felt her fingers draw small circles on his palm. She hesitantly pulled back and pushed her breasts together. "So, who was she and why on earth would she break the heart of a man who looks as enticing as you do?"

With a nerve hit, Gavin cleared his throat and glanced past Jessica. He raised his hand for Miguel to bring them another round. He rolled his neck, leaned back, and tucked his hands into the pockets of his khaki cargo shorts. Face impassive and eyes pinned on hers, he cocked his head to the side. "Let me clarify a few things for you. Jessica's your name, correct?"

Looking slightly thrown off by his question and tone, she nodded.

"Well, Jessica," Gavin continued, "one: My life, and who used to be in it, is none of your business. Don't ask me about it again. Two: You may think you can remedy my problem, but I'm pretty fucking sure you can't. However, I'm more than sure I can fuck you into oblivion, remedying the recent tough times you've had right out of your mind. I might be younger than you, but you're not my first walk in the park. Get where I'm going with this?"

Eyes wide, Jessica parted her lips but didn't speak. She nodded again.

"Good. I'm glad we're on the same page." Gavin handed his credit card to Miguel, who'd approached with their drinks. "Three: I've been around many intriguing women, so don't take my statement as a compliment. I know how to flatter a woman better than telling her I find her under-sexed, crazed approach intriguing. Four: If you want to fuck, we can fuck. My house is a two-minute walk from here. But I'll warn you now, that's all it'll be. Don't expect a sleep over. I'll fuck you, and fuck you *very* well, but I'll send you on your way once our escapade is over. I won't give you my number, and you'll never enter my thoughts again. So now, Jessica…" Gavin cupped his chin, the crease of his brows showing he was trying to remember her last name.

"Layton," Jessica answered, her voice cracking. "My last name's Layton."

"Ahh, that's right. So now, Miss Jessica Layton, the ball's in your court." Gavin ran a hand through his hair and shot her a wink. Once again, Miguel approached the table with Gavin's credit card. After shoving it back into his wallet, Gavin looked across the table at Jessica sitting speechless, her fingers rubbing up and down her neck. "Make the call, Jessica, because honestly, if we don't do this," he said with a light shrug, "I'll just go back to my joint and milk my own dick."

With shock twisting her face, Jessica stood, slipped her sandal back on, and reached for her clutch.

Assuming his curt response had scared her off, Gavin gave another shrug as his eyes landed on the family he was admiring earlier. He watched them make their way, hand in hand, over to a small, two-door clunk of shit. He knew his riches couldn't compare to their happiness. He wanted that happiness. He wanted that clunk of shit.

"Well, are you ready?" Jessica asked, her voice laced with sexual urgency.

Gavin tore his attention from the fading dream and watched Jessica pluck his bourbon from his hands. She finished it in one long gulp. After placing the empty glass on the table, she brushed her fingertips across Gavin's temple, down the side of his cheek, and over the curve of his jaw. Gavin momentarily stiffened, trying not to flinch at her touch. He rose and grabbed Jessica's hand. His feet, as if they had a mind of their own, led them toward his place.

"So, aren't you a little curious as to why I'm in Mexico alone?" Jessica questioned as they made their way down a small wooden walkway.

Looking out onto the tumbling waves, the last of the sun falling asleep below the horizon, Gavin shook his head. "Not really."

"You know, you're really not a nice guy." She pulled her hand away. Its absence didn't affect Gavin either way. Still, she followed closely by his side.

"No. I'm too much of a nice guy," Gavin mumbled, idly wondering where Emily was in that moment. Loneliness flooded his chest, but he welcomed its suffocating presence. This was something he knew. It was all too familiar to him. He almost considered it an old buddy.

"Right," Jessica huffed, her tone tight with skepticism. "Well, considering what we're about to do, maybe you can try to be a little... pleasant?"

Stopping just shy of his place, Gavin looked at her, his brow drawn up. "Look, I laid it all out. I can do sex, but I won't do pleasantries. Take it or leave it." For the barest second, Gavin felt ill to his stomach. He'd been raised to always treat women with respect, and he pictured his father's disgust with the way he was acting. Still, the thought was fleeting. His old habit screamed, waving its self-medication in his face.

Shut down. Shut off. Disconnect.

Jessica pursed her lips. "Fine. Only because I need this more than you know."

Once on his porch, Jessica whipped her crimson hair to the side, and Gavin was suddenly engulfed by the scent of her body. Her jasmine perfume aroused memories he was trying to forget. It shook him, nearly staggering his balance. He took a deep breath and steadied himself. Looking down at her wanting green eyes, he brought his hand around the back of her neck and pulled her hard into his mouth. She pressed her chest against his and let out a soft moan, her hands coming up to grasp his hair. Her moan, although filled with seductive, feminine yearning, wasn't the moan he wanted to hear. Her lips, sweet in their own way, didn't feel right locked on his. They didn't mold to his like a piece to a puzzle.

Anger swelled, and Gavin started kissing her with ravenous intensity. He pinned her against the wall, reached for her thigh, and drew her leg up around his waist. She breathed out heavily as he roughed his hand under her sundress, skimming below her panties. In one swift motion, he had three fingers buried inside her. Her hips bucked against each hard thrust, and she clung to his neck, fisting the collar of his white linen shirt. Her pussy, though wet and as ready as any man could ever want, felt foreign, and at this, Gavin fingered her deeper, harder.

"Wait," she purred, trying to catch her breath. She towed her head back and stared into his eyes. "What are you doing? Are you going to fuck me right out here?"

With a smug grin, Gavin backed away, leaving her panting body lax against the wall. "Not as fun as you originally appeared, I see," he muttered, fishing his keys from his pocket. He slid them into the door, unlocked it, and held it open as he waited for Jessica to adjust her clothing.

Sighing, she picked up her clutch from the ground. As she walked past him, she rolled her eyes. Dropping the clutch onto an antique, claw-footed table in the foyer, Jessica's gaze swept across his expansive beachfront home. "Nice place." She faced him, her smile showing she was impressed. "So now, where were we?"

"You were about to strip for me." Gavin tossed his keys onto the table and started unbuttoning his shirt. After slipping it off, he leaned against the doorjamb of the kitchen and crossed his arms as he watched her undress.

Jessica peeled the last piece of clothing from her body and moved toward Gavin. She took his face in both of her hands and pulled him into her mouth. It was then Gavin shoved Emily back into his aching heart's closet, locked the door, and threw away the key. As he unbuckled his belt, one clear thought attacked his mind.

Emily would be proud he was taking a "void filler" to bed tonight.

CHAPTER FOUR

Broken

With fear eating away at her stomach and a desperate ache for Gavin consuming her, Emily handed her bags to the flight attendant as she stepped into Blake Industries' private jet.

Olivia raised a playful brow. "Hmm, maybe I need to break a few hearts in order to get special treatment like you… Yes. It's been decided. While you're gone, I'm gonna find me some rich dude, fuck around with his head a little, and get his brother to send me to where he is in absolute fucking luxury so I can reclaim his love."

Emily stared blankly at Olivia, her mouth agape.

"You know I'm only kidding, Em." Olivia laughed and grabbed Emily's hand, tugging her toward the back of the jet.

Trying to keep up, Emily sighed and shook her head. "What are you doing, nut job? You're not coming with me. Or is this something else you've decided on a whim?"

"This is Blake Industries' new jet, and if you think I'm stepping foot off it before I see every inch, you're just as flighty as I thought." Olivia halted and snorted. "I just made a joke. Flighty, flight, fly, flying. Get it?"

"Yes. I get it, Liv. Wanna know what I've decided on a whim?"

Olivia tilted her head, her eyes wide. "You're not changing your mind, are you? I said I was kidding around, Em. You know I'm your biggest fan right now. I know this is scary for you—the whole flying thing and Gavin possibly not taking you back—but you have to do this. The pilot doesn't look drunk, well, not *too* drunk, so it's pretty safe to say you're in good hands. Besides, if you don't go, you'll never find out what could've happened with you and Gavin. You'll regret it for the rest of your life."

Emily placed her hands on Olivia's shoulders. "I'm not changing my mind, Olivia, but I've decided you're no longer allowed to drink cappuccino." Emily dropped her arms and smiled. "For someone who practically vibrates after one cup, two cups and you look like you've been smoking crack."

"Oh. Right. My mother tells me the same, minus the whole smoking crack part." Olivia reached for the back cabin door. "She usually says I look like I've committed a murder."

"What are you doing? We can't just go in there."

Olivia whipped her head around. "Why not?"

"Because it's Gavin and Colton's private cabin."

"Big deal." Olivia shrugged and pushed open the door. "Like I said, I want the grand tour before I get off."

Emily shook her head and watched Olivia disappear into the cabin. When the engines roared to life, she squeezed her eyes closed and clawed the tops of leather seats on either side of her. The vibrating sound immediately ignited her sickened fear of flying. She shivered. With a trembling breath and heart bouncing against her ribs, Emily mentally flipped through her one and only reason for being there.

Gavin...

Swallowing down her instinct to get the hell off the jet, Emily steadied herself, wiped away the sweat gathering on the back of her neck, and took two tentative steps forward. She tried to breathe deeply through her nose as she took another step, her fingernails nearly puncturing the cold leather. Grabbing the smooth, mahogany doorframe of the cabin, Emily peered in and found Olivia sprawled out on a king-sized bed, her lazy smile showing she was comfortable.

"You need to get up," Emily stated. She shakily made her way across the room.

Smile faltering, Olivia sat up and pursed her lips. "You're seriously no fun."

"I know." Emily frowned and rushed a hand through her hair. Her eyes darted around the room and landed on a blue Yankees cap hanging on a hook next to the minibar. Momentarily, she froze. Ignoring both her fear of flying and Olivia's bitching about something as she slipped off the bed, Emily stared at the cap before moving toward it. Lifting her hand, she gently grazed her fingertips against it, her heart heavy with memories of Gavin's smile shining in the sun as they sat at the game just a few months before.

As if the cap had seared her skin, Emily dropped her hand, hot tears blurring her vision. Backing away, she once again resisted the urge to flee. Run. So used to running from everything, the habit consumed her, but it faded as a slow smile curled her lips. She closed her eyes, a tear slipping down her cheek, and allowed Gavin's sweet, dimpled smile to wash over her. Allowed it to propel her into the unknown of what was to be of their future. If anything at all.

Emily felt a hand on her shoulder, and she swept away her tears, not wanting Olivia to see she'd been crying. Quickly, she turned around and made her way past Olivia.

"Are you okay?" Olivia asked, following her out into the aisle.

Slipping into one of the seats, Emily rested her head against the window. "I'm fine."

Arms crossed, Olivia arched a skeptical brow. "You know, you're really not a good liar."

"Yeah. My mother used to tell me that," Emily whispered, facing Olivia.

With a weary smile, Olivia leaned over the cream leather seat. She cupped Emily's chin in her hand. "Right here, right now, you're exactly where you're supposed to be. Everything's going to be fine. I know you don't believe me, but I think I have some kind of psychic thing going on. It's going to be bucketloads of babies in a nasty green minivan with Mr. Gavin Fuckable Blake. You'll see." Olivia popped a kiss on top of Emily's head, straightened, and walked away. "Text me the second you land!" she called out as she exited the jet.

After declining a beverage and a snack from the flight attendant, Emily closed her eyes and tried to concentrate on that baby-filled minivan. Gavin's face flashed through her thoughts, bringing with it a flutter of anxiety and hope as she felt the jet rolling forward. The sound of her rapid heartbeat was devoured by the screaming engines. She calculated the flight from New York to Playa del Carmen at four hours and fifteen minutes, after which she knew her life would be forever changed, more so than it already had. Gripping the sides of the seat, palms sweaty, Emily Cooper found herself in a very different situation than the last time she was en route to a new destination, a new beginning. Sighing, she watched the city's steel giants disappear beneath the blanket of clouds. Her heart sank as she inwardly prayed that what she was doing would indeed change her life.

This time for the better...

This time no longer afraid…

This time fighting for the man fate slated her to be with…

After an hour of standing in line to clear customs, Emily made her way through the crowded airport, her black suitcase rolling behind her. She weaved through a mixed array of tourists of every ethnic background as her nerves steadily built with each step. This was it. She was here, and there was no turning back. She only prayed that when she left, she'd have Gavin at her side.

However, it wasn't something she was expecting.

Upon emerging from the packed building, her flesh hit with heat, she squinted in the bright sun. She searched for the driver Colton's secretary told her would be waiting. Through the mass confusion of vendors peddling handmade blankets, dolls, and T-shirts, Emily's gaze landed on a short, dark-haired man holding a sign with her last name on it.

Approaching him, she smiled and flashed her passport. "Hello, I'm Emily Cooper."

"Yes. Yes. Hello, Señorita Cooper." Reaching for Emily's luggage, the man returned the smile and led her toward a black limousine parked among several collectivos in the busy streets. "Is this your first time in Playa del Carmen?" He opened the door for her.

Emily slid in, welcoming the air-conditioning. "Thank you. Yes, it is."

After closing her door, he placed her belongings in the trunk, rounded the vehicle, and settled into the driver's seat. Twisting the mirror slightly, he stared into it as he spoke. "Well, welcome. Our town is beautiful. My name is Javier. I make sure to give you nice tour on the way to your hotel. Si?"

"Oh. Actually, I wasn't planning on going to the hotel right away." Emily dug in her purse and pulled out the paper with Gavin's address. Not wanting to let another minute pass without seeing him, she slid across the bench and showed it to Javier. "I'd like to stop here first if I can, please?"

Nodding, Javier pulled away from the curb and smiled, his warm brown eyes twinkling in the reflection. "Absolutely, Señorita Cooper. Wherever you like. I have you to your destination very soon."

"Thank you, Javier."

Emily sat back and tried to process every emotion working through her mind. The innate need for Gavin hit her again, intensified beyond anything she'd ever felt. Anxiety coiled in ribbons around her body. She shifted restlessly, each breath a struggle as she watched tour buses, mopeds, and Fifa, the Mexican police, fly by. Though the ride into the heart of Playa del Carmen took less than twenty minutes, the wait felt like forever. With edgy nervousness pumping though her veins, Emily found it hard to concentrate as the limousine turned onto a desolate, narrow road lined with a few mansions.

When the vehicle rolled to a stop in front of Gavin's home, she drew in a deep breath and swallowed down every instinct telling her Gavin wasn't taking her back. Emily opened the door before Javier had a chance to exit the limo. She stepped out and took in the mammoth structure. Classic Mexican terracotta shingles crowned the white-stucco jewel sitting on a hill overlooking the pristine Caribbean waters. Brushing her windblown auburn hair away from her face, Emily found her mind frozen, yet her body ignored its plea to not move. Her body, nauseous with anxiety, felt Gavin's pull, that deep, familiar pull she'd felt from the first time she saw him. Before she knew it, she was slowly walking up to his home. Javier called out from behind her, but she held up a hand, signaling him to wait.

Standing before the dark mahogany and beveled, etched glass door towering over her tiny frame, Emily fought back tears, lifted a trembling hand, and rang the doorbell. Her heart sped, its thumping rushing through her ears, as a blurred figure made its way over to answer. Body taut with fear, a fear she'd brought on herself by doing this to her and Gavin, Emily closed her eyes and tried to grasp some minuscule hope that she wasn't about to face the disaster her head was telling her was coming. Before the door swung open, flashes of Gavin's blue eyes crept into Emily's thoughts, however when it opened, those weren't the eyes staring back at her.

Raven-colored hair twisted into a tight bun and wearing a maid's uniform, the lanky woman smiled. "Puedo ayudarle?"

"Umm, yes. Is Gavin here?" Emily asked, tying to quell the shakiness in her voice.

"No. El Sr. Blake no está aquí. Se fue a beber a Akumal."

Emily shook her head. "I'm sorry. I only speak English."

"No entiendo lo que esta diciendo. El Señor Blake no está aquí."

Emily turned around and waved at Javier where he was waiting in the driveway with her luggage.

"Si, Señorita Cooper," he said, climbing the steps to the covered porch. "I bring your bags in for you. Good?"

"No, thank you for that, Javier. I don't need my belongings brought in. I think Mr. Blake's not home, and this woman's trying to explain to me where he is. Can you translate for me, please?"

"Ahh, of course." Smiling, Javier swung his attention to the woman. "Juanita, buenas tardes."

The woman nodded. "Buenas tardes."

"Colton me envió al aeropuerto a recoger a esta joven y traerla de vuelta a ver Gavin. Está en casa?"

Emily waited as patiently as possible while they spoke. When they were done, the woman nodded before closing the door.

Javier looked at Emily. "Señor Blake's at a bar in Akumal. It's not too far of a drive. Maybe twenty minutes. Come. I take you there now."

Emily watched Javier bolt down the steps and across the driveway. After placing her luggage in the trunk, he opened the door to the limousine for her. Still standing on the porch, Emily hesitated. Her mind was spinning over every possible reason she shouldn't show up in a public place to see Gavin. She couldn't. It wouldn't be right. They needed privacy to discuss everything. Though pain of waiting to see him, even just a little while longer, throbbed in her chest, Emily decided she would get settled in her hotel room and come back later in the evening. With that, she started making her way over to Javier to let him know her plans.

As she neared the limo, she snapped her head in the direction of the sound of a vehicle's tires kicking up gravel in the distance. Holding her hand up to shade the sun from her eyes, she squinted and watched the charcoal gray sports car cut a hard left into the driveway. With its windows tinted as black as an iron kettle, Emily couldn't make out who was driving. That didn't prevent her heart, which was beating like a drum, from coming to a complete stop for a long second. As she tried to pull in a breath, the organ stuttered back to life when Gavin stepped out of the vehicle, a grin on his face. Emily's eyes flickered with uncertainty at his demeanor, considering he hadn't looked in her direction yet. In a complete fog at what she was witnessing, chills shot and prickled across Emily's skin as not one but two reasons for Gavin's jovial mood slid out of the car. Taking an unsteady step back, panic flooded Emily's limbs when Gavin's gaze caught hers. His grin disappeared immediately. She could read the question in his eyes, and she was sure she was about to pass out.

Tilting his head in confusion, Gavin halted mid-stride. He knew the past few days had taken their toll on him, mentally and physically, and he also knew he had some alcohol running through his system, but he was pretty fucking sure he wasn't seeing things. "What the fuck?" he whispered. He whipped off his sunglasses and scrubbed the heels of his palms across his eyes.

"What's the matter?" the auburn beauty asked, grazing her pouty red lips against his jaw. "You look like you've seen a ghost."

Gavin rolled his shoulder, shrugging her off his arm. "I have," he bit out, cutting his narrowed eyes her way.

The platinum knockout snapped her gum. "Jeez, talk about split personalities. What's up?"

Gavin tore his attention from the two soon to be "void fillers," his gaze intent on Emily who was turning to get into the limo. Without saying another word, he jogged over to her, his body reacting to Emily the only way it'd ever known how. Heart in his throat and confusion hammering through his head, Gavin reached out, grabbing her elbow. "What are you doing here, Emily?" The feel of her soft skin seared into his mind, kicking up memories he was trying to forget.

Frozen, Emily didn't turn around. She couldn't. Breathing heavily from his simple touch, she nervously swallowed and tried to find her words. "I came to talk to you," she whispered.

Gavin released her and stepped back. "Turn around and look at me," he commanded, his voice low.

Pulse quickening, Emily slowly turned, her gaze locking onto his. Staring into his confused blue eyes, she curled her fingers around the top of the door to steady herself.

Her beautiful face nearly stole the breath from Gavin's lungs. His eyes fell from hers, immediately landing on her quivering lips. Lips God created to fit his. Lips that'd haunted his every dream since he'd left. Her silky auburn hair whipped around in the warm breeze. Hair made to tickle his face as she hovered above him while making love. Gavin tried to breathe while his need for her snaked through every tense muscle in his body, culminating in a torturous, slow burn. His chest constricted with love, but anger at her boiled beneath his skin. A slow smirk curled his mouth. "You have permission from your husband to come see me? I never took Dillon for one who would grant his wife an open marriage."

Emily's knees went weak, her eyes steeped in confusion. "I didn't marry him, Gavin. You know that. I... I called. I left you messages." Though she tried, she couldn't keep tears from pooling in her eyes as she stared at his shocked expression. Suddenly, she found her words tumbling from her mouth. "I left Dillon that night and went to your penthouse. I've called your phone every day over the past few weeks. Colton called and left your housekeeper messages. Trevor, Olivia, we all did." Emily looked away, her eyes locking on Gavin's two companions. Leaning against his Jaguar, they peered in Emily's direction as she shook her head and brought her gaze back to his. "I don't expect you to take me back, but I needed to come here and tell you how sorry I am. I needed to tell you how much I love you, Gavin. How much I need you in my life."

Looking at the ground, Gavin grabbed the back of his neck with both hands. He snapped up his head and looked at the driver. "Javier, dame sus cosas."

Javier nodded. "Por supuesto, Señor Blake."

Emily watched Javier retrieve her luggage from the trunk and pass it to Gavin. After thanking him, Gavin grabbed Emily's hand, his grip tight as he led her toward his car. Struggling to keep up, Emily's heels clicked frantically against the pavement. She stared at the two women.

The brunette quirked a brow and placed a hand on her hip. "Um, we're not opposed to adding a fourth, but I still think you should've asked us first."

The blonde nodded and straightened her pink tank top. Emily bit her lip, her eyes wide on Gavin.

Gavin released a weighty breath, pulled Emily to the passenger side, and opened the rear door. He tossed her suitcase into the backseat. Opening the front door, he looked at Emily. "Get in."

"What?" she questioned, shock shimmering in her eyes.

"You heard me, Emily. Get in," he replied as he rounded the car.

The blonde cocked her head to the side. "Where are we going?"

"You two are going home," Gavin answered, his tone clipped. He looked at his driver, who appeared equally confused. "Necesito que lleves a estas dos a su casa, de acuerdo?"

"Si, Señor Blake." Javier waved the two women over.

This time, the brunette cocked her head to the side. "You're making us leave? You can't do that."

"I just did. Have a great day, ladies," Gavin replied, staring at Emily over the roof of his car. With a casual shrug, he brushed off the gasp one of them emitted. "Get in the car, doll."

Bending to his will, Emily snapped her mouth shut and ducked into the vehicle. After closing his door, Gavin pushed a button and started the car. He punched the gas a few times and the engine roared, warning the two women still standing behind the vehicle. Taking him seriously, they stepped back onto the grass and crossed their arms in clear annoyance. Once out of his way, Gavin floored the gas, and the sleek Jaguar careened in reverse out of his driveway.

Gavin lowered the window and called out to Javier, who was about to get into the limo. "Sabes en que hotel se esta quedando?"

"Si, en El Real, Señor Blake."

"Gracias," Gavin replied. With one hand gripped tight around the wheel and the other on the shift, he looked at Emily. "Get your seatbelt on."

"What did you just ask him?"

"I asked him what hotel you're staying at. Now get your seatbelt on."

Feeling the tension pour off of him, Emily pulled the belt over her waist. After it clicked, Gavin slammed the gear into first and took off. Dust from the gravel road swamped the rear and sides of the car. Out of the corner of her eye, Emily watched Gavin, his eyes focused on the road, his face painfully impassive. Her heart clenched against the long stretch of silence taking hold in the air around them. Gavin turned onto a highway, and adrenaline washed through Emily's veins as he kicked through the gears effortlessly. Ripping in between slower vehicles, the odometer neared 85 mph.

Emily tensed, grabbed the handle above her head, and looked at Gavin. "You're going to kill us."

"I'm already dead," he answered, clenching his jaw. He gripped the steering wheel tighter and punched the gas again, this time harder.

The force jerked Emily's body back. "Gavin! Have you lost your mind?"

Without looking at her, Gavin cut the wheel hard right, and the car fishtailed to a screeching stop on the side of the road. Other drivers blared their horns, flying past Gavin and Emily as dust settled around the vehicle. Both heaving for air, their gazes caught one another.

Clung.

"I'm already dead," Gavin repeated, the words spoken low, but the undertone of anger as clear as the cloudless sky. As angry as he was at her, like a rubber band, something snapped inside of him as he stared at Emily's lips. In one swift movement, he reached for her, lifting her over the console and onto his lap.

Emily straddled him, and her breath faltered as she stared at his face, his pained eyes staring back. Unable to contain her want, she crashed her mouth to his and gripped the back of his hair, her apologies whipping past her lips as she soaked in his familiar taste with each stroke of her tongue. "I'm so sorry, Gavin. I can't take away what I've done to you. I know I can't, but I love you. God, I love you so much."

Gavin squeezed her thighs and slipped his hands under her sundress. Gripping Emily's waist, a groan ripped through his throat when she arched her chest against his. He could feel her hardened nipples through the thin cotton, and he swore he would lose it right there. Licking fast through her mouth and trying to savor every moan she expelled at his touch, Gavin fought against doubt plaguing his mind. With one hand still caressing her waist, he took the other and fisted her hair, pulling her down harder to his lips. She moaned and circled her hips, grinding hard against his rising dick. Her panting breaths echoed in his ears along with the words she'd spoken to him the night of her rehearsal dinner.

"Fuck!" he snarled, tearing his mouth from hers. Hand still tangled in her wavy curls, he stared at her with narrowed eyes.

Before Emily could catch her breath, he swung open the door and slipped out of the car, leaving her on her knees in the driver's seat. She curled her fingers around the head rest and watched him pace on the side of the road, both of his hands gripping his hair.

"Fuck!" he yelled out again, reaching down to the ground.

Eyes wide and breathing heavy, Emily jerked with sudden fear as he pelted a rock against the back window. The glass split into a cobweb. Without hesitation, he rocketed another against the taillight. Emily gasped, but with confusion and anger bubbling in her stomach, she hauled her suitcase over the seat and tore out of the car. She headed away from Gavin, tears streaming down her cheeks as she tried to pull the wheeled luggage through the rocks.

"Where are you going, Emily?" Gavin called, following her.

Without stopping, she flipped him the bird and continued her pursuit into nowhere land.

Coming up beside her, Gavin grabbed her elbow and spun her around, a lopsided smirk tipping his lips. "You're in the middle of Mexico, doll."

"And you're an asshole!" she hissed, defiance glittering in her eyes. She wiped the tears away from her face.

"Ahh, still so beautiful when you're mad." He cupped her chin and smoothed the pad of his thumb under her eye. After wiping the smudged mascara from her face, he stepped back and crossed his arms. "And you still love calling me an asshole, huh?"

Throwing her arm out to the side, she stepped forward, her chin jutted up. "What do you want from me, Gavin? I came here to apologize. You knew damn well I didn't marry him, but yet you didn't take my calls and you say you're dead? I'm dead right now!"

"I am fucking dead, goddammit!" He stepped closer, curled his arm around her waist, and pulled her against his chest. Staring into her watery, green eyes, he resisted the urge to kiss her again. "You killed me, Emily," he breathed, brushing her hair away from her face. Leaning into her ear, he yanked the suitcase from her hand, his voice a heated whisper. "I didn't know you never went through with it. I chucked my phone the night I came out here, and I haven't read any messages my fucking housekeeper left for me. I threw each and every single one of them away." He whipped around and headed for the car.

"Gavin, wait!" she called out. He came to a stop and shook his head, refusing to face her. Inching toward him, Emily swallowed nervously, her head more confused than when she'd first showed up. "What are you trying to say to me?" she asked, taking a cautious step forward. "Say it if you have to, Gavin, but I need to know. What are we doing?"

Gavin turned around and raked his hand through his hair. "I don't know what we're doing, Emily." He paused, his gaze shifting between her and the highway. He shook his head again, then brought his attention back to her. "I don't know what I want right now."

"I've broken us," she whispered, slowly bringing her hand up to her cheek as she stared at the ground. Trying to catch the breath that'd been stolen from her, she lifted her head. Her eyes locked on Gavin's. "I have. I've broken us."

Gavin cupped the back of his neck and stared at her a long moment, his mind fighting against what his heart wanted. "Yeah. I think you have," he answered softly. He pulled in a deep breath and turned around. "Come on... I'm taking you back to your hotel."

Emily felt lightheaded. Felt the blood drain from her face. She knew when she got there he could reject her, but no amount of mental preparation could've prepared her for the loneliness slamming through her. In a daze, she made her way back to the car and settled into the seat. Barely able to make sense of her emotions, Emily couldn't look at Gavin when he slipped in and started the engine. She rested her head against the seat and blankly stared out the window. With everything in her, she tried to contain herself from breaking out into hysterics as Gavin eased the car back onto the highway.

"How do I know you're not going to go back to him?" Gavin's soft, broken voice cut through the silence. "And what makes you think I can trust you won't?"

Emily snapped her head in his direction, her lips parted as she gazed into his eyes. They held so much pain, and it was then she realized how badly she'd hurt him. She took a calculated risk and reached over, brushing her fingertips along the dark stubble on his jaw. She felt him tense, and it stung her heart. She dropped her hand into her lap and looked down. "I'm not taking him back, Gavin. I love you," she whispered, swiping away a tear that'd trickled down her face.

"You say that now." He dragged his attention from her and brought it back to the road. "You love me while you're here, Emily. What about when we get back to New York? What happens when you see him again?"

She cupped her hand over her mouth, and a sob crawled up her throat as she stared at him. "I don't know how to get you to trust me other than giving me the chance to prove it to you, Gavin. I don't."

Exhaling, Gavin gripped the steering wheel and didn't say another word for the remainder of the ride.

By the time they pulled up in front of the hotel, Emily wasn't sure if her heart was still beating. She wasn't sure if she could move... could breathe. However, she was sure her soul had shattered into a million tiny pieces, scattered somewhere along a highway in Mexico. With hues of pinks, purples, and orange replacing the lazy sun disappearing from the sky, Gavin slipped from the car and retrieved Emily's luggage. Handing it to the bellboy, Gavin reached in his wallet for a tip and spoke something in Spanish.

Emily climbed from the car and walked over to Gavin. Staring up into his eyes, her words softly fell from her mouth. "Do you know how scary it is to want something so bad you're willing to change your whole life for it?"

Gavin searched her face. "You mean the way I was willing to change mine for you?"

"Yeah. I guess we were both willing to do that, Gavin. I was ready to take that plunge and never look back. Never. I was ready to risk everything for you, to push away the overwhelming fear I had because I knew you and I are worth it. We fell in love in a second. I was barely able to blink, and you had my entire world upside-down. I was scared you weren't… real. I was scared no one could be as magnetic as you are to me. It still scares me. You still scare me." Pausing, Emily shook her head. "Then I saw Gina, and all my fears came back. My heart wanted to believe you, but my head wouldn't allow it after I'd already taken that risk on us. I'm so sorry, Gavin. I don't know what else to say other than I love you and need you with everything inside me."

Gavin cleared his throat but didn't say a word.

Once again unable to resist her want, her need, Emily moved closer, pushed up on her tiptoes, and placed a soft, lingering kiss on Gavin's cheek. She closed her eyes as his heat radiated over her body.

Gavin lifted his hands, burrowing his fingers tight around Emily's waist. Emily felt his lips brush against the crown of her head and heard him suck in a steeling breath, but before she could open her eyes, he let go. With her heart pounding, she watched him duck back into his car, his tires screeching as he veered out of the parking lot.

Feeling as though Gavin couldn't get away from her quick enough, Emily hugged her stomach, sickened by what she'd done to them. All hope gone and head in a daze, she looked at the bellboy who'd been waiting with her luggage. Sporting a warm smile, he nodded and led her into the hotel lobby. She followed, her breathing shallow as she tried to unscatter her thoughts long enough to show the proper ID to the woman seated behind the front desk.

After handing Emily's passport back to her, the young, dark-haired woman smiled. "Thank you for choosing the Royal Playa del Carmen, Señorita Cooper. Rafael will show you to your room. The presidential suites are located in a separate building, but they're within walking distance." She slid a pamphlet and room card across the clay-colored marble counter. "Any information about your suite and the amenities the resort offers can be found here, or you can call the concierge desk at any time. I hope you enjoy your stay."

"Thank you." Emily turned to Rafael and shook her head. "I don't need any help with my bag, but thank you."

"Are you sure, señorita? I'm more than happy."

"I'm sure."

He nodded, and Emily made her way out of the pristine lobby and into the humid night air. Glancing at the pamphlet with her room number on it, Emily rounded the corner and followed a cobblestone path to the back of the resort. A mariachi band in the distance and laughter from vacationers hummed through her ears. She pulled her luggage and tried to drag her attention from several happy couples dancing under the woven diamond of stars above. Envy pierced Emily. That should've been her, and she'd ruined any chance at having that. At her building, she slid the room key into the glass door, shuffled into the small lobby area, and slipped into the elevator. With her heart aching for Gavin, she wondered why she was even staying the night. She didn't belong there, and she knew it. Her reason for being there was gone, lost from her life forever, and there was nothing she could do to change his mind.

When the elevator doors slid open, she stepped into a hallway housing six suites. Scanning the numbers on each, she eventually found hers and swiped her card through the entryway scanner. Emily pushed open the door and flipped on the lights. Pain continued to crush in around her as she made her way through the expansive suite. Exhausted and mentally spent, she curled her hand around the sleek bamboo of one of the four posters of a king-sized bed. She slid off her heels and dropped them onto the cold marble floor. Feeling depleted—mind, body, and soul—she sank onto the bed and pressed her face into the pillow, a rush of tears falling from her eyes. He was gone. Her Yankees-loving, bottle cap-giving, dimpled smile other half was gone, and there wasn't anything she wouldn't do to turn back time.

However, her time was up.

CHAPTER FIVE

Collide

Eyes fluttering open, Emily rolled to her side and yawned. For a second, she didn't know where she was. Her gaze caught the clock on the nightstand. It was just past two in the morning. Then reality hit. Unrelenting sadness lashed her as she sat up on the edge of the bed. Staring around the empty suite, visions of Gavin swam in her mind. He clearly wasn't coming back. She sank deeper into a cesspool of pain. She gazed at the clock again before grabbing her luggage and tossing it onto the bed. After rummaging through it, she padded into the bathroom.

Weariness pulled at her, and regret weakened every muscle as she stepped into the shower. Standing under the hot spray, she decided to leave. She couldn't stay, even if leaving meant she had to spend the night in the airport. Though a part of her begged her to call a cab, head over to Gavin's house, and plead with him to take her back, the other part shielded her from any further hurt. She heaved an exhausted sigh, reached for a towel, and wrapped it around herself. After blow drying her hair, she changed into a pair of jean shorts and a T-shirt. She tugged her bag from the bed, gave the breathtaking room one last look, and left.

In the hallway, Emily turned and felt her legs buckle. Her eyes locked on Gavin stepping from the elevator. When their gazes caught,

Emily tried to swallow, but her throat felt too dry and tight. She drew a shuddering breath and let it out as he moved slowly toward her. Her heart tripped, stopped, and restarted when he came within inches of her. His heady, masculine scent engulfed her.

His gaze zeroed in on her mouth, his voice soft. "I stared at the ceiling half the night wondering if I could honestly go the rest of my life without kissing these lips ever again." Gavin grazed the pad of his thumb against Emily's mouth. Letting it linger, he traced the top and bottom. She parted her lips, her mind desperately trying to remind her how to breathe as she stared into his eyes. Gavin stepped closer. "I paced the house when I couldn't sleep, imagining another day of not feeling this body against mine. This body was made to fit me in every possible way." Gavin's fingertips ghosted across her cheek, along the curve of her neck. Coiled heat simmered through Emily's stomach as his hand drifted down her shoulder, brushed the side of her torso, and finally settled on her waist. He squeezed, and desire jolted up her spine.

Trembling, Emily dropped her head to the side, but Gavin found her chin and gently lifted her face. She swallowed back tears and turned her green eyes to him.

He rolled his tongue over his lips and took a breath. "The thought of not seeing your eyes when I wake up, or not hearing your heart next to me when you're asleep made me sick. With all of that, I decided no, I can't go another day without you. I don't *want* to go another day without you." Gavin stepped closer, and suddenly, Emily's back was against the suite door. "You're mine," he added. "The second you showed up at my place that night, you sealed your fate." Emily's heart pounded. He placed his hands on the sides of her head. "Do you love me, Emily?"

Her belly knotted, and her breathing became shallow. "Yes, I love you," she whispered, staring into his blue eyes.

He licked his lips, dropped a hand to the door, and leaned into her ear. "Do you know you're mine?"

She heard the door unlock. "Yes," she breathed.

"Say it," he growled, his lips hovering above hers.

Her nipples beaded. "I'm yours."

"Say it again, Emily." He curled his arm around her waist, yanked the bag from her hand, and jacked her tight against his chest.

The blistering heat of his body sent Emily's emotions crashing over a cliff. "God, Gavin, I'm yours. Forever. No one else."

Before Emily could blink, Gavin's lips seized hers, the kiss instantly desperate and hungry. Breathing heavily, they plunged their tongues inside each other's mouths as if dying to taste one another completely. Gavin flung open the door, dropped her bag, and backed her into the suite. Gasping, Emily twisted her arms around his neck, her hands gripping his hair as he started unbuttoning her shorts. He roughed them and her panties down her thighs. Wiggling out of them, Emily tore her mouth from his and whipped her T-shirt over her head. With no hesitation, Emily worked the button on his pants. Hands knotted in her hair, Gavin yanked her head back and trailed open-mouthed kisses down her neck. Somewhere between Emily's bra slithering to the floor, along with Gavin's shirt and pants, Emily wound up on her back on a crushed velvet chaise lounge in the middle of the living room.

Standing above her, Gavin's stared at the woman he loved, his heart swelling as he watched her waiting for him. His gaze crawled over her body, taking in her succulent pink nipples drawn up tight in her arousal. So. Damn. Lush. She ran her tongue across that pretty bow of a mouth, swollen from his kisses. Just looking at her could be his undoing, and he knew it. He knew it the first time he saw her. He was desperate to be inside her and feel her sweet little pussy wrapped around him. Running her hands down her legs, opened wide for him, Emily let out a dejected sigh and it was then a deep, raw, primal urge to reclaim every inch of her body forged through Gavin's thoughts. A sickening need to wipe Dillon clear from her mind forever hit, kicking him in the gut. The first time Emily had shared herself with him, Gavin told her there wasn't a part of her body that wouldn't feel him.

Tonight, he knew he was going to remove every speck of Dillon from her.

Blue eyes hot with possessiveness and breathing heavily, Gavin dropped to his knees, easing Emily's leg over his shoulder. Staring at her, needing to catalogue her reaction, Gavin tripped two fingers across Emily's clit. Her moisture seeped, coating his fingers. Before she could release the gasp perched on the tip of her tongue, Gavin settled his mouth over her smooth pussy.

Arching her back, her body jerked and bucked, her nipples budding hard as he speared his tongue in and out of her. Dear God, she couldn't breathe and she didn't want to. Simply lost in the feeling of him, all she wanted to do was drown in his familiarity. His heat crashed over her as he pushed his fingers in deep and slow. On a long groan, he curved them, pressing on her core as his tongue stroked, swirled, and flicked tiny circles over her sensitized bud.

"Please don't stop, Gavin," she panted, circling her hips against his mouth. "I'm so close." And she was. Body starved for him, Emily knew it wouldn't take much to bring her there. Not that it ever did with him. All he needed to do was take one look at her and she'd melt, but the burning wait wasn't helping in the prolonging department. As if her words sent him into a frenzy, Gavin worked his fingers harder, deeper, their steady rhythm relentless as Emily leaned up and pulled his face against her wetness. He groaned, and the rich, deep, erotic sound vibrated, resonating against her sensitive flesh. Emily came apart. Falling, her body hurtled into orgasm. She tossed her head back, moaned, and curled her fingers tight in his hair. Her body convulsed with surges of heat pooling low in her belly.

With her addictive flavor fresh on his tongue, Gavin swept her up and carried her toward the bedroom, his mouth plastered to hers. As he inhaled her scent, Gavin set her on her feet.

Emily watched, entranced, as he slid the briefs from his body. His dick sprung free, and he palmed it, stroking it slowly. She could barely breathe.

Eyes locked on hers, carnal, fierce with passion, Gavin stepped closer, his chest pressed to hers. "I'm going to fuck you right now, Emily. I'm going to bring you so much pleasure you'll never think about walking away from me again. " Conviction rang in his tone, and his primal demand made Emily's pussy weep with need.

He closed his eyes, and his head fell back as a groan rumbled up his throat. Bringing his gaze back to hers, he slid two fingers over her clit and gathered her moisture. He lifted his hand, dragging his fingers across her mouth. Emily parted her lips and released a soft moan as he slipped them in. She grabbed his wrist and pinned him with a saucy stare as she sucked her juices from his fingers, her teeth lightly grazing his flesh. "After I'm finished fucking you, I'm going to make love to you. From the minute my body touched yours, there was never going to be anyone else. I'm in love with you, but I have to fuck you first. Do you understand me?" he asked.

"Yes," she breathed, reaching for his cock.

"Say it, baby." He delved his hand in her hair, gently massaging his fingers through her soft waves. With the other, he helped her stroke his long, hard length. A muscle ticked in his jaw, his voice ragged. "I need to hear you say it before I do."

Pressure rose and heat swelled between Emily's legs. She whimpered, running her tongue along his jaw. "Please, Gavin, I want you to fuck me. Fuck me... hard."

A feral smile spread across his mouth, his voice eerily calm as he whispered, "Turn around."

Breathless, Emily stared at him and swiped the tip of her tongue across her lips, her pert nipples hardening against his chest. Slowly, Emily turned, feeling Gavin's hands slide down her waist. A shiver wound through her as he grabbed her thigh and lifted her knee onto the bed.

Fitting his hips against her ass, Gavin bent her over the bed. He trailed his knuckles down the gracious curve of her spine before he laid his chest over her back. He flicked his tongue against Emily's ear, his senses soaking in her gasp as he pushed the crown of his dick into her drenched opening. With one hand palming her stomach and the other curled around her neck, he surged into her. Instantly, her pussy clamped down, sucking him in deeper. Her quick little breaths and hungry moans set his skin on fire, sent hot lava pulsing through his veins. God, she felt so hot and tight; it was all he could do to restrain his need to get deeper inside her.

"Tell me how much you love me, Emily," he groaned, thrusting into her harder. He dropped his hands to her thighs and clutched them possessively.

He pushed deeper, stretching her painfully, however, the sensation felt wonderful to Emily. Then he withdrew completely, leaving her with a raw ache down to her knees. Emily cried out, her panting breaths nearly begging. "I love you more than anything, Gavin." She clawed at the sheets and wriggled her ass against him. "Please don't stop. Please."

He dragged the tip of his cock though her warmth, pressed one scant inch of himself inside her, and withdrew again.

Need flared through Emily, balling in her belly. A giant rush of air filled her lungs. Her voice trembled. "What are you doing? Oh my God, Gavin. Please."

He tucked his face into the crook of her neck and brushed a thumb over her nipple, the fingers of his other hand swirling over her clit. "Tell me you're mine." He spoke the heated whisper into her ear.

Emily flung her head back against his chest and moaned. "I'm yours. Only yours. Now fuck me!"

Gavin nipped the back of her shoulder, pressed his palm against her stomach, and thrust every hard inch back into her. Emily tensed and gasped, her pussy clenching him tighter than before. His cock throbbed. Her flesh set fire to his skin as he forged deeper, spreading her wide. Pleasure cut through him like a knife as Emily cried out his name, her body heat surging into him with each shallow breath he took. He rocked into her again, one steady stroke following another, but still, he needed to get deeper. He wanted her boneless, her mind completely sated with nothing but thoughts of him. Lifting her other leg onto the bed, he pumped hard and steady into her. After he pushed her hair away from her sweaty neck, he fisted it and pulled her head back.

Emily whimpered, her body melting against his. Her lungs whipped hard and fast, her body hummed, feeling deliciously split in two as he moved with ruthless control.

Gavin branded her neck with his mouth, his tongue laving up and down hungrily. "Fuck. Tell me again. Tell me how much you love me, Emily."

Emily clutched his hair and looked over her shoulder at him, her breath coming in quick pants as she stared into his eyes. It was then she sensed his fear that if he blinked, she would disappear into thin air. Guilt spilled over her. With that, she stopped moving against him.

Gavin also stopped, worry filling his face. "Did I hurt you?" He grazed his thumb along her lips. "Jesus, baby, I'm sorry if I did. I would never hurt you, Emily. Never."

She shook her head, straightened, and turned around. "No, you didn't hurt me, and I know you never would." She laced her hands around his neck. Relief crossed his face, and his perfect mouth found hers, his kiss urgent and hungry. Emily pulled back, her voice soft. "Gavin, please stop."

Eyes steeped in confusion, he stepped back. "What's wrong?"

"I'm not going anywhere, Gavin. I'm not," she whispered and reached for his hand, gently guiding him to the bed. "Lay down for me."

With a dark brow raised, his gaze drilled into hers as he did what she asked. Propped up on his elbows, he watched Emily crawl toward him.

They both sucked in a ragged breath when she sank down on him. Emily leaned over and brushed her lips against his, soft and gentle. Gavin's eyes slid shut, and he gripped her waist.

"No," she breathed, circling her hips slowly, her body pulsing around his. "Look at me, Gavin. I want you to look at me while I make love to you."

His eyes flew open, and Emily reached for his hands. She drew them up to her breasts. Gavin cupped them, his fingers kneading against each one. Body riveted, Gavin groaned and pushed up inside her. He felt Emily tense and clamp down around him. Her slow friction spiraled, blistering through his muscles.

Sitting straight up, movements calculated, Emily massaged her hands against his as he caressed her breasts. "These are yours, Gavin. Only yours." Arching her back, Emily slithered one hand down her stomach and rubbed her clit. Eyes locked on Gavin's, her hips bucked slightly faster, her breathing picking up. "This is yours. No other man will ever touch this." Her voice trembled as a fiery ache shot, tingling through every nerve. She watched Gavin drag his bottom lip between his teeth, felt his body go rigid. She reached around and grazed her fingernails under his balls.

Pleasure broadsided Gavin. "You feel so good around me." He sucked in a harsh breath, his hands dropping to her thighs. He gripped them tightly, guiding her body up and down his cock. Her slick, wet pussy was hot, turning him harder than ever. "I fucking love you, Emily. You're mine. You've always been mine." Bucking his hips up, he thrust her down onto him. "Tell me you love me."

She started riding him faster, harder, her need to get him to understand driving her to the brink of insanity-filled desire. The feel of him inside her drugged her system beyond words, beyond coherent thought. "Goddamn you, Gavin, I love you! I love you so much. I'm so sorry. I didn't mean to do this to us. Do you understand me? I'm sorry." With tears slipping down her cheeks, she dug her nails into his shoulders and pulled his body flat against her sweat-dampened chest. He buried his face against her breast, his mouth sucking and swirling her beaded nipple. Her body burned as she gripped his hair. His neck went taut as a bow, his eyes boring into hers. "You're all I see. All I hear. All I dream about. I came here for you. I'm not leaving. I'm not going anywhere. It's you, Gavin. Only you."

She crashed her lips to his, their pounding hearts and short, panting breaths in sync. Gavin curled his hands around her nape, his hands fisted in her hair as tight as hers were in his.

The sound of wet flesh smacking together echoed through the room as their orgasms hit. Their every sense attuned to one another like never before. In each of them, fire danced into a violent explosion of pleasure, and every stolen moment, hurtful word, and accusation fell away, disappearing as their bodies jerked and shuddered together. They were no longer on borrowed time and each of them knew it. Soaked it in. Emily felt Gavin's strong arms wrap around her waist, his breathing shallow against her chest. As the sensations liquefying them settled, Gavin snagged Emily's gaze as she looked down at him. Gavin smoothed her damp hair away from her face and guided her lips to his. Deep and passionate, slow and gentle, he kissed her. Warmth centered deep in her womb as she moaned into his mouth.

Lying back, Gavin pulled Emily on top of his chest. Tenderly gliding his hands up and down her spine, he breathed a sigh of relief. For the first time since he'd met her, Gavin felt relaxed. At ease. Emily was finally his.

Other than their sweet breaths starting to calm, the air was filled with the sound of waves crashing in the distance beyond French doors leading to a balcony. Moonlight bathed the bedroom while Emily listened to the steady rhythm of Gavin's heart beating against her ear. The heart she nearly destroyed. Feeling unworthy of him, she dusted kisses across his chest and looked up at him. "I'm so sorry," she whispered. "I can't believe I almost ruined us."

He trailed a finger along her cheek, his blue eyes intense. "I know you are, and I don't want you saying it again. We're not ruined. We're better. Understand?"

Nodding, she laid her head back down on his chest and clenched his shoulders. "I didn't think you were coming back."

"Well, I knew I was coming back the moment I left."

Emily lifted her head, her hooded stare meeting Gavin's. "Oh, did you, Mr. Blake?"

"Why, of course I did, Miss Cooper," he said with a grin. "I figured I'd let you sweat it out for a while." A slow smile spread across his face. "Apparently, I made you moan while you sweated it out."

With a pseudo pout, she batted his arm playfully. "Wiseass."

"It's part of my charm." He chuckled and skimmed his fingers down her back. Pulling her closer, Gavin fastened his mouth to hers. Emily's lips went pliant and goose bumps rose over her body. "Get used to it. You're stuck with this wiseass."

She nipped at his lip and smiled. "I'll take you whatever way I can." After indulging in his kiss a little longer, Emily rested her head against his chest, her body deliciously sore.

A stretch of silence filled the room as Gavin sank into the sensations of Emily tracing his tattoo. Her touch tossed him into heaven, yet his thoughts cast him into hell. Guilt hit him and decided to play a little game. He'd planned on telling her right away about his brief encounter with the woman he'd met a few days before on the beach, but God help him, he couldn't when he'd arrived at the hotel. Seeing Emily in the hallway with her luggage, ready to leave his life again, sent his intentions flying out the fucking window. Hell, he knew he had every right to do what he did, but that didn't stop it from weighing heavily on his chest. Gavin cleared his throat and brushed his hands through Emily's hair. He cupped her face, bringing her gaze to his. "I have to tell you something."

She blinked, met his stare for a moment, and then laid her head back down on his chest. "How old were you when you got this, and why did you choose to get it on your ribs?" She grazed her fingers along the dragon's wings.

Head downcast, examining her delicate fingers flowing over the black ink, Gavin stroked the long line of her back. "I got it right out of college, so around twenty-two or twenty-three." He ran his hand through his hair and released a breath. "I decided to get it there because I wanted it hidden from eyes I didn't want to see it and traced by beautiful fingers that I did."

She peered up at him, her smile soft and her touch softer as she skimmed the dragon's body. "These fingers?"

"Yes," Gavin whispered. "Those fingers." He watched Emily smile at his words and lay her head back down against his chest. Hesitation rolled through him for a second, but he knew if he didn't tell her, it would eat away at him. "I have to talk to you about something."

"Did it hurt when you got it?" Emily didn't look up as she continued to trace the art.

Gavin lifted her chin, his brows furrowed. "Emily, I did something I have to tell you about."

Swallowing, Emily nodded. "I know you slept with those two girls." She touched his cheek with the back of her hand and stared into his eyes. Those beautiful blue eyes, edged by thick, dark lashes holding her future. "And I don't care. You thought I married Dillon. I know you wouldn't have if you knew otherwise." She placed a soft kiss on his lips and nuzzled her face in his neck.

Gavin caressed her hair and pulled in a breath. "I didn't sleep with them."

"You didn't?" she asked, shock evident in her voice as she pulled her head back.

"No. You thankfully intercepted that train wreck when you showed up."

She let out a sigh of relief. "So you won't have any children running around in Mexico. Thank God."

Gavin watched her expression ease, and fuck if it didn't seize his heart in a single second. Bringing her face closer to his, he ran the pad of his thumb across her lips. "No. I won't have any children running around in Mexico because I used protection with someone you didn't intercept." He paused, his eyes searching hers. Emily bit her lip and nodded. "I'm sorry," he whispered, his voice riddled with guilt.

Emily swept her gaze over his face and found nothing but regret. Guilt of her own tripped through her stomach, knowing she was the reason for it. As she searched her mind for a way to free him from his remorse, to show him it didn't matter to her, a devious smile crept up the corners of her mouth. Sitting up, she straddled his lap, pinned his hands behind his head, and brushed her lips against his. Staring at him, she spoke against his mouth. "Gavin Blake, I love you so much, it's literally dangerous to us both. You know that?"

He cocked an incredulous brow. "Dangerous?"

"Very," she purred, raining kisses along his jaw.

Freeing his hands from her hold, Gavin threaded his fingers through her hair. A grin touched his mouth. "Mmm, I like a naughty Emily. You can be as dangerous as you want to with me."

Emily's stomach rolled with heat as Gavin brought her down to his lips. While kissing him, she heard Gavin's stomach roll with a growl of hunger. She laughed. "Hungry?"

"What?" he asked innocently. He turned on his megawatt smile.

"Okay, I'm not deaf, Blake." She leaned over and flipped on a lamp. "Either you've caught a bug while here in Mexico, or you're hungry." After pulling a menu from the nightstand drawer, she handed it to him. "I'm *praying* for the latter."

Gavin barked out a laugh and then slowly sobered. "What is that?" He slid his thumb over her eyebrow and placed the menu on the bed.

Emily's stomach plummeted. She felt all kinds of sick as she curled her hand around Gavin's wrist, pulling it away from the spot where Dillon hit her. Panic set in, but she covered it up with a smile. "Oh, that? It's nothing. I was at work, I bent over to pick up something from behind the bar, and I slammed my head against the countertop."

Gavin sat up, snaked one arm behind her back, and lifted the other to her brow again. He studied it for a second. Something in Emily's tone didn't sit right with him. He shifted his eyes to hers. "It happened at work, huh?"

"Yes, Gavin," she said, mustering up all the confidence she had left. "My moment of grace happened at work. Luckily the place was empty, or I would've been even more embarrassed." She plucked the menu from the bed and started looking over it. "So what are you in the mood for? They have everything from burgers to filet mignon." She swung her legs off him, pulled the sheet around her body, and stood to go to the bathroom. "Just order me the chicken Caesar salad."

Emily flipped on the light switch and closed the door. Leaning against it, she drew in a breath, hoping she'd successfully pulled off the lie gnawing away at her. This wasn't the way she'd wanted to start off with Gavin. Not even close. Keeping anything from him bit at her conscience. However, visions of Gavin going after Dillon tightened her chest, and Dillon's threats the night of her rehearsal dinner screamed loud in her ears. With that, she settled the internal battle. She was protecting Gavin and wouldn't say a word about what'd happened that morning. Emily turned the handle to exit the bathroom. On the other side, she found Gavin with his arms crossed, leaning against the doorjamb. His probing blue eyes made her heart lurch into her throat. Though her nerves skyrocketed, she couldn't keep her gaze from sweeping over his naked form. The utter masculine perfection of his solid body had her instantly breathing faster, unconsciously biting her lip.

"You startled me." She pushed up on her tiptoes and planted a kiss on his cheek. "But I've always known you were a stalker." She feigned playful and draped her arms around his neck, but his stare was all over her, as if he was waiting for her to tell him the truth. All she wanted to do was 'fess up, but she wouldn't. "Speaking of stalker, how did you get a key to the suite?" Emily knew it was a poor attempt at a subject change, but she was grasping at anything to keep Gavin's attention from Dillon.

"I called Colton from my house and told him to add my name to the reservation." Gavin leaned down and brushed his lips against her forehead. "So, what happened the night you left him?"

Emily swallowed back the bile rising in her throat and clenched the sheet to her chest. She looked at him from beneath her lashes. "Nothing really happened."

Gavin pulled back, his expression tight with skepticism. "Nothing? He just let you walk out the door and didn't say a word?"

She grappled for an answer as she crossed the room. Sinking onto the bed, she slid a stare back at him and shrugged. "Yes. I left his townhouse after he fell asleep, stopped by your place, and then went back to my apartment. He came over the morning of the wedding, and we got into an argument. In the middle of it, my sister and her husband showed up, and Michael made him leave. That's it."

Forehead creased, Gavin palmed the back of his neck and stepped closer. "And he hasn't bothered you at all?"

"No, he hasn't." One truth she could admit. Shockingly, other than Joan calling to bitch her out after bailing Dillon out of jail, Emily hadn't seen or heard from him since the cops dragged him out of her apartment.

Gavin closed the distance and knelt in front of Emily. His hands glided effortlessly under the sheets to grip her waist. "You would tell me if anything had happened, right?"

Nearly paralyzed by her lie, Emily struggled against tears. She lifted her hand to his face, cradled his cheek, and nodded. "Of course I would," she whispered.

Rubbing his thumbs in slow circles on her skin, he closed his eyes. "I'm sorry I wasn't there when you told him. You shouldn't have had to do it on your own."

"Gavin, no," she choked out, standing. She buried her hands in his hair and pulled his face to her stomach. Looking down at him, guilt thudded through her heart as she watched him kiss her flesh. He clenched her waist tighter, his mouth urgent. His guilt seared her stomach. "Please, Gavin, I was fine. You thought I'd married him. Please don't do this to yourself." Emily sank down on his lap and wrapped her legs around his waist.

"I'm so fucking sorry, baby." Gavin kissed her deeper as he scooted back against the nightstand. "I shouldn't have left. We said we were going to tell him together."

Emily tore her mouth from his and took his face in her hands. Tears broke loose as she stared into his eyes. "Please stop," she begged. Heat whipped over her flesh as she fitted his heavily veined dick between her wet folds. A paradox of the worst kind splintered through her as she relished feeling him inside her. Blinding and beautiful, in that moment, Gavin owned her and she owned him, yet guilt held them both captive, its chains heavy, exhausting.

Eyes flaring with hunger, Gavin's kiss became possessive as he licked into her mouth, taking total domination of her body. His every muscle hardened, tightening his arms around Emily's waist. He consumed her flesh, pulsing energy colliding with their love and chemistry as he filled her thicker, deeper.

Quickly, with reckless abandon, Emily fell into every sensation Gavin bestowed. His eyes controlled her very soul. His touch filled her inner being. It was then, in that moment, she knew she had to remove every speck of guilt from Gavin's body.

She only prayed she could.

CHAPTER SIX

Do-Over

Sunlight peeked over the horizon and streamed into the bedroom as Gavin lay awake, soaking in the sound of Emily's sleeping body. She was curled on her side, both hands tucked under the pillow, as his eyes traced every line of her face. God, she looked sweet, an angel so beautiful next to him. Wanting to reach out and touch her, he blew out a breath and resisted the urge, deciding to let her sleep. He watched, mesmerized, his mind replaying the last few weeks as the exhaustion of it all lifted from his chest. Each complicated, tangled layer they'd started off with disappeared. A smile lifted the corners of his lips as Emily burrowed against him. She let out a sleepy sigh and snuggled closer, her leg coming up over his thigh. Fuck. All good intentions of allowing her to sleep were demolished. Gone.

Rolling her naked body into his arms and onto his chest, Gavin fused their lips together and held her tight. "I tried. I honestly did."

A purr of pleasure crawled up her throat as her eyes fluttered open. Smile on her face, she cocked a brow. "My ass."

"The ass that's officially owned by me?" Gavin caressed his hands down her waist, settling on said ass. "This one? Ah, yes. Yes, this one. I love this ass."

"Owned?" Emily playfully questioned.

"Yes… owned. Never to be leased by another. I'm king landlord, sweets." He nipped her lip, and she laughed. "I don't take checks, but I do accept most forms of foreplay and sex as payment."

Emily filtered her fingers through his hair and shook her head. She wiggled her ass that'd been thoughtfully cupped in his hands. "I only do wild, hanging from a chandelier sex."

"Mmm, that's a tough one." Gavin bit his lip, primal satisfaction glassing his eyes. "I'll accept your offer as long as I can rope you to the chandelier and have my way with you in whatever way I please."

Giggling, Emily kinked her head to the side. "Who are you? Christian Grey?"

Hands gliding up her back, a furrow appeared between his brows. "Who's Christian Grey?"

Eyes wide, Emily sat up and pinned Gavin's hands above his head. She brushed her nose against his. "You don't know who Christian Grey is?"

"Not a clue." Gavin craned his head up, catching her mouth with his. "Is he someone you went to school with?" Before Emily could answer, he gently tugged her lip between his teeth. "Wait. You've never been roped up by someone, right?"

"No, not yet." Emily laughed, lacing their fingers. "And I didn't go to school with Christian Grey. But I'm pretty sure there's not a woman on earth who hasn't heard of him." Gavin sent Emily another confused look. "Never mind." She sat up, wrapped the satin sheet around her body, and slipped off the bed. "I'll explain it one day."

"Wait. Where are you going? I hope you're not thinking about showering without me." Wearing a grin, he leaned up on his elbows. "Remember, I'm the landlord. You need my permission to do anything."

Eyes piqued in humor, Emily watched Gavin swing his legs over the bed and take a ground-eating step toward her. "Caveman much?"

Gavin didn't reply. Nope. Instead, he swept her off her feet. Slanting his mouth over hers, he kissed her hard, inhaling deeply, as if trying to breathe her into him. He carried Emily into the bathroom and set her on the vanity.

Gavin's hard body instantly sent a welcomed shiver up her spine, making her forget about the cold granite under her ass. Her blood sang, and she felt a blush creep up her neck as he slowly pulled the sheet away from her.

His gaze trekked over her body before settling on her lips. "God, you're amazing." He positioned himself between her thighs. Gripping her legs, he drew them up and wrapped them around his waist. "A certified fucking wake up call."

Pleasure to come clouded Emily's mind as she watched him shove his fingers into his mouth. Achingly slow, with his eyes pinned to hers, he pulled them out and trailed them down her stomach. Goose bumps erupted, dancing all over her skin. The breath left her as he palmed her pussy and slid his fingers deep inside. A whimper escaped her as he curled his other hand along the side of her neck and eased her back against the mirror.

"I want you to finger yourself with me," he roughed out, his breathing ragged.

"What?" Emily moaned, unable to keep her voice from shaking. "I've never—"

"Fingered yourself?" He circled his thumb around her clit.

Arching her back against the mirror, Emily started to pant. "No, I've only used a vibrator."

Gavin bit his lip and closed his eyes. A groan rumbled in his chest as he pumped his fingers in and out, their fluid motion slow and steady. Opening his eyes, he dragged his hand from Emily's neck and reached for her wrist. Guiding it down between her legs, he placed her fingers over her clit. "No vibrator today. Rub it for me."

Emily batted her eyelashes shyly but found herself doing what he'd asked. She sucked in a breath as she slid two fingers over her swollen flesh. Lips parted at the multiple sensations, she stared at Gavin and clenched down around his fingers. With every nerve ending awakened and a burning urge for climax nearly disintegrating her, she moaned as she circled her hips. "Oh my God, Gavin," she breathed, rubbing harder.

Gavin stroked himself with his free hand, ruthless arousal flaring in his eyes. "That's right, baby," he grunted, "now push them in with mine."

His demand, so raw and primal, had Emily surrendering. Sinking two fingers in with his, she trembled and shuddered. Her blood rushed with the force of a freight train, shutting down her thoughts. The faster Gavin stroked himself, the faster he worked his fingers inside her. Gazes locked, both of their breathing erratic, their faces twisted in total ecstasy.

"Christ, your pussy's so perfect." Gavin's head fell back for a second, a groan pushing up his throat. Bringing his eyes back to hers, pleasure surged and seized deep within his balls as Emily sank farther against the mirror. She unwrapped her legs from his waist and planted her feet on the vanity. Completely exposed, she continued to thrust her fingers inside herself with his. The hard stalk of his dick pulsated in his hand as he watched her eyes flutter closed. "Fuck. I have to taste you," Gavin bit out, his nostrils flaring. "Take your fingers out and rub that hot clit for me."

Aching for release, Emily gasped and removed her fingers, sliding them over herself. She watched Gavin kneel. Clenching her hips, he pulled her ass to the edge of the vanity. He latched his mouth to her pussy, his tongue laving urgently. Instantly, need grew, magnifying in Emily's core. Tightening, her body was totally lost to the passion of the intimate act. She'd never opened herself like this with anyone, but it felt so natural with Gavin. Rubbing herself faster, her breathing grew choppier and then completely stopped. Gavin brushed her fingers out of the way and stroked his tongue over her, pulling her clit into his mouth, nipping, sucking. She melted. Done.

She gasped a long, shocked intake of air. "Oh my God, Gavin… I'm… I'm… coming." She couldn't breathe. Couldn't think. Lost to the sensations crashing through her system, her body quivered as she reached for Gavin's hair, tugging him against her as she rode out the last bit of her climax.

Standing, Gavin continued to stroke himself and grabbed Emily by her nape, pulling her against his lips. He swirled his tongue over hers. The taste of their juices mixing nearly sent him over the edge. Emily moaned into his mouth, and it was the hottest fucking sound Gavin had ever heard. She slid her fingers under his and started stroking him, their hands gliding in unison along his cock. Gavin surged his tongue deeper into Emily's mouth and groaned, his entire body tightening as his orgasm wracked through his muscles.

With a snarl, he lifted his hands and fisted Emily's hair as he let her finish him off. And she did. Every last bit of what he had to give flowed over her fingers, their breathing heavy as Gavin ripped his mouth from hers. He buried his face in the crook of Emily's neck. A moment later, Gavin pulled back and found Emily's gaze, her green eyes sated as she kissed his lips. Soft and gentle, bodies relaxed, they fell deeper in love as they slowly absorbed one another; as if in shock that now, time… time was on their side.

Time was all they had.

An hour and a long, hot shower later, Gavin and Emily stepped from the hotel into the afternoon warmth. As they waited for the valet to bring his car around, Emily sent Gavin a wide smile that made his heart ache. Her eyes glowed with happiness, and it did things to him he never imagined.

He moved behind her and draped his strong arms around her stomach. "Thank you," he whispered against the back of her neck, reaching for her hand. He brought it to his mouth and kissed it.

Emily craned her head toward him, pushed up on her tiptoes, and brushed her lips along his jaw. "No. Thank you."

Gavin smiled and leaned over to kiss her. They both sank into the drugging feeling until the valet pulled up with the car.

The driver stepped out and approached Gavin. "Muy bonito carro."

Reaching for Emily's luggage, Gavin looked at her and back to the driver. A reverent smile broke out across his face. "Muchas gracias. Además de esta hermosa mujer que tengo a mi lado, los carros son mi segunda pasión."

The man glanced in Emily's direction, nodding enthusiastically. "Claro que si, los dos son muy hermosos."

Emily looked at Gavin. "What are you two talking about?"

"Cars and you. My two favorite things." Gavin shot her a wink as he placed her luggage in the trunk. Emily shook her head and smiled. Walking over to the driver, Gavin dug in his pocket, fished out his wallet, and handed him a tip. "Gracias de nuevo." The driver nodded his thanks and went to give Gavin the keys, but Emily plucked them from his hand.

She looked at Gavin and shot him a wink back. "So I assume you won't mind if one of your favorite things drives your other favorite thing?"

Gavin's lips slid into a grin. "It's a stick, doll."

With a little cock of her head, Emily's mouth dropped open. "You just assume I don't know how to drive a stick?"

Gavin wrapped his arms around her waist and whispered into her ear, "Well, I know you've mastered driving a *certain* type of stick." One eyebrow crept up on Emily's face, and Gavin chuckled. He cupped her cheek and kissed the top of her head. "But yes, I naturally assumed you didn't know how to drive the other."

"Well," Emily purred, slinking her arms over his shoulders, "one of your favorite things knows how to drive stick, and she knows how to drive it very well." She brought his lips down to hers. "I also like to drive fast."

"That's pretty fucking hot." He grazed his lips against her ear. "You can drive every stick I own whenever you want."

Excitement bubbled in Emily's stomach as she turned on her heel and headed for the driver's side. Opening the door, she slipped in and adjusted her seatbelt. When Gavin sank into his seat, Emily looked over at him, a smirk on her face. "Now it's *my* turn to tell *you* to get your seatbelt on."

"A dominant woman. I love it." Gavin reached for the seatbelt. "Just don't get us killed."

Emily playfully smacked his arm. Keys in hand, she frowned when she couldn't find the ignition. "How do I start it?"

Gavin couldn't hold back his smile. "Miss Indie 500, the car's already on, and it's a push button."

Emily rolled her eyes, stepped on the clutch, and eased out of the parking lot. "Don't make fun of me, wiseass."

Her cute, sassy words made Gavin chuckle.

"This Indie 500 woman's not used to driving expensive cars like this. The ones I've owned usually yell at me when I start them up."

Gavin mocked shock, his blue eyes wide. "They literally yell at you? Bastards."

Glancing in the rearview mirror, Emily smiled and nodded. "Actually, they curse me out." Gavin barked out a laugh, and Emily stopped before turning onto the highway. She looked at him. "How did you get the window fixed so quickly?"

"Money has its advantages, sweets." He grinned, curling his fingers around the nape of her neck. "Now turn your landlord on and show him what you got, speed demon."

Emily smiled like the Cheshire cat and pulled onto the highway.

Gavin watched soberly as her shapely legs, belonging to him, moved under her silk sundress each time she pressed down on the clutch. Her delicate fingers curled around the shift as she glided through the gears. Her auburn hair falling in loose curls had him shifting in his seat. Fuck. He was getting turned on. Heat sliced through his stomach. But hell if she wasn't driving like his grandmother.

He cleared his throat and hit a few buttons on the touchscreen panel to turn on the satellite radio. "You *can* drive a little faster."

Emily sent him a questioning stare. "I'm doing the speed limit."

"I thought you liked to drive fast?" Gavin lifted a confused brow.

"I said that so you'd let me drive, considering how fast you drove yesterday." She shrugged. "I never speed."

A wicked grin twisted Gavin's mouth. He leaned over, rested his hand on her right thigh, and pushed down. To add a little fuel to the fire, he caressed her flesh in a slow, circular motion. He had her now. The car sped up, jolting forward and passing other vehicles. "I feel like I'm in *Driving Miss Daisy*. You're supposed to be showing this landlord what you've got, and so far, you've fallen flat on your ass."

"Gavin," Emily gasped, her eyes wide as she tried to ignore just how enticing his hand felt. "You just told me not to get us killed, and now you want me to speed?" Emily pressed harder against the gas, feeling as though she had to prove herself to him. "Fine. To our deaths we go."

With the Lumineers ho'ing and hey'ing from the speakers, an unmistakable air of satisfaction crossed Gavin's features as he watched the odometer climb. Hand still on her thigh, he propped his feet on the dashboard and pressed the button to roll down the window. A rush of warm air flew into the car. He pumped the radio louder. Tapping his other hand on his knee, he looked at Emily, his full tooth, sexy smile wider than she'd ever seen.

Emily giggled and started tapping the steering wheel in unison with him.

"Wait! Pull over here." Gavin dropped his legs to the floor. He put his hand over Emily's and threw the gear into neutral. Reaching for the steering wheel, he yanked it to the right, and the car rolled onto the side of the road. Gravel crunched as the car screeched to a stop.

Confusion peppered Emily's face. "What are we doing?"

Staring into her eyes, expression serious, Gavin didn't answer. Instead, he leaned over the console and gently brushed his lips against hers. Emily closed her eyes and tried to breathe. Voice low and lips on hers, he cupped her face. "Get out of the car."

Eyes still closed, Emily sighed when she felt his hand and lips leave her face. With Etta James streaming out of the speakers now, she watched breathlessly as Gavin ducked out of his seat. She tried to regain her sudden spiked composure as she followed suit and slipped from the car. One foot in front of the other, she moved around to where he stood. Capturing her gaze, Gavin stepped closer, reached for her hand, and slowly swept her against his body. In the heat of the late afternoon sun, Emily nearly froze. Gavin slid his arm around her waist, took her hand, and cradled it to his chest.

"What are we doing?" she asked again, nearly breathless.

Gavin leaned down and touched his lips to hers. Skimming lightly, they tantalized but didn't quite fulfill her need. Emily's nerves lit up, wild and electric.

He looked into her eyes. "A do-over," he softly replied, rocking them back and forth. He nibbled on her lip, his free hand gripping her waist. "This is where we argued yesterday. I want a do-over so when you think of this road, this is what you'll remember. Me holding you... you staring into my eyes... and us kissing." Maddeningly, he played with her lips again, giving her just a little bit more. He rolled his tongue in slow and deep. Emily moaned into his mouth, her senses engulfed in the feel of Gavin's hand floating down her hip. "Do you know what song this is?" he asked, his eyes pinned to hers as they slowly swayed to the music. "Better yet, do you know who sings it?"

Above the roaring blood rushing through her veins and cars whipping by, Emily registered the sound of Etta James's sultry voice. It purred from the speakers of the opened car doors. "*At Last* by Etta James." Emily stared into his eyes as he pulled her closer.

"Very good, Miss Cooper," he crooned against her ear. "Have you been studying jazz?"

Emily swallowed and shook her head. "My... my grandmother used to—"

Gavin covered her mouth with his. He parted her lips and slid his tongue in, groaning as he brought both hands up to cup her cheeks. He dominated the kiss, his tongue plunging, caressing, and dancing over hers. He licked into her ravenously as if he couldn't get enough.

Emily's breath caught. Her womb clenched. Feeling like a delicate flower against his chest, she went languid. Her body melted into his. Heat built between them, and his love and devotion surrounded her with warmth and passion beyond words.

"I love you," Gavin whispered, slowly breaking the kiss. Still cupping her cheeks, he dipped his head and leaned his forehead against hers. "I want to break the rules with you. Kiss you passionately every day. Make you smile when you're about to cry. I want no regrets with us. I want us to laugh together until we can't breathe and it hurts. No man will ever love you the way I'm going to love you, Emily. You're it. My last. My forever."

Breath stolen, a lump formed in Emily's throat. "I don't know what to say," she whispered, tears misting her eyes. "You breathe life into me, and I love you in more ways than I thought I was capable of loving, but you're more than I feel I deserve."

"No, I'm *what* you deserve." Gavin ducked his head, kissing her again. "You deserve a man who remembers your grandmother used to listen to jazz while she cooked."

Emily's heart skidded. "You remember me telling you that?"

Gavin grinned against her mouth. "I remember everything you told me." He smoothed his hands through her hair. "I'm going to break you, Emily Cooper. I'm going to break you down and slowly build you back up. Second by second, piece by piece, and memory by memory, I'm going to make you realize you're worth what I'm going to give to you. If I have to open a dictionary every day and make you stare at the word 'worth,' I'll do it." Gavin pulled her closer and chuckled. "I'll even paste a picture of myself next to it."

Emily sniffled and let out a light giggle. "A picture of you, huh?"

"Yeah. A picture of me." Gavin tightened his hold, his strong arms cradling her as he leaned into her ear. He grazed his lips along the shell. "I can make it a nude one if you really insist."

Resting her cheek against his chest, Emily smiled. "What am I going to do with you?"

He looked down at her, and Emily met his gaze. Expression softening, Gavin angled his lips above hers, his eyes searching. "Move in with me."

Emily pulled in a breath and went to speak but hesitated. Anxiety rained down on her, and her pulse leapt. She touched his jaw, her big green eyes staring up at him. "What?"

He cupped his hand over hers. "You heard me. I want you to move in with me. I know it's—"

"Crazy," she interrupted.

Gavin's hands found the curve of her neck. "Yeah. It's crazy, and it's quick. It's dangerous, reckless, and intoxicating." Gavin paused, drawing her face closer. "But it's what makes us. It's what's made us since the moment we met. Move in with me, Emily. Stay crazy, dangerous, reckless, and intoxicating with me. Just do it waking up by my side every morning."

Emily dropped her gaze to the ground and nibbled on her thumb nail. The whole idea was more than intoxicating. God, everything about Gavin bled her dry of anything negative. However, her uncertainty of whether or not she could truly make him happy hammered through her thoughts. It was enough he'd taken her back, trusting her again with his heart, but something inside screamed she'd never be able to fulfill what he needed.

"I don't know," Emily said, looking up at him. "Let's see what it's like when we get back to New York. Give it time maybe."

A slow smile smeared across Gavin's face, and without warning, he picked up Emily, hauling her delicate body over his shoulder like a sack of potatoes. "Emily Cooper, are you asking me to wait longer than I already have?"

"Gavin Blake, are you insane?" she gasped, curling her fists in the back of his T-shirt.

"I'm the one asking the questions." Chuckling, Gavin strolled over to his car and set Emily on the hood. She gasped again and jumped off. "What?" he questioned.

Eyes wide, Emily swiped the hair away from her face. She frowned. "The hood burnt my ass."

Gavin smirked and pulled his T-shirt over his head. He spread it out across the hood, picked Emily back up, and set her on top of it. "And here I was thinking your ass couldn't get any hotter." Smirk holding steady even as Emily stared at him as though he had ten heads, he shimmied between her legs. Leaning in, he softly kissed her lips. "Is that better for you? If not, I can take my shorts off to give that sweet ass added cushion." He started unbuckling his belt.

"You *are* crazy." Emily reached for his hands, her eyes skirting over every ripple of his sun-kissed abs. "Certifiably crazy."

Gavin lifted a single brow and nodded. "Crazy in love," he replied, slowly leaning in again to kiss her. Sliding his arm around her waist, he pulled her closer. "Hook 'em."

"What?" Emily breathed, her head tilting of its own accord as Gavin ghosted his mouth down her jaw.

"Your legs," he said, draping her arms around his shoulders. "Hook 'em around my waist."

Emily flushed. "We're on the side of a highway, Gavin."

"I know. Kinky, right?" With a wide smile, he didn't wait for her to do as he asked. He took it upon himself, curling his hands around her calves and wrapping them tight around his waist. "Ahh, there we go."

Noticeably embarrassed, Emily bit her lip, her gaze shifting to the highway of speeding cars. Gavin laughed when her eyes widened as a car flew by, honking, with a passenger whistling out of the window.

Gavin lifted his hand from one of her calves and placed a finger under her chin. He brought her attention back to him. His eyes scanned over her lush, berry-colored lips, his pulse automatically thudding. "Move in with me, Emily. Fuck, we fell in love like this… Let's crash the rest of the way."

Staring into the sea of his blue eyes, Emily swallowed and clenched her hands around his bare shoulders.

Gavin leaned in closer, brushing his lips against hers. "I can't promise you it'll always be sweet and tender because you and I fight hard. But I'm pretty sure it won't be a horror ride either because you and I love even harder. What I can promise is you'll always mean more to me than my next breath, and it'll always be you in my life. No one else."

In that moment, everything Emily ever feared fell away, disappeared, muted along with every sound in the background except for her and Gavin's breathing. Her heart, that was so empty just days before, felt as if it was about to bust at the seams. Pulling him closer, she nodded, the smile on her face rising in succession with tears falling from her eyes. "Okay, Mr. Blake. Let's crash."

Matching her smile, a hint of surprise flashed in Gavin's eyes as he pressed his lips to hers. "Really?"

"Yes." Emily giggled against his lips. "Really. Let's fucking crash."

With his infamous smirk, Gavin swept Emily off the hood. She squealed, her feet dangling over his arms. "That was pretty easy. I figured you'd fight me a little bit more. It was my strip tease, am I right?"

"Yes, Gavin," she replied simply, but the hilarity in her eyes was tangible. "The strip tease did me in. Lord, help me."

Gavin sank his lips to Emily's, and it was there on a long stretch of highway in Mexico, he knew wholeheartedly they would get their do-over.

CHAPTER SEVEN

Confessions and Broken Promises

Emily looked up from her desk to the clock on the wall. "One minute left."

Scurrying from their seats and into a jumbled line, fifteen first graders slung their backpacks over their shoulders, tripping over one another to be first to the door.

"Miss Cooper, will you be here tomorrow?"

Emily walked over to the wide-eyed girl, her dimpled smile waiting patiently for Emily's answer. Emily knelt down in front of the child. "I sure will. Mrs. Nelson won't be back until next week." The little girl's smile widened as she brushed wisps of blonde hair away from her face that'd made their way out of a tight braid. The bell chimed, and the race began. "Don't forget to bring in your permission slips for the field trip next month." Emily glanced down the line as each child hastily shuffled past her. A percussion of "Okays" erupted along with a rumble of chatter through the hall as they fled from the room, excitement dotting each tiny face.

On a sigh, Emily stood and made her way to her desk where she gathered papers she needed to grade. After shoving them into her canvas bag, she scooped up a novel she'd begun reading during her lunch break.

Walking over to the door, she gave the classroom one last glance and exited the room. She'd barely turned the corner when she ran smack into Laura Fitzgerald, another substitute teacher who'd started a few weeks before. Native to New York and what Emily would consider a "Club-O-Holic," Emily was pretty sure what she was about to say.

"Just who I was looking for. We're going out tonight." The tall, leggy brunette smiled, her brown eyes wide with excitement. "Webster Hall's having ladies night this evening. Wanna come? Brooke, Cary, Stephanie, Angie, and Melinda are going. I know it's a Thursday, but hey, you only live once, right? We'll all snooze while they're in library tomorrow."

Clubbing assumption correct, Emily smiled and continued making her way past the front office. "I can't. I'm going out to dinner tonight with my boyfriend." Emily shrugged into her coat. "Next week?"

Laura frowned, then realization crossed her features. She raised a plucked-to-perfection brow, a curious grin sliding across her lips. "The new boyfriend?"

Smiling, Emily nodded and made a show of checking her watch. Wanting to pick up something to wear for the evening, she'd planned on trekking a few blocks over to a small boutique Olivia had showed her when she'd first moved to New York. Still needing to stop at the post office to drop off a change of address, she knew she'd be pressed for time to get ready.

"Maybe swing on by after dinner?" Laura asked hopefully, keeping pace with Emily as she pushed through the front doors.

"Yeah. Maybe. I'll text you later." As they stepped out into the frigid, mid-December air, Emily wrapped her scarf around her neck. "I have some papers to grade. If I can get them done early enough, I'll come out for a while."

"Shit," Laura exclaimed, turning back into the building. "I forgot my keys. Sounds like a plan. We'll be there after ten."

Emily waved and watched Laura disappear into the school. After sliding on her gloves, she started down the stairs. The parking lot had mostly emptied, the school busses gone. A winter breeze plucked at the hem of her pencil skirt as she reached in her purse for the forms she would need to give to the post office. Her heart fluttered when she glanced at Gavin's address. Still afraid they were possibly moving too fast, Emily soaked in the fact that when Gavin looked at her, his eyes moved over her face as though memorizing every line and curve. He'd easily led her through the maze of conflict they'd found themselves in with love and determination she'd never experienced. In difficult conversations, he'd mentally held her hand as though keeping her from falling off a cliff. He soothed her, loved her, and admired every flaw she had. But above everything, he'd never given up on her. Two magnets drawn together from the beginning, even when she'd threatened to tear them apart, Gavin was the one who kept them together. Emily simply cemented their fate when she showed up in Mexico. A trip she'd never regret.

Sighing with warmth from a future filled with the unknown, but one she was sure would bring them to where she and Gavin needed to be, Emily's stomach fell away when she heard Dillon's voice calling her name. Her pulse pounded, the sound of it loud in her ears. A small gasp left her lips as her eyes widened, her vision filling with darkness in the bright, late afternoon sun. She shivered and turned in his direction. Arms crossed, leaning against his car, he stood across the street, his eyes pinned to hers. Without a second thought, Emily pulled her phone out of her purse.

"What are you going to do, Em? Call the cops?" he yelled, his voice stinging through the air like a hive of angry bees. "I'm more than a hundred feet away from you, and I'm not on the school property."

Emily didn't look up, nor did she answer him. She opened her phone, her fingers trembling as she dialed 911. When the dispatcher came on the line, Emily heard Dillon laugh.

"911. What's the nature of your emergency?" the female asked.

"I need an officer at Hamilton and Stone Avenues," Emily stammered. Her eyes snapped between Dillon and the half-empty parking lot.

Dillon shook his head, his smile maliciously bemused as he strolled across the street, both hands tucked in his pants pockets.

Unable to move, terror chained Emily to the ground as she watched him step onto the sidewalk. Panic beaded in her stomach. "I'm in the parking lot of Brody Elementary School. I have an order of protection against my ex, and he's here."

"What's your name?" the dispatcher questioned. Her tone was so insanely calm, it scared Emily. Staring at Dillon, Emily swallowed, her words stuck in her throat. She didn't answer. "Miss? Are you still there? I need your name."

With each uneven breath Emily took, and memories warning her mind, Dillon's whispered threats pulsated through her thoughts. *"You'll force me to hurt you both."*

Both...

Her natural instinct to run turned into something else. Sliding her phone closed, Emily waded through her dread of him being there as her fear bubbled into anger. She had pure, honest, and good now with Gavin, and she understood the evil in Dillon more so. She had happiness beyond comprehension and loathed the misery she'd once allowed. She had pleasure and no longer endured pain. Though she felt as if she couldn't breathe and a clamor of nerves danced in her gut, the desire to no longer remain his prisoner, or allow him to hurt Gavin, overtook her. She stepped forward, her shaky legs leading her straight in Dillon's direction.

Standing just beyond the chain-link fence surrounding the school, Dillon cocked his head to the side. He sent her a shark's smile, all teeth. "I'll repeat it for you, so maybe you'll understand this time. I'm not on the property. I'm on the sidewalk. I may not have measuring tape with me, but I'm good at math. I'm still more than a hundred feet away."

"The cops are coming, Dillon." She meant the words to sound strong, but somehow Emily sensed he knew they weren't.

"I loved you, and you actually made me hate you," he growled, his eyes liquid poison. "How could you do this to me? I took care of you and you fucking embarrass me the way you did?"

"You think you took care of me?" Shocked, Emily stared at him, her tone sharpening. "You know what? I take that back. For a while, you had me convinced you were taking care of me, but you had me fooled. You knew what I went through as a child. What I saw. You promised you'd never turn into those men, and you did. I just didn't realize it when it started happening. You used my mother's death against me. You knew I was vulnerable, and you ate it up. That's not love. That's sick and twisted. And just a bit of information for you, Dillon. Love's not being embarrassed at what happened. Love's being heartbroken over the way things ended between us."

"You don't think I'm fucking hurt?" He went to step forward but stopped.

"No," Emily answered. "I don't think you're hurt. I think your ego's bruised. You never loved me. Never."

Fists balled at his sides, he clenched his teeth. "I did love you, but you fucked my friend!" Emily felt that all too familiar fear creeping back in. She fought against it as she continued to stare at the man who'd meant everything to her before he tore them apart. "And just a bit of information for *you*, I didn't use your mother's death against you. You fell the fuck apart, and I didn't know how to deal with it. I did the best I could."

"Did you think I wasn't going to fall apart?" Emily choked back a sob. "She was my mother, Dillon! My mother!"

Dillon shrugged, a wicked chuckle flying past his lips. "Your relationship with her was strained. Give me a break."

Emily eyes went wide, her pulse thudding wildly. "What does that have to do with anything? Strained or not, she was all I knew." Emily paused, unable to believe the monster he'd hidden beneath a camouflage of good for so long. "You're a fake. A chameleon. Where, in that shallow heart of yours, did you even conjure up the ability to do what you did for her before she died? Tell me. Because I can't begin to even understand it."

"Neither can I." Another shrug as his darkened eyes stared into hers. "As fucked up as she was, she didn't deserve my help. No wonder you gave up on her right before she died. Even you knew the mess she was. You couldn't even help her. Or should I say—didn't want to help her."

Even though she knew he was continuing his rampage to hurt her, Emily's world stopped, anger coiling deep in her veins. "Go to hell," she hissed. "You're cut from your mother's evil flesh. It's obvious you enjoyed being in jail because you're about to go back. This time, it'll be longer than a few days. I only wish they could drag her with you for giving birth to such an asshole."

"Fuck off, whore," he growled. "I'm not going to jail. I know my rights and my limits." He leisurely rocked back on his heels. "Again, I'm on the sidewalk, and there's not a fucking thing you can do about it, Emily. Not one fucking thing." He looked down the block at a group of teenagers crossing the street and brought his eyes back to hers, the malice in them pinning her like a target. "That is… unless you want to call Gavin and tell him I'm here." Pausing, he shook his head and laughed. "Now, that would be some fun. I'll go back to jail—and enjoy every single second—knowing you had to watch me beat his ass to a fucking pulp right here on this very sidewalk. That'd be worth a few nights of my freedom."

As though he'd turned on a switch in her head, something inside her shifted, something words couldn't describe. She clenched her canvas bag, her fingers digging into her palm. She made her voice sound unaffected though she felt anything but. "That's right, Dillon, idle threats. Something you've always been good at." She cocked a brow, feigning disinterest. "You barely draw blood. I, out of anyone, would know that. Right?" She lifted her hand, rubbing the spot on her lip where he'd hit her. "Just so you know, it barely stung. My first graders can throw a better punch."

"You fucking cunt," came his retort, the words spewing out of him as if they tasted of acid. Mindful to remain on the sidewalk, he inclined his head and spit at her.

It didn't reach, but Emily didn't dodge it either. She stayed as still as stone. Her breath rattled in her throat as she stared at him, her heart thumping. A man's voice caught her attention. Stepping back, she watched an officer ease from a patrol car, the casualness in his stride unnerving.

Hands on his hips, deep lines gouged his face as he approached. "What's going on here?"

Emily shoved her hand in her purse, pulling out her court documents. "I have an order of protection—"

"Nothing," Dillon said. "She's wasting your time." He shot Emily a glare, and yanked his wallet from his back pocket. "Here's my PBA card." He passed the card through the fence. "My uncle's been a detective at the Brooklyn North narcotics in Bed-Stuy for the last twenty years."

The officer looked it over. He nodded, a smile lifting his mouth. "Look at that." He slid the Patrolmen's Benevolent Association card back through the fence. "I bet he knows Anthony Armenio."

"I grew up with Anthony Jr. and Anna." Dillon looked into Emily's eyes, his stare cold as he slipped the card back into his wallet. "My uncle used to bring me down to the—"

"Excuse me," Emily interrupted, shoving the documents into the officer's hand. "I hate to interfere with this friendly conversation, but he's violated an order of protection from the court."

"I haven't *violated* anything," Dillon argued, a smirk pulling at his lips.

Patience depleted, Emily snapped her head in Dillon's direction. "Yes, you have! You're not supposed to fucking be here!"

"Hey, hey," the cop warned as he glared at Emily. "Calm down."

"I will not calm down," Emily rebuked, flicking her eyes to his badge. "It's your job to keep him away from me, *Officer McManus.*" She stepped back and crossed her arms. "*Please* do the job my tax dollars pay for, and take a look at the order."

With a lift of his brow, the cop rubbed his chin. Aggravation danced over his features, but nonetheless he tore his stare from Emily's. Looking at the papers in his hand, and appearing to be in no hurry, he flipped through them. "He hasn't violated this order, Miss Cooper." He handed the papers back to her. "As far as I can tell, *you* may have violated the order, though."

"What?" Emily questioned, her eyes wide. "How did *I* violate the order? He showed up at my place of employment."

"No, he didn't," the cop corrected, pulling out a small pad. As he scribbled on it, Emily looked at Dillon. He sent her a smug smile. "It says Mr. Parker can't step foot on Brody Elementary School's property," the cop continued, his white hair blowing in the frigid air. He ripped the small piece of paper from the pad and handed it to her. "As far as I can tell, he hasn't. He's right outside of the property on a sidewalk owned by the city. But what I'm wondering is why *you're* so close to the fence. Now, unless Mr. Parker has some kind of magical powers that made you float across the parking lot, *you* willingly approached *him*." Emily opened her mouth, but the cop cut her off. "That paper you're holding's a warning. You get another one of those, and your order of protection will be rescinded." The cop didn't say any more. He turned on his heel, heading for his patrol car. Once settled into his seat, he lowered the window and smiled. "Mr. Parker, I'm going to sit here until you leave, but I'm starving, so make it quick."

Smirking, Dillon nodded and turned toward Emily. Keeping his voice low, he dug his hands into his pockets and slowly backed away. "I never make idle threats, Emily. Remember that."

As Dillon did an about-face, crossing the street and slipping into his Mercedes, the fear Emily was trying to remove prickled across her skin. It anchored her, seeding deeper than before. Clenching the paper she so easily assumed signified her protection, Emily watched Dillon and the officer drive away. The cocoon of her past unraveled right before her eyes. However, a beautiful butterfly didn't spring free. Instead, an emotionally unhealthy woman was left standing in the parking lot alone, her delusional thought that she would be all right a distant blur. There would never be reprieve from Dillon's mayhem. A machine had replaced his heart somewhere along the way, and she knew in that very second, she would never be truly safe from him.

"Hey, you can't just walk in here like that." Olivia rose from the couch. She placed her hands on her hips, a playful smile breaking out across her face. "You're no longer a resident, and besides, I was just having sex in the middle of the living room."

"I moved out three days ago." Emily looked at her with a raised brow. "And you're having sex by yourself, fully clothed?"

Olivia shrugged. "I have my ways."

Emily dumped her belongings on the foyer table. She slid off her coat, walked into the kitchen, and grabbed a can of soda from the refrigerator. "You have no idea what happened," she said, taking a seat at the table.

Olivia squinted and studied her a moment. "Okay, I've seen this expression before. Please don't tell me you and Gavin are already having problems." She plopped down on a chair across from Emily. "If so, I swear, I'm writing you both off. Besides, you two already have plans to spend Christmas at your sister's house. Surely you're not going to fuck up the holidays."

"Gavin and I are fine." Shaking her head, Emily's nerves caught again. "Dillon came to the school today."

"You called the police, right?" Olivia asked, impatient. "He's back in jail?"

"No. He's not. I did call the police, and the asshole who showed up said *I* was in the wrong, not Dillon."

For once, Olivia seemed almost speechless. Almost. "What? I don't understand. How could you be in the wrong? That makes no fucking sense. The order's supposed to protect you, not him."

Emily sighed. "I walked over to where he was standing behind the fence."

Olivia's eyes went wide. "Why would you even attempt getting that close to him? You know what he's capable of. If Dick-wad's showing up at the school, who knows what he planned on doing?"

"Maybe that's the point, Olivia. Maybe for a second, I didn't want him having the power to make me afraid of what he would do to me."

Olivia blew out a puff of air and crossed her arms. Leaning back, she peered out of the kitchen window and tucked a strand of her blonde hair behind her ear. "You need to tell Gavin."

"I know." Emily's stomach lurched, but withholding the truth from Gavin was no longer an option. "We had plans to go out to dinner tonight, but I sent him a text and told him I didn't feel well. I'll tell him when I get home."

With a weary smile, Olivia reached for Emily's hand. "I'm thinking you'd better stop off and pick up a few bottles of wine on your way. It might ease the reaction when you tell him."

Snorting, Emily stood. "Right. Gavin drunk when I tell him won't make the situation any better."

"I didn't mean him. I meant you." Olivia rose and shrugged. "You're the one who's going to need a few glasses. He's going to bug the fuck out, but I'm sure you know this."

She did. Anxiety settled over Emily, but before she could dwell on what she was about to face, a flutter of movement in the hallway caught her gaze. "Is Tina here?"

Olivia bit her lip and shook her head.

"Trevor?"

Remaining quiet, Olivia shook her head again and smiled.

Emily's forehead crinkled about the same time a tall, slender man sauntered into the living room, sporting nothing more than Olivia's finest pink cotton towel.

"Oh, shit. I didn't know anyone was here," the unnamed guest said, sliding a rugged hand through his damp, chocolate-colored hair.

He went to turn around, but Olivia swiftly made her way over to him. She stood on her tiptoes, placed a luscious, lingering kiss on his lips, and linked her arm in his.

Dragging Mr. Fluffy Pink Towel to the kitchen, Olivia smiled. "Emily, this is Jude. Jude, this is my best friend, Emily."

After snapping her mouth shut, Emily reached out to shake the hand Jude extended. "Uh… hi. It's nice to meet you," Emily said, trying to keep the greeting from sounding like a question.

With a smile highlighting his pearly whites and light green eyes, Jude hooked his thumb in the towel, cinching it tighter to his waist. "Yeah, you too. Sorry. I'd figured the first time we met I'd be wearing clothes."

"Why?" Olivia asked, curling under his arm. She ran her hand down his hardened abdomen. "I like showing these off."

Jude grinned, pulling Olivia in for a long, drawn out kiss.

"I have some running around to do," Emily said, her desperation to get out of there mounting by the second. "It was nice meeting you, Jude. I'm sure I'll see you around."

"Cool. Without a doubt," he replied, breaking the kiss. He headed down the hall, leaving Emily and Olivia alone.

"Well," Olivia drawled, "what do you think? I have my own certified eye-candy now, huh?"

Emily pulled on her jacket and slung her purse over her shoulder, a smile toying on her lips. "Where did you meet him, and what happened to Tina?"

Olivia shrugged. "She was too quiet for me, and her family wasn't exactly fond of the whole girl-on-girl thing." Walking Emily to the door, her eyes gleamed with sudden light. "Jude came into the gallery looking for a piece, and somehow I convinced him to let me paint him… naked."

Emily laughed, quickly covering her mouth. "You painted a portrait of him naked?"

"No, friend." Olivia tossed her arm over Emily's shoulder, her smile as wicked as the devil himself. "I painted *on* his body *while* he was naked."

"You crack me up. You know that?" Emily pulled her in for a hug. "You really do, and I adore you for it."

"Oh, I crack myself, but I love the way Jude cracks me more." Olivia released Emily and elbowed her ribs. "Catch my drift?"

"Yes, I catch your drift, nutter."

Olivia gave a satisfied smile. Opening the door, her features sobered. "Call me tonight, and let me know how things went, okay?"

Emily nodded, reality coming fast into view. "I will." She stared at Olivia a moment before her eyes swept over her first home in New York. "I love you, Liv."

"Love you, too."

As she stepped into the hallway, leaving her past behind her, Emily felt a surge of unease about her future. But nonetheless, she knew she had to face it. No longer hiding and slowly beginning to change, nothing would chain her to herself… but herself.

And this… this she wouldn't allow.

The smell of garlic bread coated the air as Emily opened the door to the penthouse. Nervousness raced up her arms when Gavin came into view, but it faded as he started toward her, his smile slow and deliciously sexy.

His gaze slid lazily over her as he pulled her into his arms. "Are you feeling any better, or do I need to play doctor tonight?" He smoothed his hands down her waist. "Although the latter could be *very* fulfilling for us both, I'd rather you be healthy."

Butterflies swarmed Emily's stomach. "I'm sure it'd be *more* than fulfilling," she replied, her eyes trained on the mouth she so desperately wanted to kiss. Giving in to the temptation, she edged up on her tiptoes and did just that. She lingered in the moment his lips melted over hers.

"Mmm, I take it you *are* feeling better," he said, backing her out of the foyer and into the living room. Lips still locked, he slipped her purse from her shoulder and dropped it onto a moving box behind the couch. "But don't think you're getting off so easily. I have the whole doctor set up in my closet, complete with stethoscope and white thigh highs for those pretty legs."

Emily reared her head back, curiosity swimming in her eyes. "Are you serious?"

"No, but I can make a quick run to Kiki De Montparnasse on Greene Street to pick out something naughty for you if you insist."

Emily giggled. "Did you just speak French?"

Gavin smiled, his dimple deepening his cheek. "Yes… As a matter of fact, I speak it fluently. I have a *very* talented tongue." He brushed his lips over hers, teasing lightly. "But that's not something you wouldn't know already. I love the thought of you in white thigh highs, but I have to admit I prefer you in black."

"And here I was thinking you preferred me naked." Another giggle as Gavin groaned. Tilting her head as he worked his lips against her neck, Emily noticed water about to bubble over a pot on the stove. "It's boiling," Emily breathed huskily. The sensation of his mouth caressing her collarbone sent pleasure up her spine.

"I'm sure it is. I've always had that effect on you." Gavin's voice vibrated over Emily's skin as he started unbuttoning her blouse. "Remember, I do things to your body no one else can."

Though utterly and completely turned on, Emily couldn't help but bust out laughing. Gavin looked adorably confused, but in that moment, all of her nervousness hit her at once, and she couldn't stop.

Brows drawn together, Gavin sent her a questioning stare. His hands fell away from her blouse as she continued her hysterics. "What?" His mouth quirked into a half smile. "I'm not a pro, but I thought they were pretty good lines."

Emily placed her hand on his chest. "I was talking about the water on the stove. Do you really think I would use the word *boiling* to describe what you do to my body?"

Gavin blinked. "Is this an attempt to make me feel better? If so, you're failing miserably."

Emily playfully pursed her lips, threading her fingers through his hair. "Aw, did I bruise my man's ego?"

"In more ways than one," he admitted. Like fire, the raw hunger igniting his features devoured her. He leaned into her ear, his voice a slow whisper. "But don't worry… my retaliation will be your *wonderful* undoing."

His promise slid over Emily like silk. A shiver prickled her flesh as he feathered his mouth across her jaw, her muscles coiling, taut with desire. Wrapping his hand around her nape, Gavin crushed his lips against hers. Leaving her nearly breathless, he tangled his fingers in her hair, his kiss intense, and just as quickly backed away. As she tried to recover from the delicious blow of his overly skilled tactics, Emily heard him stifling a laugh. He wandered into the kitchen. Half in a daze, she slumped onto the leather couch, slipped off her heels, and discarded them on the marble floor.

"Emily," Gavin called.

Still dizzy, she swallowed and took a deep breath. "Gavin."

"I just made your body *boil*, sweets," he pointed out with a raised brow and a smirk. "Would it be safe to say I'll achieve the same results once I have your naked body pinned beneath mine tonight?"

Knowing the man staring at her was nothing short of enthralling, exhilarating, powerful, and all-consuming, Emily found herself simply nodding. His words wiped her clear of her own. He grinned that sexy grin that'd caught her off guard from day one and made his way into the kitchen.

He opened a box of pasta and tossed the noodles into the pot of water. Steam drifted up, wreathing around him. He flipped on another burner, drizzled a touch of olive oil into a pan, and layered a few pieces of chicken breast coated with flour into it. After washing his hands, he grabbed two plates from the cabinet. Sitting back, Emily took in the way he maneuvered around the space with ease. He had this shit down. A real life Emeril, but one who was completely hot and undoubtedly worked out. Considering he sat behind a desk all day, there was no other way his body stayed magnificently in shape. Her eyes traced the faded jeans hanging perfectly over his trim waist. She watched soberly as his muscles flexed with every movement underneath a black T-shirt. He was so casual, yet so powerful. She wondered if he knew it.

Since her extent of cooking knowledge went no further than ramen noodles or a box of mac and cheese, Emily knew she had some catching up to do in the cooking department. Considering Gavin had a private chef prepare most of his meals, she found it amusing he even knew what he was doing. However, this wouldn't be the first time something Gavin did or said shocked her. A warm feeling of comfort spilled through her. Dillon had never cooked for them. They'd always gone out to dinner. Not that she didn't enjoy being spoiled to some extent, but she loved the small things Gavin did. Somehow, as she watched Gavin pull out a bottle of white wine from the refrigerator and pour them both a glass, she knew he was going to fill her life with countless small things that would equate to more than anything any other man would ever give her. For a brief second, she smiled. Then the reality of what the evening would consist of attacked her nerves again. She cringed, regretting that she'd lied to him. Swallowing, she took a deep breath and rose to her feet.

She moved into the kitchen and came up behind Gavin at the stove. She circled her arms around his waist, stood on her tiptoes, and perched her chin on his shoulder. "I didn't know you cooked. You keep getting sexier and sexier."

At that, he chuckled. "Wait. I thought I was shmexy?" He forked a piece of pasta out of the pot and reached back to feed it to Emily.

She took it into her mouth. "Shmexy?" she asked, chewing and clearly confused. "Is that your take on the word?"

Turning, Gavin lifted a brow, amusement in his eyes. "No, doll. It's *yours* after you've had too much to drink." He placed a kiss on the crown of her head. "And I think it's very shmexy."

She stared up at him and smiled. "I have no idea what you're talking about, but I'm just gonna go with it."

"Smart woman," he said, the corner of his mouth crooked upward. "Go take a seat, shmexy. Everything should be ready in a minute."

"Shmexy." Emily laughed. "Well, what can I help you with, Mr. Shmexy?"

"Bring this to the table." Gavin plucked a basket of garlic bread from the counter.

"That's it?" she asked. Walking away, she set it on the table. "There's nothing else I can do for you?"

Grinning, Gavin leaned against the counter and crossed his arms. "How can you make such a simple, innocent question sound so sexual?"

Wearing a grin of her own, Emily placed her hands on her hips. "Maybe it's a gift?"

Gavin bit his lip and moved toward her. Standing inches from her body, he whispered in her ear, "Can I unwrap it, then?"

Emily drew in a shuddering breath at the feel of his soft voice so close to her. "We have to eat first."

"See? You just did it again, Miss Cooper." He lifted his hand to her neck. Massaging his fingers into her hair, his eyes glassed over with a want Emily couldn't mistake. "You know I love eating... *dessert*."

Heat curled through Emily, settling in her stomach. God, he made himself nearly irresistible. Blowing out the breath she was holding, she shook her head. "You, sir, need to learn how to control yourself." Trying to exercise her own self-control, but more concerned about the dramatic turn the conversation was about to take, Emily backed away and settled into her chair.

With slight shock in his eyes, Gavin watched her for a second and then turned back to the stove. "You deplete me of any control I've ever had." He strained the pasta and poured some tomato sauce on it. "But you know this already."

Truth. There it was smashed right in her face. Emily knew he couldn't control himself around her, and although she felt the very same way on so many levels, in that moment, she couldn't stomach that he wanted her. She couldn't stomach herself. Her question hit the air before she could think about it. "Why, Gavin?" She looked up from the table. "Why would you choose me? You can have any woman you want. Why me?"

Turning, Gavin drew his brows together. "Why wouldn't I want you, Emily?"

She lifted her shoulder in a casual shrug. "Because there's absolutely nothing to me. I'm weak in so many ways, and you... you're strong." Emily paused, shifting in her seat. "Nothing about me fits what you need or deserve."

Gavin stood perfectly still, his stare unwavering. "Why are you saying all of this?"

"I can list more reasons why you shouldn't want me." Another shrug as she stared at him.

"I don't want you to list any more bullshit reasons why you *think* I shouldn't want you." He moved to her, completely unknowing where all of this was coming from. Reaching for her hand, he gently pulled her up from the chair. His eyes danced over her face. "Do you want me to list the reasons *why* I need you, Emily? Because that's what you are to me. You're a need. Not a want." Tears welling in her eyes, and lips trembling,

Emily shook her head and started to speak, but Gavin cut her off. He cupped her cheeks, drawing her face closer to his. "I'm not sure you'll ever understand, but I told you I need you more than I need my next breath. Since the day we met, from the second I laid eyes on you, there's never been anyone else worth taking up a fucking inch of space in my mind." He stroked his thumbs along her lips, laying his own against her forehead. "God created me to love you. Let me heal the cracks in your heart. I know this broken woman didn't exist before Dillon. I refuse to believe that."

Love over lies. Trust over mistrust. Heart breaking and swelling, Emily pulled in a deep breath. "I lied to you," she croaked, wiping tears from her eyes.

Gavin swallowed down a sudden feeling of unease, slowly dropping his hands from her face. "Wait... what? What did you lie to me about?"

His gaze burned into Emily, making her step back. Mind in turmoil and unable to breathe, nausea hit her with pounding force. Cupping her hand over her mouth, Emily bolted toward the bathroom, nearly tripping over moving boxes scattered throughout the penthouse.

"Emily," Gavin called, following her.

She reached the bathroom, slammed the door, and locked it. Hunched over the toilet, she dry heaved repeatedly. Her stomach had been void of any food over the last several hours, so nothing came up.

Gavin banged on the door, worry evident in his tone. "Emily, let me in."

Another vicious lurch plowed through her stomach. She shook her head and stared into the toilet. "I... I need a second, Gavin."

"No, Emily," he retorted, jiggling the handle. "Open the door. Now."

Though she heard the concern in his voice, she also heard authority, and she didn't put it past him to break in if she didn't do what he asked. Straightening, Emily drew in a gulp of air and inched over to the door. With so many emotions pummeling through her, she couldn't decipher if she was coming or going. Eyes glassed over, she swung open the door. Her words belted from her mouth before Gavin had a chance to speak. "Did you know one in three women wind up in a mentally or physically abusive relationship?"

Though his muscles tensed immediately, and blood raced within his veins, Gavin stared back wordlessly.

Sniffling, Emily nodded. "But the funny part is, it doesn't start off that way. It starts off wonderful, as close to everything you imagined something solid should be. Then little by little, the relationship changes, and you wonder if you're going crazy. You literally start to question your own sanity. One minute, the person you're in love with is kind and caring, and the next, they're flipping out. The first few times you write it off, assuming they're having a bad day, but then it becomes a regular pattern of behavior. The person on the receiving end isn't oblivious to it but starts blaming themselves."

With his entire body on alert, Gavin clenched his jaw and tried to school his tone. In a low whisper, he brushed his fingers across her cheek and stared into her eyes. "Did Dillon lay his hands on you?"

Shaking, Emily swallowed. "Did you know mental abuse can make a victim feel depression, anxiety, helplessness, nonexistent self-worth, and despair? But that doesn't matter because your feelings don't count, and you don't realize they never will. Sometimes the abuser makes you think they count. Then you're back to thinking that *you're* the one who belongs in an institution, not them. But on the norm, your needs or feelings, if you actually have the fucking courage to express them—and most women don't—are ignored, ridiculed, minimized, and dismissed. You're told you're too demanding, or there's something wrong with you. Basically, you're denied the right to feel… anything."

Crying hysterically, Emily started for the living room. Sitting on the couch, she stared up at Gavin as he walked into the room, his eyes pinned on hers. "Sometimes you distance yourself from friends or loved ones. Sometimes you're not even allowed to have friends. Though you've given this person your heart and soul, their behavior becomes so erratic, it's as if you feel like you're walking on landmines. But you continue to love them because they weren't like this when you met, so it only seems obvious it's your fault. Then—here's the hysterical part and just how twisted this whole thing becomes—*you* start making excuses for *their* inexcusable behaviors in an effort to convince yourself it's normal. In an actual, damn effort to convince yourself you're the one who's made them become the monster they've turned into."

Heart pounding, Gavin knelt in front of her. Anger-filled electricity zipped through his nerves as he reached for her hands, lacing his fingers in hers. "For Christ's sake, Emily, tell me what he did to you."

With tears streaming down her face, Emily started laughing. "Wait, Gavin, here's the kicker. A couple of ladies from an organization fighting against domestic abuse told me I allowed this to happen because 'I'm a product of my environment.' I mean really, how clichéd is that? Did I ever tell you about my parents? Did I ever tell you how after my father left us, my mother continued pursuing assholes?"

Wanting to rip the answer out of her, Gavin simply shook his head. Emily had never opened up like this to him, and he knew he needed to let her speak. He squeezed her hands as his chest constricted with every unsteady breath she took.

"Well, she did. She went through them like the world was going to end the next day. I get that being a single parent was hard for her. I do. But she definitely had a thing for picking up the local drunk at the nearest bar in order to help pay the next month's rent. They'd help for a while before they bounced out like my father did, but that never came without a price. She let them smack her around a bit if dinner wasn't cooked by the time they walked in the door, or if the house wasn't cleaned by the time they kicked off their filthy boots. They all looked different, but they came from a mold. Each and every single one of them was cut from the same piece of abusive wax."

Shaking her head, Emily squeezed Gavin's hands this time. "So, those women told me witnessing my mother's weakness drove my own, and her watching my grandfather beat my grandmother was what drove hers. They told me I was raised thinking it was okay for a man to do that to a woman. I was raised thinking self-worth was gained by catering to a man's needs at whatever cost. Even if it meant degrading myself time and time again.

"But the apple *can* fall far from the tree. Fifty percent of children who grow up seeing that will never walk in their parents' footsteps, whether it's a boy watching his father beat his mother or a young girl watching her mother get hit. But this apple landed on the tree's stump, Gavin. This apple took the same path as her mother." Pausing, Emily looked at her hands tangled around Gavin's. When she brought her equally pained gaze back to his, it was all she could do to get out the words. "They also told me because I physically fought back against Dillon the day of our wedding, I'd finally broken the cycle."

And there it was. The question answered right before him. The question Gavin already knew the answer to. His stomach bottomed out.

Feeling his face go pale, he slowly rose as blades of wrath sliced through his chest. Blood. He wanted Dillon's blood, and he wanted it now.

Emily surged to her feet, her legs shaky. "Don't. Please don't," she whispered, staring into his venom-filled eyes. Bringing her hands up to his cheeks, her body trembled with his. "I'm here with you, Gavin, and I'm fine." Silence fell, its presence suffocating as she watched Gavin try to control his features. It wasn't working though. She could see he was about to explode. "I didn't tell you because I don't want you getting hurt. I don't want you getting in trouble or going through any more than you have already. Please, don't hate me for lying to you. Please don't."

Gavin had known she lied to him that night. Something deep within his gut told him she did. However, another part tricked him into believing her. Gavin gave her a look of confusion, a scowl marring his face. "I could never hate you, Emily. Do you believe me when I say that?"

Emily nodded, tears trickling down her cheeks.

"And you're worried about *me*?"

"Yes," she admitted faintly. "I have to protect you from all of this. I caused everything."

"Protect me after what he did to you?" he asked, the exasperation in his tone cutting through the air. Gavin lifted his hands to her face, his eyes boring into hers. "My God, Emily, you didn't cause any of this, but you can't ask me not to do anything to him."

"Please," she cried.

Gritting his teeth, Gavin turned away. "No."

Fear shot through Emily's stomach as she watched him yank his keys from the counter. As she moved toward him, her mind on fire with images of what he was about to do, Emily broke out into hysterics she never thought possible. She'd cried many times throughout her life, but nothing held a candle to what her tiny frame was producing at this very moment. She couldn't breathe, couldn't think. Legs feeling as though she was trudging through mud, she barely made her way across the penthouse. Emily curled her fingers around the back of Gavin's arm as he was about to open the front door.

Gavin turned, his expression fierce, his stare raking over her. "You're asking me not to be a man, Emily, and I can't fucking do that. I can't. You're mine, and if I didn't leave, this wouldn't have happened. Don't ask me not to make this right in the only way I know how."

Breath seized and heart disintegrating from the notion he blamed himself, Emily hesitated a moment before lifting her hand to his face. Stroking his jaw, she shook her head, her voice a soft whisper. "Gavin Blake, you're more of a man than any man I've ever known. You're gentle. You're kind. You're strong and witty. You're personable and warm, and you can reduce most females into blithering puddles of goo with the simplest words. " Dragging her fingers from his jaw, she trailed them down to his chest. "You have a heart you wear on your sleeve, and you couldn't do a thing to make me fall more in love with you. Not a single thing." Pressing up on her tiptoes, she experienced a bout of nerves as she twined her hands behind his neck, bringing his face to hers. "And you're not to blame for this."

Struggling against the fury burning a hole in his stomach, Gavin leaned his forehead against hers. "No, Emily. If I didn't leave—"

"And if I didn't take him back."

"He shouldn't have fucking touched you," he breathed, trying to contain his rage. "It's not the same thing."

"I know it's not. But you want to know what is?" Gavin placed his hand on her hip, his fingers digging into her side as he looked away. Emily touched his cheek, bringing his gaze back to hers. "If you walk out that door and go after him, you're no different than any man I've come across. Please don't take this man away from me, Gavin. Please."

Damn it all to hell. The look in her puffy green eyes, combined with the soft plea falling from her lips, had Gavin feeling as though he was backed against a wall. His mind was fucked, completely bulldozed over by her words. Torn between the need to beat Dillon within inches of his life and not wanting to drag Emily through any more shit, tension bristled deep within Gavin.

She'd bled herself out to him, burrowing her hurt and painful memories beneath his skin. Before this, she'd seemed unreachable, but today, she drowned every fear she had into a sea of trust Gavin knew only he possessed. But for fuck's sake, he wouldn't be able to escape his own hostility if he let Dillon get away with what he'd done. Every male instinct in Gavin screamed to demolish the man who had hurt the woman he loved. The woman who was his. Utterly… fucking… screwed.

Stuck in his thoughts, Gavin clenched his jaw until it ached. Staring into the eyes of the woman he knew he couldn't live without, he made a decision he hoped wouldn't haunt every waking hour of the rest of his life. "I won't go after him." He cringed when the words slipped from his mouth. "I promise I won't. But you're telling me where he hit you. Do you understand me? I need to know."

Emily could see the reluctance in his eyes, but sincerity rang true in his voice. Emily released a breath and nodded tightly. "Yes," she cried.

Gavin's chest twisted at the slice of pain in her voice. Grabbing her hand gently, he led her into the kitchen where he shut off the burner holding the seared-to-a-crisp chicken. Gavin could feel the way Emily's grip tightened when, a moment later, he made his way into the bedroom with her. Staring at one another, they stood silently, as if neither knew what to say.

Trying to wipe all traces of anger from his features, Gavin looped his arms around her waist and pulled her tight against his body. Within seconds, she was limp in his hold, her tears coming hard and fast. He nuzzled his nose in her hair, pulling in the sweet smell of her shampoo, as he attempted to prepare himself for what she was about to tell him. His brain couldn't come close to computing how anyone could hurt her. She was fragile. Loving. Vulnerable. With all his possessions, Gavin knew her touch was all he had that was true, pure. Dillon had methodically unpeeled her layer by layer, exposing parts of her no woman should have to bare. In that moment, Gavin feared he would break his promise about not going after the sick fuck. With each passing second she came undone in his arms; Gavin was becoming perilously close to losing any semblance of control.

When Emily's cries dulled to a low hum, and her breathing slowed to a normal pace, Gavin gently tipped up her chin. Understanding flashed in his eyes. "Are you okay?"

Emily wiped her nose. "I am. Are you?"

He wasn't. Not even close. He was unhinged. But wanting to keep her as calm as possible, Gavin nodded. "God, you haven't even eaten yet." Letting out an exhausted sigh, he slanted a hand through Emily's hair. "Are you hungry?"

"No," she whispered. She wasn't. Still feeling as though she could throw up, food was the last thing on her mind.

"Okay. I'm going to toss some water on my face." He lowered his mouth to her lips and kissed her softly. "I'll be right out."

Emily nodded and watched him disappear into the bathroom. After he closed the door, she inhaled deeply in an attempt to ebb the tension from her body. It wasn't working. She didn't want to give Gavin details about that morning. Hell, rehashing it could be the last devastating blow to his sanity. It was bad enough she could see he was fighting his instinct to leave and go after Dillon. This could definitely send him over the edge.

She yanked herself from her evil thoughts and rummaged through a few moving boxes still holding some of her belongings. Searching for a pair of pajamas, she came across a picture of her mother and sister from a trip to Santa Cruz many years earlier. Forced smiles dowsed the photo. Those small pieces of reprieve had served as a sliver of good among the chaos consuming their lives, but that's all they were. Slivers of peace. Slivers of something that was never constant. As she stared at it, Emily choked back tears, knowing she was about to shed enough for the evening. She shoved the memory underneath a pile of sweaters.

By the time she'd slipped out of her work clothes and into a pair of sweatpants and a T-shirt, Gavin reemerged from the bathroom. Stripped down to nothing but a pair of boxer shorts, his face angrier than a few minutes before, Emily watched him sink onto the edge of the bed. Something in the set of his body alarmed her. It was as if the few minutes he had to himself had turned him into one huge combustible ball of pissed off alpha-male. Emily swallowed nervously and crawled onto the bed. God, all she wanted to do was soothe him from the battle she knew he was fighting. Coming up behind him, she placed her hands on his shoulders and massaged, trying to remove the tension tumbling off him in hot waves.

She chose her words carefully. "Gavin," Emily began, her voice soft, "why don't we just go to sleep? We're both mentally shot right now. We can talk about this tomorrow."

Without answering, Gavin shook his head. After rolling his neck, he leveraged himself back against pillows tucked up along the headboard.

On her knees, Emily turned and stared at Gavin. Shadows of cold hostility danced on his face and all it did was make her feel guilty for not allowing him to do what she knew he so desperately wanted. She moved her eyes from his, unable to witness his pain any longer.

"Look at me, Emily," he commanded in a tortured whisper. Her gaze flickered back to his. Gavin sensed her nervousness, her hesitation, and fuck if it didn't mess with his thoughts. "Come here," he said, holding out his hand.

She reached for it, and he guided her to his side. Nuzzling against him, Emily rested her head on his chest. Though tension of her own poured from her body, the tantalizing aroma of his cologne and the steady thumping of his heart calmed her and brought her mind to a place she felt safe. His hand drifting up and down her back eased her further into a cave of euphoria only Gavin could provide.

"Where did hit you?"

She knew it was coming, but his question still elicited a full, bone-deep shiver, pulling her right from those few seconds of calm. Curled into a tight ball and molded to him, Emily lifted her head and looked into his searching blue eyes. She brought up her hand and pointed to the spot above her brow, where only a few days before, he had questioned her about it. Where only a few days before, she lied to the man she loved. The man she needed to trust her. Emily felt his body go taut with tension. Like an inferno, anger blazed in his eyes. Emily watched the muscle in his jaw tick as he gazed at her. Other than Gavin's increased breathing, silence hung in the air, weighing heavily on Emily's heart.

"I'm okay, Gavin," she whispered, feigning reassurance.

Gavin seethed. The need to wipe Dillon from the face of the earth seeded itself in every cell, tendon, and muscle in his body. However, the need to comfort Emily pulled at him as he forced his composure to remain intact. Gently, he lifted her on top of him, straddling her legs over his hips. He could feel her shaking, and it wracked through his head. Fucked with him... bad.

Staring at the tiny scar, he brushed his thumb across it. Though barely noticeable, just knowing how it got there gutted Gavin beyond words. How could a man, a true man, do that to a woman? It was something Gavin couldn't even begin to process. Leaning up, he circled one arm around her waist as he wrapped his free hand around the back of her neck and guided her face down to his. For a second, he stared into her eyes before grazing his lips across the mark that would forever brand her beautiful face. A brand placed there by an asshole who'd never deserved her.

"Where else did he hit you, Emily?" Gavin flicked his eyes to hers. He realized he was setting himself up for more self-inflicted pain, but a part of him needed to put himself through it. Emily had suffered far worse than he was. Or not. That was a question he definitely couldn't answer because this was a suffering he'd never had to endure.

"My lip," Emily softly answered, watching Gavin's eyes turn fierce. She froze.

Gavin cringed, fighting back the compulsion to rip out of the house. "Your lip," he stated calmly, once again trying to school his tone. "He hit your fucking lip?" Hesitantly, Emily nodded. Watching her beautiful lips tremble, Gavin caught a whisper of her perfume. In that moment, all he could think about was re-branding those lips. He pulled her down to his mouth hard and fast.

Emily let out a soft whimper as their tongues met, hot and wet. His kiss was desperate, urgent, and devouring. Though his possessiveness took her by surprise, she knew he was stamping her. She knew it, and she didn't care because she wanted him to. She needed this from him, and she knew he needed to mark her. She tangled her fingers in his hair, tugging hard as her heart sank.

"I can't believe he fucking hurt you, baby," Gavin breathed. "I'll only ever worship these lips. I'll only ever worship this body." Gripping the back of her neck tighter, Gavin deepened the kiss. "When I look at you, I feel like I'm looking at the other half of myself. You've filled the empty space in my soul, and because of that, you're a Goddess to me. That's the way I'm always going to treat you. For the rest of your life. I promise you that. I fucking promise."

Emily kissed him harder. His words tattooed themselves in her heart, his kiss nearly depleted her of air she didn't want in her lungs. She only wanted to breathe him in.

As Gavin pulled Emily's T-shirt over her head, he knew those promises would be easy to keep. He'd rather burn in the lowest pits of hell than go back on his word because she *was* a Goddess in his life. His lover. His friend. His forever.

But damn him into those flaming pits of hell, as he began to re-brand his lover, he knew there was one promise he wouldn't be able to keep because he would protect her until the day he died.

The most fucked up part, and God help him…

He couldn't wait to break it.

CHAPTER EIGHT

Fuck It

"Gavin, could you go ahead and answer Mr. Rosendale's question regarding our approach?"

Without warning, Colton's deep voice intruded on Gavin's thoughts. Wicked thoughts that'd consumed him over the last sixteen hours since Emily explained what Dillon had done to her. Sitting in a meeting, surrounded by executives representing one of the country's leading pharmaceutical giants—one in need of a massive advertising campaign—Gavin knew he should be paying attention. But he wasn't. His world had been turned inside out, his heart ripped open. There weren't adequate words that could possibly convey his mental state of mind on this late Friday morning.

His sleep-deprived state of mind, that is.

In the darkness, Gavin had stared at the ceiling as he held Emily. Listening to her soft breathing, wide awake with adrenaline pumping through his veins, Gavin attempted to purge visions of Dillon hurting her from his head. No matter how hard he tried, it didn't work. His brain fucked with him. The insistent clatter of wanting to feel Dillon's blood on his hands screamed loud in his ears. He had seethed until the sun rose. Gavin would've never thought it was possible that Emily's soft body, intertwined with his, couldn't bring him down from the cliff of murderous destruction from which he was so eagerly waiting to jump. Last night proved that even though holding her dampened some of the anger boiling under his skin, Emily couldn't extinguish the flame fueling it.

Colton repeated his earlier request, yanking Gavin back to the present. He lifted his heavy head and settled his eyes on his brother. Colton stared at him with a look of confusion shadowing his face. Gavin rummaged through the paperwork in front of him. When he heard one of the four gentlemen seated across from him clear his throat, Gavin broke the silence.

He shook his head and glanced back at Colton. "No. I can't answer his question." He tossed the stack of papers onto the conference table. "Why don't you go ahead and give them the information, Colton." It wasn't a polite question but more so a statement that said '*now's not the time to fuck with me.*' The eldest man's face went gray, its color mimicking his hair. Once again, silence cloaked the room.

Brows cinched together in what Gavin easily recognized as aggravation, Colton cleared his throat. He dragged his stare away from Gavin and focused on the impatient executives. "I apologize, gentleman. It appears my brother woke up on the wrong side of the bed this morning." Colton gave a casual shrug, a smirk tipping the corner of his mouth. He shot Gavin a sideways glance, humor replacing his aggravation. "Clearly, he must not have gotten laid last night."

Within a few seconds, the table erupted in an orchestra of chuckles, none of which included Gavin's. Though he wanted to bitch-slap his brother for the catty remark, he was impressed by the asshole's quick witted response. Colton had always had a knack for it, and Gavin had to admit it smoothed over the tension in the office. Gavin mirrored the stupid smirk on his brother's face as he leaned back, rubbing a tired hand over his chin. He flicked his attention to the clock on the wall, ignoring the bullshit spiel Colton was working over the group in an attempt to gain one of the largest accounts Blake Industries could acquire. Money was the furthest thing from Gavin's mind as he noted the time. Eleven fifteen. A little over an hour until he had to meet Emily. Before falling asleep last night, she'd sweetly suggested a quiet lunch at a small café in Battery Park since she was getting off of work early. Gavin knew she was trying to calm his nerves. That was one of the many things he loved about her—the way she evened him out. God, he fucking loved her. He'd give up everything for her. Travel across the world at the drop of a hat if she insisted. There wasn't a limit he could reach or a line he wouldn't cross in order to make her happy. Now, he just needed to convince her she was worth every bit of it.

A moment later, Gavin's thoughts were interrupted again as the group of men rose from their seats, each sporting a satisfactory smile. Gavin stood and regarded Colton with amusement. He was looking at Gavin with a smug grin. Gavin knew that was his way of letting him know he'd landed the account without his help, and Gavin was pretty damn sure Colton was going to word vomit his displeasure with him once they all left. Gavin could give a flying fuck.

"Sounds like a game plan, Colton," said Mr. Gray-Haired Executive as he shook Colton's hand. "We'll get the contracts sent over by the end of the business day tomorrow."

Colton flashed his winning smile. "Excellent. We look forward to making this come together for you. You went with the right choice."

"Let's just hope your brother here is getting laid while you're putting the campaign together," the man said dryly, leaning in to shake Gavin's hand. Again, the room burst into laughter. Again, Gavin didn't. "I have a few connections in the city if you need some help in that department. They don't come cheap, but they sure as hell are worth every penny."

Gavin accepted his hand, his grip tighter than normal considering he didn't like the asshole's comment. It didn't matter. Gavin knew how to handle his type without being *too* offensive. Or not. Again, he didn't give a fuck. Gavin's mouth slid into a sly grin. "I'm sure they are, and I appreciate the offer, but I've never had to pay for services like that. They usually come willingly to me. But hey, you do what you have to do." The man's smile fizzled, a tight frown replacing it, but Gavin didn't give him a chance to speak.

"We look forward to receiving those contracts, Mr. Rosendale," Gavin said, walking to the office door. He held it open for the group of polished wealth staring at him. "My brother's correct. You went with the right choice. Blake Industries is about to rock the shit out of your campaign. We're going to keep you all very wealthy. Dry martinis and expensive call girls galore."

The frown creasing the man's forehead eased as his mouth crooked upward into a slow, smartass smile. "I have the utmost faith you and your brother will do right by us, Mr. Blake. But just so you know, kid, I don't do dry martinis. I prefer Scotch. A Dalmore 1962 Single Highland Malt Scotch to be exact."

"Excellent choice," Gavin said, unbuttoning his $22,000 blue Ermenegildo Zegna suit. He knew the guy was being a dick, trying to push a $58,000 bottle of scotch in his face. Gavin smiled with every intention of being a dick right back. "I'll have our secretary send you two cases so you're properly stocked. Sound good?"

The man hesitated a moment, his eyes sharpening. "Sounds very good. We'll see you again come March." Without another word, he nodded in Colton's direction and walked out of the office, his crew of equally arrogant bastards behind him.

Gavin strode across the office and chuckled when he heard Colton slam the door.

"What the fuck was that all about?" Colton bit out. "It's not enough you were in a daze during the meeting, but you almost kill the damn contract in typical Gavin fashion."

Gavin turned, his eyes narrowed. "What the fuck is that supposed to mean?"

"Do I need to spell it out for you, little man?"

"Yeah. Maybe you do," Gavin replied dryly. Crossing his arms, he perched on the edge of the table, awaiting his brother's response.

Head tilted, Colton shoved his hands in his pockets. "Seriously, we worked on that bid for months. Where the fuck were you?"

His sentences were clipped, and Gavin could tell Colton was losing his patience. Though he was having a shitty day, guilt spilled through Gavin. Damn. Colton was correct. They'd worked endless hours to gain the account. To hell with himself; his brother had spent night after night away from Melanie and his kids, making sure everything was on point for the meeting.

Gavin's face softened. "I'm sorry, all right?"

Colton sighed, his tone calmer. "What's going on with you, man? I could tell something was bothering you when you came in this morning."

Gavin glanced at his watch. He had a limited amount of time to explain what'd happened. Bringing his attention back to Colton, he felt his blood surge through his body. "Dillon hit Emily the morning of their wedding."

Colton's mouth dropped open. "What?"

"Yeah. He fucking hit her, and he showed up at her job yesterday." Standing, Gavin plowed his hands through his hair as he thought about the conversation he and Emily had after making love last night. She'd further tilted his world on its axis when she'd explained that Dillon went to her school. Though Gavin wanted to make her quit her job that second, he couldn't. Teaching meant too much to her and she loved her students. But it was all good. Without Emily's knowledge, Gavin had already placed a call this morning, making sure she would be followed everywhere. A little cash and an old buddy who'd just finished a seven-year bid upstate would hang in Dillon's shadow for the rest of his fucking life. "Did you know he hit her?"

Colton's eyes went wide. "Jesus Christ, Gavin. Why the fuck would you assume I knew about it? No, I didn't know."

"I assumed you did because apparently Trevor knew and didn't tell me." Gavin stalked across the office to retrieve his keys as his head hammered through round two of last night's conversation. He tried to shake off the mess of emotions that'd also taken up residence in his mind. Though Emily insisted Trevor made her promise to tell him if they got back together, it didn't sit right with Gavin. He'd seen Trevor the day she moved into his penthouse. As a matter of fact, the fucker acted as if life was just dandy. Little did Gavin know *his* life was about to become more complicated than ever.

"He knew and didn't say anything?" Colton questioned, sitting at the table. "And let me make myself very clear. I'm your brother. I'd never hide anything like that from you. Got it?"

"Yeah, I got it. But he's like a brother to me," Gavin murmured, flicking his eyes down to his watch. No doubt his driver had already picked Emily up from work. He needed to leave to make it across town on time to meet her. "I haven't spoken to him yet, but I plan on making sure I do soon. I'll deal with him then."

"I see." Colton nodded. "Besides, I'm sure dealing with Dillon is on the top of your priority list." Colton rolled his neck and cracked his knuckles, a wicked smirk tipping his mouth. "I'm slightly older and not as buff as you are, but if you want some help, I'd be more than willing to go a few rounds with the prick."

Gavin hesitated a moment before turning toward the door. "Look, I have to get out of here. I'm meeting Emily for lunch in forty-five minutes."

"Wait," Colton blurted, standing to his feet. "How come you just gave me that look? Don't tell me you're not going to toss the asshole around a little for what he did to her. I know you better than you think. What's up?"

Sighing, Gavin stopped shy of the door and turned around. "Emily made me promise I wouldn't go after him."

At this, Colton drew his brows together and chuckled. "Gavin, you're dealing with a woman who also made you promise not to buy her a car because she thinks they're unnecessary in Manhattan."

Gavin couldn't help grinning. "I know, right? Who gives a shit that it's Manhattan. She has no idea, but I already ordered her one."

"Exactly." Colton laughed and sat back down. Features serious again, he tented his hands beneath his chin. "Now go order up a side of kicking some Dillon ass. What Emily doesn't know won't hurt her." Colton paused, his stare unwavering from Gavin's. "But what you're sitting on will *kill* you."

Colton stated those last three words with an air of simplicity, but the truth in them shot through the room. Battling to stay true to his promise to Emily, no matter how badly he could taste Dillon's blood, Gavin simply walked out of the office.

No matter if it was the middle of early morning traffic, midday traffic, or late afternoon rush hour, traffic in Manhattan blew. Fucking. Blew. Gavin was starting to think Emily's reasoning for not wanting a car wasn't so bad after all. But try as he might, he was addicted to driving. Sure, he could easily have his driver cart him around in his limo like the rich prick some perceived him to be, but Gavin couldn't let go of the sense of control he had behind the wheel. He loved it. Windows rolled up and stereo blaring, cluster-fuck of Manhattan traffic or not, it was one of the few stolen moments he had to himself that actually calmed his nerves and levied his thoughts. However, as Gavin maneuvered through the tidal wave of vehicles clogging the streets, calm wasn't something he was feeling. No. Not even close. His head was jarred. His thoughts became more fucked with each passing second. Though Chevelle's "The Red" was bursting from the speakers, the only thing Gavin could hear was Colton's words reverberating through his head.

"But what you're sitting on will kill you."

Sitting on it would kill Gavin. This he knew. He also knew if he stayed dormant, it would turn him into a bitter man. Although the thought was something Gavin couldn't register now, he feared he would come to resent Emily as the years dwindled on. With the café he was supposed to meet Emily at clear in his line of sight, Gavin pictured her sitting at a table waiting for him. Only a few hundred feet and he'd be there. Another few minutes and he'd be able to keep his promise to her. At least for today.

"But what you're sitting on will kill you."

"Kill you…

Kill you…

Kill…

You…"

"Fuck it," Gavin bit out. Before his brain had a chance to grasp what his body was doing, from the farthest left lane, Gavin cut the wheel hard right when the light turned green. He couldn't hear or see them, but a symphony of horns and display of middle fingers from pissed off New York drivers were directed at him. His new destination? Dillon's office in the financial district. Punching through the gears, Gavin managed to plow through the busy city streets without killing anyone. That didn't mean he didn't come close. His blood surged as he blew through a red light crossing over Church Street, nearly clipping the back of an open double-decker bus filled with tourists. Another burst of horns went off. Again, Gavin couldn't hear them. He couldn't see pedestrians jumping onto curbs to get out of the way of his speeding Ferrari FF because his vision went blood red.

Blood. Fucking. Red.

With one hand gripping the wheel, he used the other to yank the tie from around his neck. As he pulled into the garage below Dillon's building, he shrugged out of his suit jacket, paid the parking fee, and shot into a parking spot. After swinging open the door and slamming it closed, Gavin made his way to the elevator and hit the button to Dillon's floor.

Gavin was no longer fighting a fucked up battle in his head. He rolled his sleeves up and sank deep into an eerie sea of calm. He was feeding his body what it craved, what it needed, and because of this, he felt high. Drugged. As he rode up to the fifteenth floor, specks and shadows of Emily's face curled through his thoughts. His heart sank as he glanced at his watch. The thought of her sitting at the café waiting for him, completely unaware of what he was about to do, bothered him. However, he couldn't stop.

Gavin broke from the elevator when the doors opened, stepping out into a shitload of commotion. It was something he was used to seeing. Wearing cheap suits from eBay and ties their grandmothers had bought them for their twenty-first birthdays, young, money-hungry cubs paced the bullpen in front of their cubicles. With Bluetooth receivers in their ears and polished wealth on the other end of the line, they talked fast, attempting to rip a piece of meat from a portfolio holding more cash than they'd make over the course of a lifetime. They jutted their chins up in greeting and Gavin knew a couple of them recognized him when he breezed through the chaos. He simply nodded back. None of them would end their calls from the potential stack of money they were trying for. Considering he'd only shared a beer or two with them through the years when Dillon invited him out, Gavin really didn't give a shit if they ended their conversations to stop and say hello or not. His focus was on the door in the left corner of the massive office. Behind it was the piece of meat Gavin was about to tear into. No longer calm, the closer he got, Gavin felt his unfed hunger splitting his stomach in two.

"Hey, Gavin," a familiar female voice purred.

He dragged his attention from the door holding his lunch beyond it, but his feet never stopped moving. "Hey, Kimberly. Is he in his office?"

The busty blonde nodded. "He sure is."

"Good," he clipped, rounding the corner of her desk.

As he approached Dillon's door, Gavin ducked his towering six foot three inch frame in an attempt to see below mini-blinds covering up half the glass. Gavin's eyes landed on Dillon's back. He stood in front of his desk, his arms crossed. In one swift motion, Gavin swung open the door and closed it. In another, he twisted the lock, sealing them off from anyone who might try to enter.

Let the motherfucking games begin.

Without turning, Dillon blew out an annoyed puff of air. "Kimberly, how many times over the last few months have I told you I'm not fucking you in here anymore? Go back to your desk, and I'll call you later if I feel like it."

"It's not Kimberly, asshole," Gavin growled. His eyes zeroed in on Dillon when he turned around. "I told you I'd kill you with my bare hands if you ever touched her again."

Narrowing his eyes, Dillon opened his mouth, but before words could tumble out, Gavin charged him, tackling him onto the desk. Though mammoth, the solid piece of cherry wood screeched a few inches from the weight of the two men landing on it. With Dillon pinned beneath him, Gavin curled his hands around his neck, barely noticing the blow from Dillon's fist slamming against his mouth. Blood from his split lip dropped onto Dillon's cheek, sliding down to his chin. As Gavin stared into the soulless eyes of a man he'd considered a friend at one point, flashes of Emily receiving his brutal treatment made adrenaline spike through Gavin's veins. His anger simmered, and Gavin had no intention of stopping it from erupting.

Hands wrapped around Dillon's throat, Gavin lifted up his head and shoved it back down against the desk. It hit the surface with a hard thud. Gavin was sure he'd cracked Dillon's skull open. "You pussy!" Gavin spewed, his body shaking. "I told you I'd fucking kill you if you hurt her!"

"Fuck you and her!" Dillon choked out, squirming under Gavin's weight.

Gavin squeezed harder, his grip tightening to the point he could feel Dillon's pulse hammering against his thumbs. At this, Dillon brought his arms up and circled his fists around Gavin's forearms in a lame attempt to pull Gavin's hands from his neck. It didn't work, and it only pissed Gavin off more. Gavin slammed his head against the desk again. After the second, possible skull-cracking blow, Gavin heard Dillon inhale sharply as he fought to breathe. Gavin also heard his own blood rushing through his ears. Dillon released his hold on one of Gavin's arms and swung again, but this time there was no speed in it. It was easy enough for Gavin to dodge. Gavin could feel him weakening beneath him. Felt him slipping away as he stared into Gavin's eyes. Gavin watched Dillon's capillaries pop to the surface, turning his face a light shade of blue.

And then it hit him.

"Gavin Blake, you're more of a man than any man I've ever known. You have a heart you wear on your sleeve, and you couldn't do a thing to make me fall more in love with you. Not a single thing."

Now, Gavin found himself fighting a completely different battle brought on by Emily's words. Something inside him twisted, a debate on whether or not to stop. The sick bastard below him might own his emotions in this very moment, but the woman he was willing to kill for would own his heart forever. Choosing love over evil, Gavin pulled in a steeling breath, released his hold from Dillon's neck, and stumbled away from the desk.

Fisting his hands in his hair, Gavin paced and watched Dillon's close to lifeless body slither to the floor, dragging stacks of paper, pens, and a telephone with it. Choking, Dillon rolled to his side and clawed to his hands and knees, his chest heaving up and down for air. A barrage of chills overtook Gavin's system as he witnessed Dillon trying to stand. It was no use. He couldn't. Gavin had stripped him of any and all energy he had. Gavin tore his attention from Dillon and latched onto the deep voices and banging coming from behind the door. Gavin didn't know if they'd just started or if they were trying to get in the whole time. As Dillon's life was slipping through his hands, time seemed to slip by, blurring from one second into the next. Swallowing hard, Gavin stalked over to Dillon and grabbed him by his hair.

Kneeling beside him, Gavin yanked Dillon's face within inches of his. He shook as he spoke, his breath a vicious whisper. "You better listen to every fucking word I'm about to say to you."

"Fuck off, asshole," Dillon grit out, staring into Gavin's eyes, his breathing still labored. "You're going to jail for this, motherfucker."

Gavin quickly elbowed Dillon's mouth. Trying to jerk away, Dillon winced. Now Gavin wasn't the only one with a split lip. Gavin gripped Dillon's hair tighter, a sick smirk twisting his mouth. "If you report this, sure, I might go to prison. You're lucky I didn't fucking kill you. But just know this"—Gavin paused, trying to tamp down his sudden urge to once again choke Dillon within inches of his life—"I'll get out one day. Oh, you bet your ass I fucking will. And when I do… *nothing* will stop me from killing you. Not even the insane love I have for the woman you threw away will keep me from making sure you never take another fucking breath. So, consider this bit of information before you go running to the cops. If you know me at all, then you'll know this isn't an empty threat from a pussy who likes to knock women around. This is coming from a man. A man who'll laugh all the way to the gas chamber as your mother cries all the way to your fucking grave. Do you understand me?"

Breathing hard, Dillon stared at Gavin and remained quiet. Simple resolution to the unanswered question. Another elbow to Dillon's mouth.

"Do you fucking understand me?" Gavin snarled, his face curled in anger.

"Yes!" Dillon replied through clenched, bloodied teeth.

"Good," Gavin replied mildly, standing. He started for the door, but before unlocking it, he turned, his eyes narrowed. "And if I find out you showed up to her job again, I'll make sure it's a closed casket funeral."

With that, Gavin unlocked the door and pushed through the crowd. Without looking back, he heard the clamor of commotion taking place in Dillon's office. Strike that. He heard Dillon yelling at everyone to get *out* of his office. The edge of embarrassment in Dillon's tone carried through the air as Gavin stepped into the elevator.

On his way down, Gavin checked his watch. With less than five minutes to make it across town, he whipped his cell from his pocket and shot Emily a text to let her know he was going to be late. By the time he made it to his car, she'd replied.

Emily: I'll be here waiting for you. Please be careful. No speeding! I love you.

Gavin pulled out of the garage. As he crawled through traffic, he couldn't help but flick his gaze down to his cell. He reread Emily's text over and over. Emotions flying high, Gavin was aware he had to walk into the café holding some semblance of normalcy. He just wasn't sure he'd be able to. Thirty minutes later, he was about to be put to the test.

After finding a parking spot, Gavin stepped from his car, slid his hands through his hair, and made his way in. He hadn't taken but three steps into the café when he spotted Emily. His breath faltered as it always did when he saw her sitting at a table and reading a book. It was then Gavin knew he was bound to her. He knew there wasn't a thing he wouldn't give up for her. Hell, as long as he was inhaling the air around her, every day would feel complete. Today, he knew he would give up his freedom for her. His life. She was in his bloodstream, and he didn't care if he spent the next twenty years behind bars, shackled in chains for what he'd done to Dillon. Gavin only hoped he could remove the shackles around her heart Dillon left behind, because no amount of kicking Dillon's ass could rid her of the scars she had from him. Gavin knew he'd always wipe away her tears, but he desperately wanted to be able to wipe away her painful past.

As if she had sensed him, Emily lifted her head, a beautiful smile crossing her face when her eyes met his. Clichéd or not, her smile lit up the room like a ball of fire in a darkened sky. Clichés were created for her. End of story. Again, Gavin felt as though the breath had been sucked right out of his lungs. He watched as her smile fell away, her face becoming troubled as she stood. Damn it. Gavin shot a glance down at his clothing. Stuck in his head on the way over, he'd forgotten to fix himself. He knew he looked like a disheveled mess. He wasn't wearing his suit jacket, and his shirt was untucked. Forget about his missing tie or the tiny specks of blood dotting the front of his crisp white button-down.

As Gavin moved toward her, raw power flowing from his body, Emily swallowed back the sick feeling seeping into her stomach. Meeting him in the middle of the crowded café, inches apart from one another, the voices surrounding her faded and figures blurred. His face blinded her to everything else. His breath was all she could hear. Though he wore a mask of cool passivity, his blue eyes said more than they should. They spoke volumes, inspiring an ache within Emily's heart. She knew what he'd done. She didn't need to ask.

Emily dropped her gaze from his swollen lip dappled with blood and stared at his shirt. Lifting her eyes, she met his steady gaze, and she could tell he was waiting for something from her. An approval possibly, words that would let him know she was okay with what'd happened. Not knowing how to begin, she simply looped her arms around his neck and brought his mouth down to hers.

Gavin pulled her into him, his hands gripping her waist and molding her body against his. "I had to do it, Emily," Gavin breathed, kissing her softly. "I wouldn't have been able to live with myself if I didn't."

Threading her fingers through his hair, Emily choked back a threatening sob. "I know you wouldn't have, and I'm sorry I expected you not to."

Gavin went to speak, but Emily kissed him harder, guilt flowing through her body. As her senses spiraled into his touch, Gavin's blood rolled around on her tongue, the taste deliciously intoxicating because she knew why it was there. She knew he'd been wounded defending her. The one thing she thought she knew was all wrong. For a brief moment, she was sure Gavin couldn't do anything to make her love him more than she already did. This proved to be false as she stood in the middle of a packed Manhattan café, kissing the man that'd forever changed her world. Her life. The man she loved a million times more than a few minutes earlier. Blind to further evil and deaf to the sound of ever crying again, Emily sank, crashed, and fell deeper in love with Gavin than she thought was humanly possible.

CHAPTER NINE

Let The Caveman Battles Begin

"I'm pretty sure if you squeeze my hand any tighter, I'm going to lose circulation." Gavin looked at Emily's sweating hand intertwined with his as if she were on a roller coaster ride and holding on for dear life. He knew she was afraid of flying, but shit, considering she was half his size, he couldn't believe the grip on her. "What good would I be to you if I lost a hand? I'm extremely talented, but only having one to work with might prove difficult during foreplay."

Emily swallowed, trying to focus on Gavin's dimpled smile. "Right. One hand's no good." She drew in a cleansing breath, slightly loosened her hold, and squeezed her eyes closed. "How much longer until we're on the ground?"

Lifting his right hand, which happened to be the one she wasn't trying to demolish, he stroked his knuckles along her jaw. "Ten minutes."

"Ten minutes," she repeated, her voice shaky. "Okay. Ten minutes. I can do this."

Gavin chuckled. "I have absolute faith you can. But really, I offered to keep you busy in the cabin, and you declined. You know I would've been good for a four hour flight and *then* some."

Smiling, Emily opened her eyes, her brow lifted. "Gavin Blake."

"Emily Cooper," he mocked, his grin widening. "I was simply trying to calm your nerves by properly initiating you into the mile high club. The only thing you would've had to fear was I might not have stopped once we landed. The jet would've been rocking on the runway." He leaned over and brushed his nose against hers, his words slow and husky. "*Oh…yes.*"

"Sick." She laughed, nipping at his lip.

"Sick in love, baby."

As the plane began its descent from the clouds, Emily re-tightened her hold around his hand, her body once again taut with fear. She leaned back and exhaled. Landing was the part she dreaded the most. "Oh… my… God."

"That sounded fucking hot," Gavin teased, but not really. She honestly sounded hot saying it. "I've said it before. You have the ability to make the simplest phrase sound sexual. I just had the sweetest vision of you sitting in a confessional booth, talking to a priest."

"Gavin!" she breathed, fighting against the smile cracking along her face.

Gavin leaned over, dragging his bottom lip between his teeth as he stared into her widened green eyes. "Pigtails. Short mini-skirt. Legs slightly parted. Black lace panties. Mmm, lucky bastard." Emily tried to breathe as he trailed his hand up her bare leg. Tingles shot down her spine. "You were confessing the naughty things I do to you that you can't get enough of." He slipped his fingers underneath her skirt, gently nudging open her legs. "The way I make you moan while sucking on those pretty little nipples. The way, right before you come, I hold you back and start over again while licking that sweet pussy. Your panties were drenched. Your breathing was heavy. Your body was… *boiling* for me like it is right now."

Emily couldn't think as he leaned in, grazing his soft lips against hers. Pulling her bottom lip between his teeth, he circled his fingers along the edge of her panties.

"Guess what?" he whispered, his voice low, his eyes intense.

She could barely get out a word. Hell, she could barely think. *Damn him.* "What?" she breathed, her mind concentrating heavily on his other hand—that'd come loose from her death-grip—floating up the side of her breast.

"We've landed, sweets." He slipped his tongue into her mouth, kissed her passionately for a damn millisecond, and stood, his megawatt grin beaming from ear to fucking ear.

Sitting lax in her seat, panties severely dampened, she watched him yank their carry-ons from the overhead compartment, his face as cool as a cucumber. "You're evil." Emily stood, her lips pursed in disappointment. "Pure evil."

Reaching for her hand, Gavin chuckled. "I'm evil?"

Emily nodded and slung her purse over her shoulder. "Yes." She laced her fingers in his as they made their way toward the front of his jet. "Don't even try to play innocent, Blake. You're evil, and you know it."

"Me? I was a Catholic altar boy growing up, and now *you* have me thinking impure, cast-me-into-hell wicked thoughts. My poor mother would be devastated."

Emily giggled, following him. They stepped out of the jet and into the clear, sunny air of San Diego. Emily inhaled, taking in the warmth.

Gavin kinked his head back, a smirk plastered across his lips. "Miss Cooper, it's apparent I'm the victim here. You, my little vixen, should be wearing diamond-studded horns on your head."

Emily snorted. "And I bet you'd find that sexy."

"Beyond reason," Gavin answered, handing their bags to his chauffeur. He pulled Emily into his arms, his smile wide. "I wouldn't mind that as my Christmas gift tomorrow. You, naked in a red bow, wearing those horns."

Emily lifted a brow, her voice husky. "You forgot about the red, six-inch stiletto heels, my hair pinned up off my shoulders, and a bottle of champagne. My belly button could serve as your glass."

Gavin's eyes flared with instant, primal need. "Get in the limo." He opened the door for her.

"Is that a threat?" Emily asked nonchalantly, trying to rile him up as she slipped in. She scooted across the cool leather seat and watched Gavin duck in behind her. "Because if so, it sounded... weak."

Without a moment's hesitation, Gavin dragged her body on top of his, straddled her legs over his waist, and hit the button for the privacy screen, sealing them off from the driver's view. Emily went warm with pleasure as Gavin eased his hands through her hair, bringing her lips down to his. He kissed her hard, his tongue licking greedily over hers. God, he tasted so good. A cross between the bourbon he was drinking on the flight over and minty gum. It made her high. *He* made her high. His smell, touch, and taste did things to her body she'd never experienced. She couldn't help but moan into his mouth as he slid a hand down her neck, along the arched curve of her spine, settling on her waist. His grip tightened in her hair, his kiss becoming desperate. Her heart took a nosedive into her stomach.

"Gavin," she breathed, "my sister's house is less than five minutes away."

Still kissing her, he slipped his hand under her shirt, his voice strangled deep with desire. "I'll tell the driver not to stop until we're finished."

Pulling back, a frown split her lips. She glanced at her watch. "We can't. It's already four. Dinner's at a quarter after. My sister's borderline OCD. She'll seriously panic if we leave her waiting."

Sighing, Gavin scrubbed his hands over his face. Staring at Emily, he shook his head, a lazy grin pulling at his mouth. "You know I'm inhaling every inch of your body after everyone goes to sleep, right?"

Emily smiled. "I would hope that you do."

"I have every intention of doing so." Resting his hands on her hips, he swept his gaze over her face. "Okay. Let's play twenty questions."

Emily gave a look of confusion. "Uh, okay."

"Emily, I have a massive hard-on right now that I'm pretty sure isn't going down anytime soon. I'm also pretty sure it won't look too good in front of your sister and brother-in-law. I need something to take my mind off of the things I was planning on doing to you on the way over. Get where I'm going?"

Covering her mouth, Emily stifled a laugh. "I do. Okay. Twenty questions. You start."

Gavin shifted beneath Emily, trying to ignore his need to rip her clothing right from her body. "My driver knows where we're going, but I forgot the name of the town they live in."

"La Jolla."

"Beach community?" Gavin asked, swiping a hurried hand through his hair.

Emily nodded, clearly able to see he was still suffering. "Right on the beach," she answered quickly.

Gavin cleared his throat. "Nice. What does your brother-in-law do for a living?"

"He's a computer engineer."

"Ah, a computer geek. Cool."

Emily smiled. "Yes. A certified computer geek."

"And your sister? What does she do for a living?"

"She's also a computer engineer."

Gavin lifted a brow, the corner of his mouth tipped upward. "Two computer geeks. That sex must be pretty dull."

Emily crinkled her forehead. "What does that have to do with it? I'm a teacher. That's kind of geeky."

"Mmm, no, that's sexy. Even David Lee Roth agrees he's hot for teacher."

Emily let out a laugh. Knowing she shouldn't but unable to resist, she leaned down and placed a soft kiss on his lips. "I'm seriously starting to think you need therapy."

Circling his hands around her waist, Gavin flicked his blue eyes to her mouth. "I'm going to need a cold shower if you do that again. Or I could tell the driver to keep going while I give you an early Christmas gift in the back of this limo. Don't say I didn't warn you."

"Deal." Emily smiled, but her features quickly softened. "Thank you," she whispered.

Confusion blanketed his face. "For what?"

"For coming out here with me for Christmas. Even though we celebrated early with them, I know it's hard for you to spend it away from your family. Especially your niece and nephew."

Emily was correct. This was the first time Gavin wouldn't spend Christmas surrounded by his family, but it was her first Christmas without her mother. He knew she should be at her sister's side. He gently ran his hands over her arms. He hoped being together on Christmas would ease some of the grief he knew they would experience. "Don't thank me. All I want to do is love and take care of you, Emily. I know you need your family right now. Nothing would've stopped me from making sure you were out here with Lisa."

His words tightened around Emily's heart, anchoring deep in her soul, a place no one else had ever attempted to gain access to. No one. Staring at perfection, both inside and out, Emily leaned down and kissed him, wanting nothing more than to pour every ounce of her love into that kiss. As Gavin's mouth whispered over hers, Emily had never felt more alive, never felt more complete than she did right there and then. At the same time, sadness set in. She'd nearly lost this man. Fate had a weird way of circling back over paths that were meant to cross. This was something Emily had always believed in and she knew it'd happened with her and Gavin. Now, there wasn't a thing she wouldn't do to make sure their paths never drifted apart from one another again.

"I liked that kiss," Gavin whispered as Emily pulled back. "But you know what that kiss did, right?"

Emily laughed. "Yes. I'm sitting on top of you, so I can *feel* what it's done."

"Okay. As long as you remember I'm inhaling you later, it's all good." Gavin shifted, trying to get comfortable as his body screamed at him. "And I don't care if your sister and Michael hear us."

Smiling, she shook her head. Her gaze shifted to the sandy beaches and rocky shorelines coming into view as the limousine made its way into her sister's hilly seaside neighborhood. La Jolla was nothing short of a pure oasis, a glorious retreat from the sweet insanity of New York. With the sun beginning its descent, the scenery popped and sparkled with vibrant Christmas lights twinkling against each home. Emily sighed. She loved this time of year.

As suspected, Lisa was eagerly awaiting them when they stopped in front of the home, her smile showing she was as excited as Emily. Emily heard her squeal, and it made her laugh. After dropping a quick kiss on his cheek, she hopped off of Gavin's lap, swung open the door, and raced into her sister's arms. She hugged Lisa tightly, comforted by her presence. Though it was just shy of a month since Emily had seen her, it'd felt like an eternity, considering everything that'd happened.

"Oooh, a *limo*," Lisa drawled, her eyes resting on Gavin stepping out of the vehicle. "Nice touch."

Emily looked at Gavin and smiled. "Yeah. He definitely has his ways." Dragging her attention from the man who couldn't even begin to know how much he was already making her Christmas bearable, Emily placed her hands on Lisa's shoulders. "I'm starving. Is dinner ready yet? Oh, and please tell me you made mom's casserole."

"It is, and I did. But before we go in, I have to tell you something."

Emily stared at her sister's face that'd suddenly taken on a look of distress. "What's wrong?"

"Phil's here," Lisa whispered.

"What?" Emily asked, exasperated. Keeping her voice low, she stepped closer. "Lisa, why didn't you tell me he was going to be here?"

"I didn't know he was coming. He stopped by on his way through to see his parents in Laguna Beach. He literally called five minutes before showing up."

Emily sighed and shook her head.

"I know. Talk about awkward." Lisa frowned. "But he's not staying the night."

"Thank God for that."

"Thank God for what?" Gavin asked as he approached the women, his and Emily's luggage in hand.

Biting her lip, Emily battled whether or not to tell him about Phil. Not that she could hide it from him, the real question was whether or not to tell him *exactly* who he was. Emily cleared her throat, deciding to take the plunge into complete honesty. "Uh, someone I used to date is here."

"Oh," Gavin said simply. Snapping his eyes between the two sisters, a smirk lifted the corner of his lips. "Should we be expecting Dillon for dinner as well?"

Emily's mouth dropped open as Lisa let out a gut-belly laugh. "No, Gavin." Lisa pulled him in for a hug. "It's good to see you again, and absolutely not. Dillon won't be attending dinner tonight."

"It's good to see you again as well, and it's refreshing to hear I won't have to break bread with, excuse my language, the biggest fucking asshole I've unfortunately had the dishonor of knowing." Lisa nodded in agreement as Gavin snaked his arm around Emily's waist. Leaning into her, he whispered, "So, how serious were you with the unnamed gentleman in your sister's house? Did you sleep with him?"

Emily let out a breath, her eyes wide. "No, Caveman, I didn't sleep with him. He became a little... obsessed with wanting to date me."

"Obsessed?" Gavin questioned, his brows furrowed.

"Phil's a good guy, Gavin," Lisa interjected. "A little quirky, but nonetheless a decent guy. I went to college with him, and we became best friends. He took my sister out on a few dates. That's all. But let's just say after her interest in him faded, he didn't give up so easily."

Gavin smiled one of those killer, sexy smiles known to drop panties. His blue eyes lit up with raw humor. "Ah well, who am I to fault the man for that? Your sister brings out an honest fight in any warm-blooded creature. As long as he didn't develop stalker tendencies, since I'm the only Caveman allowed to get like that with Emily, I see a very enjoyable evening in our future."

Again, Lisa laughed as Emily let out another breath.

Gavin shot Emily a wink, his lips grazing her ear as they followed Lisa to the house. "You know I'm going to have a little fun with this guy if he pushes the wrong buttons, right?"

"You?" Emily playfully questioned as they stepped into the foyer. She closed the door and cupped Gavin's cheek. "You're not only known for your stalker-ish tendencies. I've come to know you as one of the biggest wiseasses I've had the pleasure of loving. Just don't be too hard on him, okay?"

After setting down their luggage, Gavin dipped his head and kissed Emily's lips. "I'll try. But I promise nothing."

She rolled her eyes and looped her arm through his, leading him into the kitchen where Phil was leaned against the counter while her brother-in-law helped Lisa set the dining room table. When Phil saw Emily, his face lit up, his smile more than showing he was happy to see her again. Emily flicked her gaze to Gavin, his smile more than showing he was definitely going to have his share of fun with Phil.

Headed right in her direction, Phil's smile widened. "There you are, kiddo. I had no idea you were coming out until Lisa told me."

Before he reached them, Gavin leaned into Emily's ear. "Kiddo? What are you, twelve years old? I already feel like smacking him across the back of the head. Please tell me I have your permission. I'll be quick. I swear to God I'll be quick."

"He's nine years older than me," she quickly whispered, nudging his ribs… hard. It was Emily whose smile widened when she heard Gavin release an audible "oof." Looking at him, she shot him a wink this time. "*Be nice.*"

Rubbing his rib, Gavin mocked severe pain for a second and then grinned. "Whatever you say… *kiddo.*"

"Hi, Phil," Emily said as he approached. "Yes, it was kind of a last minute trip."

Phil smiled. "The one who got away from me. It's been way too long. You look absolutely beautiful. Actually, you look stunning." Sweeping his gaze from Emily, his eyes landed on Gavin. "And who do we have here?"

"We have here this stunning woman's boyfriend." Gavin held out his hand. Phil shook it, and Gavin found his grip weak. Yeah. He'd easily be able to knock him around. "I'm Gavin. It's a pleasure meeting you, Phil. Emily's told me a ton about you. It's always good putting faces with the names of men she got away from."

Stepping back, Phil rubbed his chin, carefully analyzing Gavin. "Odd. She never once mentioned your name the last time I spoke to her."

"Which was over a year and a half ago," Emily blurted out, staring at Gavin who now had his eyes narrowed on Phil. "I wasn't dating anyone at the time."

"Right. Right," Phil agreed, his eyes locked on Gavin's. "That would make sense, I guess."

Gavin was far from an asshole. He could tell the guy was trying to ruffle his feathers. Time to pluck some feathers from the fucking turkey. "I knew you looked like a smart man, Phil," Gavin said calmly, sweeping his arm around Emily's waist. "I can spot them a mile away."

"Talent of yours?" Phil questioned.

Gavin lifted a brow, a smirk toying at his mouth. "One of many. Ask Emily. She seems happy with my… talents. I'm pretty sure I can keep her from getting away."

Oh Jesus. If Emily had a knife, she could've cut right through the alpha-male tension filling the air.

"Hey, hey, hey!" Michael approached the group, his jovial voice music to Emily's ears.

Tension deflating like a balloon, Emily leaned into her brother-in-law's embrace, hoping he could bring a little balance to the semi-heated situation. She let out a weighted breath. "Hey, big brother."

"Hey, little sister," Michael laughed, releasing Emily from his bear hug. "Looking good."

"You're not looking too bad yourself," Emily said, her smile growing by the second.

Michael patted his stomach. "You like the extra cushion?"

Emily giggled. "Love it."

Wearing a proud smile, Michael turned to Gavin. "Hey, buddy. Good to see you again."

Gavin accepted Michael's hand. "You too, man. How've you been?"

"You know. Same old. Just be careful with this one," he said, jerking his chin in Emily's direction, a grin smothering his face. "If you stay with her long enough and she ever learns to cook, she might turn you into a fat slob the way her sister did me."

Gavin chuckled. "I'll take whatever she can give me. Even the clogged arteries."

"Good man." Michael patted Gavin's shoulder. "We're about to get this show started. Who's ready for some kickass food?"

Feeling her stomach growl, Emily grabbed Gavin's hand and started for the dining room, dragging him along. "I am." She plucked a basket of rolls from the counter and craned her head back to look at Gavin. "You're ready to eat, right?"

"Depends on what I'm eating," he whispered into her ear, his tone seductive. Wrapping his free hand around her waist, he pressed his pelvis against her ass. "Unless my assumption of keeping you from getting away was wrong, I'd like to enjoy my dessert somewhere on your body after dinner."

Sucking in a deep breath and tingles overtaking every inch of her, Emily stopped and watched Michael and Phil breeze into the dining room. Phil's eyes locked on hers until he disappeared around the corner.

Emily spun around, her gaze catching the sexiest baby blues ever placed upon a man's face. "Gavin Blake, you listen to me right now." Her eyes dropped to his luscious lips forming a smartass smirk. She bit her own lip in an effort to cause pain that might possibly distract her. It didn't work. Gavin stepped closer, and the smell of his cologne completely fucked up her plans. God, she wanted him. Bad. Her heart jumped into her throat as he nuzzled his nose against her hair. She tried to breathe. "You're not listening to me."

"I'm all ears, sweets," he said, his voice low. "Talk to me."

"You're making it difficult," she breathed.

And he was because his hand was now lightly rubbing the back of her neck, his eyes drilling into hers. "I'm making it difficult for you to speak?"

"Yes, you bastard. You are," she whispered.

Gavin chuckled. "God, I love it when you get nasty. You have no idea how much it turns me on."

Wanting to melt into him right there, Emily poked her head into the dining room. Everyone was already seated and waiting for them. She turned back to him, her voice becoming heated. "Gavin, are you going to make me beg you to stop?"

Gavin blinked. "Are you trying to get me to take you right here in the kitchen?"

Shaking her head and about ready to let him do exactly that, Emily laughed and reached for his hand, once again pulling him along. The escape into the dining room was quick but comical as she heard Gavin release a dejected sigh. She felt bad, but considering he commanded a room by simply being in it, she loved knowing she had power over him.

"So how'd she do on the flight, Gavin?" Michael asked. "Did you need to drug her up?"

Emily rolled her eyes as Gavin pulled out her seat. "No, he didn't have to drug me up."

Lounging into the chair next to her, Gavin smirked, slipped his hand under the table, and rested it on Emily's thigh. Drawing tiny circles along her silk skirt, he smiled when he felt her shift. "I was able to talk her down. It was easier than I expected, though."

"Good," Michael said, dumping a pile of green beans onto his plate.

"I'm sure being on a private jet helped some," Lisa said, reaching for a bowl of mashed potatoes. After scooping some out, she handed them to Emily. "Those seven-forty-sevens scare the shit out of me."

"Private jet?" Phil stared in shock across the table. "Did you hit the lotto?"

Gavin turned to Emily, a lazy smile on his face.

She leaned over and kissed his cheek. "In more ways than one," she whispered. Gavin squeezed her thigh, his smile widening. Emily shoveled some mashed potatoes onto her plate. Looking at Gavin, her eyes questioned if he wanted some. Gavin nodded, and she served him up a pile. "No, Phil, the jet's Gavin's. And, Lisa, you're correct. It's better than flying on seven-forty-sevens. But either way, you're still in the air where humans *don't* belong. I hate it."

Gavin and Michael chuckled.

"Shit," Lisa chimed, standing to her feet. "What are you two drinking?" she asked, looking at Emily and Gavin.

"Red wine," Emily answered.

"Thank you," Gavin said. "I'll take a beer if you have one."

Lisa nodded and whisked off to the kitchen.

Leaning back, Phil crossed his arms. "A man who owns a jet drinks a simple beer? I would've thought someone who could afford such a luxury would prefer something more refined. Looks can be deceiving."

Emily's eyes flew from Gavin—clenching his jaw—to Michael, his hand halted with his fork inches from his mouth. She swallowed nervously, placing her hand over Gavin's on her thigh.

Amusement at the asshole's statement glimmered in Gavin's eyes as he leaned back, crossing his arms. "I wasn't aware there were rules to what one should drink whether they're rich, poor, or somewhere in the middle, Phil. It'd be interesting to hear how you formed this opinion, though."

Lisa emerged from the kitchen and handed Emily and Gavin their drinks.

Gavin popped the top off the bottle, leaned over, and placed a luscious kiss on Emily's lips as he slid the cap into her palm. Leaving Emily breathless, he returned his attention to Phil. A simpering smile broke out across Gavin's face as he continued. "What's your source of information? *Reader's Digest? Newsday?* Perhaps a woman's magazine?" Before he let Phil answer his barrage of questions, Gavin leaned back over to Emily and whispered, "I owed you a bottle cap since the last few times I drank, I forgot to give you one. I'm sorry."

Cupping his cheek, she stared into his eyes. "I love you. And I love your bottle caps more than you'll ever know."

Gavin quirked a brow. "Yeah? Even though I have a fuckload of money, you love my bottle caps? Should my caps be more… refined?"

"No," she said breathlessly. "They're perfect."

"Are you sure?" he whispered, his eyes searching her face. "Phil and his semi-bald head might disagree."

"Phil's an asshole, and you're perfect," she whispered back, lacing her hands around his neck and pulling him in for another kiss. Uncaring that everyone seated at the table was most definitely watching them, Emily indulged in his lips for a few more seconds before pulling away.

Staring into her eyes, Gavin mouthed the word "*Inhaling*" before once again shooting his glare back to Phil. "Sorry about that. I find it hard to control myself where Emily's concerned. I'm sure you understand. Oh wait. You couldn't. She's the one who *got away*." Gavin threw him a wink and picked up his fork. "Back to what I was saying. Your source of information on such an outlandish assumption would be… what?"

Phil shifted and cleared his throat. "No *source* of information. I guess it was just an assumption."

Lisa's eyes went wide, clearly confused by the conversation that'd taken place while getting their drinks.

Smiling at her sister, Emily shook her head, trying to stifle a bout of laughter threatening to erupt from her belly.

"That's what I figured," Gavin said, bringing his unrefined bottle of Budweiser to his lips. "So, what do you do for a living, Phil?"

Phil adjusted his tie, the uncomfortable set in his body palpable. "I own a real estate development company."

Seated to Emily's right at the head of the table, Michael swung his head in Emily's direction, his voice low. "Phil's a moron. Always has been and always will be. But I deal with him because I love your sister." Emily nodded, admiring the way Michael always put Lisa's feelings before his. "Gavin's one badass motherfucker. I like him."

With a light smile, Emily glanced at Gavin, who appeared to be paying attention to Phil detail how he started his company, but she knew the conversation was boring him. She swept her gaze back to Michael. "Yeah, he is. Thank you. I'm happy you approve."

"How can I not?" Michael gave her arm a little nudge. "Besides the fact Lisa told me he dug into Dillon for what he did to you, you're glowing, and I respect him for making you happy. I wish you two the best of luck."

"Thank you, Michael." Emily leaned over and popped a kiss on his cheek. "I appreciate that."

"No problem."

As everyone ate, whether it was because Gavin had set him straight or because he simply didn't try again, Emily enjoyed not having to listen to Phil act like an ass. The tension that'd started the evening disappeared, bleeding away into laughter. With Christmas music spurring through the air and good home-cooked food in their bellies, they all conversed easily. After clearing the table and bidding Phil an eager goodbye, Emily helped Lisa put the kitchen back in order as Gavin and Michael chatted it out about who would win tomorrow's basketball game. Staying faithful to his New York roots and showing Michael his wiseass side, Gavin egged him on, saying that the New York Knicks were going to wipe the floor with the Lakers.

Needless to say, the two men agreed to *disagree*.

Feeling a yawn lurking, Emily decided to grab a hot shower before turning in for the night. She popped a kiss on top of Gavin's head, left the two men to themselves, and laughed to herself when she heard Gavin mention something about his beloved Yankees beating her Birds. She dragged her luggage into the guest room, closed the door, and shook her head, sure he would never let her live that one down. As she hauled her suitcase onto the bed, she wondered how many times he would harass her over the course of the upcoming baseball season. She was positive it would be too many times to count. She just hoped her Birds would make a sweet comeback, making her harassment even sweeter.

After indulging in a long, hot shower, she towel dried her hair and slipped into soft cotton shorts and a tank top. When she emerged from the bathroom, not only did she find Gavin's clothing strewed out across the bed, she also found the door to the balcony wide open. A breeze curled through the room, causing a shiver to prickle up Emily's spine. Though it was Southern California, the evenings usually brought cooler temperatures. Pulling a chenille blanket from the queen-sized bed, she wrapped it around her body and made her way onto the balcony.

Sitting in an Adirondack chair, his bare feet perched on the iron railing, wearing a pair of shorts and a T-shirt, Gavin sipped on a beer as he watched the waves tumbling in the distance. Another shiver, one that didn't have to do with the colder air, moved through Emily when Gavin turned. He caught her gaze, his blue eyes beckoning her in an instant. Longing lit up in the hard angles of his face.

Odd. She was no longer chilly.

After placing his beer on the ground, the glass clinking on the concrete, Gavin dropped his legs from the railing. Widening his knees, his smile was slow and deliciously sexy. Emily stepped between his thighs and crawled into his lap. She rested her back against his hard chest, curled the blanket over their bodies, her senses immediately drowning in the raw heat emanating from him.

Gavin pushed her hair away from her shoulder and lowered his mouth to the crook of her neck, his breath hot as he sucked lightly. "I've been waiting for you," he whispered, his husky words telling Emily what she already knew. He was about to inhale her. Snaking his hands under her tank top, he ghosted them across her belly, sliding them upward, until he had both breasts cupped in his hands. "You like leaving me hanging, don't you?"

Butterflies swarmed Emily's stomach, her body quivering under his touch. "It's the only control I have over you," she breathed, her voice shaky. She could almost hear the smile on his face. She could definitely feel his growing erection pressing against her ass.

With his thumbs, he slowly stroked the swell of her breasts. "Do you want me to keep touching you?"

Nipples hard as pearls, Emily arched her back against his chest. She bit her lip as he nipped her shoulder. "We're going to stay out here?" she asked. Her attention flew to the beach below them where a group of rowdy, apparently drunk teenagers were setting up a bonfire. "They might see us, Gavin."

"It's too dark up here. They won't see anything," he whispered. His low, primal voice vibrated over her skin as he twirled her nipples. Pinching them lightly, he licked behind her ear and pulled her tank top up over her head, dropping it beside them.

The cool night air danced across Emily's bare chest. She tried to breathe, tried to think. Words entirely left her mind.

"Now answer my question," he whispered, running his tongue up her neck. "Do you want me to keep touching you?"

She wanted him. Wanted him desperately. With each feather-light touch, she felt her core tighten, throbbing, begging to have any part of him inside her. Gavin pinched her nipples again, and she let out a soft moan. Desire won the battle of her embarrassment about possibly being caught, shattering any thought of not allowing this to happen. Suddenly hyperaware of her body, her cheeks flushed. "Yes," she whispered, "I want you to keep touching me."

"Tell me where you want me to touch you, Emily," he commanded, his voice caressing her name.

"My pussy," she managed to get out.

"I'm sorry. I couldn't hear you. Can you repeat that?" he asked in a low growl, his hands grazing the sides of her ribcage.

Dear, God. His fingertips brushed fire against her skin, simmering heat deep within her belly. "My pussy," she repeated, trying to keep the undertone of begging from her voice.

"You want me to touch that pretty pussy?" He hooked his thumbs in her shorts, the hard edge in his tone dripping with carnal need. "Is that what you want?"

"Yes," she moaned, slightly lifting her ass, as he slipped her shorts and panties past her thighs. With her toes, she yanked them down, the blanket following behind them to the ground. To hell with not begging. She was beyond it at this point. She'd do anything he asked her. "God, Gavin, please. Please touch it." The words tasted like chocolate-covered strawberries, sweet and delicious.

With one hand around her stomach and the other nudging open her thighs, Gavin couldn't help but groan as Emily whimpered before he'd even touched her. Fuck. She drove him mad. Dismantled him to pieces. He wanted her spread wide. "Put your feet on the edge of the chair."

Pulse racing wildly and already soaked in anticipation, Emily did as he said. Gently, he pushed two fingers inside of her, and she flung her head back against his shoulder, her arms instinctively flying behind her. She tensed, fighting her fear of being discovered. Quietly moaning, she dug her fingers into his hair, her clawing grip tight as she moved in synch with his strokes. With the sound of the tide ripping in and out in the cool night air, and their breathing picking up pace, Emily shamelessly ground harder against his fingers. Her muscles clenched, drawing them in deeper.

Trailing his lips along her shoulder, Gavin dragged his free hand from her stomach, up over the lush swell of her breast, and settled it around her neck. He pushed deeper inside her warmth. Emily's breath caught as he swirled his thumb in quick circles over her wet clit, his low groans and greedy mouth devouring her flesh, arousing her further.

Pulling her back by her neck, fingers slowly pumping in and out, Gavin angled her face and crushed his mouth to hers. "Take your hands out of my hair and squeeze those beautiful tits for me," he groaned, licking through her mouth.

His voice so carnal, so full of lust, made her body shake. With his words twisting deliciously in her mind, Emily untangled her hands from his hair, and once again, did as he said. Bringing her hands to her breasts, she palmed them for a second before tugging on her nipples. Tension built, growing fierce between her legs. She rode every screaming wave of desire he brought her with each thrust of his fingers. Spasms hurtled through her body, sending her higher and higher. Though she was close, so close, she needed him inside her and she needed him now. She couldn't wait.

As if sensing what she wanted, Gavin eased his fingers out of her, leaving her pussy hot and wet in their wake. She could feel the protest crawling up her throat, but it died on her lips as he hoisted her up, his one hand sliding underneath her ass as the other yanked his shorts and briefs down just enough. Within a split second, he'd pulled her down onto him. Emily sucked in a ragged breath as she felt the head of his cock spread her swollen flesh, the pleasurable burning nearly sending her into orgasm. Her eyes went wide. Though still in shock over where they were, his growls and heavy breathing made the risk of getting caught worth her while. Hot and hard, he was nothing but pure, primal, fierce, consuming alpha male. He filled her. Claimed her. Broke and owned her.

Brought her full circle from the woman she once was to the woman she was becoming. The woman she was meant to be with him.

"Fuck," Gavin bit out, his voice strained. Digging his fingers into her hips, the pressure and need that'd built up throughout the day nearly exploded as Emily thrust down hard onto his aching cock. His muscles jumped and twitched. He brought the fingers he'd had buried inside her to her mouth. "Taste yourself on me. I want you to lick your sweetness off my fingers."

And she did. She sucked on each one with an intensity she'd never before shown him. So entranced by her, Gavin felt lightheaded as her hand curled around his wrist, licking and stroking her tongue along his fingers.

"Tell me how good my pussy feels, Gavin." The demand burst from Emily's lips as she pulled his fingers from her mouth, leveraging forward to place her hands on his knees for balance. She moved up and down, her speed increasing. "Tell me."

Holy shit. Gavin swore he was about to lose it right there. Fisting one hand in her hair, he took the other and gripped her waist, guiding her body in vicious strokes up and down his cock. "You feel like heaven wrapped around me. Fucking heaven." And she did. Soft velvet over hard steel. Her slickened warmth, so tight, had Gavin's balls nearly climbing into his stomach. He wanted to spill every ounce of himself into her. But he would wait.

Wanting to always get her off first, he slipped his hand from her hair to her clit and rubbed hard and fast. Fuck. Emily gasped and her muscles tightened, constricting and clamping down around him so fiercely, he wasn't sure he was going to make it. She saved them both when she arched her body against his chest, her movements a sexy, sensual rhythm. However, it was all the more devastating to Gavin's already heated senses because now he could feel her core in its entirety, felt each flick of her hips as she circled his cock.

"Jesus Christ," he groaned, skimming his palm from her waist to her breast. He cupped it, squeezing. With the other, he kept steady pressure on her clit, stroking and teasing the swollen bud. "That's right, baby. Fuck me slow. Nice and slow. Let me feel every bit of you."

So turned on, Emily drew in a breath, overwhelmed by the sensations. "Please don't stop rubbing me." She whispered the plea, bringing her arms up and entangling her fingers in his hair. God. Between his mouth closing over her shoulder, his hand playing with her breast, and the other tripping over her clit, Emily was close to done for. Licking her lips, she whimpered. "Please, Gavin."

Unrelenting, unforgiving, and unstopping, Gavin bucked his hips, filling Emily completely. No longer breathing, thinking, or worried about who might be watching, painful pleasure shot through her body. It exploded, unfurling a release so intense, so deep, and wicked in its potency, she thought she was going to lose her mind. She cried out his name, her voice louder than expected, but she couldn't help it. It was pure fucking bliss. *He* was pure fucking bliss.

Spasms tore through every one of her muscles as Gavin slid his hand over her mouth. He held it there as she felt his orgasm hit, felt his hot, silky semen spilling into her. His body tightened, shuddering violently beneath hers, his breathing coming rough and fast against her ear. With shockwaves still possessing her and her body limp like a wet rag, lost in a haze of passion, Emily's breathing started to slow. She turned her head to the side, catching Gavin's mouth with hers. For a long moment, he kissed her deep and hard as he groaned, palming her breasts.

Spent and completely sated, Gavin reached for the blanket and covered Emily's naked body. Moving her long, damp hair away from her bare shoulders, he feathered his lips along her neck. "I love you, Emily, and I need you to know there's nowhere else in the world I'd rather be than here with you."

Turning, Emily stared into his eyes. They held so much passion and dedication, her heart swelled. With an intensity bordering obsession, she kissed him, thankful their roads had crossed paths once again. She drew strength from him she never knew she possessed. She blossomed when he was near. Holding her life in his hands, he was nothing short of carbon to a flame within her, waiting to ignite. Slowly breaking the kiss, Emily turned back around, taking in the heat of Gavin's strong arms wrapped around her stomach. Her gaze fell from the clear sky blooming with stars to the dark waves, dappled silver by the light of the moon. Emily released a satisfied sigh, her soul warm with a love she was certain she'd never find with anyone else. She knew tomorrow would be hard, but somehow, she also knew this might be one of the sweetest Christmases she would ever have. As Gavin pulled her closer, she was pretty sure she was correct.

CHAPTER TEN

A Shift In The Road

Emily awoke when the bright sun coming in through the blinds hit her face, its warmth not so welcomed considering she and Gavin had stayed up into the late hours of the night. Pillowed against his chest, his peaceful breathing in her ear calmed her. But that only lasted so long. Emily's thoughts struck, just as unwelcome as the early morning wake up. Flashes of last Christmas hit, a day spent in the hospital next to her dying mother, nearly yanking the air from her lungs. Dillon was also there in her mind, further souring her stomach.

Lifting her head, she glanced at Gavin's beautiful face, beyond grateful for him. Though she was happier than she could ever remember, her mood shifted as emptiness anchored deep in her gut. She didn't want to look back, but ghosts from her past wouldn't allow her to move forward. Her ache for her mother hovered like a dark storm, bringing a cloud of sadness.

Trying to escape the despair taking hold, Emily slipped from the bed. The yearning for her mother followed her with each quiet step she took across the cold wood floor. She shivered as she reached for the door handle, careful not to wake Gavin as she opened and closed it. Being it was just shy of a quarter to eight, the house wasn't alive yet. Void of any sound and clear of any movement, Emily was alone in her thoughts.

On a sigh, she moved toward the Christmas tree. Her gaze fell upon several ornaments she and Lisa had made for their mother when they were little girls—paper angels glued to clothespins and silver, red, and gold glittered reindeer highlighting each of their names tossed themselves into her memory. Emily ran her fingertips across the fading reminders of the past as tears gathered in her eyes. She swallowed, her body instantly shaken, her heart instantly crushed. Had she already been without the only parent she'd ever known for close to a year? The same parent who'd brought her love and insanity in equal parts? Her mother's voice danced in her ears as she tried to compose herself.

Emily didn't hear Gavin come into the room, but she didn't need to. His soothing presence blanketed the air. He wrapped his arms around her from behind as she wiped away an errant tear slipping down her cheek. Still staring at the ornaments, she shook her head and sucked in a deep breath. "How do I let her go?"

Gavin placed a soft kiss on the crown of her head, and without saying a word, he gently reached for Emily's hand and led her back to the bedroom. Confusion dripped into her mind as she watched him haul his luggage onto the bed. After unzipping it and pulling out a small black velvet box, he sat on the bed, motioning Emily toward him. When she approached, he stared at her, his eyes soft with concern. Once again, he reached for her hand and guided her onto his lap. With her back against his bare chest, he moved her hair away from her shoulders.

"You don't let her go, baby," he whispered as he clasped a diamond-studded, platinum oval locket around her neck. "You hold onto her with everything you have. You carry her with you through every joyous moment in your beautiful future. Your accomplishments. Seeing your children's eyes for the first time. Your life in general. You shoot for the stars with her in mind. She'll be there, watching. You forgive her for the mistakes she made while you were growing up, and during the bad times you have to face, you lean on whatever words of wisdom she gave you. But you never let her go. Ever. She wouldn't want you to let her go."

Opening the locket, Emily's breath caught. Her eyes swept over a picture of her mother as a teenager. With the sun shining against her dark hair and her smile highlighting the warm, carefree glow found only in one's youth in her eyes, Emily couldn't help but think it was the happiest she'd ever seen her mother. Emily sniffled and more tears fell. However, these tears were delivered by a man who couldn't even begin to understand the empty space in her heart he'd filled so many times.

Turning, Emily straddled his waist and stared into Gavin's eyes. The emotions swirling behind them riveted her. She was in awe he was hers. "My God, are you even real?" she whispered.

Holding her gaze, a sad smile lifted his mouth. "I think I am."

"You make me feel like I'm in a dream," Emily confessed, wrapping her arms around his neck. "Like I'm sleepwalking and I don't even know it." Continuing to take in the pure, honest, unselfish man in front of her, Emily lost herself in the fact he *was* real. "I'm able to close my eyes and just… trust you. You're the color on my blank canvas, the light in my dark, the air in my lungs, and I almost let you go. I almost erased us from ever happening. I can't imagine not having you here with me. Please tell me you know how much I love you, Gavin. I need to hear it right now. Please."

Gavin swallowed, his senses reeling. She owned him, mind, body, and soul. Words. God, he didn't have enough words to let her know how much he knew she loved him. Even if he did, how could he ever begin to let her know how much he knew she'd risked changing her life for him? Words weren't meant for this moment and Gavin knew it. He brought his lips to hers, kissing her softly. He kissed her the way she should've been kissed the first time a man was ever allowed to feel her body. He kissed her hoping he could banish every headstone of grief that'd taken up an ounce of space in her heart. Wanting to wipe away every sick moment and twisted memory her eyes ever witnessed, he held her closer, trying to shield her from the demons he knew she was battling.

In the silence, with only the sound of their beating hearts, Emily slowly pulled away. The heaviness in her chest lifted, its weight no longer suffocating, no longer draining.

Gavin ran his hands through her wavy hair, his smile soft. "Merry *first* Christmas."

"Merry *first* Christmas," Emily whispered, placing another kiss on his lips. After a moment, she edged off him. She hopped to her feet, strolled across the room and dug in her luggage. Pulling out a white bag, she lifted a devious brow. "Now it's my turn to give you your gifts, but I have to warn you, you have to start using each of them today."

With an equally devious brow lifted, Gavin ran a hand through his messy hair and leaned against the headboard, the grin on his mouth wide. "These gifts wouldn't happen to include a black lace ensemble worn by you, double 'A' batteries, and your shmexy legs shaking uncontrollably around my head, would they?"

Eyes wide, Emily belted out a laugh. But shit if he didn't look so hot waiting for her, shirtless no less. She swallowed, suddenly aware of the throbbing between her legs. All humor left her face as she slowly crawled onto the bed. With the bag in one hand, she slightly lowered his sweatpants with the other. She rained kisses along his hip, following his glorious tattoo all the way to the side of his left rib cage. Sighing in pure contentment, she moved her lips back over every delicious peak and dip of his washboard abs. She felt Gavin tense, his muscles tightening. He buried his hands in her hair as she hovered, lightly skimming her tongue along the edge of the evil-looking beast's wings. In all its evilness, it tasted like the sweetest cotton candy.

Emily brought her eyes up to his, their light-blue sexual intensity shocking her system. She smiled. "So you never told me why you got *this* particular tattoo."

Gavin blinked, a rush of puffed air escaping his mouth. "Are you honestly going to ask me that after you just *achingly* licked your way up my body?"

"What?" Emily giggled, straddling his waist. Looking down at him, she frowned. "I want to know. You told me *why* you got it where you did, but you left out why you picked a dragon."

Eyes zeroed in on her lips, Gavin smirked. "I got the dragon because I knew women would never... *ever*... *ever* be able to resist licking it."

Emily playfully swatted his arm. "You bastard. Are you saying I'm *not* the first to lick it?" In one quick movement, Gavin slipped his arm behind her waist and flipped her onto her back. Emily gasped, her heart nearly stopping as he hovered above her, lightly brushing his mouth against hers. "Oh my God," she breathed. "I was right. You are crazy."

"And you're trying to kill me with your questions," Gavin countered, nipping her bottom lip, which she started to realize was something he loved to do. "You're no longer allowed to say the words 'lick it' in my presence. Is that understood, Miss Cooper?"

His demand drifted over her like a caress, but she was about to push a few buttons. She popped a brow, her mouth curled into a smirk. "*Lick... it...* Caveman."

Gavin's eyes went wide right about the same time he dove his hand under her tank top. Emily squealed, squirming under his embrace. She yanked his hand away from her breast. "Gavin! No, I want you to open your gifts."

"It's a done deal," he replied, his voice a desperate groan. "I'm convinced you're seriously trying to kill me. I thought I was pretty on point with my game. Where did I go wrong?"

Emily released another giggle. "You could never go wrong, and I swear I'll make it up to you later."

Grinning, Gavin shook his head and sighed.

After kissing his cheek, she eased out from beneath him and straddled his lap as he sat cross-legged. Reaching for the bag that had gotten lost under the tangled mess of blankets, Emily smiled and pulled out a small envelope. "Here. This is something that you have to use for the rest of your life."

Gavin looked at the envelope. Written across the front in Emily's handwriting was:

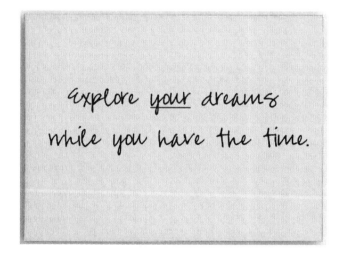

With a small smile, Gavin pulled out a thin card, showing Emily had purchased him a lifetime subscription to *Architectural Digest*. It was then he realized she also remembered things he'd told her. Wrapping his arms around her waist, Gavin ducked his head, whispering a soft kiss on her lips. "You'd be happy with me if I was an architect?"

"I'd be happy with you if you picked garbage up off the side of the road if that's what you wanted to do."

"You would?" He knew Emily wasn't with him for his money, but her answer somewhat shocked him. Most, if not all, women he'd encountered would've told him to stuff his dreams up his ass if he wasn't making the millions he did with Blake Industries. Though a career as a sanitation worker would never be his choice, his heart warmed. He'd found a woman who would accept him under any circumstance he might find himself in.

"Of course I would," Emily replied, tossing her arms around his neck. A teasing smile crept across her lips. "And I'm thinking you'd look pretty damn hot in the uniform."

"Ah, always an ulterior motive." Gavin popped a kiss against her forehead. She smiled, and his features sobered as he stared into her eyes. "Thank you. I love it."

"No. Thank you," she whispered against his lips. Unwrapping one of her hands from his neck, she reached into the bag and pulled out a small box. "I have more gifts for you. This one kind of coincides with the subscription in a weird way."

Gavin smiled and started unwrapping it. Once he'd peeled the red wrapping paper away, he found a black box with the name *Patek Philippe Calatrava* engraved on it. Shocked, because he knew his time pieces as well as he did cars, Gavin knew it held a very expensive watch. Upon opening it, his suspicions were correct. Trimmed in gold, the piece was amazing and something Gavin could easily see himself wearing. He ran his fingers over the soft black leather wristband, his eyes taking in the fine, Switzerland-made contemporary design. Though the Breguet piece he was currently wearing dented his checkbook a cool $260,000, this particular Patek Philippe Calatrava must've cost Emily upwards of $25,000.

Emily smiled, and handed him a second card with the words:

Don't let <u>time</u> slip away without doing what you truly want to do.

Now he understood how the two gifts fit together. Gavin cupped her cheek and placed a soft kiss on her lips. "Thank you," he whispered, stroking her hair. Emily smiled, but Gavin couldn't help wonder how she was able to afford the watch. "Did you use the funds I put into your bank account to buy me this?" Gavin searched her face. Though she'd argued with him about dumping any cash into her account, spending it on him was the last thing he wanted her to do. "I told you not to buy me anything with that money."

Emily rolled her eyes. "Do you like it?"

"Of course I like it. I love it. But I don't want you spending money like this on me, Emily."

With a sigh, Emily rolled her eyes again. Bringing his face close to hers, her expression became serious as all hell. "Gavin. First of all, I didn't use the funds you gave me to buy it. I have my own, and I used some of it to purchase that for you."

"Emily. Even though you make some extra cash waitressing, I highly doubt a substitute teacher's salary would allow you to spend this much on a watch."

Emily reared back, her brow raised. "Thanks for the compliment."

Gavin pulled her closer, tucking her hair behind her ear. "I didn't mean it like that, baby. But come on. I have a pretty good idea how much this cost. If you didn't use what I gave you, how could you afford this?"

"Dillon—"

Gavin reared back in shock this time. "What?"

"Are you going to let me finish, Caveman?"

Eyes locked on hers, Gavin nodded. His words came out slow. "Yeah. I'm listening."

"Thank you," Emily replied, running her hands through his hair in an effort to settle him. "Dillon took the money I had from my mother's life insurance policy and threw it into some IRAs, mutual funds, and different CDs. After I called off the wedding, I went through my financials. I took my name off several credit cards we'd had together, and I pulled my accounts from him. I transferred them over to a broker Trevor suggested. Let's just say, if it's the only compliment I can give him, Dillon knows how to grow a bank account. It nearly tripled over the year. I took a small loan against one of the accounts and bought you the watch. So again, I used my own cash. Not what you gave to me. Happy?"

"Happy?" Gavin parroted, pulling her closer. "I'm happy the woman I love was smart enough to yank her funds from her asshole ex's control." Trailing his hands along her back, Gavin brushed his lips along her jaw. "But I'm not happy she spent some of it on her charmingly sexy current boyfriend after he asked her not to spend that much on him."

Emily laughed. "Oh, now all of a sudden you're charmingly sexy?"

"You know it." Gavin smiled, shooting her a wink. After replacing the watch he was wearing with the one Emily bought for him, Gavin's face softened. "Really, Emily. Last big spending spree you waste on me, okay? I have everything I need sitting right here in my lap."

Emily sighed and eased the last gift from the bag. "We'll see. Now here. This is the one I *insist* you start using today."

Gavin eyed her suspiciously and pulled the red bow from what appeared to be a clothing box. "Your expression tells me this is some kind of payback gift."

"Sweet, sweet, Mr. Blake, you know me so well," she purred, tossing her arm around his neck.

With another shake of his head and a smile, Gavin slowly, so slowly, peeled the green wrapping paper from the box. He hesitated, bringing his eyes to Emily's. He could see she was becoming impatient. He chuckled when she tore the rest of the paper from the box and flipped off the top. Before he had a chance to get a look at what was in it, Emily yanked out a piece of bright yellow clothing. However, she was holding it balled up in her lap.

Oh, and she was laughing. Hard.

"What is it?" Gavin asked, unable to keep the laughter from his voice.

Emily stopped laughing, cleared her throat, and tried her hardest to keep her face serious. "I really hope you like it." She batted her eyelashes, bringing a hooded Los Angeles Lakers sweatshirt up to his chest. "I know Michael will *love* that you're wearing it during the game today."

Gavin shook his head. "Nope. Not a chance."

"Yes chance," Emily retorted.

"No way."

Emily frowned. "Yes way."

"Nope. I love you, but I'm not wearing that in front of Michael. Besides, I'm diehard New York. I have my Knicks sweatshirt with me."

Sighing, Emily drew her brows together, her frown deepening. She knew how to get him. "You know, I had many reasons for picking out that gift."

"I'm sure you did," Gavin admitted, circling his arms around her waist. "My misery being one."

Emily laughed. "No, it wasn't bought *solely* for your misery. But it could've, considering you made me prance around in that *hideous* Yankees sweatshirt."

"The Yankees are hardly hideous," he replied easily with a smile. "And let's not forget I made you prance around wearing it in the privacy of my home without another soul on earth watching."

"Yes, that's true. But, it's just… well, I have a thing for guys in yellow." Emily shifted. She wrapped her arms around his neck and made sure to circle her hips over his as she did. Ah, yes. He was getting hard. "There's something about the color that makes me get… *wet.*"

Gavin bit his lip, his eyes tracing Emily's face. "You're so full of shit."

"Oh no, but Mr. Blake, I'm really not. Between watching you wearing it and suffering the little bit you'll have to, I'll be a guaranteed good time for your efforts."

Sliding his hand up her back, Gavin tangled his fingers in her hair, tugging just enough. With a clear view of her gorgeous neck inches from his mouth, Gavin took the opportunity to indulge. He dragged his lips across her collarbone as he gripped her hair tighter. "I've created a woman who thinks she's going to win me over with sex."

Sinking into the feeling of him gently biting her shoulder and then lightly sucking on her neck, Emily wasn't sure who she was fooling. She'd backed herself into a corner and had no desire whatsoever to come out. "Is it working?" The questioned filtered out as a moan.

"Possibly," he answered, slowly lifting her tank top over her head. He tossed it onto the bed and reburied a hand in her soft hair. The other cupped one of her breasts. Eyes locked on hers, he licked her nipple. Another moan crawled up Emily's throat and Gavin got off on knowing he was beating her at her own game. "Are you willing to work to get me to wear this sweatshirt today, Miss Cooper?"

Yep. Completely backed in a corner. Emily lost the battle. But not really, because by the time the early morning hours had come and gone, not only was she achingly rejuvenated by her boyfriend's *multiple* Christmas gifts, she was also looking forward to seeing him sport the hideous color yellow for the remainder of the day.

With Brenda Lee belting out "Rocking Around the Christmas Tree" from the speakers in the living room where Michael and Gavin were getting ready to sit down and watch the basketball game, Emily giggled while Lisa jerked her hip in rhythm against hers as the two of them finished rolling up the last bit of cookie dough. Emily placed the tiny chocolate chip ball onto a baking sheet and popped the tray into the already heated oven.

"Remember how much mom loved this song?" Lisa's tone was cheerful as she reached into the refrigerator for a pie shell that would eventually hold homemade apple filling. "God, it was so fun watching her dance around to it. She loved Christmas."

A light smile touched Emily's face at the bittersweet memory. She flipped on the faucet and placed her hands under the warm water. "Yeah. She did love Christmas."

Lisa set the pie shell on the counter, once again bumping Emily's hip in tune with the music. Emily sighed, enjoying the jovial mood her sister brought to the moment. It didn't shock her though. Lisa, in a sense, had replaced their mother long before she'd passed away and she always made sure Emily was tended to. From helping Emily with homework to showing her how to apply makeup when she was old enough, Lisa willingly fell into the role thrust upon her after their father left. And not once did she ever throw her responsibilities resentfully into Emily's face. When long days and nights came and went without their mother, whether it was because she was working late bartending to put food on the table or out with one of her newest boyfriends, Lisa kept a certain level of consistency in Emily's life. A calm. An unwavering sense of peace.

As Emily stood with a dish towel in her hands, not only did slight hostility toward her mother bloom in her gut, she started to wonder why she'd allowed her mother's words to anchor her to Dillon for as long as she did. Sure, her mother didn't live to see what Dillon had morphed into. Before she took her last breath, Patricia Cooper left the earth thinking her youngest daughter was being swept off her feet by a true knight in shining armor. Emily was pretty sure if her mom had witnessed his change, she would've told her to get rid of him. Still, Lisa was the mothering force in her life, and during long conversations, she had always let Emily know if he wasn't treating her well, she should walk away.

The signs had been there. Warning flags were waved in every direction from most of the people surrounding her. However, she blanked them out. The few times she'd spoken to a counselor after leaving Dillon, she was told it was possible she leaned into Dillon after her mom died because he was a piece of something that no longer existed anymore. He was a witness to a soul another man in her life would never meet. In a sense, holding on to him was holding on to her mother. Holding on to her past. Although that past was painted with specks of sorrow, it was still familiar, understood. It was cold, yet warm, dark, yet filled with bright light she would never experience again. It was something that was forever... gone.

As Emily dried her hands, Gavin's words from this morning filtered into her thoughts. Not only did she have to forgive her mother for the mistakes she made, she also needed to forgive herself. And that's exactly what she did in those seconds in her sister's kitchen on this particular late Christmas afternoon. Though she knew she'd never begin to fully understand the way her mother was or the way she'd followed in her path, Emily reached into her heart and stripped away the last bit of negativity she held toward herself and her mother.

"Hey, I lost you there for a few." Lisa's soft voice lulled Emily back. Placing her hand on Emily's cheek, she gave a weak smile. "Are you okay?"

Emily didn't answer as she pulled her sister in for a hug. As if sensing what Emily was going through, Lisa squeezed her tight. Her comforting hold seized Emily with love as it always did.

"Uh oh. We've interrupted a sisterly moment." Michael chuckled as he and Gavin strolled into the kitchen. "We suck, man."

Staring at his jewel, Gavin smiled and leaned against the arched entryway. He watched Emily back away from her sister, love gripping him by the neck as her gaze caught his. Even dressed in sweatpants and a sweatshirt, she was so goddamn beautiful she took his breath away. With a smile on her face that filled him completely, she made her way toward him. Warmth spilled through his body as she looped her arms around his neck, her soft auburn hair draping down her back as she looked up at him. She seemed genuinely happy, and he could feel it.

"Have I told you that you look amazeballs in yellow?" Emily laughed, snuggling against his chest.

Michael snorted, reaching for an olive on a platter filled with cold cuts and cheese. "Yeah right. He looks like Big Bird on crack." Lisa smacked his arm and pulled the cookies from the oven. "That hurt, babe." Michael mocked pain and rubbed his arm.

Gavin shook his head. "You might be right, Michael, but if you'd received the… *gifts* I did in exchange for wearing this, you might find yourself on a crack high modeling a Knicks sweatshirt."

Emily blushed and laughed.

"Not a chance, buddy," Michael replied, popping the olive into his mouth. "No matter what my sister-in-law gave you, considering your big, goofy ass looks like it was hit with a hearty blast of sun, I'm thinking you need to withhold your last Christmas gift and give it to me instead. Hell, I'd be your girlfriend *and* wear a Knicks sweatshirt. Me love you long time, Gavin."

"Michael!" Lisa gasped, smacking his arm again.

Michael chuckled, and Emily looked at Gavin, her expression confused. "Last gift? I thought we were done exchanging?"

Gavin popped a knowing brow, a smirk on his face. "Ah. That's what I had you thinking, sweets. To be quite honest, I'm filled with surprises that'll keep your mind... blown... constantly." Dipping his head, he pulled her closer, his lips brushing her ear. "And I'm not just talking about when those gorgeous, shaking legs are wrapped around my head while you're moaning my name."

Emily whipped her head around, glancing over her shoulder at Michael and Lisa. Thankfully, they weren't paying attention. Quickly, she pulled Gavin down for a heart-stopping kiss, and then she whispered into his ear, "Thank you so very much for making my legs shake the way you do."

Gavin grinned, his eyes filled with considerable male appreciation. "The pleasure's *always* mine." Emily smiled, and Gavin looked at Michael. "Hey, Lakers loser."

Michael snapped his head up from where he was digging into the smorgasbord of food piled on the counter. "What's up, New York Knicks-don't-have-a-chance-in-their-wildest-fucking-dreams nobody?"

Gavin threw his head back and laughed. "Whatever you say."

"Yeah. We'll see." Michael swiped a beer from the refrigerator. "What can I do for you?"

"I forgot to grab the, uh"—Gavin looked down at Emily and back to Michael—"you know, those things, from you last night."

Leaning against the counter, Michael took a long pull from his beer and shrugged. "I'm not sure I know what you're talking about."

For the third time in less than five minutes, Lisa swatted his arm. "Michael. You know what he's asking for. Stop being a jackhole."

"Damn, babe. It's Christmas." Lisa rolled her eyes. Shaking his head, Michael snorted and dug into his pocket.

Gavin let out a puff of air, turned Emily around, and slid his arms around her waist. Walking behind her, he moved her toward Michael and yanked something from his hand that Emily couldn't see.

"What are you all up to?" Emily's eyes flicked to her sister, whose face looked as if it was about to burst at the seams with joy.

"Does she have sneakers on?" was Lisa's answer, clapping as Emily and Gavin rounded the corner to the mudroom flanking the back end of the house.

"Nope," Gavin called. "What size are you, Lisa?"

"Six," Lisa answered.

"Sit," Gavin commanded, pointing to a bench as he released Emily's waist.

With a curious look molding her face, Emily sat. "What am I, a dog?"

"Mmm, I bet if you were, you'd have a sexy bark."

Smiling, Emily shook her head as Gavin knelt down and scanned a row of shoes underneath the bench. He plucked what appeared to be a size six Nike woman's running shoe off the floor and propped Emily's foot on his thigh. After slipping her foot into the sneaker and tying it, he repeated the process with the other.

Once finished, he looked up at her, his smile wide. "Comfortable?"

Emily crossed her arms. "What are you doing?"

"You didn't answer my question. Are they comfortable?"

"Yes. They're comfortable."

"Good," Gavin said, lacing his fingers in hers as he stood, pulling her up from the bench. "You ready?"

Emily slid her sweatshirt hood over her head. "To go running? Sure. Why not? I'll need to burn off today's calories anyway."

"First: I'll help you burn off those calories later. I'm the best workout you can get." Emily rolled her eyes and giggled. "Second: we're running and we're running fast. But not with our feet." Gavin stopped short at the garage door.

"Okay. Now you're scaring me."

Dipping his head, Gavin cupped the back of her neck and stared into her eyes. "Emily Cooper, the only thing you have to fear is how much I'm going to love you for the rest of your life. And… how many times I'm going to make those legs shake. But that's beside the point. Never fear me, sweets. Understand?"

With a breezy smile, Emily lifted her hand in a salute. "Yes, sir, Mr. Blake. I completely and fully understand, sir."

Amused and somewhat turned on, Gavin chuckled and swung open the door to the dark garage.

Before flipping on the lights, Emily could see the smile splitting his face, and she couldn't help but sigh in contentment. God, she loved the charismatic energy he released. She knew it bled from his pores the moment she met him, and it captivated her. It gripped her, drew her in, anchoring around her heart.

A click…

Presto…

Lights…

When her eyes adjusted, Emily's pulse quickened and her breath caught. Her gaze fell upon the most elegant vehicle she'd ever seen. White, sleek, and wrapped in a larger-than-life red bow, its sophisticated design was something she pictured Hollywood movie stars cruising in.

"Oh my God, Gavin. You didn't," she breathed, stepping down the stairs in a haze. Her eyes shifted between him and the car.

After walking down the stairs as well, Gavin wrapped his arms around her waist, resting his chin on her shoulder. "I did. Do you like it?"

"Like it? I love it." Sliding her hand along the magnificent contour of the hood, she moved around the extraordinary machine, her heart slamming in her chest. "What is it?"

"That would be a car, Emily."

Pulling her gaze from the vehicle, she turned around, tilted her head, and laughed. "I know it's a car. I mean, what kind is it? I've never seen one like this."

Gavin chuckled, slid the hood from her head, and placed a kiss on her crown. "I knew what you meant." He winked. "It's a Maserati GranTurismo S, and we're about to *run* it through the streets like two certified maniacs in love. I insist on speeding. Got it?" Stepping back, he tossed her the keys, and she caught them, a smile beaming from ear to ear.

Throwing her arms around his neck, Emily pushed up on her tiptoes and dragged Gavin down to her lips. She kissed him hard, pulling his body closer. "Yes. Got it. But you didn't have to do this. I told you I didn't need one. Are we driving it back to New York?"

"No, I'll have a shipping company put it on a trailer and drive it across the country. And it's too late to not buy it for you now. C'mon." Grabbing her hand, he walked her to the driver's side and opened the door. "She's an automatic. I figured that was better for you since your sexy ass will be in the city. But she's holding over 400 horsepower under her hood. I'm not kidding when I say you're opening her the fuck up. Let's see what she can do."

Emily squealed, popped a kiss on his cheek, and slid behind the wheel. Smoothing her hands along the soft red leather interior, she watched Gavin hit the garage door opener on the wall. He pulled the bow off the car and rounded the vehicle to the passenger side.

Once he was nestled in his seat next to her, she looked at him. "Push button?"

With a grin, Gavin nodded. "You're getting good at this."

"Wiseass." She giggled, tossing the keys to him. "Okay. We're opening her up. Speed. Here we go."

Emily pushed the button and the engine purred to life, its sound nearly nonexistent. A far cry from the cars she'd owned that threw up when she started them. As she backed out of the garage into the bright sun of the late afternoon, Gavin synched his cell to the car, pumping the stereo to near-deafening levels.

"Who is this?" she yelled over the smooth, sultry voice of a man singing about a girl who was his angel. The slow beat was eerily dark and sexy. She checked her mirrors before pulling into the street. "I like it."

"Massive Attack. The song's called 'Angel,'" Gavin answered, staring at Emily as he wet his lips. "When you're not with me, I've often... *thought* of you while listening to this, among other things."

Emily glanced at him, her senses heated by his sexual tone. "Oh, have you?" She cleared her throat, pulling her eyes from his as she pressed the gas harder than intended. The car leapt forward as she made a quick right out of the development. "And what are the other things you've done while listening to this song with me in your thoughts?"

Still gazing at her, his mouth turned up in a wicked grin, his voice low as he lifted his arm, massaging the back of her neck. "I'm usually in the shower with hot water spraying all over my body."

Emily's breath hitched, stuck in the back of her throat as he dragged his hand from her neck, down her shoulder, brushing against the swell of her breast. "And then?" she breathed, trying to concentrate on the ramp leading onto the San Diego freeway. She rolled down the window, allowing fresh air into the small space that'd suddenly become sweltering. "Please tell me what you do to yourself."

Oh yes. Gavin had created a sexual monster, and he loved Every. Fucking. Bit. He flicked his blue eyes to the speedometer. She didn't realize it, but his sexual angel was nearing 80 mph as she weaved in and out of other vehicles, her shiny hair whipping around her heart-shaped face. Continuing his pursuit along the side of her body, he adjusted his seat back slightly as his hand slowly moved down to the waist band of her sweatpants. Nice easy access.

He teased his fingers against her stomach, lingering before dipping below the material. He felt Emily tense, the car jolting forward, faster as he slipped his hand lower still. Holy shit. She wasn't wearing any panties. Dick hard as a rock, Gavin couldn't help the groan rumbling up his throat. With Nine Inch Nails now pummeling through the car, screaming about fucking like animals, Gavin was more than pleased with his playlist. As Emily parted her legs, Gavin glided his hand down the smooth, bare flesh of her pussy, his fingers instantly slick as he pushed them inside her. A moan tore past Emily's lips, and Gavin watched her hands grip the wheel tighter. He slid his fingers in and out with the steady beat pulsating from the speakers. Faster, the vehicle surged forward, nearing 110 mph as Emily lifted her left foot onto the edge of her seat. Emily tilted her head back, her eyes fluttering closed as he pushed deeper, harder.

"Eyes on the road, Emily, or else I stop," Gavin commanded, his breath becoming ragged as she ground on his fingers.

Emily snapped her head forward, another moan filtering past her lips.

Staring at her beautiful face twisted with pleasure, Gavin leaned into her ear. "I take my cock and stroke it slowly while thinking of you."

"Please keep going," she begged shamelessly, her concentration faltering by the second. Her actions were dangerous and she knew it, but hell if she could stop. She was completely high, teetering on the edge of ecstasy, and she wanted nothing more than to jump. "What else do you think of?"

"I think about the way we fuck until our bodies are dripping with sweat and we can't take anymore." Gavin groaned, his senses drowning in the feel of her wetness coating his fingers. "I think about the way your hot pussy feels around me as you beg me to take you harder. The way your body shudders like a fucking leaf when you come for me. "

"Oh my God," Emily moaned, her need to pull over and ravish him escalating with each stroke he pushed inside of her. He circled his thumb over her clit, heightening that need beyond any control she had left. Mind made up, Emily eased off the gas. Before she could seek out a spot, any damn spot, her gaze caught the blazing red and blue lights of a highway patrol car pushing up her ass.

"Gavin!" she wailed, her nerves shot and her body a tumbling mess. "I'm getting pulled over!"

Gavin barked out a laugh and eased his hand from her sweatpants. "That's my speeding vixen," he said as if unaffected by the situation. He licked his fingers, adjusted his seat, and smiled. "Don't worry. I'll just let them know what I was doing to you. I'm sure they'll understand."

Mouth agape, Emily shook her head, trying with all her might to calm her heated body. She reared off onto the shoulder, her attempt to calm down in vain, because she was shaking uncontrollably. Sure, some of it had to do with the not one but two towering state troopers flanking either side of the vehicle, but more of it had to do with her aching desire for release. Eyes wide and body pulsing with what she was sure was pure unleashed torture, Emily reached for the purse she never brought. "Holy shit! I don't have my license with me!"

"Emily, calm down." Gavin lifted his ass, pulling his wallet from his jeans pocket. "Relax, baby, really."

"You're telling me to relax?" she questioned, her words clipped. "I was doing ninety, and I don't have my license. They're going to haul me off to jail."

Gavin popped a smirk, sliding out his ID. "One: You were doing a hundred and ten if you want to get technical. Two: They're not hauling you off anywhere. Three: I just had the sweetest fucking vision of you wearing a black and white prison jumpsuit. You were even wearing the little cap on your head. Mmm, simply beautiful."

"You need help," Emily whispered as the two officers approached, their hands resting on the pistols tucked in their holsters. She swallowed, smeared a smile across her face, and glanced up at the officer on her side of the vehicle. "Hello, sir."

Eyes shielded by dark sunglasses, the older gentleman pressed his mouth into a hard line before he spoke. "License, registration, and insurance."

With a smartass smirk brighter than she ever witnessed, Emily watched Gavin reach into the glove compartment and pull out the necessary documents. Handing them to her, he shot her a wink.

She rolled her eyes and looked at the officer peering down at her. "Um, I don't have my license with me. I'm visiting from New York, and we left my sister's house in a rush. I forgot to bring my purse."

After examining the information she gave him, he slid his glasses from his face. "Is there a reason you thought it was okay to do 111 miles per hour on the freeway?"

"That's my fault, officer," Gavin piped up, inclining his body toward the driver's side window. "I told her I was in dire, excruciating pain and needed to be examined by a nurse." Gavin cleared his throat. "I mean a doctor. But I'm happy to say I'm feeling better now."

With a suspicious eye, the trooper glared at Gavin for a long second. "I need your social so I can run a check for a license," he said, looking back to Emily.

She gave him the digits and nervously glanced in the rearview mirror as he walked to the patrol car.

Still standing on the passenger side, the younger trooper leaned in the window. "So you're a Yankees fan?" he asked, his eyes pinned on Emily. "I'm from the Bronx. Nothing beats a Yanks game at home."

"I'm not a Yankees fan, but my boyfriend is," she answered, shifting in her seat. The small talk soothed her nerves slightly.

The trooper furrowed his brows. "You're not? Your plates say otherwise."

Now Emily furrowed her brows as she looked to Gavin. "And what would my plates say, Gavin?"

Smile full-toothed and wide, Gavin cupped the back of her neck. "Ah. You must've missed that while we were in the garage." He chuckled, running his fingers through her hair. "I had them shortened up to say 'New York Yankees Lover.' Emblem and all. I have to admit, they look pretty cool."

Palming her cheek, Emily looked down and laughed. "A living, breathing, walking wiseass."

"You left out shmexy," Gavin clipped.

Before Emily could toss him her own wiseass remark, the older officer returned. "Okay. Your New York license checked out. I need to issue you a correctable violation for not having it with you, though. Just bring the ticket and your license to any station in the San Diego area, and it should get dismissed. Sign your name by the X." Emily nodded, and he handed her a white slip. After scribbling her name on it, she gave it back. He ripped the yellow carbon copy off from underneath, once again repeating the process of paper exchanging.

"Seeing you look like a nice girl and I don't want to do the paper work, I'm not going to arrest you. Which I could, considering how fast you were driving. But you're getting a speeding ticket for doing forty-six miles per hour over the posted speed limit. It could carry a fine up to $1,000 and a possible thirty-day suspension of your license." The trooper paused, hunched over, and looked into the car. Though his glare was aimed at Gavin, his statement was directed at Emily. "I suggest you rethink your speed the next time the gentleman next to you tells you he's *sick*."

Emily nodded, holding in a sigh of relief. "I will. Thank you, officer."

He gave a curt nod. After the two troopers walked away, Gavin busted out laughing, slapping his knee.

Emily pulled onto the freeway, mindful of her speed. "I can't believe you're laughing," she said, trying to keep herself from doing the same.

Running his hand through his hair, Gavin popped a smile. "Your face was absolutely priceless."

"Bet you wish you had a camera."

"Sweets, you have *no* idea what I would've done for one."

Once again, Emily rolled her eyes. Though it took double the amount of time to make it back to her sister's house, because she was driving as Gavin would refer to as "like his grandmother," nonetheless they arrived. This time, less… *heated* than when they began their trip.

After hopping from the car, Emily glanced at the tags. Sure enough, Gavin had the letters *NYYLVR* put on the plates.

Upon entering the foyer, after dowsing her Yankees lover with a few kisses, Emily heard Michael hooting out that the Knicks had their shit handed to them by the Lakers. Now it was her turn to bust out laughing. Gavin playfully swatted her ass and made his way into the living room. Shaking her head, she started for the kitchen and found Lisa pulling a honey glazed ham from the oven. The second the savory smell hit Emily's nose, a lurch of nausea hit her. It coiled and simmered, stopping her dead in her tracks. Her eyes glassed over as she curled one arm around her middle, the other cupped over her mouth.

"Are you all right?" Lisa asked, placing the ham on a cooling rack. "You don't look so good."

Another whiff and Emily was done for. Turning on her heel, she belted through the kitchen, nearly tripping over a stool next to the island. She barely made it into the lower level bathroom, and she didn't have time to close the door. She slid onto her knees in front of the toilet. With another twisting lurch scraping though her gut, Emily pulled back her hair, her body viciously releasing the hearty breakfast and lunch she'd enjoyed earlier. Her throat burned hot from the acrid taste. She gasped for air, choking as she heaved.

"My God, Emily!" Lisa ran into the bathroom, helping Emily hold her hair.

"The door," Emily croaked. "Close the door."

As Lisa closed it, Emily pulled herself from the floor, her nerves shot from her body's sudden reaction. Hunched over the sink, she flipped on the cold water and slipped her hands under it.

"What the heck was that?" Lisa asked, her eyes wide.

Emily shook her head and sipped water from her hands. As it slid down her throat, easing the fiery burn, she shook her head again. "I have no idea," she breathed. "I came in, and the smell of the ham made me sick."

Lisa leaned against the wall, her arms crossed. "This isn't the first time you've felt sick recently."

Reaching for a hand towel, Emily dried her face. "Right. I've been under a lot of stress, Lisa." She tossed the hand towel onto the vanity and whipped open the medicine cabinet. "Do you have an unused toothbrush?"

"Not in there. Underneath the sink."

Ducking, Emily pulled open the cabinet. After rummaging through a small basket, she found the pack. Quickly opening it, she stood, snatched the toothpaste, and squirted some onto the bristles. She shoved it into her mouth and plowed the brush over her teeth, wanting to remove the nasty taste.

"I know you've been under a lot of stress, Emily, but did it ever occur to you," Lisa paused, placing her hand on Emily's shoulder, "that you might be pregnant?"

Staring at her sister's reflection, Emily immediately stopped brushing. She pulled the brush from her mouth and turned around. "No. Why would I even think that? I'm on the pill."

"Have you kept up with it?"

Emily sighed, rinsed her mouth, and shut off the water. "Yeah, I think I have."

"You think you have?" Lisa scoffed. "The pill only works when you take it on a regular basis. When's the last time you had your period?"

"Jesus," she puffed out. "It's just my nerves. Everything that happened with Dillon while we were engaged, not to mention everything with Gavin between the engagement and after. I'm not pregnant."

Lisa's green eyes softened with concern. "Answer the question, Emily. When's the last time you had your period?"

Trying hard to remember the last time she did receive a visit from "Aunt Flo," Emily rushed her hand through her hair. "I'm not sure. The second week of October, maybe."

"Right. The second week of October." Lisa reached past Emily and opened the medicine cabinet. She plucked out a box and handed it to her. "Michael and I are still trying for our own. There're two tests in there. Get peeing."

Emily opened the box and pulled out both pregnancy tests. "I can't believe this."

"My thoughts exactly. What can't you believe?" Placing her hands on her hips, Lisa gaped at her. "You haven't had a period since the middle of October. Every time I've spoken to you since I left New York, you told me you were fighting some kind of nausea. You pawned it off as nerves. I get it. But everything's fine now. There's no reason for you to be nervous. If it's as simple as nerves, sit down and take the test. No biggie."

On a sigh, Emily slid down her sweatpants and popped a squat over the toilet. Waiting on Mother Nature, she tore open both tests. "Can you stop watching me? You're making me feel like a child getting a potty training lesson."

"Oh give me a break." Lisa rolled her eyes and messed with her hair as she stared at her reflection. Throwing the dark curls into a messy bun, she shot Emily a sideways glance, a smile lifting the corner of her mouth.

"I did potty train you. Let's not forget I'm ten years older. I've wiped your ass one too many times for either of our own good."

With way too much information pelting through her head, Emily didn't dare keep the conversation going. But it was all good because Mother Nature finally showed up. Holding both tests, Emily slipped them under the flow, making sure both were saturated. Once finished, she placed them on the toilet paper Lisa had neatly squared up on the vanity.

Emily washed and dried her hands, her head starting to become fuzzy as the sisters hovered above the tiny sticks that, in that moment, scared the shit out of Emily. Through the past few weeks, she'd dismissed her nausea as nerves, but all of a sudden, that no longer seemed plausible. The words denial, fear, and plain out stupidity came to mind. With sweat gathering just above her lip, she yanked up the empty pregnancy test box, flipping it over to read what a positive and negative would look like. Making note that one line represented a future void of diapers, and two lines initiated her straight into motherhood, Emily started nibbling nervously at her thumb nail. "How long do these take?"

The question had barely escaped Emily's mouth when a single line on one of the tests started turning a light shade of pink. With a sigh of relief perched in the back of her throat, a tiny smile crept across Emily face. However, that tiny smile quickly fell when the line's twin screamed for a little attention as it, too, started blushing. Emily flicked her eyes to the other test, already beaming two bright red lines.

Standing above two plastic sticks signifying her life was about to change in more ways than she could even begin to understand, Emily tried to breathe.

Breathe…

Numbers.

Dates.

Times.

Calculations of every sort pounded through her head. A mental calendar, wicked in all it was, flashed in Emily's mind. Its pictures reminded her that the first time she'd made love to Gavin, the night of his mother's benefit, was within days of her and Dillon breaking up. Within days of her and Dillon making love.

Breathe…

Days.

Hours.

Minutes.

Memories of every kind arrowed through her heart. Each second she and Gavin had spent together over the last few weeks, slowly mending what was once close to broken, felt as though it was about to be ripped from her. Gone. There was no denying the child she was carrying might not be his. The chances were slim to none. In the two glorious nights they shared, she'd slept with Gavin a handful of times. In the weeks leading up to and after that night, she'd been with Dillon many times. Arms open wide, forgiving every confused indecision she'd made, Gavin had taken her back, but he'd never signed up for this. A stand-in father to the child of a man he hated. A man he loathed with every fiber of his being. This could surely break them. What they were, and what they had yet to become, would be nothing but an almost that… never was. A mirage.

The possibility of losing Gavin forever tore through Emily's chest as she hunched over, her arms wrapped around her stomach that would soon bloom with life. A beautiful life that shared her blood, but may not share the blood of the man she couldn't live without.

Breathe…

"Emily." Lisa's soft voice barely broke through her thoughts... her nightmare. Emily felt her sister's caring touch on her neck. "Emily, look at me."

Covering her mouth, tears pooled in Emily's eyes as she shook her head. "It might not be Gavin's," she cried, trying to keep her voice to a whisper. "Oh my God, Lisa, it might not be his."

Lisa leaned into Emily, cradling her the way their mother would when she was hurt. "I know, sweetie. I know." Dangling over the edge of near insanity, Emily shook, her cries muffled against Lisa's chest. "Listen to me, okay? I want you to lie down. I'll tell Gavin you were tired and went to take a nap. It'll hold him off until after we're done eating dinner. You'll have some time to think about what you're going to say to him. All right?"

Lips trembling, Emily nodded. She swiped her hands through her hair, plucked a tissue from the container, and looked at her reflection. Her eyes, puffy and blackened with smeared mascara, would soon stare into the eyes of the man she loved so desperately. The man she may very well lose. After scrubbing her face with soap and water, she gave Lisa a hug and made her way to the guest room. Her heart dipped lower in her chest when she heard Gavin bark out a laugh as he accepted a few more jabs from Michael regarding the Knicks' loss.

With the click of the door, her thoughts spiraled out of control. She was about to ruin him. How would she even begin to tell him the news that was about to change them forever? Words. Her mind felt stripped of the right words to say. Would he just up and leave her in California? Visions of his face the second he found out hit, plowing through Emily's head. Bile burning like acid rain rose in her throat. In a haze of not only fear but a loneliness so dark, she sank onto the bed, pulling her knees against her chest. As she lay there, she tried to go over what she would say, how she would say it. But as the minutes ticked by, she was fast becoming aware no amount of right words would make any of it simple. Life was about to change. She didn't have to lie there too long, praying Gavin would remain by her side when it did, because a moment later, the door creaked open and in walked the man who would forever steal the breath from her lungs. The man who, no matter what decision he made in the next few minutes, would forever own her heart.

Emily swallowed and sat up. She tried to keep the edge of despair from her voice. "You're already finished eating?" She watched him pull the hideous Lakers sweatshirt over his head, leaving him in a white T-shirt and Dolce and Gabana jeans that hung just below the glorious V that sculpted his abs. He ran his hand through his messy black hair and stretched. She swallowed again as he made his way toward her, his contagious smile reminding her what she could potentially lose.

Sinking onto the bed, he gathered her in his arms and pulled her on top of his chest as he leaned against the headboard. "Michael was right. Though we leave in two days, staying in this house could turn me into a fat bastard." Chuckling, he popped a kiss on her forehead. "I was full from the ten pounds of chips and dip I inhaled before your sister said dinner was ready, so I decided to skip. Besides, once I knew you were in here alone, I couldn't resist."

Emily gave a weak smile as her eyes soaked in his dimple, drowning in every inch of slight stubble on his chin. They followed the contour along each line and plane of his beautiful face, a face that'd kidnapped her heart and held it hostage from the second she saw it. A face that might soon be nothing more than a memory that'd touched her life for the briefest moment.

"Hey," Gavin said, dipping his head, his eyes searching hers. "What's the matter?"

And there it was. The question that would lead them both down a path that could break them. Their pieces scattering along a road that held so much hope. So much love and promise.

Breathe…

"I have to tell you something," Emily whispered, her body as numb as it was when Gavin was gone.

A current of worry zipped through Gavin. He leaned up, straddling Emily's legs over his waist. Cupping her cheeks, he searched her eyes again. "Talk to me, doll. What's wrong?"

"I… I'm…" The words, wrong or right, caught in her throat as she tried to pull in a breath. Tried to get them to come out. This was it. She had to say them. *Breathe…* "Gavin, I'm pregnant."

Relief, pounding like a crashing wave, washed over him. The woman he'd loved from the minute she stepped into his life, who he was sure he would have a family with, just told him he was going to be a father. *Father.* The word ricocheted through Gavin's heart, the proud feeling behind that title reminding him of his own. This wasn't bad news. Surely Emily was scared, as was Gavin, but she had no reason to be. He would do everything in his power to make sure she and their child were loved beyond any measure he could ever show. With excitement unlike anything he'd ever known flowing through him, Gavin brought Emily's mouth to his. Kissing her hard, a cascade of moments to come filled his soul.

However, when she immediately pulled away, so did his excitement. The empty look in her eyes screamed out something that hadn't crossed his thoughts. The choking feeling in his throat nearly consumed him as he waited for her to say something. Anything. He just prayed it wasn't what he thought it was, because no matter how much he loved her—and

God, he loved her—he'd never allow Emily to get rid of something that was a piece of them.

"Gavin," Emily whispered, her heart exploding because, in the few seconds he'd kissed her, she felt a love so deep from him, she knew he didn't understand what they were about to face. "It might not be yours." She paused, her body trembling as she stared into eyes suddenly empty of emotion. Void of the spark she'd fallen in love with. She heard him swallow, heard his breathing pick up, and she shivered before she continued. "My last period was a few days before you and I were together the first time. I have an idea how far along I might be, but..."

"You're most likely carrying Dillon's child." The brokenness in Gavin's voice cut through the air. No longer able to hear what he was, he slipped from the bed and started pacing, his mind a complete clusterfuck of emotions he couldn't come close to dealing with in that moment. Anger at the situation thrust upon him and the woman who filled his life beyond words spread through his body. Reaching for his sweatshirt, he pulled it over his head and looked at Emily. His heart fell when he saw her confused eyes staring back. "I have to leave."

"What?" Emily breathed, standing. "Where are you going?"

Seeing the panic bleed from her eyes made him feel like an asshole, but he couldn't stay. Trying to soften the confusion he knew was all over his face, he walked over to her and placed his hand along the delicate curve of her jaw. Her lips trembled as she stared at him, the deep green pools of her eyes begging him not to go. Fuck. Pain ripped through his muscles as he fought to do exactly that. Stay. Talk with her. Figure out how they could make this work. God help him. Though he wanted to, he couldn't. He needed out, and he needed out now.

Without saying another word to her, Emily watched him turn and make his way out of the room. He took her scarred heart right along with him as he closed the door. The reality that he might not be able to handle the pressure of it all bulldozed through her mind, leaving her speechless and broken. A single tear slipped from her eye as she sucked in a shuddering breath. Once again alone with her thoughts, Emily tried to pull herself together as she flipped off the light next to the bed.

In the darkness, she sank onto the mattress, her gaze catching the shadows dancing across the ceiling. She slid her hand across her stomach, realizing the enormity of the torture to come. Day in and day out of not knowing whose child she was carrying would surely crack her. Emily found herself on a road she didn't think she would cross so soon in her life. Definitely not under these circumstances. However, she needed to believe there was a reason this was happening. Continuing to cry, she fought hard to find that reason, but she couldn't. It didn't appear. As seconds blurred into minutes and minutes disappeared into hours, the only thing she knew she had to find was the missing piece of her heart that'd walked out the room a broken man. Without another thought, she stood, plucked a light jacket from her suitcase, and rushed into the hall. Brushing her tears away, Emily rounded the corner, running right into her sister.

Lisa reached out and steadied Emily by her shoulders. "Jesus, are you okay? I was just coming to check on you. I figured I'd give you some time to yourself."

Breathing frantically, Emily shook her head and hurried into the kitchen. Lisa followed. Assuming Gavin had taken off in the car he'd bought her, Emily swiped Lisa's keys from a hook on the wall next to the refrigerator.

"Where are you going?" Lisa asked.

"I have to find him," Emily breathed, making her way toward the garage.

"He never left."

Lisa's words stopped Emily in her tracks. She whipped around. "What?"

"I mean, he didn't drive away. I think he took a walk down by the pier."

Emily's heart stilled for a moment as she replaced the keys on the hook. But that only lasted for a second because as she turned, her heart rate picked back up as she approached the French doors off the side of the den. Swimming in a sea of hurt, she swung them open and stepped out into the cool night air. Shivering from a breeze skirting off the ocean, Emily threw on her jacket and started up a hill, just beyond her sister's home, leading to weathered wooden stairs.

It didn't take her long to spot Gavin, and when she did, her breath caught. As Lisa thought, he was sitting on a bench down by the pier, the ambient glow from a dockside light shining above his body. He looked like an angel, but she knew he was in hell. Overlooking the ocean and the man she loved, tiny beads of sweat formed along her forehead. With the wind blowing through her hair, Emily brought her hands up to her mouth and sucked in a breath, trying to find the courage she needed to go to him. Somewhere between remembering what they had been together and what they were always meant to be, Emily found that courage. Up until now, Gavin might've only represented a small part of her past, but she needed him to fill every second, minute, and hour of her future, and she wasn't about to let him go for anything. She couldn't. She refused.

Gripping the rusty metal railing, she slowly started down the stairs, her pulse fluttering with each step she took. By the time she made it to the sand, Gavin stood from the bench, catching her gaze. In an instant, Emily froze, her breath faltering. As the waves kicked up, pounding against the pier, she watched Gavin make his way toward her. He shoved his hands in his pockets, his eyes locking on hers as he stopped a few feet away. Even with distance separating them, Emily could feel his heart burning through her, felt the undeniable connection they shared.

"I love you, Emily Cooper." He paused, looked at the ground, then back to her. "I think I loved you before I knew you existed." His voice was so soft, Emily could barely hear him. He stepped closer and brought his hand to her cheek, his touch gentle as his blue eyes caressed hers. "I'm pretty sure you were in my dreams before you walked into my life. I felt it the first time I saw you. You pulled at me. Took hold of my heart and never let go. Even if you had, I wouldn't have let you. I wouldn't have been able to. Something about you was… familiar, and it scared the shit out of me, but I knew somehow we needed one another. I've never been a man who believed in any type of fate. I considered it fluffy bullshit women read in romance novels, but sitting down here for the last couple of hours, I started thinking about you and me. Our romance. Our novel." Once again he paused, his head tilted as he wiped away a tear that'd trickled down her cheek. "Did you know I was supposed to go on that trip to Ohio with Trevor when you were in school?"

"I did," she whispered. Though her nerves started to calm, she wasn't sure if this was his goodbye. "Olivia told me."

"Right." Stepping closer, he wrapped his arm around her waist and brushed his lips against hers. "You were never supposed to be with Dillon. You were always supposed to wind up with me, but fate interrupted us for a while. This baby may not be mine, but it's a piece of something I need in my life. Something I'll cherish even after I'm long gone. I wasn't kidding when I said the good, the bad, and the in between. This is just our… in between right now." A small cry escaped Emily's lips, and God, Gavin's heart broke. Melted. "Standing here before you tonight, I give you my word as a man, as your friend, and as your lover, if this baby isn't mine, I'll love it *no less* than I do the angel carrying it. I can't tell you I'm not scared because that would be a lie, and I promised you I'd never lie to you. I'm scared to death, and I know you are too. So, Miss Cooper, if you'll forgive me for acting like an asshole by leaving you alone while I got my head on straight, the next few months, you and I are going to be absolutely scared to fucking death together. No matter what, we'll figure it out. Sound like a deal?"

Body warm and breath stolen, Emily nodded and pulled him down to her mouth. She'd stepped out of her sister's home swimming in a sea of hurt and confusion. But now, as she stood on this beautiful Christmas night kissing the man who would stay by her side through anything, she was drowning in a sea of relief so deep, words couldn't even begin to describe it.

CHAPTER ELEVEN

Change is Coming

The New Year had come and gone, bringing with it a mountain of emotions for Emily. As she sat in her doctor's office, holding Gavin's hand, Emily couldn't help but wonder what it was like for her mother when she'd found out she was pregnant with her. Given her father started showing signs of abuse somewhat late in their marriage, Emily's mother never hid the fact that Emily was an unplanned pregnancy. Her intentions were to leave Emily's father shortly before she found out she was having another baby with him. Nonetheless, she always told Emily she was the greatest surprise of her life. That simple statement rang loud in Emily's ears as the receptionist called her up to the window to fill out paperwork.

"Do you want me to go with you?" Gavin asked as she rose from her chair.

Emily shook her head, trying to ignore her full bladder that'd just screamed out in pain. "No, I'm good. It'll just take a second."

Gavin nodded.

After reaching for her purse, Emily made her way to the window. While waiting for the blonde, bobbed-hair girl to finish up a call she'd taken, Emily glanced around the small office at the other couples waiting to be seen. Emily wondered if any of them were in the same situation as her and Gavin. From their smiles, she highly doubted it. On a sigh, she rummaged through her purse, plucking out her insurance card and license.

"Sorry about that. It was my boyfriend," the receptionist squeaked, sliding a clipboard through the window. "If nothing's changed, you can just sign at the bottom, and Dr. Richards will be with you shortly."

"I have a new insurance carrier, and my home address has changed." Emily handed her the card and license. After snapping her gum, the girl rolled her eyes, flipped her hair, and turned to go make copies. Emily shook her head at the obvious lack of professionalism. When the girl finally returned, she slipped them back through the window, and Emily filled in the necessary sections on the form. Afterward, she sat next to Gavin, feeling as though she was about to burst.

"You don't look so hot," Gavin whispered, his lips turned down. "Do I need to make a scene in here if they don't let you pee within the next two minutes? You know I can deliver."

Trying not to giggle because she knew it'd be the end of her bladder, Emily laced her fingers through his. "Oh, I know you can." She leaned over and kissed his cheek. "But I'm okay. At least for another few minutes."

Gavin smiled and brushed his thumb along the top of her hand. "You're in dire need of my twenty questions game." Emily looked at him as though he'd sprouted a new head. "I'm serious. It'll help take your mind off this whole non-urination thing. I go first."

Emily frowned, nudging his arm. "You always get to go first."

"That's because I invented it, sweets." Grinning, Gavin stared into her eyes. "Silk or lace?"

Emily lifted a brow. "That's a question I should be asking you."

"Nope." Gavin leaned in closer, his lips grazing her ear. "My game. My rules. Now answer the question. Silk... or... lace?"

Emily pulled in a breath, his husky tone instantly making her forget her bladder issue. "I... like... silk."

Gavin smirked. "Nice answer. Can't beat Emily Cooper in silk." He leaned back, sliding his arm over her shoulder. "Stone or brick?"

"Hey." Emily nudged his arm again. "It's my turn. And how do you go from silk or lace to stone or brick?"

"My game. My rules, so I decided to change the rules and go again." He smiled at her pouting lips and leaned into her ear once more. He nipped it and held it between his teeth, loving the way he could feel her shudder. "Don't worry about how I go from one subject to the next. Just answer the question. Stone... or... brick?"

Emily puffed out a breath, convinced he'd spent years studying the art of driving women to the brink of losing control in public. Full bladder a distant memory, Emily brought her gaze to his, her ear desperately missing his teeth. "Stone," she said slowly. Now she'd play his game, knowing she could drive him as physically crazy as he did her. "I like anything...*hard*." Gavin's eyes honed in on her lips, so she puckered them, feeling high as she watched his pupils dilate with lust. Oh yes, she had him. "Not that brick isn't... *hard*, but if I'm not mistaken, and I could be, so forgive me if so, but isn't stone... *harder... much... harder* than brick?"

Gavin flicked his gaze from her lips to her eyes, a smirk spreading across his face. "I know what you're doing."

"Oh, do you?" Deadpanned, Emily stared at her nails, trying for disinterest. "Am I doing it well?"

"Very," Gavin whispered, leaning closer. "And if you keep doing it this well, we're about to leave so I can show you how well *I* can do it. But

I won't hold any punches, Miss Cooper. I'll be relentless, only stopping once you beg me to."

Emily smiled and puckered her lips again. "Do you like when I beg?"

"Is that your question for the game?" Gavin's gaze drifted from her saucy eyes to her lips. Damn her. She was getting good at this shit. "You only get one. Choose wisely."

"Yes, that's my question for the game." Emily sighed and crossed her legs. "Now answer the question, Mr. Blake. Do. You. Like. When. I. Beg?"

With the answer on the tip of his tongue, which he wished was gliding along Emily's body, the receptionist opened the door and called Emily's name.

Emily giggled as she watched Gavin stand and adjust his pants. Unable to help it, she giggled all the way into the back office.

After turning on a sonogram machine, flipping off the lights, and draping an exam sheet over a less-than-comfortable-looking table, Unprofessional Hair-flipper turned to Emily. "I need you to unzip your jeans, pull them down just below your pubic bone, and lay down for me."

Taking a seat next to the table, Gavin lifted a brow, a slow smirk curling his lips as he watched Emily do as she was told. "This might turn out to be a little more entertaining than I anticipated. My *stone* is very *hard* right now."

Emily's eyes landed on the girl, who was blushing a deep shade of crimson, as she hopped onto the table. Shimmying in an effort to get comfortable, Emily looked at Gavin and belted out a laugh. "Leave it to you to continue getting sexual in a doctor's office after you *lost* at your own game."

Gavin shrugged. "The game will resume once we leave, and I never claimed to have limits when it comes to women who love stone over brick."

Wide-eyed and staring at Gavin, the unnamed blonde cleared her throat. "Dr. Richards will be right in." She hurried out of the darkened office.

Smiling, Emily shook her head. "You scared her off."

Gavin leaned forward, propping his elbows on his knees. "I turned her on."

"Oh my God. Could you be a little more conceited?"

Another casual shrug. "I call it self-assured."

Emily rolled her yes. "You also said you weren't a stalker, and now look at us."

"You've rendered me speechless, and that doesn't happen all too often." Gavin chuckled. "I couldn't conjure a comeback if I wanted."

Emily grinned, and a moment later, the doctor breezed through the door, his tall, lengthy build towering over Emily as he approached. Clipboard in hand, he slid his glasses up the bridge of his nose and looked at Emily, the wrinkles under his eyes pulling together as he smiled "Good to see you again, Miss Cooper."

"Hello, Dr. Richards."

"I see you took two pregnancy tests that came out positive, but you're not quite sure as to when your last period was." Emily nodded. He placed the clipboard on a counter, washed his hands, and slid on a pair of gloves. Reaching for a small white bottle, he gave it a good shake. "A little cold," he warned, squirting a blob of aqua gel onto Emily's stomach. She jumped and shivered when it hit her. The doctor looked at Gavin as he started pressing what looked like a microphone against the gel. "Father?"

With a weak smile, Gavin flicked his eyes to Emily. His heart sank a bit as he watched her shift uncomfortably. Reaching for her hand, he threaded his fingers through hers and pulled his chair closer.

"He might be the father. We wanted to speak to you about that," Emily started, glancing at Gavin. She shifted again, not only from the awkwardness of the situation but from the amount of pressure the doctor was putting on her lower stomach. "I'm... not really sure who the father is. I did some quick research online regarding amniocentesis, but I read there's some risk."

Whoosh...

The doctor cleared his throat. "I see. Yes, there's some risk to the amniocentesis, however, if done properly..."

Whoosh...Whoosh...

"The benefits can outweigh the risks in some cases..."

Whoosh... Whoosh... Whoosh...

"Especially in a situation like the one you've found yourselves in."

Whoosh...Whoosh...Whoosh...Whoosh....

"What's that sound?" Gavin asked, his eyes darting between the doctor and the black and white glowing monitor.

"That's the heartbeat of your... of the baby." The doctor twirled a few knobs on the machine. Pointing to the screen, he brought his eyes to Gavin's. "And that little dot right there is the baby."

Gavin swallowed, his heart pummeling his ribcage as fast as the one that could potentially be his child. *My child...* He felt Emily squeeze his hand as he started to feel sweat forming above his brows. Staring at the screen, he nearly lost his breath. He watched the tiny, unborn life twitch and jerk inside its little cocoon. Hell, it was so fucking small, he swore if Emily sneezed, she would hurt it. God, not that the last couple of weeks since they'd returned from California wasn't spent praying this child was his, but here and now, he needed to believe it was. Flashes of teaching a little blue-eyed boy how to play baseball in the backyard of a home he'd have built dowsed his thoughts. Visions of a little girl in a pink tutu, singing and dancing for him and Emily, stoked his need even further.

Gavin pulled his chair closer, released Emily's hand, and brushed his fingers through her hair. Gazing into her eyes, he swallowed again. "Can you... feel it moving inside of you?"

Emily shook her head, her voice a whisper. "No."

"She's too early to feel any movement. That happens somewhere around the fifteen week mark." After some more prodding, button twirling, and *whooshes*, the doctor shut off the machine. He sauntered over to the wall, flipping on the light. He plucked a cardboard wheel from the counter and looked at it a moment. "Based on the size of the baby, you're approximately ten weeks along. Conception took place within the last week of October. My estimated due date is July twenty-first. My office isn't equipped with the latest technology, so I'll have the receptionist schedule a transvaginal ultrasound for you. I may be close to retirement and a little outdated, but I'm pretty sure I'm correct. Been doing this long before you two were a twinkle in your parents' eyes. " He handed Emily a paper towel, gesturing to her stomach. "Use that to wipe off the gel and feel free to use the restroom. When you're finished, you can meet me in my office. Second door on your left when you exit the room. We'll go over the pros and cons of the amnio."

As the doctor walked out, Emily wiped the gel from her stomach. The only words she could remotely concentrate on were when conception had taken place. The last week of October. She'd only been with Gavin a handful of times during that week, but it still put him in the running. Even if by a few days, that's all that mattered to Emily. Sighing, she slipped from the table and quickly used the restroom. After relieving herself, she walked out and caught Gavin's eyes. She could tell he was stuck deep in his own thoughts, and hell if it didn't cut through her heart.

"Are you okay?" she whispered, walking over to him as she buttoned jeans that were starting to become a little snug.

Standing, he snaked his arms around her waist. "I am. Are you?"

She nodded, snuggling against his chest. However, she wasn't okay. She was far from it. The pain Gavin was going through was killing her. Pulling in his smell and drowning in the sound of his heart, she fought back tears.

Gavin kissed the top of her head. "I didn't know you looked up that amnio… or whatever it's called."

"Yeah. I did the other day while I was at work."

"You mentioned risks." He reached for her purse and handed it to her. "What kind of risks are there, and how do they perform the test?"

Sliding the strap over her shoulder, she paused a moment, remembering what the procedure entailed. An involuntary shiver worked through her. "They would stick a needle through my stomach and…"

With shock crossing his face, he cut her off. "A needle? In your stomach?"

"Yes."

Gavin blew out a puff of air. "Emily, I'd rather a needle *not* go near your stomach."

"Umm, Gavin, *I'd* rather a needle not go through my stomach either. I mean, it can cause an infection."

Gavin's eyes went wide. "What type of infection?"

Emily smiled at his confusion and worry. "Amniotic. It's the sack of liquid the baby's in. It can become… infected."

"Then what happens?" he asked, swiping his hand through his hair, his tone showing his worry was mounting.

Emily pulled in a slow breath. "It can lead to a miscarriage."

Gavin swallowed, his words slow. "Are you serious?" Emily nodded. "No way. You're not getting it done." Intertwining their fingers, he started for the door. "Jesus, Emily, why would you even think about putting the baby or yourself through that?"

They rounded the corner, heading in the opposite direction of the doctor's office. Emily came to a stop. "I looked it up because I can see you're suffering. That's the only test I found that could prove who the father is now." Looking away, her voice trailed. "It's enough you took me back. Now you have to deal with this?"

Gavin cupped her face, bringing her gaze back to his. "It's enough I took you back?" Emily nodded, her eyes glassing over. With his thumbs, he gently swiped away her tears. "Despite all the pain and hurt I went through losing you for just that little amount of time, Emily, I wouldn't change a thing. Not a thing. I'd take you back a million times over. Pain and all." He brushed his lips over hers, his voice soft. "*We're* dealing with this. Not just me. *Us.* I'd rather not know than have you put yourself or the baby in any kind of danger. I'd never be able to live with myself if anything happened to either of you because you think I need to know."

Leaning into his intoxicating warmth, Emily rested her head against his chest. "Are you sure?"

He slid his hands through her hair, pulling her closer. "As sure as I know we're growing old together. I can see it now. Two rocking chairs on a porch, watching our grandchildren make a fucking mess of our yard. It's all good. We'll sugar them up and send them home with their parents in retaliation." Emily giggled. "Though you might have to feed me applesauce because these pearly whites will be gone. You're stuck with me."

Emily looked at him. "Applesauce, huh?"

Gavin shrugged, a grin pulling at his mouth. "Eh. I like pudding, too."

Pushing up on her tiptoes, Emily popped a kiss on his nose. "Deal. Applesauce, pudding, and grandchildren running loose on sugar highs in retaliation." Gavin smiled, and Emily reached for his hand. "Okay. But I still need to schedule the transvaginal ultrasound before we leave."

Gavin cleared his throat as they approached the window where Blondie was chatting away on the phone. "Right. About this transvaginal thing. I don't like the sound of it."

Emily rolled her eyes. "What now?"

"Well, I'm not a doctor, so I'm just assuming here, but I'm thinking some dirty old man's going to have center view of your—"

Emily quickly covered his mouth, her eyes wide as saucers. "Gavin!" She could feel his lips lift in a smile, his blue eyes shimmering with humor. "You, sir, need to get used to this."

"I'll do no such thing," he said, the words muffled under her hand. Turning, effectively releasing his mouth from Emily's hostage grip, he rang the bell, jolting Blondie from her conversation. Eyes wide, she hung up the phone. "We need to schedule a transvaginal amnio for my girlfriend, but we'd like it performed by a woman." Emily belted out a laugh. Gavin looked at Emily, his smile wide. "What?"

She shook her head. "It's not called a transvaginal amnio, psycho Caveman." His smile faltered, and if Emily wasn't mistaken, he appeared slightly embarrassed. Nonetheless, he looked adorably sexy.

"It's called a transvaginal ultrasound," said Blondie, looking equally embarrassed by the conversation. "Dr. Richards sent the paperwork up. Will two-thirty next Tuesday over at the Freeman building work for you?"

"Will a woman perform this test?" Gavin questioned, no longer looking embarrassed or confused. Now he just looked all-out concerned, and Emily couldn't help but laugh again.

"I can put in a request, but I can't *guarantee* it'll be a woman who does it."

"That's fine." Emily reached for Gavin, quickly leading him toward the exit. "Two-thirty, next Tuesday, the Freeman building. I'll be there. Thank you."

"A woman," Gavin called out as Emily tugged him into the hall. "We want a woman."

Emily stepped out into the frigid night air, the mid-January wind needling her face as she waited for Gavin to pull around to the front of his building. With her glove-covered hands tucked deep into the pockets of her pea coat, she shook as she watched motorists fly by. Glancing to her left, she caught Gavin's Ferrari rounding the corner of the underground garage. She puffed out a smoky sigh of relief and made her way to the curb. Reaching for the handle as he stopped, she swung open the door and climbed in, her body nearly frozen from the few seconds outside.

Gavin frowned, a perplexed look on his face. "I was getting out to let you in."

She pressed the control panels on the dash, blasting the heat. "You're too ki… kind," she stuttered as she pulled the seatbelt across her waist. "But I wasn't waiting. It's cold as hell out there."

"Hell's not cold, sweets." He stroked his knuckles against her neck as he eased into traffic. "But you are. Why didn't you wait in the lobby?"

"I think I'm a glutton for punishment." She pulled out her cell from her purse and hit the button for Olivia. After a few rings with no answer, she sent a text instead. "It's either that or... yeah. I'm a glutton for punishment."

Gavin stopped at a light. Sliding his arm over the back of her seat, he lifted a brow. "You did pass on a romantic evening of watching reruns of the *Honeymooners* with your man. Maybe you do deserve a little punishment."

Bringing her eyes to his, she slid her phone closed. "You're just saying that because we're meeting everyone at Pacha."

"Right. A crazy club. Somewhere you don't belong considering you're pregnant."

Emily sighed, amused at his remark. She knew where it came from. She'd won the dispute while getting ready, but he wasn't hot on the idea. "Gavin Blake?"

"Miss Emily Cooper."

"Stop being an ass."

Gavin chuckled. "An ass?" Traffic light green, he brought his arm down to pop the car into gear.

"Yes. An ass. We went over this. It's a club, not a mosh pit. We haven't been out with everyone in a while, and in a few months, I won't be able to." She kissed his cheek, placing her hand over his as he glided through the gears. "So, I suggest you zip it, Caveman, and show off your hot girlfriend before it's too late."

Grinning, he shook his head. "That's twice today."

"Twice what?" Emily questioned, pulling down the visor. "That I've called you Caveman?"

"Yes. But it's also twice today you've rendered me speechless." Gavin tried to keep his eyes on the road, but it was close to impossible.

Emily's vanilla-scented perfume drifting through the car was making him high. Shifting in his seat, he glanced in her direction, taking in her sweet, puckered lips. "I'm starting to like it more than I should." She smiled as she checked her makeup in the mirror. "Either way, this caveman's keeping his hot girlfriend tucked close while we're there." He pulled his eyes from her beautiful smile back to the road. "I'll deal with your punishment later, *Cavewoman*."

By the time they found parking, Gavin had explained, in great detail, the many ways he planned on punishing her when they returned home. Needless to say, Emily was starting to regret ever going out. His pleasurable torture tickled her senses as they slipped from the car, heightening her regret. After a short but very cold walk around the block to the club, they cleared the VIP line. Gavin pressed his hand against the small of her back, guiding Emily upstairs to the Mezzanine level where Olivia was gyrating against Mr. Fluffy Pink Towel's pelvis. Music pounding through her ears, Emily could still hear Olivia's squeal from a few feet away. She all but sprinted toward Emily and Gavin.

"My friend!" After a near fatal collision with a metal pole and a few tables, Olivia pulled Emily into her arms. "You won the battle with the man! I'm so happy you didn't let him defeat you, *and* I'm wasted. Yay me! This is going to be a night!"

Emily giggled, slipping her coat from her body. "Yes. I did win the battle." She smiled at Gavin. He grinned, taking her coat. "And, yes, you're looking mighty toasted."

"I plan on constant, warm fuzziness tonight." Olivia smiled and reached for Emily's hand, dragging her to the balcony overlooking the dance floor. "See, Emily!" she yelled, her arms flared open wide. "The world is my people!"

"Holy shit, Olivia!" Emily belted out, shocked because Olivia was hanging over said balcony. Emily curled her arms around her waist to keep her from plummeting to her death. She guided her back to Jude and Gavin.

Olivia frowned, but Emily's worry didn't stop her from plucking a fiery red shot in a tube from a waitress walking by as Jude pulled out his wallet to pay for the drink. She slammed it back, handed the waitress the glass, and smothered a wet kiss on Jude's cheek. "You remember my human canvas, right?"

Emily smiled. "How can I forget?"

"Cool seeing you again," Jude yelled over the music. "At least I'm dressed this time."

Emily smiled, having no clue how to respond to that one.

Yeah. That statement piqued Gavin's curiosity. Just a little. After placing his and Emily's coats on a suede couch, he walked back over to the group, his eyes pinned on Jude. "I'm Gavin, and *I'm* happy to see you're dressed. You are?"

"What's up, bro?" Jude said with a toasty smile. He held out his hand and Gavin shook it. "I'm Jude, or you can call me the human canvas. Either one. It's cool."

Gavin nodded and leaned into Emily's ear. "Okay, he just mentioned being dressed this time around and now he's calling himself a human canvas." He curled his arm around her waist. "I'm left with the assumption that you've somehow seen him naked, and possibly paint brushes were involved. I would've let you paint on me if that's what you needed."

Sliding her arms around his neck, Emily popped a brow, a smirk lifting her mouth. "Would you let me paint a pretty rainbow on your stomach?"

"Mmm. I'd let you paint whatever the fuck you want on me wherever the fuck you want to paint it." He nipped her lip and pulled her closer. "Remember, I hold not one sexual limit with you. But I draw the line at you painting on any male bodies other than mine."

Emily hooted a laugh, grazing her mouth along his ear. "I've never painted on a man's body, but I plan on doing so when we get home. Oh, and I've only seen him partially naked. He has a nice build, but it's not nearly as rock hard and hot as yours, so don't worry about it. Again, it was just a partial view."

"You had me going until that last bit, but I'll let it slide." Staring at her, he rolled his tongue over his bottom lip. "Are paint stores open this late?"

"Hey!" Olivia chirped, yanking Gavin away from Emily. Stumbling into him, she swiped a hand through her blonde hair and smiled. "One: I never got my hug from you, Blake. Two: She's already knocked up. I'm pretty sure you can't double-impregnate her. Back up, my brother. You two were looking a little heated there for a second."

After enduring Olivia's swaying bear hug, Gavin shook his head. "I'm surrounded by women who've left me speechless today."

Wearing a full-toothed, Cheshire cat smile, Olivia swung her arm around Emily's neck. Her brown eyes zoned in on Gavin. "Get used to it, buddy. We're here to stay." She belted out a burp, looking at her watch. "Damn, my brother and Fallon. Hopefully he's not off somewhere knocking *her* up. He said they'd be here by midnight, and it's already a quarter after."

Emily crinkled her nose, stepping back. "Jesus, Olivia."

"What?" Trying to steady herself by grabbing Jude's arm, which was no help because he stumbled back, she frowned. "I overdid the whole 'knocking up' thing, didn't I? Me sorry. But you are. Oh my God, Emily!

You're having a baby! We get to go shopping for little kids' clothing. Well, not little kids 'cause it won't be a kid when it comes out, 'cause it'll be so tiny. Tiny like a pencil eraser." Olivia lifted her hand, tapping her forehead. "We need a mane. I mean a name. A mane. A mane. Oh! I got it! Olivia! Boy or girl, mane it Olivia in my honor."

Completely dumbfounded at Olivia's drunken display, Emily had the sudden urge to yank a shot from the waitress making another round. "Olivia, I wasn't talking about the baby. I was talking about the burp you released in my face."

Olivia touched her mouth. "I burped?"

No sooner had Olivia dropped the burp question than, hand in hand, Fallon and Trevor approached the group. Squealing in delight, Olivia clamored them both with an overly drunk, overly tight hug. After answering several questions about possibly knocking up Fallon, Trevor sent Olivia and Jude out to the dance floor, telling them to go burn off some alcohol.

Against a gnawing feeling in his gut telling him not to, Gavin allowed Emily to join the group. Fallon was with her and didn't plan on drinking because of an early morning communion, so he felt slightly better. Nonetheless, it didn't sit well with him. With his hands clasped, Gavin leaned his forearms on the railing of the second level. He watched with a hawk's eye as Emily made her way out onto the crowed club floor.

"I heard what happened between you and Dillon." Trevor—also intently watching the girls—spoke up, and Gavin could hear the weariness in his tone. "A couple of guys from the office called and told me about it."

Eyes locked on Emily, Gavin didn't bother turning to look at him. "You fucking hid what he did to her from me."

"I didn't hide anything," he retorted, adjusting his glasses. "I talked with Emily, and she promised she would say something to you if you guys got back together." He clapped his hand over Gavin's shoulder. "I assumed you already knew."

Jerking away, Gavin shrugged off his hand. He dragged his eyes from Emily and pinned Trevor with a look he was sure told him he was about to get knocked over the railing. "You fucking assumed I knew? What the fuck is wrong with you? You came over the day after she moved in with me. That was the first time I saw or spoke to you after we got back from Mexico. You don't think I would've said something if I knew?"

"Come on, man, what did you expect me to do? She promised. I assumed. It was a mistake. That's all."

The more Trevor talked, the more tossing him over the railing became that much more appealing to Gavin. "Yeah. A fucking mistake. What did I expect you to do? You should've flown to Playa del Carmen the fucking day it happened. That's what I expected from a friend I've known half my life. Someone I consider a brother." Gavin glared at him another second, then focused his attention back on Emily. Watching the woman he'd saved from a lifetime filled with nothing more than pain and hurt, he grit his teeth, trying to calm himself down. "I love her more than anything. I would've come back that day had I known. You should've done something. End of fucking story."

Over the ear-blowing music zipping and pounding through the air, Gavin heard the resignation in Trevor's sigh. Either way, Gavin wasn't sure the friendship could be salvaged. Hell, he wasn't sure it was worth trying to save at this point. Other than feeling as though he could kill him right there, Gavin felt burned.

Before he could dwell over the torn friendship, Gavin watched Emily and the girls exit the dance floor. Making their way up the stairs, human canvas in tow behind them, they stepped into the lounge area. Gavin flicked his attention one last time in Trevor's direction, paying no mind to the impassive look on his face he could tell was for show. Gavin saw thoughts moving behind his eyes, and he didn't give a shit. Emily wrapped her arms around his waist, pulling Gavin from the standoff he was having with his former best friend.

Gavin turned, brushing his fingers through Emily's dampened hair. She smiled, and he was nearly done for. God, between the raging male hormones running rampant through his system and sweat glistening off her body, he could've eaten her alive right there. Hungry in more ways than one, Gavin pulled her into his mouth. Wanting to drown in everything that made her, he kissed her hard, his body seeking release. He could feel the vibration of her moan dance over his tongue, and fuck if it didn't drive him mad. "Have a good time?"

"I did," Emily breathed, her body tingling. Her skin. Her pulse. Every damn hair on her flesh stood on end. A sizzling, demanding ache started to build between her legs as her eyes stroked from his face to the luscious bump of his Adam's apple hidden between the collar of his white button-up shirt. Sighing, she ran her hands across his gray, tailored V-neck sweater, her fingers burning to feel his bare chest. She swallowed. "I have to make a quick run to the restroom. I'll be right back." Still holding her, she watched Gavin lift a single brow, his blue eyes slowly fucking her right there. She swallowed again.

He jerked his chin toward the exit. "I'd like to get out of here when you're done."

The intimate edge in his tone said all she needed to know. It surrounded her, pulling her under like a rolling wave. Legs weak and body limp, Emily nodded. "You don't have to ask twice, Mr. Blake."

"Good girl." The triumph in his voice pulled her under further, sweetening the surrender to his request. "I'll see you back here in a few, Miss Cooper."

Emily turned on her heels and started for the restroom, only to be stopped a few feet away by Olivia. Swaying more than before, she smiled, and Emily couldn't help but giggle. Grabbing Olivia's hand, Emily dragged her toward the restroom only to be stopped by Fallon. Sandwiched, Emily linked arms with them and finally made it to the bathroom. After a twenty-minute wait on a long line snaking through a decent amount of the second level, the girls got in and did their business.

"Country," Fallon chimed, pulling mascara from her clutch. Looking in the mirror, she swiped it through her lashes. "Did Gavin tell you about the argument he and Trevor just had about you?"

Emily lifted her eyes from digging through her purse for lipstick. Brows furrowed, she tilted her head, confused. "No. What happened?"

"Gavin's pissed because he never told him what Dillon did to you."

Emily sighed. "I told him that was my fault for not saying anything. I'll talk to him again."

"I hope so." Fallon tossed the mascara back into her clutch. She fluffed her hair, its fiery crimson vibrant under the overhead lights. "He shouldn't catch shit for something *you* should've told Gavin to begin with. You need to make this right."

Emily jerked her head back. "I know he shouldn't, Fallon. I just told you I explained to Gavin it was my fault. I also told him Trevor made me promise to tell him if we got back together and I didn't. What do you want me to say? I'm going to talk to him about it again, okay?"

Fallon blew out a noisy breath and nodded. "All right. I'm sorry. I came off snotty, but I love Trevor, and he's pretty upset right now."

"Trevor's always upset about something," Olivia blurted, swinging open the stall. Untangling a necklace that appeared to be growing from her hair, she rolled her eyes and yanked it out. Her expression twisted in pain for a moment before she smiled. "Thank God. That thing was fucking killing me. Don't ask how it got in my hair, either. I think it happened when I bent over to wipe myself. Oh, and I'm pretty sure I peed on my heels."

With her arms crossed, Fallon leaned against the sink. "Trevor's not always upset, Liv."

"Pfft. To hell he's not," Olivia scoffed and started washing her hands. "He's a bitch on wheels. Even my father says I was supposed to be the boy in the family. If he didn't have a dick, I'd call him a pussy."

Emily covered her face, trying to stifle a laugh.

A slow smile curled Fallon's lips. "Well, I can guarantee you he has a dick and he knows how to use it."

Olivia dried her hands with a paper towel. Once finished, she balled it up and chucked it at Fallon's forehead, hitting her target dead on. Olivia snorted. "And I can guarantee you if he doesn't bag all two inches of it, you'll wind up with a little bun in the oven just like our friend here, except yours won't be as cute and it'll bitch just like his father. Wa-wa."

Sighing, Emily rolled her eyes. "Enough with the pregnancy jokes, Liv."

Olivia shrugged. "Well, it's the truth. Your kid would definitely be cuter." Pausing, Olivia pressed her lips in a hard line, her eyes squinting. "Wait. I take that back. If it's Douchelord's spawn, you're in trouble. That'd be one ugly baby."

While Fallon's mouth dropped open, Emily's parted in a gasp. "Olivia! How could you say that?"

"Emily, I speak the truth. Especially while I'm drunk. You're golden if it's Gavin's, but if Dumbledick's the baby daddy, I would look into giving it up for adoption. This whole ordeal's already a clash of Maury Povich meets Jerry Springer for an all-out battle of 'who's got the most drama going on.' Seriously, I love you. But honestly, I shudder thinking about what it'll look like."

Emily yanked her purse from the counter and zipped past Olivia.

Olivia grabbed her arm. "Wait! Emily, I'm sorry. In Deputy Dillhole's defense, and you know I never defend him, I still think it's wrong you and Gavin aren't telling him about the pregnancy until you find out whose baby it is. It's no secret I'm not his fan, but he could be the father. In the long run, if you don't tell him and he is, it can look bad for you."

Emily pulled in a slow, deep breath, attempting to calm her nerves. "You know what, Olivia? You're drunk. In the last thirty seconds, you've called my child a spawn, told me it's going to be ugly, and suggested adoption. You're also giving your *unwanted* opinion as to how Gavin   and I should handle telling or not telling Dillon. If you weren't so trashed, you'd remember Gavin's reasons for not wanting to tell him. You'd also remember my reasons for agreeing with him. Now if you'll excuse me, *friend*, I'm leaving. You can go ahead and call me tomorrow after   you've woken up with your nasty hangover."

Emily exited the restroom feeling hurt, confused, and also burned on what was supposed to be an exciting night out with close friends. Change, in many wicked shapes and forms, was becoming the norm. Emily only hoped it wouldn't tear her or Gavin away from people they cared for.

People she hoped still cared for them.

CHAPTER TWELVE

Stolen Breaths

With the *New York Times* in one hand and a bottle of water in the other, Gavin's thoughts were abruptly interrupted when the doorbell chimed through the air. He placed the water on the end table, stood from the couch, and glanced at his watch. He wasn't expecting anyone, and he was pretty sure Emily wasn't either. When he opened the door to see Trevor standing in the hall, he was shocked.

"Hey, bro." Trevor rushed a hand through his hair. "Can you talk for a few?"

Gavin gave a halfhearted shrug, turning toward the kitchen. He heard Trevor close the door and took a seat at the island.

Rubbing the back of his neck, Trevor rounded the island and cleared his throat. "Is this a bad time? You look like you're about to leave."

"Emily and I are driving up to my parents' house for dinner." He answered with stiff coldness he wasn't about to hide.

"Oh." Trevor paused and looked around. Puffing out a heavy breath, he brought his eyes back to Gavin, his unease tangible. "Let them know I said hello."

Gavin crossed his arms and nodded, wondering when Trevor would get to the point.

Staring at Gavin, he shook his head. "I'm sorry, man. You're right. I should've come to get you. I fucked up a lot during all of this. That was just the last thing on a long list of things I should've done differently." The cavernous, low timbre of his voice sounded scratchy, exhausted, and resigned. "I should've been by your side from the beginning, from the moment you told me you needed Emily right down to the second I watched the fucking asshole take a swing at you. I don't know what else to say except if you don't talk to me again, I understand why."

Watching his friend sweat through an attempted amends, Gavin thought about the conversation he and Emily had before going to sleep last night. She'd verbally thrown him into a corner, bringing up his words from California. She reminded him he said she needed to forgive her mother for her wrong doings, and in their case, Trevor should be treated the same. "Forgive fast and forget even faster" were her exact words. Though he felt Trevor had made an already shitty situation worse and Gavin was still struggling with a sense of betrayal, he knew harboring ill feelings toward him wouldn't be good for anyone. His friend was waving a white flag, and Gavin needed to consider this. Emily's threats of beating his ass down gave him a little push as well. Trying to keep any lingering resentment from his eyes, Gavin stared at Trevor for a beat before reaching out his hand in a gesture of acceptance.

Trevor heaved in a deep, shaky breath and released it as he gripped Gavin's hand in a firm shake. "Thanks, bro." He gulped back a swallow. "I appreciate you not giving up on our friendship. It means a lot."

Resting his arm on the back of a stool next to him, Gavin rolled his eyes, a crooked smile on his lips. "Enough with the sentimental shit. Any more, and I might have to buy you a girdle."

Trevor shook his head and chuckled. After a moment, his grin faded, his features serious. "So, how are you doing with all of this? Seems like heavy shit for you both."

"Yeah. It's not something I expected, nor did Emily, but we'll get through it." Gavin eased out of his seat and swiped a bottle of scotch from the bar. He held it up, gesturing to Trevor, who nodded. After dropping some ice into glasses and pouring them both a shot, Gavin set Trevor's in front of him. "I love her, and that's all that matters."

Trevor nodded. "What do your parents think?"

"Only my father knows," Gavin answered, tossing back his drink. Swirling the empty glass, he stared at Trevor a second. Gavin zoned in on not only the sound of the ice clinking against the glass, but also his mother's reaction when they would tell her this evening. "That's the point of dinner."

Trevor's eyes barely widened, but Gavin could see the shock he was failing to hide. "What do you think she's going to say?" Trevor asked.

Gavin shrugged. Not that he didn't care what his mother thought, God knew he did, she meant the world to him. But his main focus was Emily and freeing her from any worry over the next several months. The situation was tough enough on her. The last thing he wanted was for her to suffer any physical effects of stress. He prayed his mother wouldn't add to that by rejecting Emily. "I'm not sure what she'll say. We'll see, right?"

"Gavin, have you seen my black heels?" Emily's voice echoed from the hall. Rounding the corner, her eyes were downcast as she secured a bracelet around her wrist.

Seeing his girlfriend had no fucking idea they had a visitor, Gavin cleared his throat. He made sure it was loud enough to catch her attention.

Emily snapped her head up and gasped, gripping the towel barely covering her just-showered body. "Shit! I didn't know he was here." Both Gavin and Trevor chuckled. Doing an about-face, she darted down the hall, her bare feet slapping against the marble. "Hi, Trevor. Bye, Trevor!" she called out.

Trevor downed the last of his drink and smiled. "Hi, Emily. Bye, Emily." After placing his glass in the sink, he walked over to Gavin. The two friends shook hands. "You're a good man, bro. She's always deserved someone like you. I hope this works out for you both. We'll have a ton to celebrate, if so."

Gavin nodded, swallowing back the evil instinct telling him the opposite would more likely be the scenario. After seeing Trevor out, he went to go check on the girl he hoped was carrying *his* child. He tapped on the bedroom door with his knuckles before tentatively sticking his head in. As he entered the room, he detected Emily's jasmine perfume drifting through the air. It engulfed him, wrapping around his every male instinct.

But hell if he wasn't at odds with a battle he never saw coming. When they'd returned home last night from the club, he began ravishing Emily, only to come to a screeching halt once he was inside her. Hovering above her, her panting driving him harder, it'd hit him like a ton of bricks that he could hurt her or the baby. The thought staggered him. In the middle of making love to the woman who owned his heart, he stopped. Cringing, he lied and said he didn't feel well all of a sudden. He'd felt like a bigger jerk-off when she tried to soothe him to sleep with a comforting massage.

Sitting on the bed slipping on the missing black heels, Emily raised her eyes to his. She smiled, and as always, Gavin wanted to drown in it. Biting his bottom lip, he drank in what was his.

"Hi, you," she purred. Standing, she moved toward him, her creamy, smooth flesh vibrant under her black, scoop-neck, silk blouse. He inhaled her hips swinging with feminine poise under a knee-length, gray twill skirt. With a seductive gleam flashing in her eyes, she slithered her arms around his neck. "You look edible."

"Not as edible as you do," Gavin countered, trying to mentally talk down his growing wood tenting his slacks.

"Well," she whispered coyly, touching her lips to his ear, "we can enjoy dessert a little early and finish up what we didn't get to complete last night. If I'm not mistaken, there's whipped cream in the refrigerator. My makeup's done. I'll just pin my hair up and shower again if you're unable to… *lick* it all off my body."

Let the full-on battle begin. Gavin cleared his throat, backing away. He tossed a nervous hand through his hair and pulled open the closet door. "We have to leave soon," he said in a strained rasp, the lie bitter on his tongue.

Taken slightly aback, considering he was just looking at her as though he was about to pin her to the bed, Emily sighed. Glancing at her watch, her lips turned down in a pout. "We have almost two and a half hours until we have to be there, Gavin. That's more than enough time. We can skip the whipped cream and get right to it. I need to burn off some of this nervous, edgy energy about tonight."

Fuck. He'd already played the "let's see if we can cover every inch of Emily's body with whipped cream" game with her. That alone was enough to give him blue balls just thinking about it. But an edgy, nervous Emily on top of him working off her stress put being in a strip club surrounded by twenty beautiful, naked women to shame.

Think, motherfucker, think. "My mother called and said dinner's earlier. We need to leave… now. Get your coat, and I'll meet you at the door."

After yanking a pair of Zelli Mario dress shoes from a rack, Gavin shamefully sat on the bed as Emily's pout deepened. After rolling her beautiful green eyes and crossing her arms over her luscious breasts, she turned on her heels and walked out of the room. Gavin's chest ached with hollow longing, his heart growing heavier with each passing second. He shoved his feet into his shoes and stood, padding over to the mirror. Adjusting his tie, he stared at his reflection, sick to his stomach.

"You're an asshole," he mumbled under his breath. Sighing, he dug the keys from his pocket, hoping the car ride wouldn't be as awkward as the evening itself.

An hour, and a not-so-awkward drive later, Gavin pulled into the driveway of his childhood oasis. Located just outside the city, the grand, Tudor-style home sat on the shores of Sheldrake Lake in the plush hills of Croton, New York. It was one of the few places Gavin always found reprieve. However, as the rich, crimson glow of the sky started to fade into darkness, Gavin wasn't sure this evening would bring much peace. As Emily slipped from the car and reached for his hand, Gavin could tell her mood had shifted. His heart sank like a rock as he swallowed her up in his arms, cradling her protectively against his chest. Her body trembled with that all-too-recognizable fear Gavin had unfortunately come to know.

"I swear to you everything's going to be all right, baby," he whispered, pressing his lips against the top of her head. The promise came out as easy and instinctive as the love he had for her.

"I hope so," she answered meekly, tears in her eyes when she looked at him. "It'll kill me if your relationship with your mother becomes messed up by this."

"I don't want you worrying," he said, tracing figure eights on the small of her back. "Everything's going to be fine with my mother. My father knows how to work her. Thirty plus years of marriage does that."

Emily gave a weak nod, wanting to believe him. She pulled in a slow breath and tangled her fingers in his as they began to climb the cobblestone steps up to the front door.

Gavin stopped, able to tell she was still a mess. "Twenty questions."

"Now?" Emily asked, confusion jumping over her expression.

"Yes now. You need it." Gavin circled his arms around her waist, pulling her into him. "I'll make sure you're not thinking about anything that has to do with my mother by the time I'm done with you."

Emily shook her head, a light giggle escaping her lips. "Oh, there's no doubt in my mind you'll have me thinking about something else. Go ahead. I know you get to go first."

A slow grin slid across Gavin's mouth. He already knew the answer to his first question. Emily always had her face buried in one. "Books or movies?"

Emily rolled her eyes. "What do you think?"

"I have no idea." Gavin shrugged, attempting to play stupid with his sexy bookworm. "That's why I'm asking."

"Books," Emily sighed. "You're not as observant as I thought."

Gavin chuckled. "That all depends on *what* I'm observing." He held Emily closer, enjoying that she looked somewhat annoyed. He'd definitely taken her mind off the mother situation. "Your turn."

"Bond or Bourne?"

Gavin's mouth twitched into a smirk. "As in James or Jason?"

"You're a quick one."

"I'm as quick as they come, sweets." Gavin brushed his lips against hers. "And of course I'm a James Bond man. Remember? My balcony?"

"I have not a clue what you're talking about," Emily replied with a furrowed brow.

"It seems *you're* not as observant as *I* thought." Emily stared at him blankly, and Gavin took the opportunity to dramatically roll his eyes. "The night we first played bottle caps on my balcony. You came out. I scared you. I said, 'No. It's Gavin. Gavin Blake.'"

"Oh my God. You're such a geek," Emily laughed, hugging him. "James Bond says it the other way around." Emily deepened her voice, adding a British accent. "'It's Bond, James Bond.'"

Gavin frowned. His sexy bookworm was right. "Okay. You win. But it was still double O seven-ish."

Still maintaining the British accent, Emily said, "Yes, it was. Kind of. Go ahead, Blake, Gavin Blake. It's your turn."

Yeah. Emily was definitely making him feel like a geek. Smiling, he shook his head. "Granite or marble?"

"Umm… granite."

"Why did your answer sound like a question?"

"I don't know." Emily shrugged. Lately, he had a freakishly odd fascination with those types of questions. She figured he was just excited to get his architect magazines. "I don't usually sit around thinking about stuff like that."

Gavin kissed her, and although Emily shivered, he could tell it wasn't his doing. She was getting cold. "I wouldn't expect you to. Come on. We'll go in now."

She nodded.

Confident he'd taken Emily's mind off his mother, Gavin turned the handle to find it was locked, so he rang the bell.

With a genuine, warm smile, Gavin's father opened the door. He shook Gavin's hand and pulled Emily in for a hug. Flicking his light blue eyes down to his watch, Chad closed the door. "You're quite early. Your mother's still at the grocery store picking up a few items for dinner."

Gavin looked at Emily, the confused expression in her eyes alerting him she was onto him. She stared, scrutinizing his face as she searched for answers he wasn't ready to give. He brought his attention back to his father, feeling like a fool caught in a web of lies. Clearing his throat, he helped Emily slip off her coat. "When I spoke to her earlier, I could've sworn she said five."

"Nope. Seven fifteen." Chad reached for Emily and Gavin's coats and hung them in the foyer closet. "Bad hearing at your age is a sign of working long hours. You and your brother need a break."

Grinning, Gavin crossed his arms. "Pop, I just got back from a break. I'm cool. Really."

Chad shrugged, his tone holding nonchalance. "Eh, another can't hurt. You're young. Live it up." Slapping Gavin's back as he led them into the den, he let out a full, hearty chuckle. "Don't tell your mother I said that, though."

Gavin smirked, depositing himself and Emily onto the chenille sofa. "She'd put you on restriction from watching CSI if she knew you were trying to get me to play hooky."

"She'd do worse than that, but I'd rather not go into details." Smiling, he clapped once and looked at Emily. "I know you can't have any liquor, but can I offer you something else? We have raspberry iced tea, water, and a few juices."

"I'll take a water, Mr. Blake. Thank you."

With a loving gleam in his eyes, he smiled. "You're part of our family now, so I insist on you *not* calling me Mr. Blake. Pop seems to be the cool name for me among my kids, including my daughter-in-law. You're no different. Good?"

His acceptance of her and the situation spread warmth through Emily's chest. In that moment, she understood where Gavin had acquired the charm and charisma he was born with. "Good. I'll take a water, Pop." The word felt foreign leaving her lips.

He shot her a wink and started for the kitchen. "Very good. I'm going to get the appetizers started. Son, a cold bottle of Sam Adams?"

"Yeah. That'll work," Gavin answered as his father disappeared around the corner. Sliding Emily's hand over his lap, Gavin pushed her hair away from her neck and leaned into her ear. "You look beautiful."

Turning to face him, she lifted a slow, suspicious brow. "Oh do I? I wouldn't have thought so considering you didn't want to fool around earlier." She watched him gnaw at his bottom lip, his vibrant blue eyes revealing more than they should. For a second, her heart took a nosedive, her words falling from her mouth faster than she could comprehend. "I scheduled an appointment at a local gym with an instructor who helps pregnant women keep in shape. I won't gain that much weight."

Gavin reared back. "You think it has to do with your weight?"

"I've gained a few pounds. What else am I supposed to think? You've never turned down sex with me, Gavin. My hormones are raging right now, and yours... well, yours are usually no better than a teenage boy. You said you were sick last night, and then before, you just... didn't want to. Admit you're turned off." Emily looked down, her voice trailing. "Oh, and nice try with the whole having to be here early excuse."

Gavin took her face in his hands, gazing into her worried eyes. "My God, I could never be turned off by you, Emily. It's taking everything in me to *not* hike up that skirt, bend your pretty body right over this couch, and plant myself so deep inside you, neither of us would know where the other begins or ends. Sex with you is a drug, and I'm a fucking addict. But hell if you aren't the sweetest addiction there is to have."

"Then what is it?" she breathed, trying to shoo away the vision of being bent over the couch. She was about to hike up her skirt and let him. She squeezed her eyes closed. Gavin holding her face so close to his wasn't helping the hormone situation at all. Not. One. Bit.

Gavin hesitated, his voice low. "I'm… afraid of hurting you and the baby."

Emily's eyes flew open. "What? We've been having sex for the last couple of weeks. You weren't worried then."

"I know. But seeing the baby yesterday on the monitor somehow made it… real." Sighing, he leaned back. "I'll wind up hurting you. It's impossible with the way you and I are during sex. We're animals."

Emily hooked her finger under his chin, bringing his gaze back to hers. "First of all, I like when you hurt me," she whispered, her brow arched. "Second: Do you expect me to believe a man with your education can be so naïve regarding a woman's body, pregnant or not? Third: You can't hurt me or the baby. Couples have been having sex for billions of years while women were pregnant."

Gavin smirked, dragging a hand through his hair. "First: When given permission, of course I like… *pleasurably* hurting you. Second: Yes, yes you can expect me to be so naïve regarding a woman's pregnant body. The key word's *pregnant*. Third"—he grinned and leaned into her ear—"never in a billion years have couples fucked the way we do. We break records. So with that, yes, I'm afraid of hurting you."

Body heated, Emily sighed deeply, then moistened her lips. Her tongue was tingling to glide along Gavin's lower abdomen. "Gavin—"

Before she could say another word, the front door swung open. Juggling three stuffed paper bags, Lillian Blake used her heel to close the door. She shook her head in an attempt to remove big, fat powdery snowflakes from her chestnut hair.

Gavin jumped to his feet, almost tripping over the coffee table as he dashed toward his mother who was about to drop every bag onto the tiled foyer floor. Snatching the bags from her arms, he popped a kiss on her cheek. "Hey, mom. It started snowing?"

Beaming, she swooshed her hand through his hair. "Yes. Pretty heavily, too." On a sigh, she looked at Gavin, her eyes filled with love only a mother could hold. "My baby boy, I've missed ya. Next time you decide to take off on a two week vacation, could you think about calling the woman who brought you into this world?"

Chuckling, Gavin shook his head. "Mom, I'm twenty-eight, I own a thriving business, and my girlfriend's sitting on the couch. You're dropping my swoon-worthy factor by the second."

Emily stood and made her way over to them. Also swishing her hand through his hair, she lifted a playful brow. "Ah, that swoon-worthy statement couldn't be further from the truth."

"No?" Gavin questioned incredulously, the gleam in his eyes predatory. "And how so?"

"Because any girl with a head on her shoulders knows a man *earns* swoon-worthy points by loving his mother," Lillian answered with a sparkling smile. "Right, Emily?"

"My point exactly," Emily agreed.

Gavin cocked his head to the side, a smirk twisting his face. "Well if that's the case, just so you know, Emily, I did ask my dear mother to marry me once."

"Yes, when he was three," Lillian trilled, pulling her purse from her shoulder. Placing it on a glass entryway table, she gave Gavin an endearing smile and cupped his cheek. "I remember it like it was yesterday. He won a plastic engagement ring from one of those bubblegum machines, and right there in the grocery store, he dropped to one knee and proposed."

Emily giggled, watching him turn the loveliest shade of crimson.

"Yep. The swoon-worthy factor just dropped a few hundred notches," he confirmed, flashing an impish, schoolboy grin as he slipped into the kitchen. "I'm out of here, ladies."

Lillian hooted out a laugh, gathering Emily into her arms for a warm embrace. "So how've you been?" She unpeeled a creamy white scarf swathing her neck and dropped it onto the table. After shimmying out of a heavy fur coat and hanging it in the closet, she turned to Emily. "It's been a while and a lot has happened. I hope you're doing well."

Unsure how much she knew about what'd happened with her, Gavin, and Dillon, Emily simply nodded. "I'm doing much better, thank you. How've you been?"

"Good. I've been busy building up the organization. We're trying to spread into New Jersey. It looks like it may happen, too," she said happily, linking her arm through Emily's. They started for the kitchen. "Let's go see if our men are attempting to burn down the house."

Once again feeling a warm, welcome flush through her limbs, Emily noticed just how opposite her and Gavin's upbringings were. Where she lacked a father figure, Gavin was raised by a strong man who trusted good would prevail over any bad situation. Though Emily's mother was there as much as possible, Lillian had stayed home with both boys until they entered high school. Sure, Lillian's situation was different since she'd married an honest, caring man, but even in her darkest hours suffering through her battle with breast cancer, she never stopped trying to achieve a sense of normalcy in their home. Two very different colored lights at opposite sides of life's spectrum. Now all Emily needed to believe was she and Gavin had been brought together for a reason. Hopefully that reason was what would be the main focus of conversation during dinner.

Once they entered the kitchen, both women were happy to see neither man was in the process of setting the house ablaze. Father and son had put the groceries away and started mixing, sizzling, and baking what smelled to be something delicious.

"Don't ever let them think you can't train them," Lillian whispered, her smile as contagious as Gavin's. "It's actually quite easy."

"I'll keep that in mind," Emily responded, completely unable to stifle a small giggle.

Turning with a frying pan in his hand, Gavin caught Emily's gaze. He grinned and did some fancy flick with his wrist, popping what appeared to be pasta up from the pan the way a trained chef would. "Quite talented, right?" he asked, reaching for his bottle of cold brew on the counter. After downing a sip, he attempted to show off again only to flop half of the noodles onto the floor. Marinara sauce coated the kitchen from one end to the other.

Gavin looked up from the mess half-laughing and half-groaning while rolling his eyes. Needless to say, he was the only one groaning, because right along with Emily belting out a laugh, so did his parents. Several damp paper towels, some cleaning product, and a quick mop of the floor later, Mr. Show Off's failed attempt was a thing of the past. Within a half hour, Lillian had everything under control.

The four sat down in the dining room for a hearty, home-cooked meal of house salad, breaded eggplant parmesan, Italian bread, and courtesy of Gavin, a tiny helping of pasta. Emily relaxed a bit, enjoying the conversation while she could. She knew their news would soon end it.

She learned Chad and Lillian met while attending Harvard Law School. Not quite your typical "love at first sight" story, but Emily found out where Gavin gained his tendency to relentlessly pursue what he wanted. Chad had chased Lillian for two semesters, insisting he was the man for her, until she eventually agreed to go out on one date with him. Emily inwardly laughed at how that apple didn't fall far from the tree. To their surprise, Lillian found out she was pregnant with Colton the following year. They agreed she would leave school for the time being to stay home and raise Colton. A shotgun wedding, another baby, a mortgage, a dog, and Little League baseball practices later, Lillian never made her way back to law school. However, as Emily took in the story of their life together, there didn't seem to be an ounce of regret in either of their eyes when they looked at one another. Instead, a lifetime of love and memories bled through every word, smile, and hoot of laughter.

After clearing the remnants of dinner from the table and waiting for his parents to bring dessert into the dining room, Gavin couldn't help but hear Emily's heel pat the hardwood floor in relentless, jerky taps. The sound echoed, pouncing off the walls like raindrops against a glass window. God, he hated that she was so nervous. It scorched his heart.

Before he could tell her everything was going to be fine, his parents breezed into the room, his father gripping a freshly brewed pot of coffee and his mother holding a homemade apple pie. With their seats reclaimed, Lillian sliced into the just out-of-the-oven dessert and served them each a slice. Staring at his father from across the table, Gavin could see he was nervous as well. His ashen, troubled expression told all. Gavin couldn't even feign a smile as he slugged back the rest of his beer in one long gulp. Hell. His nerves were lighting up, but he knew he needed to strike up the damn conversation. However, his voice got tangled up in his racing thoughts, his words sticking to his tongue like molasses.

His father looked at him once more, nodding as he cleared his throat. "Lillian, Gavin and Emily have some… news they want to share." His eyes locked on Gavin's with such solemn seriousness, Gavin wanted to leave and take Emily as far away as possible to somewhere no one would ever find them. "Go ahead, son. Let your mother know what's going on."

Reaching for Emily's hand, Gavin turned to her and placed a soft kiss on her quivering lips. "I love you." His eyes traced over her face as he pulled away.

"I love you too," she said softly.

"What's going on, Gavin?" Lillian asked with a furrowed, wary brow of a probing mother.

After a moment's hesitation, the confession. "Mom, Emily's pregnant and… the baby may not be mine."

Lillian's face melted into pure astonishment, her shock clear in the bloodless paling of her white skin and flabbergasted, slacked jaw. Bewilderment shadowed her once vibrant green eyes like a cloak. Her gaze roamed over Emily suspiciously. "You're with my son, yet you may be having a child with someone else?" Pushing her plate away, she leaned back, bringing her hand to her chest. "I guess my impression of you was incorrect, Emily. I mistook you for a woman who would stay faithful to my son."

Emily opened her mouth, but she couldn't sort through the thousands of words flying around in her scattered brain.

"Now, Lillian, wait a minute. She's been faithful to Gavin. There's more to the story than you know," Chad pointed out with the shake of his head. "Hear them out for a minute."

Lillian sucked in an indignant breath, her eyes battering her husband. "You knew about this and didn't tell me?" Her attention flew to Gavin. "Is there a reason I've been left in the dark?"

"Yeah, mom, there is." Gavin leaned his elbow on the table. "I anticipated this exact reaction from you. Are you going to let us explain? If not, then we'll go ahead and leave right now."

Thick, tense silence coated the room before Lillian blinked her heavily mascara-painted lashes and nodded. As though she might turn into a statue if she accidentally met Emily's gaze, her eyes avoided Emily's path, focusing solely on Gavin. "What happened?" she asked, her voice softer while she raised both eyebrows at him.

Emily stared at her, stricken by the depth of anger and sadness clouding her face. She felt ill, and in that moment, she swore she wasn't going to make it through the conversation without heaving. Lips parting without a word, Emily lifted her watery eyes to Gavin, waiting for him to respond.

"Emily and I were together after she and Dillon broke up the first time."

"This is the same Dillon you're friends with?" Lillian interrupted. "Your broker?"

"The same man I *used* to be friends with, yes. He's no longer my broker."

"Well how does something like that happen, Gavin? I'm just assuming here, but it doesn't sound like any of this ended very well." Lillian swung her eyes to Chad, her face dripping with mortification. "Did we raise our sons to just go off with their friends' girlfriends?"

Chad lifted a brow, his tone resolute. "No. But we didn't raise our sons to give up on something they believed in, either."

"At what expense, Chad?" she asked, seeming astonished by his answer. "Since when did stealing a friend's girlfriend become popular?"

"He didn't steal me away," Emily softly spoke up. She looked from Lillian to her hands, tangled nervously with Gavin's, in her lap. As her thoughts tossed her back to the first second she saw Gavin, she was unable to keep the barest of smiles from her lips. She brought her eyes to his, her gaze stroking his beautiful face. "Well, he did steal my heart away from Dillon. But when that happened... your son wasn't aware he did it."

With a light smile that matched hers, Gavin palmed Emily's cheek, his heart falling further in his chest. Holding his breath, he still couldn't believe she was his. After a moment, he dropped his hand, inhaled deeply, and glanced at his mother. She seemed more confused than before. "The fact is, our love is so far past the point of return, it's actually scary. It has been for a while. We just had a few kinks to work out. No, the way we got together wasn't right in the opinions of some, but I couldn't care less. I'm pretty sure the woman sitting next to me couldn't either. We're in love. A deep, sick, twisted love like they make movies about. We're looking fear in the face together and telling it to take a hike. This baby might not be mine, but even if it's not... it is. It's a piece of Emily, mom, and there's not a piece of your son that couldn't love it. There's not a piece of your son that couldn't love her."

As tears soaked Emily's lashes, she noticed a tear fall from Lillian's cheek and land with a plop onto the white linen tablecloth. Swallowing, Emily watched Lillian stand, her almond-shaped eyes flashing between her and Gavin.

"I don't think I can support this relationship," she choked out though a frown. "I just..." She brought her hand to her throat, stroking her long, delicate fingers across her flesh. She looked at Chad, who released a heavy, defeated sigh and reached for her hand. He squeezed it before she turned and walked out of the room, her sniffles echoing throughout the home until they disappeared into whispers of nothing with the closing of a door.

No longer able to witness the grief she'd brought to this once solid family, Emily scrambled out of her chair, her heart breaking a million times over as she swallowed back a sob.

Gavin surged to his feet, catching Emily's arm as she headed for the front door. He stroked the hair away from her face. "Wait! Emily, listen to me—"

"No, you listen to me, Gavin." She cradled his face in her palms, as she gulped for air. "Do you remember telling me you almost picked up the phone to call me when I left you, but you didn't?"

With confused, worried eyes, Gavin searched her face. "Yes. What does that have to do with this?"

"I hated myself because every time I looked at my phone, I wanted to call you. I wanted so desperately to call and tell you how sorry I was for not believing you, but I couldn't. Something held me back. You also told me you got in your car and almost drove to my apartment, but you didn't. I did the same. I jumped in a taxi and had them drive me to your building. I stood outside looking up, wondering what you were doing and fearing who you were doing it with. I wanted so badly to see you. My heart was torn, broken into pieces, Gavin. I felt physical pain while we were apart. I didn't believe that kind of pain existed. It was something so entirely different than what I felt when I lost my mother. It cut deeper. But I couldn't bring myself to get in that elevator and go to you. I didn't want Dillon. I wanted *you*."

"Emily, stop." Gavin gripped her waist, pulling her against his chest. "Why are you saying all of this?"

"I'm saying this because it's said breaths are stolen during a passionate kiss. That's not true, Gavin, because I literally can't breathe before your lips even touch mine. I try, but I'm unable to. I can't think when you look at me. You strip my mind bare. You always have, and it's beautiful and consuming. It's magical and everything a girl is supposed to feel. It's said you're truly in love with someone if your skin tingles from their touch. Mine tingles when I hear your voice; I don't need you to touch me. I can feel you when you're not near me. I feel you in my dreams. I felt you when you were a thousand miles away.

"You scared me the moment I saw you, and I think it's because I knew, I just knew, I was going to fall in love you. I didn't know our worlds were already intertwined, but my heart somehow knew it belonged to you from the start. I didn't believe a pain so deep existed while we were apart, but I also didn't believe a love like ours existed. You've shown me it does. You've shown me good when there was bad. You've given me pleasure above all of my pain. You've given me life when I thought I was dead."

Emily paused, tears streaming down her face in a rush. "It's also said if you love someone enough, you'll let them go if all you're doing is causing them pain. That's all I've ever caused you, Gavin. From the moment we met, I've turned your world upside down. And now this. I can't have you not speaking to your mother because of me. I love you enough to let you go so she can continue to love you."

Gavin recoiled. Feeling knocked off balance, a flash of pain shot through his chest. He swallowed, inhaling a deep, broken breath as he stared into her eyes. "You can't leave me," he said, hearing the desperation shaking in his voice.

"I have to," she choked out, dying from the fear she saw on his face. "I can't be the reason your family falls apart."

"You won't be," Lillian's soft voice hummed through the air, reassuring certainty filling her tone. Emily faced her, blinking her wet eyes in surprise. Head spinning with confusion, she swiped her fingers across her cheeks, her body shaking. "You won't be the reason our family falls apart because I wouldn't allow a woman who loves my son as much as you do to walk out of his life." Stepping closer, Lillian placed a tentative hand on Emily's shoulder, her eyes spilling over with tears. "I wouldn't allow you to walk out of *our* lives. What you were about to give up, though it would've hurt my son, was selfless. I once knew a girl who loved a man so much it scared her, too." Lillian paused, her gaze falling on Chad. The corner of her mouth turned up in a small, sad smile as he made his way toward her. Bringing her eyes back to Emily's, Lillian shook her head. "It would've killed me if I had to give up those stolen breaths before he kissed me. Whether or not the baby you're carrying is my grandchild, I'd be honored to call you my daughter."

Emily's breath caught, her heart pounding so hard she could hear it as Lillian pulled her in for a long hug. Emily cried against the shoulder of the woman who brought life to the man she loved so desperately. Not only was Emily thankful she didn't have to give up the stolen breaths he took from her, she was thankful that somehow on this cold, snowy night, in the year her life would change in multiple ways, she gained a mother.

CHAPTER THIRTEEN

Something Wicked This Way Comes

Emily closed the penthouse door behind her, smiling when Gavin stood from the couch, holding a box of Valentine's Day chocolates. She peeled her coat and scarf from her body and tossed them onto the couch as she moved through the living room, toward him. "You do realize those are almost two weeks old, right?" She smiled as she looped her arms around his neck. "And do you *ever* eat anything healthy?"

With a chocolaty smile, he kissed her. "I do realize they're almost two weeks old, and no. The unhealthier the better."

She smacked her lips together, tasting the small bit of chocolate he stamped on them. Considering he had teeth any dentist would be proud to say they worked on, she was surprised he basically lived off of anything coated in sugar. The sweeter, the better. Over the last couple of months, she'd discovered other little things about Gavin that made him who he was. Who she kept falling in love with. Without fail, twice a day, he'd spend at least thirty minutes, sometimes longer, in the shower, filling up the bathroom with hot steam while blasting Breaking Benjamin from a surround sound system built into the walls. Oh, and in his best efforts, he sang along. To her surprise, but without a doubt to her liking, he had a wonderful addiction of sleeping nude. She was a lucky girl who awoke every morning to nothing but rock hard, naked alpha male.

He wasn't without odd habits either. Emily considered him borderline OCD and possibly in need of therapist intervention. He was a clean freak in the worst possible way. Shit, if he found a crumb from a sandwich she'd eaten, it didn't take him but a split second to grab some paper towels and Windex and swiftly wipe down the surface. This she'd laugh at, confused, because he had a housekeeper who came to clean four days a week. It was as if he needed the penthouse sparkling before the woman came to do her job.

Needless to say, Emily was attempting to break him of that quirk, easing him into the fact it was indeed okay to leave some laundry piled up in the corner. However, that was a battle she usually lost. Either way, she considered every one of his little quirks and idiosyncrasies ravishingly cute. She couldn't help but love his many layers.

With a smile, she dropped her purse and a towering stack of mail onto the kitchen island. Gavin followed her and lounged into a chair, watching Emily pull open the refrigerator. Shuffling through the slush pile of invitations to local charity balls, Gavin plucked out his first delivery of *Architectural Digest*.

"You have a letter here," Gavin informed her, sliding the envelope across the granite countertop. Opening the magazine, his eyes scanned a luxury Italian villa in Agropoli, straddling the Tyrrhenian Sea. "I also paid off your Visa. I suggest if you're going to hide your credit card statements in a horrible effort to dissuade me from taking care of your bills, you should come up with a savvier hiding place than your jewelry box." Sporting a devious smirk, he lifted his shoulder in a casual shrug. "There's a surprise for you in the lower level compartment. Now we're both sneaks."

Pressing her lips together, Emily lifted two guilty brows, but she couldn't deny he was correct about finding a better spot to hide her bills. Challenge accepted, she yanked the envelope from the counter and popped a kiss onto his sneaky temple. "What did you get me?"

Eyes locked on his magazine, his tone was as cool as a lazy fall breeze. "I'll pass on that question and let you figure it out for yourself." With a slight jerk of his head in the direction of the bedroom, those baby blues still glued to the magazine, a smile curled the corner of his mouth. "Go."

On a sigh and a smile of her own, Emily started for the bedroom. She slid her finger under the lip of the envelope, tearing it open. With a small gasp, she stopped, looking down at the finger that'd been assaulted with a fresh paper cut. She sucked the wound, trying to ease the pain. With the envelope in her uninjured hand, and the burn starting to dissipate, she flipped over the envelope, her heart nearly stopping when her gaze triggered in on the handwriting on the front.

Though it was void of a return address, there was no mistaking Dillon's scrawl. She swallowed and pulled out the paper, quickly unfolding it. Heart jumping wildly, she scanned a photocopy of an explanation of benefits from her old insurance company. It was a detailed breakdown of her doctor's visit from a few weeks earlier. Confused, because she specifically remembered giving the receptionist her new insurance information and address, Emily didn't understand how the paperwork wound up with Dillon. With a blood red marker, he'd circled the words "First trimester fetal sonogram." At the bottom of the paper, he wrote:

Counting backward from the date of service,
you and I were happily engaged.
I think you have something to tell me????
If you don't call me the second you open this,
I call a fucking lawyer.

Swiping a shaky hand through her hair, Emily turned around, slowly making her way back into the kitchen. Gavin had insisted they didn't tell Dillon. He firmly felt Dillon didn't deserve to know she was pregnant until they had a definite answer as to who the father was. Not wanting to buck against his decision, though she had reservations about hiding it, Emily had reluctantly agreed.

Olivia's words from the club a few weeks ago went off like loud sirens in Emily's head. This *could* look bad for her. There was no doubt in her mind Dillon would use this against her in court if he turned out to be the father. The thought chilled her to the bones, flashes of him trying to take away her child sent icicles needling through her heart.

Quietly placing the paper in front of Gavin, Emily pulled in a deep breath, waiting for his reaction. She watched his expression go from slightly confused to impassivity as he read, bleeding into full-blown anger. His eyes lit up like hot coals, rage burning raw behind them. Another shiver spiraled through Emily as he shot to his feet, tossing the magazine onto the counter.

"How the hell did he get this?" he questioned, the confusion he was wearing on his face seconds before returning.

"I have no idea," she breathed, still in shock.

Gavin shoved his hand through his hair. "Were you ever on a health insurance policy with him?"

Emily nodded. "When I moved to New York, he paid for a private policy because he couldn't add me to the one he has through the firm without being married. He knew I wouldn't qualify right away for insurance when I began teaching. But I changed the information with the receptionist the day we went for the test. I don't understand what happened." Nervously fingering the locket Gavin gave her for Christmas, Emily started to feel as though she was about to hyperventilate. "He's going to drag me to court and try to take the baby away from me for not telling him. I need a lawyer. I can't, I can't go through this." She gulped back a sob, her body hunched over. Resting her arm on the cool granite counter, she felt Gavin's hand on the back of her neck.

"I wouldn't let him take the baby away from you," Gavin said, his tone resolute. Trying to catch a breath, Emily shook her head. "Emily, look at me," he commanded in a soft whisper. Body shaking, she straightened, her watery eyes searching his. "If I have to hire every lawyer in the fucking city, I will. I'd never allow him to hurt you like that. Do you understand me?"

She wanted to believe Gavin, but she couldn't. Her carefully trained thoughts wouldn't allow for it. Dillon was gone, but his influence wasn't far enough removed from her life. This would be his payback. Dear, God. This would be more than payback. She could feel it. Everything manipulative and hideous he'd turned into would surely have its time on stage in the grandest of battles fought out in front of a judging court system that would punish her for hiding this from him. She knew wherever he was at this very second, he was seething and waiting on her call.

"I have to call him," she puffed out, heading for the office.

Gavin caught her elbow. "We're not calling him, Emily."

Eyes wide, she yanked her arm away. "If you think for one minute I'm going to attempt to play any more games with him, you're wrong. Our glorious plan of not letting him know has blown up in our faces, and I'm not about to chance losing custody rights to him."

A sense of foreboding slithered up Gavin's spine and hell if it didn't fuck with him. "You're assuming the baby's his considering what you just said. You do realize this, right?"

"I'm not assuming anything!" she retorted, her vehemence undeniable. She continued down the hall into the office. Picking up the phone, she started dialing Dillon's number, but Gavin's large hand plucked it out of her grasp. "What are you doing?" she questioned with a gasp. "I'm calling him."

Face a mask of anguish, Gavin gently stroked his thumb along her trembling lips. Voice soft, he shook his head. "Emily Cooper, you're going to calm down. I love a good fight with you, doll, it turns me on, but I'll be damned if I'm going to fight with you over this asshole ever again."

"But—"

"Sit down."

Her hand flew to her hip. "You can't tell me what to do."

"Keep going." With a wicked smirk, Gavin crossed his arms. "My dick's growing harder with every word you shout." Yep. Sure enough it was. Tenting his sweatpants, there was no denying he was getting turned on.

Emily bit her lip and fell into the leather chair in front of his desk. Cocking her head to the side, she narrowed her eyes. "I'm not surprised it's growing. We haven't had sex in a few weeks. Not only have you starved me of getting some, it looks like you've starved yourself."

Gavin chuckled, amused by the wit she was starting to so easily display around him. Yeah, he was turning his girl into the tiger he always knew she was. "We're not here to discuss sex."

Emily rolled her eyes. "Or lack thereof."

Hunching his body over hers, Gavin placed both hands on the sides of the chair, his nose barely grazing hers. "Now that you've calmed down some, are you ready to talk to me?"

The low, sexy timbre of his voice whispered across her flesh. Damn him. She felt like a schoolgirl getting reprimanded by a teacher. A teacher whom she wanted nothing more than to fuck right there. Pulling in a slow breath, she feigned disinterest. "Fine. Let's talk."

"Thank you," Gavin whispered, slowly backing away. He slipped around his desk, easing into his chair. Tenting his fingers under his chin, he stared at Emily and searched for words that would properly relay what was running through his head. "One: Woman I love more than Valentine's Day chocolates, woman I would lay my life down for in front of a speeding bullet train, you need to understand the chances of him being able to take this baby away from you are slim to none. He hit you. The courts have that on record." Emily went to speak, but Gavin held up a silencing finger. She sighed and he continued.

"Two: What you said before… bothered me. I heard the assumption in your voice. Neither of us is stupid. We both know the amount of times"—Gavin cringed at the thought—"you had sex with him in that week pales in comparison with the amount of times you and I did. But I'm banking on my sperm having an insane amount of muscle. Dillon's a weak man, therefore, he has a weak… army if you will. That puts me as far up in the running for being the father as Asshole. There's a blue-eyed, black-haired kid hanging out in that pretty stomach of yours as far as I'm concerned." Gavin shot her a wink, mentally getting off on his girlfriend's mouth falling open.

"Three"—he reached for the phone—"no, I can't tell you what to do. But I can tell you if you call him right now, he's going to be the spineless motherfucker he's always been. He's going to put demands on us we may not want. Whatever decision you make, I'll back you because you're a walking box of chocolates and I love you, but I don't want to hear you bitch once Asshole confronts us with any delusional ideas he may have."

Emily stood, walked around the desk, and deposited herself onto Gavin's lap. He smiled, his eyes warming her body as she snuggled against his shoulder. She drew circles on the black, worn out Linkin Park T-shirt he was wearing. It'd definitely seen better days. "Mr. Blake, do you think I can talk now?" She smiled, feeling the deep rustle of his laugh vibrating in his chest.

The sun catching the deep streams of dark, red highlights in her hair made Gavin's fingers itch to touch it. Giving into the temptation, he buried his hand under her waves, stroking the back of her neck. "By all means, if you think you can talk, please do so."

"Thank you." She nestled closer, enjoying his touch. "Okay. One: A few days after Dillon… hit me…" She paused, looking at Gavin when she felt him tense. She curled into him, bringing her knees up to her chest as he circled his arm around her waist. "A few days after, I visited a local battered women's shelter. The ADA suggested it, so I went, trying to gain as much insight as I could from other women who'd been through the same thing. I met several of them with children. Not only were these women scared to death for their lives, but they were devastated because the courts had let them down. Those animals weren't denied the right to see their children. They're allowed supervised visits. It doesn't matter how much money they have. Believe me, there were women in there from every walk of life. Rich, poor, young, old, black, white, and every color in between. Some of them had the highest paid lawyers in the city. It didn't matter. If the child isn't being physically abused, most, if not all, judges grant supervised visits."

Pausing again, she looked into his eyes, her voice soft. "That's what I'm afraid of. In more ways than one, you're the most powerful man I've ever met. But in this situation, your money can't help." Gavin went to speak, but it was her turn to hold up a silencing finger. She straddled his lap, pressing her lips to his for a long, passionate kiss. After a moment, she broke the connection, hoping she could mend the little piece of his heart she was sure she broke.

"Two: I'm sorry you heard the assumption in my voice. I let fear take hold. But knowing you're pretty sure your... army may win this battle, I promise you won't ever hear it again. As far as I'm concerned, there is a blue-eyed, black-haired kid hanging out in my *less* than pretty stomach right now. Boy or girl, in my mind, they're already a diehard Yankees fan."

Grinning, Gavin lifted a skeptical brow. "Your stomach's perfect, so add that 'less than' statement to the list of things I never want to hear again. And you're giving me the Yankees?"

"I'd give you the world if I could."

Little did she know, she already had. Gavin guided her to his lips, kissing her deeply as he slid his hands along the glorious curve of her waist. With his thumbs stroking her beautifully perfect stomach, Gavin envisioned that tiny Yankees fan. His heart dipped, bringing with it a feeling so thirsty for this to be his child, he was sure he would drown in it.

Emily slowly pulled away, her lips flushed from their kiss. With soft eyes, she tilted her head, her voice a whisper. "Three: Yes, I think we need to call him, Gavin. Now that he knows, it'll only further complicate things if we don't. I'm not sure if I'm prepared for whatever crazy demands he might conjure up, but I promise I won't bitch about them."

After a moment's hesitation, Gavin nodded. With a knot blistering hot in his gut, he reached for the phone.

Repositioning on Gavin's lap, Emily swallowed nervously as she watched him hit the speaker button, followed by Dillon's number. A few rings later, there it was, the voice Emily didn't think she'd ever have to hear again.

"Ah. I figured I'd get a phone call today," he said, his arrogance echoing through the office as if he was standing there. "So I heard our little trio's expecting? What a tangled web we—"

"What the fuck do you want, asshole?" Gavin grit out, wrath wicked in his voice.

Silence blanketed the air, its presence as heavy as an elephant sitting on Emily's chest.

"Let me explain something to you, Gavin," Dillon said, his sneer ominously low, cold. "The game's changed, motherfucker. You're playing by my rules now. The first rule of the game? You and *my* beautiful ex are about to get in your fucking car and meet me at Big Daddy's Diner on Park Avenue South between Nineteenth and Twentieth. Second rule: You pull anything funny, and I'm on the phone with the cops to report an incident from a few months ago. I'll be at the diner in thirty. If you're not there in forty, say peace to your freedom."

The line went dead, the dial tone flat lining, whispering promises of death in Emily's ear.

Breathe…

"Remember what I told you," Gavin said, his arm wrapped securely around Emily's waist. His towering frame shielded her from the blistering February winds howling through the city streets. "You don't talk to him at all. Don't even look at him."

Shivering, Emily nodded, her eyes adjusting to the vibrant red and yellow neon sign in front of the diner. Gavin opened the door, his hold instinctively tightening on Emily as he scanned the retro, 1960s diner. His eyes slipped over an array of pastel vinyl booths and narrowed when he spotted Dillon alone in a back corner booth. Immediately, Gavin's body went on alert. His pulse jumped, the blood in his veins speeding through his system. Flashes of what the fuck did to Emily dissected his thoughts as fresh as the day she told him about it.

"Two?" a young waitress wearing jeans and a T-shirt with the diner's logo asked, her perky voice blending with the frenzied atmosphere.

"No. We're meeting someone, and he's already seated." Gavin jerked his head in Dillon's direction. "Thanks."

Beaming, she whisked off, taking a seat at the chromed-out counter.

Gavin slipped his hand in Emily's, leading them toward Dillon. "Remember, don't say a word. Let me handle this." He felt the clamminess coating her skin, and he stopped, looking into her nervous eyes. His heart slowed a moment, but with it came a crushing pain. He bent his head and kissed her soft lips. "I love you."

Emily swallowed, her nerves pummeling her limbs. "I love you, too."

Inwardly cringing and mentally calling Dillon every name in the book, Gavin approached the booth, his eyes pinned on Dillon. Wearing a cocky smirk, the asshole had his back against the wall, his long legs resting on the cushioned seat. Gavin slid into the booth first, making sure he was directly in front of him.

Without looking at either of them, Dillon stared at the front doors. "Kickass place, right?" His voice was eerily monotone. "You can't deny kids eat this shit up. I mean, look at these cartoon logos everywhere." He dropped his feet to the wood floor and swiveled to face Gavin and Emily. "All of these cereal boxes are vintage, you know. The food's some of the best in the city. Maybe when the baby's old enough, we'll bring it here for a nice family outing. What do you think, Em?"

Emily jumped when Gavin's fist thundered down against the table. The silverware and condiments jiggled from the impact. With his elbow digging into the table, and finger pointed at Dillon, she could see the veins in his neck bulging.

"You listen to me, motherfucker," Gavin growled, his eyes alight with murderous venom. "I don't give a fuck about your rules. I'll gut you open with my fucking teeth if you talk to her again."

Apparently unaffected by Gavin's threat, Dillon's mouth twitched into a smirk. His eyes never left Emily. Crossing his arms, his words came out unrushed, his tone almost a whisper. "Oh no, my *friend*. We're all going to play by my rules, and I'll tell you why." He brought his gaze from Emily to Gavin, narrowing it like a hungry wolf. "I come from a long line of men who've served on the NYPD. Those men are extremely close with our local judges. Maximum sentence for assault in the third degree by means of strangulation is seven years. I can go ahead and push for attempted murder as well. I don't know how many times you... *fucked* my ex while we were together, but considering you have a small chance at being the bastard's father, I'm pretty fucking sure you'd hate spending almost a decade, or possibly longer, of its life upstate. Orange isn't your color."

Wild, panicked ringing pierced Emily's ears. Mouth parting in a silent gasp and body a twisted pile of nerves, her wide, tear-filled eyes honed in on Gavin. His brows angled down, deepening the sharp crevices splintering his face. His lips curled over his teeth as though he was fighting a poisonous taste. His eyes, those hypnotizing, beautiful eyes, turned a shade of blue so deep, dark, and vengeful, she swore he'd become possessed. She gulped as she prepared for his fury.

Gavin sprung to his feet, his hand darting forward. Clutching the collar of Dillon's red polo shirt, Gavin dragged him up, their bodies inclined over the table. Faces as close as lovers about to share a passionate kiss, Gavin's knuckles turned white. "Don't throw your fucking threats at me, pussy," he snarled. "I'll kill you right here in this diner."

Palms resting on the table, Dillon's eyes flashed like brushfire. His words came out in a loud, barking laugh. "Did you hear that, everyone? This man said he's about to kill me in front of all of you. Who wants to watch?"

With her chest heaving fast in quick, shallow breaths, Emily whipped around, taking in the curious onlookers. Every pair of eyes in the diner was focused on the display. A mother with two young children gasped in stupefied horror, shooting a scrutinizing glare at Emily. Seconds before the manger reached the table, Emily grabbed Gavin's elbow in an attempt to diffuse the situation. "Gavin," she choked out, blinking rapidly in mounting panic. "Gavin, sit down. There's a manager coming."

"Yes, Gavin," Dillon said in a low sneer, his face inches from Gavin's. "You might want to be careful. He might've already called the cops. Maybe your bid upstate will begin tonight?"

"Excuse me," said the middle-aged manager standing in front of their table. Clearly flabbergasted by the scene, he dug his hands in his hips, his voice firm. "I need to ask you gentleman to calm down, or I'm going to have to throw you both out."

Eyes aflame with black fury, Gavin slowly released Dillon. Head jarred and body shaking with unleashed hunger for Dillon's blood, Gavin pulled in a deep breath and cleared his throat. "We're actors." Gavin stared at Dillon, his tone so calm, it sent a shiver screaming through Emily's bones. "We were just acting out a scene." Taking his seat again, Gavin looked at the manager. "Please accept my apologies. The rest of our stay will be uneventful."

"Actors?" the manager asked, skepticism heavy in his question.

"Yes. Actors," Gavin answered coolly, watching Dillon sit again.

The man nodded. "Okay, *actors,* don't let it happen again. If you do, you're both out of here." On that note, he turned and walked away.

"What do you want?" Gavin asked. His eyes were murdering Dillon from across the table, but his tone held sickening composure.

Dillon lifted his shoulder in a casual shrug, an evil grin bleeding over his mouth. "I want in. I want access to each and every single doctor's appointment. I also want to be present during the birth." He paused, slid a hand though his slicked back, dirty blond hair, and aimed his gaze at Emily. "I've always wondered what the screams of a woman sounded like when she's being split in two from the pain that comes with pushing another human being from her body. *Especially* the women who deserves every minute of that pain."

Gavin surged forward, but Emily quickly lifted her hand to his chest. Nearly speechless, her face twisted in shock. "You're out of your fucking mind," she breathed, wiping a tear from her face. "You don't want any part of this baby, and you know it, you bastard. You're not even supposed to be near me."

Dillon leaned back and crossed his arms. "You're right about a few things, Em. No, I'm not supposed to be near you. But let's not forget what the cop said at the school. Once again you've been a bad, bad girl breaking the rules." He wagged a disciplining finger at her. "I did a little research. You can have the order of protection amended in a situation like this so I can attend all of these joyous events coming up in our lives. And you're also correct in that I really have no desire to have any sort of relationship with the little fucker. Either way, I'm—"

"How much?" Gavin questioned, a bid upstate looking more appealing with every word dropping from the asshole's mouth. "How much do you want to walk the fuck away? Walk away and never bother us again."

Dillon threw his head back, laughing as he cupped his chin. "You see, Gavin, I'm not as stupid as you may think I am. Don't ever forget that. I knew you would try to buy your way out of this. I know your fucking kind, the rich sleaze walking this fucking earth thinking they can purchase everyone around them. I don't need your fucking money. I have my own. Don't think for one second you fucked me by pulling your accounts because you didn't. Now, sure, even Trump would be a madman, passing up a little more cash. But no amount of green you can pay me will provide the same satisfaction I'm going to get from watching you two squirm under the pressure of having me around during all of this. I'm already fucking warm and fuzzy just thinking about it. One million or ten million of your filthy dollars couldn't buy that feeling. If I could, I'd bottle it up. I'm hitting you where it's going to hurt you the most, and that's not your wallet. It's sitting right next to you looking mighty fine this evening."

Gavin clenched his jaw. He felt backed into a corner as Dillon stood.

"I have to drain the snake. In the meantime, I think you both have a few things to go over. I'm a nice guy, so I'll recap everything before I leave you two lovebirds alone. So, let's see." Brows furrowed, Dillon crossed his arms and stroked his jaw in mock concentration. "Not only do I have surveillance footage of every second of you choking me on my desk, but I have witnesses. I have a crowd of witnesses here tonight who saw you attack me, and I have a slew of family members who play golf, drink, and barbeque with the highest criminal judges in Manhattan's court system. How fucking lucky am I? Now, you two think very carefully about your decision. We can make this somewhat easy or really fucking hard." Without another threatening reminder spoken, Dillon spun in the direction of the bathrooms.

Squeezing her eyes closed, Emily released a shaky breath and rested her elbows on the table. She caressed her temples in an effort to combat a pulsating headache, feeling as if it was splitting her skull open. Tension jittered through every muscle in her body. "We have to let him, Gavin. I'll go to the district attorney on Monday and make whatever changes I have to make to the order of protection."

"No fucking way. My father's a lawyer. We're not agreeing to anything this asshole wants until I talk to him."

Emily lifted her head, her gaze tracing Gavin's face. He looked as exhausted as she felt. Her voice came out quiet but sharp. "I'm not waiting. I'm not taking a chance you'll get thrown in jail. You might be this baby's father, and I need you in its life. In my life. Please? We're both shot from this. I can't deal with any more."

"Jesus Christ, Emily," Gavin whispered, turning to face her. "He wants to be in the goddamned delivery room. Do you know what that'll do to me? It'll put me in my grave. Think about what you're saying. It's bad enough I'm forced to reason with what he did to you, but you want me to share the birth of a child that could be mine *with him*?"

"You don't think that's going to kill me too?" she choked out, trying to keep her voice down as she stared into his eyes. "My heart's stopping just thinking about it, but the alternative is you not being there at all. How would I even make it through the delivery without you? Forget about just the delivery. You could be in jail for years." Tears streaming down her face, she caressed his hair. "You'd miss holding this baby within a few minutes of it coming into this sick and beautiful world. You wouldn't hear its first cry or first word. You wouldn't see first smiles or steps. You'd miss birthdays, recitals, and the first day of school. I need you to think about what you're saying. But more than anything, I need you to think about every first you'll never get back."

Completely. Fucking. Torn.

Gavin's heart split at the seams; he swore he heard it ripping open. He couldn't deny the truth in Emily's words. He knew missing any one of those things could put him in his grave. Every single one of those reasons owned a little piece of something that added up to everything he was looking forward to. Everything he existed for. On the other hand, his gut wretched at the thought of sharing any of those moments with Dillon. The whole situation was poisonous on its own, but now, Dillon would douse it with the last bit of arsenic. In those seconds, as Gavin watched Dillon emerge from the bathroom, something Gavin's father had said to him years earlier flittered through his mind.

"Son, sometimes being a man means you have to know when to drop the heavy sword you're holding during a battle. If the reason you're fighting for is already wounded, you need to count your losses and put a stop to senseless pain. While your head may hang low in defeat, the outcome will end in your favor. Honor isn't found in victory. It's found within the wounded reason that needed you from the start."

Dillon was the battle…

Emily was already wounded…

And here and now, she needed him to concede defeat. He only prayed the outcome would indeed end in his favor. Gavin leaned into Emily, his lips a whisper away from hers. Closing his eyes, he inhaled the vanilla scent of her skin. "I need you to trust me right now, Emily. With everything you have in you, I need you to trust I would never do wrong by you or this baby. Can you do that for me?"

"Yes," she quietly cried, her breath warm against his face.

"Good. I need you to play along with me starting right now. Get up."

Emily nodded, her gaze ripping from Gavin's when Dillon took a seat. She stood, and Gavin slipped from the booth, reaching for her hand.

He looked at Dillon, who appeared confused. Placing his palm on the table, Gavin hunched over, his eyes narrowed. "You think you've won, but you haven't, Dillon. Not only have you tried to insult my intelligence by assuming I'd cave to your psychotic requests before seeking legal counsel, you've insulted the woman I love. That *really* pissed… me… off. You think I'm the type of man who would allow you in the delivery room while you get off on seeing Emily in pain? Wrong again, asshole. I'd rather die in prison than watch you enjoy any more happiness from her pain."

Letting go of Emily's hand, Gavin leaned in closer. Dillon slid away, his back flush against the wall. "While you were draining your snake, I called my family. They're prepared to take care of Emily and the baby for as long as I'm away. And let me remind you my father's a lawyer. He also spends weekends playing golf, drinking, and barbequing with some of Manhattan's highest criminal judges. But that's not even the best I have for you, Dillon. In all the confusion and mayhem over the last thirty minutes, my head became... twisted. When that happens, I sometimes forget things. It just occurred to me I know some information about you that can send your whole world spinning to the fucking ground as well."

At this, Dillon lifted a curious brow, his eyes as narrowed as Gavin's.

"Ah yes, my *friend*," Gavin continued. A slow *"I've got you now motherfucker"* smirk slid across his mouth. "I know about your big ticket. You're churning out your transaction-based accounts in order to make more money on the buy and sell side with your clients. Your return on assets is higher than some of the most powerful drug lords in Columbia. No wonder you don't need my cash flow any longer. I wonder where you're harboring all that money. You don't live like you're on top of the world, so I'm sure it's buried somewhere. When one partakes in illegal doings, it's safe to assume they need to appear... frugal in their spending."

"Fuck you," Dillon hissed. "I only make money for my clients."

"Right," Gavin drawled. "Will that be your defense when the Security Exchange Commission starts ripping into your files? The investigation's a phone call away." Gavin slid into the booth right next to Dillon. If it was possible, Dillon leaned farther against the wainscoting. Gavin chuckled at Dillon's attempt to all but camouflage himself alongside a signed photo of Magic Johnson. "Emily," Gavin said calmly, staring into Dillon's eyes. "Go ask the hostess for a piece of paper and pen for me, sweets."

"Okay," Emily answered, turning to do as he said.

Nostrils flaring and breathing picking up, Dillon cleared his throat. "What the fuck are you doing?"

Gavin popped a smirk, resting his chin in his palm as he continued to stare at Dillon. "I'm getting rid of poison. We're about to come to a… truce, Dillon. A halfway mark. You're going to sign, in your finest penmanship, a piece of paper saying you're no longer going to fuck with me or Emily. I'm no fool. I know you can petition the courts to try to gain access to the doctors' visits and delivery. I'm willing to be a nice guy and allow you to the doctors' visits because I'll be there and I'm more than sure you'll be on your best behavior in front of *my* girlfriend. That's where I draw the line.

"You will *not* be in the delivery room while she gives birth. You have no right. That's reserved for her and me, no matter whose child this is. You're also not dragging me to court because I beat your ass when you deserved nothing less than a slow death. Try to challenge me by not signing, and I'm on the phone first thing in the morning with my lawyer, who's a pitbull who'll rip you to shreds in court, and the SEC." Gavin paused, his smirk widening. "Looks like you and I might be doing a bid upstate together, Dillon. And orange would most definitely look better on me than you."

Before Dillon had a chance to mutter a word, Emily returned with a blank piece of paper and pen. She handed them to Gavin, and he started writing down everything necessary to cover his ass. Once finished, he slid the paper and pen to Dillon. Gavin's dimple deepened with his beaming smile. "Your John Hancock makes this relatively easy for us all. No Hancock, and my phone call tomorrow makes it quite difficult. Wouldn't you agree?" Gavin could recall two times in his life when he wanted to stop time dead in its tracks. Hold the minute hand down, preventing it from ticking by another second. The most important was the first time he saw Emily. Next was right now, staring at the man he loathed more than words could define. Gavin observed Dillon's eyes drooping in this battles defeat. His shoulders slumped, and his face held not a hint of victory. After what appeared to be a moment's hesitation, Gavin watched Dillon sign the paper. Rising from his seat, Gavin swiped the paper from the table. For the second time tonight, without another threatening reminder spoken, Dillon surged to his feet, exiting the dinner like a flaming bat out of hell.

Eyes like two confused saucers, Emily looked at Gavin. "What just happened?"

Gavin twined his fingers through hers, leading them through the diner. "I just saved us from arsenic with an insurance policy."

Gripping Gavin's hand tighter, she shook her head. "I don't understand. What was all of that Security Exchange stuff? How did you know he did something wrong?"

"I didn't. It was a guess," Gavin said, reaching for the door.

"A guess," Emily repeated, the exasperation in her voice heavy.

As they stepped into the cold air, Gavin pulled her into his arms. "Well, it wasn't a complete guess."

She tilted her head. "Can I get some elaboration, please?"

Gavin chuckled. "Ah. Let me think." He dipped his head, resting his lips on her hair as he spoke. "Over the summer, Trevor came to my house and we indulged in a wicked game of Texas hold'em. I have to add, I took him down." Gavin heard Emily sigh, and he smiled. "He got pretty fucking trashed and started talking about some illegal dealings with annuities Dillon said he was thinking about getting involved with. I was pretty tanked, so I didn't think too much about it. I did start watching the funds Blake Industries had tied up with him more closely though. I never found anything wrong with our accounts, so I allowed him to keep making me money.

"What did I just do in there? One: I rolled the dice that even though Trevor had a good bit of Jagermeister running through his system, he wasn't making the shit up. Two: I banked on your ex following up with his plan. I think we got lucky."

"I think we did too," Emily said, looking at him. "Why didn't you bring that up earlier?"

"I honestly didn't remember what Trevor said until I was halfway through my little speech. I hoped my father being a lawyer would get the asshole to back down without me resorting to murdering him at the table."

"You'd murder for me?" she asked softly.

"There's not a thing I wouldn't do for you, Emily."

She draped her arms around his neck and pushed up on her tiptoes to kiss him. The temperature might've been below freezing, but Emily felt warm through and through as Gavin's mouth coated hers like a glaze of honey. His heat surrounded her like a heavy down comforter. Slowly pulling away, she bit her lip. "How do we know he won't go to the cops even though he signed that paper?"

Gavin reached for her hand and led her toward his car. Opening the door, he gestured for her to get in, but she didn't. She stared at him, her nervous eyes waiting on an answer. He lifted his hand to her cold cheek and shook his head. "I don't want you worrying about what he's going to do."

Asking that of her was like asking her not to love him, like asking her not to breathe. She was scared to death Dillon would find a way to work holes through whatever agreement he and Gavin came to. Right about the same time her heart jumped into her throat at the thought of Gavin being sent to jail, so did something else. However, this jump was in her stomach. A little flip-flop that almost made her bust out in laughter. Emily quickly placed her hand on her slightly protruding belly, and her lips turned up as another burst of butterfly wings fluttered.

"Oh my, God, Gavin," she breathed, reaching for his hand. She slipped it under hers. "The baby's moving. It's moving."

Gavin swallowed, his eyes locked on the bright smile kissing Emily's lips. His hand shook, but not from the cold. He'd suddenly become scared, yet a surge of excitement rushed through his blood.

"Can you feel it?" she asked, her hand pressing harder against his. She giggled, leaning back against his car. "Can you?"

Gavin shook his head. "No," he whispered, finding himself fully consumed by the undeniable happiness filling Emily's expression. God, she looked more beautiful than ever. His heart pounded with a burst of adoration, and his fingers tingled to feel what she was. Gavin realized the decision he made tonight was the right one. Dillon had wanted to bottle up the contentment that would come from watching him and Emily squirm, but in that moment, Gavin wanted to bottle up the feeling he was experiencing watching Emily.

He also added a third moment in his life he wished he could stop time dead in its tracks.

CHAPTER FOURTEEN

Just Take It

`

"Did I hear you correctly?" Olivia's brown eyes shone wide like pennies. Hand in midair, holding a bundle of French fries, she cocked her head to the side. "He's going to be at each doctor visit with you guys?"

Emily swallowed down a bite of her burger. After taking a sip from her bottle of water, she nodded. "Yes, you heard correctly. Why do you seem so shocked? Besides, you still think he should've known all along."

Olivia let out a deep, heavy sigh and stuffed the fries into her mouth. "Yeah. I think he should've known," she said, chewing. "But I never said I think Dilly the small Willy should be allowed at your doctors' visits. And you know why I said that, so please, let's not go there again. I love you too much, friend."

Emily rolled her eyes.

Fallon stabbed her fork into a piece of iceberg lettuce drowning in ranch dressing. "At least Gavin got him to back off the delivery room." She swiped her tongue over her lip ring. "Everyone wins. No one goes to jail. No battles in court."

"True," Olivia chirped, sucking down the remains of a vanilla shake. "But it would've been cool to see Gavin gain some street creds."

"Street creds?" Emily asked.

Olivia nodded. "The slammer. Joint. The clink. Crowbar hotel. The big house. Any amount of time in jail gains you street credit."

Emily jerked her confused head back. "Liv, why would it be cool to see him gain street credits?"

Clearly trying to contain a grin, Olivia drew up a perfectly plucked brow. "Well, he already has a delectable tattoo. Adding jail time to his background can only make him hotter. I'm telling you, Em, after he got home, you'd appreciate the spectacular sex you'd get from that boy. Jail turns them into fiends."

"Like they're already not two sex fiends. To top it off, I remember reading that women turn into a ball of walking hormones while preggos." Fallon nodded knowingly at Emily, her mouth puckered into a smile. "I bet you're keeping him busy in that department."

Ouch. Sore topic. To avoid eye contact with Fallon and Olivia, Emily plucked a fry from her plate and glanced around the café. Her gaze landed on a couple buckling a toddler into a highchair. Appearing frustrated by his confinement, the hyper, little blond-haired boy squeaked his displeasure and kicked the table. A chuckle from the father, a stern finger wagging from the mother, and a juice box later, the child fell into a quiet state of bliss.

Emily sighed, wiped her mouth, and reached for her purse. "Are we ready to go?"

Olivia squinted at Emily, her forehead pinched. Emily prepared for the smart-allecky statement she was sure was coming. "Holy shit, Em. You're withholding sex from him, aren't you?"

Yep. There it was. Cue eye roll and another sigh. "No, Liv. I'm not withholding sex from *him*. He's withholding it from *me*." Annoyed, Emily flagged down the bouncy teenage waitress.

With a smile, the girl approached, her brown hair secured into pigtails. "Can I get anything else for you, gals?"

"No. We'd like our check please," Emily replied, pulling her wallet from her purse as she stood.

"Actually, I'd like to order your double fudge chocolate sundae," Olivia piped up, staring at Emily. "Extra fudge."

The waitress scribbled down the order. "Be right back."

"Aww hell no, Em," Olivia clipped, patting the chair. "You can't just drop a bomb like that without divulging what's *not* happening in your bed." Olivia looked at Fallon for back up. "Am I right, or what?"

Fallon nodded, patting the chair too. "Completely. Sit and spill, Country."

"You two suck," Emily whispered as she reclaimed her seat. "What?"

"What?" Olivia parroted, blinking in surprise. "Like Fallon said... Spill."

"I've already spilled. He hasn't had sex with me since we went for my first sonogram." Looking away, she shrugged, her chest expanding on a deep, sexually frustrated breath. "He's afraid he's going to hurt me or the baby."

"What, does he have a sword for a penis?" Fallon asked. "It's the end of February, and you two haven't had sex since the beginning of January?"

Chin lifted, Olivia crossed her arms, accentuating the cleavage spilling out of her hot pink cashmere sweater. "For real? Are you being serious?"

Emily puffed out a sigh. "No, I'm lying. I felt like making up some ridiculous story today." She loosened her hair from its bun. The dark, wavy curls spilled down her back. "Yes, I'm serious. He's... nervous."

"He's being an asshole," Olivia vehemently noted, accepting her sundae from the bouncy teenager.

"I agree." Fallon dug her spoon into Olivia's dessert. "Something's up. Do you think he's cheating? I mean, I've read that some dudes get freakish about doing the deed when their girl is preggos. Maybe he's hitting it elsewhere."

Emily's eyes went wide.

Olivia shot Fallon a look. "That's twice you've mentioned reading shit on pregnancy. You and my brother better not have any ideas flying through your heads."

"I like to stay informed," Fallon answered, going in for another scoop of ice-cream.

"And I'd like to answer your question," Emily said, insistence heavy in her tone. "No, I don't think he's cheating." Well, the thought hadn't crossed Emily's mind until now. Damn Fallon. Emily shook the idea from her head as quickly as it entered. "He wants to talk to the doctor at my next appointment and get all the facts."

Fallon sucked on her spoon, her brow raised in speculation. "Are you trying to tell me Gavin Blake—money mogul, pretty smart cat—hasn't sought out information on the internet about this?"

"He doesn't trust the internet," Emily answered with a sigh. She picked up her spoon and started digging into what was left of the sundae. "He said there's too much conflicting information and he'd rather talk to the doctor personally."

Fallon shrugged. "I ain't buying it. Either he's turned off, or he's dropping his seed somewhere else." Emily's jaw dropped open. Fallon belted out a laugh. "I'm kidding, Country. Kind of. But on the real, keep your eyes open. It just seems… odd. A man as smart as he is can't just become dumb. And if he was interested, why is he waiting? Why not drop by your doctor's office and ask?"

Emily snapped her mouth shut and pondered Fallon's statement. She hadn't really thought of why Gavin hadn't attempted to find out on his own. Her stomach wasn't a protruding balloon yet, but considering she was nearing sixteen weeks, it definitely wasn't flat anymore. She didn't think he was cheating, and she felt self-conscious about her less than flattering physique, so Emily went with the assumption he was turned off by what she was slowly turning in to.

Olivia frowned at Fallon. "Are you trying to upset her?"

"No, I'm not trying to upset her." Fallon wiped her mouth and tossed the crumpled up napkin onto the table. "You just never know. That's all."

Olivia shook her head and rolled her eyes. "Don't listen to her, Emily. Gavin would never, not even on his worst day, cheat on you. Now, I think you need to smarten his ass up. Maybe grab some pamphlets from your doctor's office and educate the man on the specifics of indulging in a little one on one while preggos. As long as nothing needs to be plugged in while engaging in these acts, I'm sure all will be well. Don't need anyone getting electrocuted trying to get some ass."

Emily rose from her seat to flag down the waitress again. After handing the girl her credit card, she sighed. "Okay, you two. I don't want to talk about this anymore. He's going to talk to my doctor at my next appointment. Conversation over."

Both women nodded, and with that, the subject was closed. After signing the bill, they all started for the exit.

Fallon swung on her coat and gave Emily a hug. "I have to go get ready for work. I love you, toots. Don't mind me. I'm just PMSing right now. I'm sure everything's going to be fine." Emily gave her a small smile and helped Fallon wrap her scarf around her neck. "Stop by the restaurant soon. Antonio misses you. Shit, we all miss you."

Emily nodded, missing everyone too. She'd given her notice a few weeks earlier, deciding that working part time as a teacher for a class of first graders was more than enough for the time being. "I will."

After bidding Fallon goodbye, Emily and Olivia slipped into a taxi and started out for a day of maternity clothes shopping. Again, her stomach wasn't quite the bursting balloon it would be in a few months, but her expanding shape definitely required some new attire. Twenty minutes later, after what Emily considered one of the scariest rides through the city ever, courtesy of an overly hotheaded driver, they reached Rosie Pope, a high end maternity boutique on Madison Avenue.

Olivia slammed the taxi door closed. "Psycho!" Olivia flicked her middle finger at the cabbie screeching away into midday traffic. "Christ on a cracker. I swear, the city needs to give these dudes some tranquilizers before they go on shift." After securing her thick blonde hair into a messy bun, she sighed and held open the door for Emily. "Why the hell didn't you bring your car? You have a brand new, slamming vehicle Gavin bought you, and you barely drive it."

"You barely drive yours." Emily scanned the posh boutique, impressed by their selection. "You've been in Manhattan a lot longer than I have. You see how scary it is out there. It's not only the cab drivers; everyone drives like a nut here."

"Right. I've turned somewhat Manhattan-ized cabbing it or taking the subway. But I could reach orgasm by merely sitting in your car. I'd have no qualms about driving it. That machine was meant for speed and sex. It's hot on wheels."

Emily signed, her mind jolted back to a glorious freeway in California. It was indeed made for… fun.

Olivia pulled a red tunic sweater from a rack and plastered it against Emily's chest. Cocking her head from side to side, she studied it a moment. She wrinkled her nose in distaste and hung it back up. "Not your color. Oh, and can I say I'm not thrilled about you deciding not to have a baby shower."

"Liv, there's no way I'm having one. The situation doesn't merit it. Stop bringing it up." Emily swiped three pairs of jeans ranging from size eight to twelve from a neatly folded stack. Staring at the astronomical price tag, she almost put them down. On his way to work this morning, Gavin had left his credit card and a note on the counter, telling her he wanted her to purchase some clothing from this particular boutique. Considering he'd spent a cool $30,000 on stunning, intricate, hand-carved, mahogany nursery furniture flown in from Italy, she wasn't sure why she was shocked. "Other than clothing and a few odds and ends, we already have everything for the baby. We don't need a shower."

"I know you guys don't *need* one, but it's a rite of passage." Following Emily to the dressing room, Olivia plucked a few tops from racks along the way. "As your best friend, what fun is my life if I don't get to see you wearing that stupid bow hat?"

Emily giggled and grabbed the tops from Olivia. "Those hats are hideous." She rolled the curtain open and slipped into the dressing room. "You're evil enough to want to see me in one of those."

"No doubt I'm evil." Olivia pulled lipstick from her purse, applying the deep red to her puckered lips as she stared into a compact mirror. "Come on, Em, I'm being serious. Let me set something up for you. If not, I'm calling the Maury Povich and Jerry Springer shows to make sure you, Gavin, and Dark Lord of Dickheads get your fifteen minutes of fame on live television."

Emily hooted out a laugh. "I can't say I don't appreciate your names for Dillon now." She whipped open the curtain and stepped out of the dressing room wearing a pair of dark maternity jeans and black V-neck top that hung slightly off her shoulders. "But I *will* kill you if you call either of those…" Emily's voice trailed off, completely sickened when she caught her reflection in the mirror.

She'd often admired the beauty of a woman's body carrying a child. The way their flesh expanded, creating a temple for a growing, unborn life, awed her. But as she stared at her reflection, Emily couldn't find any trace of beauty. She brought her hands to her stomach and smoothed them over her widened hips. The fact that she hadn't reached the halfway point of her pregnancy only made her realize she was half the size she'd be once she gave birth.

Through the reflection, Emily watched Olivia come up behind her. "I look horrible," Emily whispered, totally convinced that was the reason Gavin was withholding sex. "I'm going to look like the Pillsbury Doughboy by the time I give birth."

Olivia placed her hand on Emily's shoulder. "You look beautiful, friend. And if the Pillsbury Doughboy looked as good as you will, he'd bake a tray of cookies in celebration."

A small smile touched Emily's mouth. "You know that wasn't funny, right?"

Olivia shrugged. "Eh. I usually hit them better than that. Give me some credit. The Doughboy's hard to work with."

Emily's smile faded as she stared at herself. Her mind took her back to a conversation she and her mother had a few months before finding out she was sick. Emily was home on break from school, and they were eating breakfast together. It was as if her mother sensed something bad was looming. She started talking about her relationship with Emily's grandmother, who'd passed away a few months before. Emily felt a pang in her heart as she listened to her mom speak of memories with her mother. Some light laughter and many tears later, she looked at Emily, her eyes distant. She told Emily if there ever came a time she wasn't there, to just always know she was. A mother's intuition she may not be around much longer.

She hadn't understood the significance that conversation on a warm June morning, in the kitchen of a home wrapped in ill and sweet memories, would hold almost a year later. Emily couldn't help but fear the impact of it all. She was about to have her first child, and though her mother might be watching, she wouldn't be there in the flesh. The gatekeeper to all of her childhood memories, whether good or evil, wouldn't see Emily's baby's eyes. She'd never shower Emily's child in the love only a grandmother could. She wouldn't be there to hold Emily's hand and walk her through the steps of what it took to be a mother. As a tear fell from her eye, Emily pushed her hands through her hair. She took another look in the mirror at the mother she was about to become.

Her road, though streaked with layers of happiness, was also paved with longing only her mother could replace.

Heavy sleet pelting the bedroom window like thousands of drumming fingers roused Emily from a deep sleep. She squinted her eyes open only to find Gavin scratching his bare stomach, his tongue moistening his beautifully etched mouth as he slept peacefully. She tried desperately to catch her missing breath. A gnawing ache grew between her legs, her body reacting to him in the only way it ever knew how. It needed him.

She needed him. Needed to touch, taste, and feel him. In her. Over her. Below her. No matter what, she wanted him and couldn't wait any longer. The air, lightly perfumed with his cologne, dug into all her senses. Her core tightened in response to his soft breathing, the low, humming cadence increasing her want. She tried in vain to stop, but when he turned, the comforter slipped from his body, exposing his glorious hip bone. She was done for. Hunger exploded in her belly.

She bit her lip, sat up, and stripped the black silk camisole from her body. Her black lace panties followed. Like a moth impossibly drawn to a flame, and with careful fingers, she slid the comforter away from his naked flesh. He stirred lightly, a deep groan rumbling in his chest, but he didn't wake. Emily swallowed, her craving for every inch of his iron clad golden skin filling her with desperation close to that of a madwoman. Her pulse, along with her breath, quickened as she slithered down the bed.

On her knees in front of his feet, she deftly spread his legs and swooped in for the kill. Curling her fingers around his semi-hard cock, she took him greedily into her mouth. She heard him moan, and his muscled body straining upward only fueled her desire. Sucking harder, she tried to satisfy her thirst for him as she licked each heavily veined inch from root to tip. God, he tasted amazing. The saltiness of his liquid silk combined with the flavor of his skin had her head bobbing reverently, her hand moving up and down each time she pulled him in.

Then he awoke.

He hauled his body against the headboard, but that didn't stop Emily. She followed without letting him go. "Emily," he breathed, his voice ragged. "What the hell are you doing?"

Eyes dilated in lust, she looked up as she slowly licked and sucked over the crest of his now rock-hard cock. "What does it look like I'm doing, Mr. Blake?" She surged down again, feeling him hit the back of her throat. Another deep, delicious groan ripped from his chest as he gripped her hair, his fingers twined tight against her skull. It made her high. Dizzy. She slid her mouth down his pulsing erection, her nails digging into his hips. She could feel the strain in his muscles, felt his body go taut and rigid, and she loved every second of it. Oh, yes, she had him now. He pushed deeper through her lips, his fingers clenching her hair harder as he guided her up and down, down and up, allowing her to take him to the hilt.

Every last one of Gavin's senses was devoured by her hungry mouth. "Fuck," he bit out. "You love the way I taste. Don't you?"

Yes. She. Did.

The sharp taste he put out mingled with a touch of sweetness had her drugged. "Mmm," she moaned, her tongue sliding over a thick bead of semen. She ran a hand over his bare stomach, her fingernails leaving deep red marks, as she continued to circle his cock with her tongue. An intoxicating whimper crawled up her throat when he pinched one of her hardened nipples, rolling it slowly between his thumb and forefinger as he pushed into her mouth again. With one hand still buried in her hair, he started to pump faster.

Hell, Gavin was about to explode. A hard swallow rippled over his Adam's apple as Emily sucked him off harder. He grabbed her shoulders, yanking her onto his chest. In a split second, he had her on her back pinned beneath him.

Breathless, Emily bucked her hips up, her raging need to have him inside her driving her as close to insane as one could get. She gripped his shoulders, her pussy clenching, burning with arousal. He hovered above her, propped on his elbows. Deep, ragged breaths filled his chest as he looked down at her as if he was debating what to do.

Hell. No.

"You're going to fuck me right now, and I'm going to love every second of it, Gavin. You're going to fuck me, and you're not going to hurt the baby. But I can tell you, if you don't fuck me right now, *I'm* going to hurt *you*."

Damn her. She just made him harder. The woman beneath him just managed to mind-fuck him on multiple levels. Want for her surged though his veins unlike ever before, yet she managed to make him reevaluate the simple act of being alive. Though stunned by her bluntness, he couldn't help the grin sneaking across his mouth. "You want it that bad, huh?"

"Yes," she moaned, her breathing labored.

"How bad?" He grazed his jaw against the buttery smooth swell of her breast. God, he missed feeling them. Missed feeling her. He circled his tongue around the tight nub of her nipple. "I want you, in great detail, to describe how bad you really want it."

Emily pulled in a shaky breath. "It's not enough you don't find me attractive anymore? Now you want me to describe how badly I want you?" She looked away, her voice trailing. "Are you trying to torture me, Gavin?"

Gavin's eyes went wide, his heart crushing in his chest. Sure, he knew she'd become frustrated over the last several weeks, but he never thought it would affect her this deeply. He knew he needed to fix it, fix her. "Look at me, baby," he whispered. Emily flicked her teary gaze back to his, and Gavin's heart fell further. Reaching for her thigh, he slowly hooked it around his waist as he brought his lips to her jaw. He grazed it lightly and the shuddered breath Emily released melted him. "I thought this body was beautiful before you were pregnant," he said, the words low against her trembling lips. "But now it's exquisite. A vision of... perfection."

He gently reached for her other thigh, repeating the process of bringing it up over his waist. He could feel her legs begin to shake in anticipation. Opened wide for him, he stared at her for a beat before lowering himself inside her. Hot, slick, and clenching around him with maddening fury, her pussy felt amazing. He contained his groan, basking in the sound of her soft gasp. A fleeting rush of fear shot through him as he slowly pushed deeper, but he kicked it back to where it belonged. Sinking his lips to hers, Gavin licked through her mouth, savoring the taste of her sugar coated sweetness. Cradling the back of her head with one hand, he cupped the gracious curve of her hip with the other. "Do you need me to tell you how badly I've craved you?" He groaned as he lapped, swirled, and laved his tongue against the delicate flesh of her neck. "I've needed you more than my next heart beat."

Undulating currents of rapture coursed through Emily's limbs as she writhed beneath him. His voice, the timbre of a man apologizing, rumbled low in her ear. His biceps clenched and flexed with each slow, calculated thrust. She was dissolving, thawing under his heat. Dragging her nails along his muscular back, her breath caught in her chest, lodged between his warm lips and seductive words. His desire for her was evident in every soft touch and stroke of his worshipping tongue. Back bowing, she bucked her hips faster, but Gavin completely stilled.

"Gavin, don't stop," she begged, her thighs clenching with vigor around his waist. "Please."

"No," he said in a strangled whisper. He stroked the dampened hair from her face and rolled his tongue over hers, talking between each heated breath. "I'm not fucking you tonight, Emily Cooper. Kill me if you want, but I'm going to slowly possess you until you can't take it anymore. My fingers are going to trace every beautiful hidden line on your body. My lips are going to caress, nourish, and feed every unsated inch of you. Is that okay?"

"Yes," she moaned.

He claimed her mouth, swallowing each moan that followed as he pushed into the soft depths of her wet, luscious warmth over and over. He filled her with the purest, sweetest, most beautiful love she'd ever experienced. His slow, agonizing pulses and deep, passionate kisses trumped anything she'd ever felt, tasted, or known. Feeding her body what it needed, Gavin wiped her mind clear of ever thinking he didn't want her.

He tossed away every insecurity…

Unraveled every doubt…

And carried her away in the eddying winds of his undeniable, unquestionable love…

CHAPTER FIFTEEN

Faults

Emily nervously bit her lip and swiped her fingers through a pregnancy magazine. Trying to ignore Dillon staring at her intently from across the doctor's office, she crossed her legs and glanced at her watch. A quarter past four. Gavin was fifteen minutes late. Anxiously, she pulled her phone from her purse, hoping there was at least a message from him. Nothing. Not a text or a missed call. She tossed it onto her lap, wondering where he was.

"Kind of sick your *loving* boyfriend's not here yet." Dillon chuckled. "Wonder if he'll be late during the delivery? Call me if you need a backup."

Ignoring him, Emily turned the page and scanned an ad claiming beet juice helped prevent neural tube defects in a developing fetus. Mental note made, she flicked her eyes to her watch again. She was starting to worry. It wasn't like Gavin not to call if he was running late. A jolt of fear shocked her system, but as soon as it did, Blondie from her previous appointment called Emily's name. After placing the magazine down, Emily ran her fingers over her cell, sending Gavin a text. She shoved her phone into her purse, stood, and started for the door to the back offices. She noticed Dillon also rose to his feet, following right behind her. She whipped around, a chill running up her spine at his proximity. "What are you doing?"

He narrowed his eyes. "What does it look like I'm doing? I'm going to see if we're having a boy or a girl."

Emily blinked, cringing at his words. "You're not going into the office with me until Gavin gets here."

With a jeering smile, Dillon pulled a piece of paper from his back pocket. He handed it to Emily. "That's a copy of the amended order of protection *you* took care of. Nothing in there says I have to wait until pretty boy gets here." He swiped it from Emily. "Looks like you may have forgotten to add a little something to it." He shoved it back into his pocket and held open the door. "Ladies first."

Emily closed her eyes with regret. Head caught in a train wreck, she'd never thought about adding that particular stipulation to the order. Gavin had been on pins and needles for several weeks, and he must have been too stressed to notice her error. On a sigh and a prayer Gavin would be there soon, she followed the receptionist into an empty office.

Blondie's displeasure with Emily was evident as she set up the necessary items for the visit. Once Emily and Gavin had found out the insurance billing error was her fault, Gavin called the office to vehemently voice his displeasure. After nearly getting his lawyers involved to file a lawsuit, Gavin wanted Emily to change offices, but since the doctor already knew their awkward situation, Emily felt it best to just leave it alone. She was more than satisfied that Blondie was reprimanded.

"You know the drill. Pants down below your pubic bone." Blondie flipped on the sonogram machine, clicked off the lights, and moved toward the door. "Doctor Richards is finishing up with another patient.

He'll be right in. In the meantime, you can't use the restroom." With that, she and her attitude walked out.

Emily sat on the edge of the table with her back to Dillon. Hands shaking, she slightly lowered the soft, stretchy cotton covering her belly. She glanced at the door, willing Gavin to open it. In the quiet room, Dillon's breathing sounded like a tornado whirling through her ears. Deciding to wait for either the doctor or Gavin, she stilled her movements.

"You let me fuck you for over a year. Now's not the time to start getting embarrassed." Emily heard the smile in Dillon's words, felt the venom lacing them. "Don't worry. There's no way what you look like right now could *ever* turn me on."

"You're an asshole," she mumbled, her heart pounding.

He chuckled. "And you're the whore who landed us all in this position. What's worse, Emily? A whore who fucks her boyfriend's friend or an asshole who's making her pay for it?"

As his sickening statement crushed through her head, the door swung open. Gavin and the doctor entered from the hall. Crossing the room rapidly, Gavin was at her side in a second, his face twisted in worry. "I'm sorry," he whispered as Emily stood and wrapped her arms around his neck.

"What happened?" she asked. She breathed in his scent, automatically calmed by his presence. She looked into his eyes, trying to keep tears from her own. "I sent you a text. You never called back."

"I left my phone at the office and didn't realize it until I was halfway through the city. I got caught in traffic. It was a mess." He looked at Emily's face, picking up that she was worried about more than his absence. Something else was there. His stomach surged, twisting with anger. He flicked his eyes to Dillon, then back to Emily. "Is everything all right?"

Emily felt him freeze as though he'd suddenly been encased in ice. She swallowed, a knot swelling in her throat. She nodded, not wanting to tell him what'd happened. Gavin was already on edge. If he thought Dillon gave her even the tiniest of dirty looks, without a doubt, there would be bloodshed in that office.

"Nothing happened?" he asked more intently, staring between her and Dillon. From the chair across the room, Dillon peered at them.

She nodded again and reached up to kiss him. Gavin sighed as her lips met his. He tried to fight off the gnawing feeling she was hiding something. A heartbeat later, he helped her onto the table, his hand smoothing over her belly as she exposed her glorious flesh. She looked at him and smiled. Warming immediately, Gavin pulled up a chair and sat next to her. As he held Emily's hand, Gavin's eyes locked on Dillon. He was starting to think the idea of allowing him to be present was something he'd regret forever. Fuck. This child could be his, and that asshole had no right to be here during something so joyous.

"So how've you been feeling, Miss Cooper?" the doctor asked, flipping through her chart. He placed the clipboard on his desk and moved toward the sink. "I see you're still having some nausea?"

"I am. But it's down to the evenings only now."

"Try a hot cup of chamomile or ginger tea," he said, washing his hands. After drying them, he padded across the room, slipped on a pair of gloves, and reached for the gel. "My wife swore on Saltine crackers when she was pregnant with all three of our boys."

"Three boys?" Dillon leaned forward, his forearms on his knees. His mouth screwed into the faintest smirk. "I'm hoping we're also having a boy."

Tension from every direction dropped in the room like an atom bomb. Feeling Gavin's hand tighten around hers, Emily whipped her head in his direction. He stared at Dillon with his mouth pressed into a rigid line, and her breath caught at the sight of Gavin's eyes glowing like burning embers. Emily squeezed his hand, attempting to bring his attention back to her, but it didn't work. Body bristling with noticeable rage, Gavin looked as though he was about to leap across the table.

"I love you," she whispered.

That broke his trance. Seething, Gavin dragged his eyes from Dillon's and focused on the reason he was there. He could do this. He would do this. He only hoped to God he would survive without killing Dillon.

The doctor cleared his throat. "Well, you're just shy of twenty weeks. If we get some cooperation from the little one, we'll know the sex in a few minutes."

Calming her, the unease of the moment faded as Gavin gently stroked her hair. Emily zoned out Dillon as she zoned in on the monitor. Praying the soft, humming heartbeat swirling through the air like a sweet melody half belonged to the man next to her, Emily pulled in a deep breath as the doctor pushed his handy microphone against her abdomen.

After a few blinking beats, the doctor chuckled. "Look at that." He pointed to the screen as he pressed a tad harder along the right side of Emily's stomach. "Not sure of the sex yet, but that's the baby with its fingers in its mouth."

Emily squinted, trying to make out the blob on the screen, and then it hit her. She could see exactly what he was talking about. Tiny, delicate fingers drifted in and out of a small mouth with the tide of the fluid it was floating in. Eyes watery, she turned to Gavin, his expression just as awed as she felt.

The doctor eased the microphone across Emily's stomach. "And if it'll just open those legs a little more, we'll know if you'll need pink or blue clothing." A series of whooshes, a harder press of the instrument, and a warm smile on the doctor's face later, he said, "Congratulations, Miss Cooper. You're having a boy."

Emily let out a choked gasp, tears falling down her cheeks as she smiled at Gavin. She watched him swallow, his eyes misting over as he stared at the screen. He'd played it off that as long as the baby was healthy, he didn't care if it was a boy or a girl. Of course she knew he honestly meant that, but the day she walked into the almost bare nursery and noticed a signed Yankees mitt and ball set up on the dresser, she knew her Yankees lover's heart wanted a little boy.

Gavin pulled his chair closer, his eyes landing on Emily's. He brushed his hand over her hair and looked at the doctor. "A boy? You're sure?"

"That little body part right there tells me yes." Pushing his glasses up the bridge of his nose, Dr. Richards pointed at the screen, his smile wide as he looked at Gavin. "They say not to do it, but considering I've seen thousands of those over the last thirty years, I'd say go out and buy some blue cigars in celebration." The doctor cleared his throat and glanced at Dillon. Wearing a composed but taut smile, his tone held awkwardness as he spoke. "You go ahead and do the same."

Dillon straightened his tie and stood. His bright brown eyes mimicked his fake smile. "I plan on doing so. My family's going to be stoked it's a boy."

Gavin felt every fucking hair on the back of his neck stand on end. He rose from his chair, preparing to break every single bone in Dillon's face, but Emily grabbed his arm and pulled him back to her side.

After wiping the gel from her stomach, Emily sat up and licked her lips that'd gone dry. "We're finished, correct?" Her breath slipped from her mouth shakily despite her attempted poise. "I can use the restroom now?"

The doctor nodded, and with the aid of Gavin, Emily hopped off the table. Staring into his eyes, she lifted her hand to the back of his neck and pulled him down for a kiss. "I love you, Gavin Blake," she whispered after a long moment. "Thank you for not doing what I know you could've so easily done. You continue to shock me. You also continue to make me fall further in love with you. My heart, soul, life, and body, you own it all."

God. Never did Gavin imagine such simple words could make *not* turning into a lunatic worth every second. But those simple words weren't spoken by a simple woman. They were thanks from his angel. Yeah, she had a way of making every struggle they'd endured worth it. He watched with adoration as she disappeared into the restroom.

Gavin swiped his hand through his hair. "Doc, while Emily's cleaning up, I wanted to speak with you in private regarding a few things."

"That's not a problem." The doctor shut down the sonogram machine and flipped on the lights. "We can talk in the hall."

"No way, Blake." With arrogance seeping through his pores, Dillon stepped forward, his eyes narrowed. "This baby is just as much my business as it is yours. No private bullshit."

Crossing his arms, Gavin cupped his chin. He cocked his head to the side, a slow smirk lifting his mouth. "You're correct, Dillon. My bad." *Bring it.* He was about to blow Dillon's fucking mind to pieces. Relaxing into a chair, Gavin's smirk widened. "So, Doc, you see my girlfriend's a total catch. The woman brings a whole new meaning to the word beautiful, right?"

The doctor cleared his throat, appearing somewhat confused. "Yes, Gavin, she's a very good-looking woman."

A reverent smile broke out across Gavin's face as he brought his attention to Dillon, who looked equally confused. Eyes pinned on Dillon's, Gavin lifted a single brow. "Yeah, she is. Well, given she and I started out with an extremely active, at least four times a day, wild sex life, I wanted to know if it should change now that she's pregnant. My concern lies in hurting her or the baby."

Gavin could see Dillon grit his teeth and wondered why the asshole was still in the room. Gavin figured his curiosity had him sticking around.

"Not at all," the doctor answered, depositing himself onto a swivel stool. "Sex is completely healthy and encouraged for both partners. The baby is protected deep within the womb. There's no chance of you hurting him."

At this, Gavin watched Dillon's face pale, yet the moron was essentially super-glued to the floor, his movements completely stilled. Gavin figured he'd take the grand opportunity to elaborate a little. Better yet, Gavin was about to reel him in…

"That's great to hear," Gavin continued, his eyes still locked on Dillon's. "But I have to be honest, I'm hung like a pro. Emily's said I'm the largest… *man* she's ever experienced. We enjoy making love, but usually, we really go at it. We both like it quite… *rough*. We love every position that's out there. We've even invented a few we're pretty sure no one's ever thought of. We're good like that. So, doc, what's your overall consensus on the facts I've provided? Basically what I'm asking is… can we *fuck* the way we've always fucked? Because if so, I'm taking my girlfriend home after this and giving her what she wants."

Baited. Hook. Line. And. Motherfucking. Sinker.

As the doctor went to answer, Dillon went to exit the room. Gavin chuckled, proud he'd hit his target dead on. Said target was giving him the reaction he knew he'd get. "Wait, Dillon, don't you want to hear the answer? I mean, the baby is just as much your business as it is mine. Let's not forget, no private bullshit."

The doctor may have attempted to answer Gavin's question, but Dillon didn't. Nope. His answer was the thundering door slamming behind his arrogant ass. Another chuckle, a few unanswered questions, and Emily emerging from the restroom shortly after, had Gavin feeling the doctor's appointment went better than expected.

By the time Emily and Gavin made their way back to his building and into the elevator, Emily was convinced her boyfriend had been possessed by a sex demon. Between the hungry looks during the drive home and his promises of exquisite pleasure to come, she believed he'd gone temporarily insane.

Leaning against the elevator wall, she indulged in his deep, passionate kiss as they rode up to his floor. Emily tilted her neck, allowing Gavin's soft mouth to worship her flesh. "And who do I have to thank for this sudden change in sexual wanting? I'd like to send them a gift. Do you have an address?"

Gavin answered by closing his lips over Emily's, caressing her tongue with needy little licks as his hands roamed her body. The elevator doors slid open, and with their arms wrapped around one another, Gavin walked her backward down the hall to his unit. Back pressed against his door, she let out a heated breath as he scrambled, fishing his keys from his pocket. His light stubble tickled her jaw as he opened the door. Walking her backward into the penthouse, his lips continued their assault on hers. Emily chucked her purse onto the sofa, circled her arms around

Gavin's neck, and giggled as he scooped her up. With her legs dangling over his forearm, she kissed him harder, her body throbbing from head to toe in anticipation.

"So are you going to answer me?" she breathed as he laid her on the massive California king, slipping off her heels. "Who do I owe thanks to?"

Grinning, Gavin slowly pulled her skirt down and tossed it on the floor. Blue eyes locked on hers, he bit his luscious lip, his finger tracing just below her belly button. "The only thing you need to know, Miss Cooper, is Dillon is very, and I mean *very*, aware of every single thing I'm about to do to your beautiful body."

Without another question, Emily spent the rest of the afternoon indulging in the mind blowing things Dillon apparently knew were going to happen to her.

"Is the blindfold really necessary?" Emily asked as Gavin led her down the hall. "I get it's a surprise, but your excitement is actually scaring me. Did you paint it black?"

"Have you no faith in my decorating skills?" Gavin asked with a chuckle. Opening the door to the nursery, he popped a smile as he took one last look at the finished room. He couldn't call it *his* decorating skills since a team of highly paid interior designers did all the work. Nevertheless, he was happy with the direction he'd given them over the last month since finding out the baby was a boy. "And yes, the blindfold is needed. But I'll strike up a deal with you. As my torturous punishment, I'll allow you to reuse it on me later tonight."

Emily giggled and went to rip off the blindfold, but Gavin grabbed her wrists. Lips turned down in a pout, she sighed. "You get off on being a wiseass. I swear you were placed in my world for that very reason."

"Mmm, I never thought of it like that." Gavin buried his face in the crook of her neck, his voice seductively low. "Placed on this earth to wiseass your world up."

"Gavin Christopher Blake, if you don't let me take off this blindfold, I'm going to do things to your ass no man would appreciate. Got it?"

Gavin let out a deep, throaty laugh, his eyes wide. "You're turning me on."

"Oh my God. You *seriously*—"

"I know. Have lost my mind or *seriously* have gone crazy." Gavin nibbled her neck. "Which is it, sweets?"

"Both."

"Good answer." He peeled the blindfold from her eyes. "Tell me. Did I lose my mind on this?"

The breath left Emily's lungs as her eyes swept over the nursery. True to his love of the team, Gavin had turned the once bare room into a Yankees paradise. Not quite overkill, it was tastefully done and could easily thrive well into her son's teenage years. Emily's gaze fell upon a single navy blue wall with massive white built-in shelving units. Each held an array of glass-encased signed baseballs, trading cards, and hats. She took in everything from autographed jerseys hanging on cast-iron Yankees emblem hooks, to a real digital scoreboard, to a row of Yankees metal lockers. One wall showcased a floor-to-ceiling black and white scene of the field right out of the early Yankees days. "The House Ruth Built" graced the top of the mural. She swore it was a real photo. Just beyond one of the windows—swathed in long, navy blue drapes—was a soft, brown leather chair with fluffy baseball pillows. A New York City backdrop circular rug covered a good portion of the space. To top it off, he had actual stadium seats in the room. Emily was struck speechless.

"Did I lose my mind?" Gavin whispered, his chin on Emily's shoulder. He wrapped his arms around her growing stomach, wishing he could see her face. "Or am I just crazy?"

Falling into the gravity of everything that made Gavin who he was, Emily faced him, her world spinning on an axis of love he provided. So many stolen moments and little things he'd said and done passed through her mind as she stared into his smiling blue eyes. Those thieving blue eyes that'd snatched her breath, heart, and soul the second she saw him. So many words, spoken and unspoken, echoed through her ears. This man, her best friend and lover, who didn't know if the child she was carrying was his, kept the promise he'd made not so long ago. He already loved her baby, whether or not it was his, because it was part of her. God willing, part of him. Bringing her hands to his dimpled cheeks, she stared at him a beat longer before pushing up on her tiptoes. As her lips melted against his, she wondered how she'd gotten so lucky. Why, out of every woman in the world, did this certified wiseass pick her?

Slowly breaking the kiss, she looked at him, her mind in a daze. "I don't even know how to thank you, Gavin. You've accepted me with every fragile weakness I have, loving me no less than a woman without faults. A woman without fears. Every look, touch, and kiss you've given without judgment of any kind. You've healed every exposed wound, old scar, and piece of pain I brought into this relationship without expecting anything in return. You've shown me what a racing heart feels like, shown me mere thoughts could easily cease with a single kiss. You've shown me what it is to feel truly, wholeheartedly, until the end of time *loved*. How do I thank you for all of this?"

"You do every single day," he softly answered, stroking her hair.

Emily closed her eyes. "How?" She leaned into the heat of his touch.

"Look at me, Emily." She opened her eyes, her watery gaze searching his. "Right there, doll. You said every look I've given you was without judgment. Well, every look you've given me is untouched, pure in all it is for my eyes. You look at me like you've never seen a man before. There's no way for me, as a man, to ever explain what that feels like." He reached for her hand and laid it against his heart. "You said every touch I've given was without judgment. Every time you touch me, your hands shake. You have no idea how that makes me shake. I'm not talking sexually, either. You shake everything I've ever know myself to be."

Pulling her closer, he ghosted his mouth against hers. "And every kiss? Jesus, don't even get me started on the way you kiss me. From the first kiss we shared that you stopped"—he softly bit her lip, sucking it between his teeth—"to this kiss right now, you sink me. You make love to me with every kiss. You confirm what this wiseass knew the second he laid eyes on a beautiful waitress with food splattered all over her uniform. I hate using the same lines, but your lips *were* made for mine. Which means each kiss was made for me. Each time you look at me the way you do, lay a shaky hand on my body, or your soft lips touch mine, you make me thank God for being a man. That's how you thank me every day, and that's the way I hope you continue to thank me for the rest of my life."

Once again struck speechless, Emily wrapped her arms around his neck, bringing him down for a kiss. She had a feeling she'd experience countless "struck speechless" moments with Gavin.

"Mmm. See? You just made love to me with that kiss." Gavin grinned, reaching for Emily's hand and leading her out of the nursery.

"I like that term. I make *love* to you with my kisses."

"Yes, ma'am, you do." Gavin winked and grabbed his keys from the kitchen counter. "Now you have me wanting to do nothing but stay home all day so I can continue to get some good ol' lovin'. I'm about to cancel this little outing."

Emily giggled and plucked a soft, knit cardigan from the closet. Opting for comfortable flats instead of her gorgeous Stuart Weitzman heels, she sat on the couch and glanced at Gavin while she slipped them on. His suggestion of canceling was becoming more appealing by the second. With his Yankees cap pulled down to his brows, he looked extremely edible swathed in dark blue jeans, a fitted graphic T-shirt, and a pair of Chucks. Emily bit her lip and moved toward her eye candy.

"We can't cancel," she said, tossing on her cardigan. The words came out like a pout as she accepted her purse from him. "We're meeting them at noon, and it's almost a quarter after eleven." She reached for his hand and dragged him to the door. If they didn't get out of there soon, they'd never leave. "Good ol' lovin' later, Mr. Blake." She smiled as she waited in the hall while he groaned, punching in the security code.

It was all good though. She kept him happy by "making love" to him several times on their way down in the elevator.

A slight mid-April chill bit at Emily, spreading goose bumps over her skin as she and Gavin climbed from her car into the bright sun. Either way, spring in New York was beautiful as the city awoke from a long, hard winter. Not that the city wasn't always alive and well, but the streets held a sense of renew as everything else came back to life. From store owners propping open their doors to let fresh air sweep through their buildings to the trees in every park springing with colorful buds, the center of the world roared her existence with the change of season. It was also something Emily had grown to love.

Locking hands with Gavin, Emily peered into several storefronts as they made their way down Lexington Avenue. Stopping just shy of 74th Street, her gaze fell on a form-fitting summer dress displayed on a mannequin. Hands poised on her hips, the offender wore the dress on her plastic body far better than any top paid model. Emily looked at her growing stomach and sighed.

"What's wrong?" Gavin asked, his eyes moving between her and the offender.

"That's beautiful, and I'm never going to fit into anything like it again." She continued walking toward Giggle, a posh baby boutique Colton and Melanie suggested they check out. "I'll be lucky if I'll fit into Hefty garbage bags after I give birth."

Gavin came to an abrupt stop. He cupped Emily's cheeks, a wide grin plastered across his face. "If you're wearing a Hefty garbage bag or a bikini, you'll still look *shmexy*." He popped a kiss on her forehead. "A hundred pounds or five hundred pounds, I'm still gonna love ya."

"You say that now. Let's see if you're saying the same thing when you have to special order me clothing to fit around my ass." Emily lifted an incredulous brow. "Better yet, let's see if you're saying the same thing while trying to pull the garbage bag off my extra-large, naked body."

A slow smile crept across Gavin's lips. "You know you're turning me on, right?"

Emily giggled and reached for his hand. "I'm making an appointment for you with a psychiatrist when we get home." Weaving down the crowded sidewalk, she spotted the boutique a few doors away. "It'll be good for you and your obsession. I really think you need one."

Gavin opened the door to the boutique, giving Emily a light swat on her ass as she walked in. "And I really think if you keep talking about your large or small naked body, I'm going to need a cold shower."

Emily shook her head, but before she could throw a comeback at him, she caught Teresa's gaze.

Beaming, Teresa ran toward Emily, her arms spread wide. "Emmy!" Emily knelt down and pulled her in for a hug. "Mommy, look! Emmy and Uncle Gaffin's here!"

Gavin's forehead crinkled as his sister-in-law approached. "You guys didn't tell them we were meeting you?"

"Yeah, right." Melanie rolled her eyes. "You'll learn very soon. Never. Ever tell a child something ahead of time. They would've bugged us to death while we waited for you."

Gavin gathered an equally excited Timothy in his arms. "Are your parents keeping things from you two?"

Timothy pouted, wagging an accusing finger at his father. "Yes! Daddy said he was bringing us to Mickey D's, but then he brought us here. We never knew you was comin. Will you bring us to Mickey D's, Uncle Gaffin?"

Gavin swooshed his hand though Timothy's blond hair. "Heck yeah, I'll bring you to Mickey D's. Uncle Gaffin's a sucker for girls named Molly and greasy French fries." Emily stood and smiled. "And always remember, kid, you're the one who controls mom and dad. They may be bigger, but you hold more power than you realize. They're actually afraid of you two. Your dad tells me that every day."

Timothy curled his lips over his teeth and roared like a lion in Colton's direction.

Colton shook his head. "Nice one, bro. You're the hero for the day, *and* you've exposed every parent's worst nightmare. Wait. You know what they say about payback."

Gavin lifted a brow, his smile devious. "Ah, well, consider it my payback for the many years of torment you put me through." He handed Timothy over to Colton, his laugh as devious as his smile. "Don't worry, I'll cover the Big Macs."

Colton looked at Emily, a smirk coating his mouth. "You're sure you're ready to hang out with this knucklehead for a while? He might drive you nuts."

"Who him?" Emily flicked her thumb in Gavin's direction. "Oh, he drives me nuts, but believe it or not, I'm the one with the control. He may be bigger and more powerful, but he's most definitely afraid of me. I'll have him trained up real good sooner than later."

Gavin chuckled, his eyes wide. "Oh really?"

"Yes really," she answered, sliding her arm around his back. "Don't try to act cool in front of them, Blake. You know it's true."

Melanie hooted a laugh. "I love it! I knew there was a reason I liked you, Emily. That's right. Never let these Blake boys think they've got you." She nudged her hip against Gavin's. "You're going to be domesticated so quick, you're not going to know which way is up or down."

Gavin looked at Colton, his voice deadpan. "Remind me to keep my girl away from your wife."

With a restless Timothy squirming in his arms, Colton shrugged. "You're already doomed, bro. They're having lunch with mom next weekend. Make it easy on yourself and already have the apron on when she gets home. If not, she'll start withholding really important… *physical* play time from you."

On that note, Gavin tossed his arm around Emily's neck, smiled warmly, and started rubbing her belly. "Darling, sweetheart, love of my life, I believe we have some clothes shopping to get done. Shall we?"

"I think we shall," Emily concurred with her own smile.

"Cool." Gavin nodded and looked around. "Which way is the clothing?"

Colton jerked his head to the side. "Just past the nursery décor. To the right of the stuffed animals and a few feet away from the activities center."

Gavin stood mute, staring at his brother.

"Bro, I've got two kids and a wife." Colton shrugged, his green eyes shimmering. "I'm as domesticated as they come."

Gavin grinned and grabbed Emily's hand, leading her toward whatever direction Colton just thoroughly explained. Gavin took in bursts of every pastel and primary color imaginable as they navigated the large boutique. He also took in every type of infant bath tub, bouncy seat, and diaper bag available. He glanced at Emily, who appeared overwhelmed by her surroundings. With smiling lips, he stopped moving.

"What?" Emily asked.

He brought his hand to her nape, his touch gentle. "Are you okay?"

She shook her head, tears springing in her eyes. "No, I'm not." And she wasn't. Between Gavin completing the nursery, her growing belly, and her increasing fear of becoming a mother, she was turning into a mental ball of nerves. A certified basket case. She swiped her hand across her cheeks and plucked a tiny newborn outfit from a rack. "Do you see how small this is, Gavin?"

Oh shit. Now Gavin was overwhelmed by her response. He nodded, careful not to upset her. "I do."

She sniffled. "That means the little person wearing it is going to be as small as it is. I've never held a baby. I have no idea how to feed him. He could starve. I'll have no idea why he's crying. What if he hates me?" Gavin went to speak, but she continued. Her words zipped from her mouth faster than a flash of lightning. "I won't know how to burp him. What if I drop him while giving him a bath? The state will take him away from me. What happens if I don't hear him in the middle of the night?" Pausing, she sucked in a breath and really broke down. "And those ointments. What if I don't put enough on him and he gets a rash? What if I put on too much and he gets an infection? What am I talking about? I don't even know how to change a diaper. Is he going to be laying on the changing table naked with too much or not enough ointment because his mother doesn't know how to get the diaper on him?"

Holy. Mother. Of. God.

Gavin blinked, swallowed hard, and slowly dragged his hand from her nape. He'd always known how to handle Emily. Shit, he was placed on the earth to do just that. But the woman before him was losing it. Thinking fast, he tossed his hand through his hair and took a shot at the only thing he thought might calm her. "Sit down on the floor with me."

Teary eyes wide, Emily furrowed her brows. "What? You want me to sit on the floor with you in a store?"

Gavin sat cross-legged on the maple floor and motioned her down. "Emily, we almost had sex on the hood of my car on the side of a road in Mexico. Sit."

Shocked, Emily nervously glanced at shoppers looking at Gavin as though he'd lost it. But she'd always known he was a tad bit crazy. After a few seconds, she sank to the floor, sitting cross-legged in front of him.

He twined his fingers through hers. With caring eyes and a warm smile, he softly kissed her lips. "Hey," he whispered.

A weak smile lifted her mouth. "Hey."

"My name's Gavin Blake, and I'm going to school you on babies, okay?"

Emily nodded, looking down at their hands. "You're trying to get me to stop bugging out." She brought her gaze back to his, her heart melting. "Aren't you?"

"I am, and I will. Give me five minutes. Good?"

She bit her lip, focusing on his eyes. "Okay."

Pulling her hands into his lap, Gavin sighed in relief. She was already coming down a notch. "First: Babies are easy to hold. They... trust right away. They know you're there to take care of them. The moment you see him, Emily, you won't be able to help it. Your arms will automatically know what to do. I guarantee you'll never want to put him down. You're so caring and nurturing. It'll come naturally to you." He leaned over and placed another slow kiss on her lips. "Okay?"

She nodded, trusting him.

"Two: When he cries, he's only crying for a few reasons. Either he's hungry, tired, sick, colicky, needs to be burped, needs to be changed, or wants to be held. Or in your case, you've dropped him and he's in severe pain, or you didn't know how to change him and he's been lying in a pissy, shitty diaper all day."

Emily popped a brow. "I thought you're attempting to calm me down?"

He chuckled and stroked her cheek. "My point is, you'll know why. You're going to know why because you're his mother. You're going to live and breathe for him. You're going to *learn* how to burp and bathe him. You're going to learn how much ointment is the right amount. He'll never starve, because you won't be able to take his crying anymore, and you'll probably wind up shoving too many bottles in his mouth."

Emily shook her head and giggled.

Gavin leaned in inches from her face, his eyes focused on hers. "And he'll never hate you. He couldn't. You love everything around you so easily, which makes you too easy to love. He's going to feel that. Believe me, he will."

Emily swallowed. "You think so?"

"I know so, doll. It's impossible not to fall in love with you."

And there, sitting on the floor with the man she couldn't live without, the man who showed her what it felt like to really be loved, Emily was no longer afraid of becoming a mother. Instead, she drowned in the fact that not only did the man sitting with her believe in her strengths and was in love with her every weakness, but another little man would soon be equally as in love with her.

CHAPTER SIXTEEN

Restored

Emily pulled open the door to a midtown Starbucks, welcoming the air-conditioned setting from the summer heat. She immediately spotted Olivia, who'd jumped up from her chair as though it were set ablaze. Emily squeezed through the lunchtime crowd, excited to see her friend. The last several weeks had been nothing short of chaotic, so their time together became limited at best. With a little over a month until she was due, Emily's schedule danced around weekly doctor's appointments, Lamaze classes, and purchasing any last minute baby items she and Gavin could think of.

Smiling, Emily approached Olivia and dropped her purse onto the table. As soon as she went to pull Olivia in for a hug, Emily noticed her friend didn't at all appear her usual self. "What's the matter?" Emily scanned Olivia's worried expression.

Olivia hesitated, the lines of her frown deepening. "I have to talk to you."

"All right," Emily drawled, her nerves spiking. She'd never seen Olivia look so panicked. Pulling a chair out from the table, Emily sat. Her head spun over every possible thread of bad news her friend could dish out.

Olivia settled into a chair and slid a Venti drink across the table. "I ordered you an iced chai latte. I figured it'll help calm your nerves after I tell what I found out."

Emily's heart dropped. "Liv, what the hell's going on?"

Olivia nibbled on her thumb nail. "Just promise me you won't get mad at me."

"What?" Eyes wide, Emily shook her head. "Don't get mad at you? What did you do?"

"Em, just promise me you won't get pissed."

Emily crossed her arms, her stomach twisted in knots. "Okay, Olivia, even though you haven't told me *what* I shouldn't be pissed about, I promise I'll *try* not to get pissed. Is that good enough for you?"

Olivia slowly nodded and blew out a puff of air. "I..." She paused, glanced around, and swiped a hand through her hair. "I called the Maury Povich show and—"

"You what?" Emily gasped, her eyes wider. "I told you not to call them, Olivia. How could you do this to me? Like it's not embarrassing enough not knowing who the father is, you want me to air my shit on national television?" Emily stood, yanking her purse from the table. "We're not doing it."

"Emily, wait!" Olivia jumped to her feet, following Emily toward the exit. She grabbed Emily's arm and whipped her around. "You're not listening to me. There's more."

"More?" Emily questioned, her brows furrowed. "What, did you tell them what positions I like during sex? Maybe you went as far as letting them know I made out with Candice Weathers at the graduation party while I was drunk?" Without waiting for a reply, Emily pulled her arm from Olivia's grasp, turned on her heel, and continued weaving through the crowd.

"Emily!" Olivia called. "There's another paternity test available, and it's noninvasive." Emily skidded to a stop. With her lips parted and shock running through her system, she turned around. "It's true," Olivia continued. "It's a simple blood test. You don't even have to go on the show, and you guys can have the results in less than ten days."

Emily swallowed, her heart pounding faster. Olivia started for the table and Emily followed. Feeling as though she'd been sucker punched, Emily dropped her purse, pulled out a chair, and stared at Olivia. "Tell me what you know," she breathed, trying to calm down.

"I'm sorry I called the show," Olivia whispered. "It was going to be a joke. I wasn't even gonna give them your real names. I had Olive Oil for you, Popeye Rodriguez for Gavin, and Norman Bates for Douchecock. I figured I'd put the tickets in a card since you wouldn't let us throw you a shower."

"Liv, I'm not worried about the show." She sighed, attempting to compute how twisted, yet hysterical her friend was. "Just tell me what you know."

"It's called a noninvasive prenatal paternity test. The woman from the show said some company, DNA Diagnostic Center, performs them at their labs across the United States. They need a blood sample from the mother and a blood sample from one of the potential fathers." Olivia shrugged. "That's it."

Emily shook her head, unable to believe what she was hearing. "How can that be? Everything I read online about the amniocentesis said you need amniotic fluid to perform DNA testing prior to giving birth."

Olivia took a sip of her frozen Frappuccino and leaned back. "I really don't understand it myself. She said something about fetal cells in the mother's bloodstream. That's it, Emily. Within ten days of the lab receiving the samples, you can go online to the DDC's website, and you'll have your results."

Ten days. Ten. Simple. Quick. Days.

Emily brought her hand to her mouth, her voice a whisper. "My God, why didn't my doctor tell me about this months ago? This whole time, we could've known." Her heart seared. Their nightmare shouldn't have lasted as long as it had. Hell, at that point, Emily felt all kinds of fucked up about taking her doctor's word for it without doing further research.

"It's a relatively new test, and let's be honest, your doctor's relatively old. His office is a throwback to the seventies. Shit, he still performs sonograms." Olivia slid her chair closer to Emily and placed her hand on her shoulder. "Maybe he didn't know about it. Either way, you do now."

Emily swallowed, trying to process what'd been dumped in her lap. There was truth in Olivia's statement. Emily now knew about the test and soon Gavin would, too. They couldn't take back the sleepless nights over the last several months. They couldn't remove every second of the agonizing wait they'd endured. Six and a half months of worrying whether or not she and Gavin would spend the rest of their lives tied to Dillon couldn't be undone. Armed with new information, Emily wasn't about to let another wicked, unknowing minute tick by. Standing, she grabbed her purse, popped a kiss on Olivia's head, and with a scared and heavy heart, headed out the door to go tell Gavin.

She only prayed their long-awaited answer would be the one they so desperately wanted to hear.

Nerves a tangled mess, Emily stepped from the elevator into Blake Industries.

Beaming, Gavin's secretary stood from her desk. "Hey, Emily!" she chirped, gathering her into a hug. When she pulled back, her smile widened as she gave Emily a once-over. "Not too much longer."

"Yeah. Not much at all." Emily shifted in her heels, wondering why she was wearing them. Her swollen belly had nothing on her feet at that point. "I'm ready to be done with this pregnancy."

"I bet. The last few weeks can be brutal, but it's so worth it at the end. Before you know it, you'll have a little life in your arms. You'll forget each second of discomfort. You and Mr. Blake won't be able to contain your excitement." Emily gave her a weak smile. Natalie was on the long list of people who didn't know the real scenario. With trepidation in her brown eyes, Natalie tilted her head. "Can I... feel?"

"Of course." Emily took her hand and placed it on her stomach. "He's very active this afternoon." And he was. Emily swore her little man was doing cartwheels. Under the silk of her sundress, her flesh rolled in waves with his squirming movements.

"God, I remember this," Natalie sighed. "Well, enjoy it. There will come a time in your life when you realize this was one of the best parts."

Emily gave another weak smile and glanced toward Gavin's office. "Is he available?"

Natalie nodded. "Yep. He just finished up a meeting, so you caught him at a good time."

"Thanks, Natalie. I'll catch up with you on my way out."

"Sounds good," she said, reclaiming her seat, her attention focused on the ringing phone.

Nerves instantly spiking again, Emily headed for Gavin's office. With a quick knock, she pushed open the door. Her heart clenched the moment her eyes landed on Gavin's smiling face. Little did he know she was about to throw a corkscrew in his day. Phone in one hand, he signaled for her to wait with the other. She sighed, taking in his relaxed demeanor. Suit jacket off and tie loose around his neck, he lazily rocked in his leather chair, talking business. Dropping her purse onto his desk, Emily settled on his lap, hoping she wasn't crushing him. He slid his arm around her waist, his hand massaging her belly. Trying to calm her anxiety, she ran her fingers through his soft black hair. God, she loved this man, but she couldn't help but feel as though she was the devil about to deliver bad news.

"That's exactly what I want to hear, Bruce. We'll be in touch." On that note, he hung up, his grin contagious as he gazed into Emily's eyes. "A midday surprise." He brushed his lips along her jaw. "Are you presenting yourself as lunch to me?"

Emily pulled in a breath, her mind telling her to just come out and say it. No skirting around. No hesitation. Just say it. Wrapping her arms around his shoulders, she pressed her forehead to his. Her eyes locked on those mystifying baby blues. "There's a blood paternity test. It has no risks, and we can have the results in days. I know we're almost at the end of this road, but we could find out a few weeks early. We can finally be done with this... this waiting." Emily watched his face pale. Watched those beautiful eyes cloud over, desolation replacing the playfulness they'd held less than a minute ago. She felt his strong, hard body sag.

His hand dropped from her stomach as he looked away... then his whispered words sank her, gutted her open. "I've known about the test for a couple of months." He brought his eyes back to hers.

His statement bounced around in Emily's head. Staring at his face, bleeding something parallel to shame, she tried to swallow. She felt dizzy as she stood, resting her hand on his desk for balance. "You've known?"

she breathed, her eyes misting over with tears and confusion. "You've known about it and didn't say anything to me?"

Gavin rose and brought his hand to her cheek, but she flinched away. For a second, he found his voice trapped, felt his heart sink. He knew the lie he was harboring would upset her, but hell, her reaction was tearing him apart. He nodded, stepping back. "I have."

"For how long?" she asked, her voice cracking.

"After we found out it was a boy." Gavin looked at the floor, remembering the day he couldn't keep his curious fingers from clicking around the internet. A son. *His* possible son had fueled a need so deep within him to see if there were other options, he'd thought he was going crazy. He spent half the day online. Once he found out they could have the answer so fast, fear shot through him. Frozen in front of his computer, Gavin realized the answer may not be what he wanted to hear, what he needed to hear. It also brought on a slew of fucked up emotions he wasn't prepared to handle. For the most part, he felt Emily was carrying his child, but as he stared at the screen, his faith vanished.

"That was months ago, Gavin." Emily swiped tears from her face, shocked at how long he'd known. "I don't understand. Why would you keep this from me?"

Stepping closer, he shoved his hand though his hair. All he wanted to do was touch her, console her, but her defenses were up, so he would tread. "I was buying time." He spoke softly and stared at her face as it became further dowsed with confusion. "That's it. I was buying time."

"Buying time? Time from what? We can't stop the inevitable. But we could've stopped Dillon from being at every doctor's appointment."

Gavin shook his head, his fears tumbling from his mouth. "No, we couldn't have. He's the father. Not me."

Emily swallowed back a breath at his admission. Her knees went weak. The man before her revealed something he'd hidden so naturally, so effortlessly over the past several months. She didn't know whether to scream at him or cry for him. However, she knew he did it for her. She could never deny his natural instinct to always protect her feelings. He'd sheltered her by keeping his fears to himself. As she watched his spirit break right before her eyes, she decided to reveal something as well. Something she'd started feeling the last few months but didn't recognize what it was until now. A pull so internal, so warming, she thought it was going to melt her. "You *are* this baby's father, Gavin Blake. Do you hear me?"

Gavin stared at her a long moment, sour thoughts invading his mind. He wanted to believe her, but he couldn't. His words came out as a whisper. "I'm not, Emily. He is."

Heart shattering, Emily stepped closer and reached for his hands. She molded them to her belly as the baby tried to kick his way out. Staring into Gavin's weary eyes, she cupped his cheeks. "You are the father, and I'll tell you how I know," Emily cried, pressing her lips to his. "I know because I can feel every bit of you running through my veins. Your blood, your heart, your soul. I can feel it. I feel his love for you. Every time you talk, he moves. Every time you laugh, I swear he vibrates like he's sharing the joke with you." Sliding her arms around his neck, she twined her fingers in Gavin's hair and buried her face against his chest. "I know you can feel him moving, Gavin, and he knows it's his father's hands on my stomach. He knows it."

Gavin had said Emily's hands shook every time she touched him. Here and now, it was his he couldn't control. He smoothed his trembling hands along the swell of her stomach, feeling the life they may have created squirm within her body.

With tears streaming down her face, Emily stared into Gavin's eyes. "I need your faith and belief in everything you know we were meant to be." She pulled in a stuttering breath and held his face. "I need it to be stronger than your fears and doubts. Don't you dare give up on us, Gavin. Don't give up on him. Please."

Gavin nodded and bent his head, brushing his lips against hers. "I won't," he whispered, pulling her into his arms. "I swear to God I won't."

And there, standing in his office with the woman he couldn't live without, the woman who showed him what it felt like to have his faith restored by her simple touch, Gavin was no longer afraid of not being this child's father. Instead, he drowned in the fact that not only did the woman with him believe he was, and was in love with every fear he had, but another life was already in love with him.

CHAPTER SEVENTEEN

Full Circle

Climbing the mountainous stairs to the second floor of Gavin's home in the Hamptons proved a more difficult feat than the year before. With a bottle of water in one hand and a hearty plate of reheated Chinese food in the other, Emily reached the last step quite winded. As she made her way down the hall, she couldn't help but stop outside the room she and Dillon had slept in the last time she was there. Tainted memories of their stay stormed her mind. But as she stared into the space, one memory trumped the rest. It knocked them all to the ground. This particular memory would never taint her. She'd hold on to it forever.

A small smile lifted the corner of her mouth as she entered the room. Placing her water and food on the large dresser, she flicked her eyes to the nightstand flanking the queen-sized bed. Simple curiosity had her pulling open the drawer. She giggled when she saw the sweatshirt Gavin had given her to wear while she played her first ever game of "Toss the Bottle Cap into the Pot" with him. She gathered it in her hands, bringing it up to her nose. Though faint, it still held his smell. She remembered wanting to burn his scent into her mind. Little did she know then she'd be lucky enough to wake up to it every morning. Warmth flooded her as she pulled it over her tank top. Closing her eyes, she hugged her chest, overcome by visions of that night. She looked around, picked up the plate and water, and made her way out of the room holding both beautiful and bad memories.

On a sigh, she stepped into the room holding her heart and future. Leaning against the doorway, Emily surreptitiously watched Gavin. Sitting cross-legged on the bed, wearing nothing but a pair of light cotton pajama pants, his focus was zeroed in on his laptop. Though he'd promised he wouldn't work over the Fourth of July holiday, Emily found that was all he'd been doing. She knew he was trying to keep busy, drowning himself in whatever he could. He was trying to avoid dealing with their new waiting game, the paternity test results game. She couldn't help but remember a year ago when their lives were very different.

Heart heavy for what he was going through, Emily moved across the room. After placing her food and drink down, she crawled onto bed and pulled the laptop away from Gavin. With a mischievous smile, she snapped it closed and straddled his lap.

Gavin lifted a brow, a slow smirk toying at his mouth. "You're very lucky I saved the doc I was working on."

"Sounds like a threat." Placing her hands on his bare shoulders, Emily cocked her head to the side and mimicked his expression. "Are you going to do harm to my body, Mr. Blake? Better yet, may I *beg* for a little pleasurable harm to my body?" He chuckled, and his blue eyes twinkled with the playfulness Emily had desperately missed over the last week since they'd gone for the test.

Gavin sucked in his bottom lip and slid his arms around her waist. "I've turned you into such a dirty, kinky, little masochist. Do you have any idea what that thought does to me?"

Emily giggled. "Yes. I can feel what it's doing to you right now."

"That obvious?"

"Very." Emily nuzzled the crook of his neck, biting him softly. Dragging his musky scent through her noise, she curled her fingers in his hair. "Your head's so consumed by my newfound dirty kinkiness, you didn't even notice something on me."

Gripping her thighs, a groan crawled up Gavin's throat. "And what you're doing is supposed to help?"

"Okay, I'll stop," Emily quipped, pulling back.

Gavin frowned. "I'm tossing out the caveman card here and demand you continue your dirty, kinkiness on my neck."

"Nope," Emily giggled. "Not until you figure out what's new on me. Seriously, it's not that hard."

Gavin buried his hands in her hair and guided her down to his lips. "Wrong," he whispered as he spoke between kisses. "It's painfully... tortuously...agonizingly, I'm-about-to-rip-the-panties-from-your-body *hard*."

Right about the same time Emily started thinking about how deliciously, intoxicatingly, and addictively wonderful his kisses were, his cell phone rang. As usual, Gavin showed no intentions of answering.

Emily pulled back and looked at him. "You really should answer that."

He guided her back down to his mouth. "No way," he groaned as he scooted against the headboard, bringing her with him. "Whoever it is will wait."

"Uh, uh, uh," she playfully warned, her smile as teasing as ever. "It could be your parents calling to let us know what time they'll be here tomorrow."

Gavin blinked. "You get off on this, don't you?"

Emily batted her lashes. "In so… many…many ways. Now answer it." She laughed and carefully maneuvered from the bed, more than enjoying the swat on her ass he gave her.

As she watched him take the call, Emily felt her stomach tighten. Though not in pain, she definitely wasn't comfortable as a Braxton Hicks contraction balled her belly. With her breath somewhat depleted, she sank into an overstuffed chair and tried to relax. Playing it safe, considering she was within three weeks of her due date, she glanced at her watch and started timing it. As her stomach loosened from the mild assault, the baby made his presence known. Hammering his foot in what Emily believed was anger at his own discomfort, he hit his mark somewhere below her right ribcage.

"I hear ya, buddy," she mumbled, rubbing the area he'd attacked. "Soon." Emily watched concern edge Gavin's eyes when his gaze landed on her.

Promptly ending his call, he moved across the room and fell to his knees in front of her. "What's wrong?" he asked, placing his hand over hers. "Are you okay?"

She nodded and pulled in a deep breath. "Fake contraction."

"Are you sure?"

"Yeah. I'm starting to get used to them." She swallowed and, with Gavin's help, stood. Smiling, she draped her arms around his neck. "So, can you tell what's new on me?"

Startled by her nonchalance, Gavin shook his head, smoothing his hands down her waist. "Emily, I think you should lay down."

"Why?" she asked, her brows furrowed.

"You're getting contractions."

"Silly man, I had a Braxton Hicks." She waved dismissively and walked across the room. She plucked her water from the nightstand, took a sip, and nearly finished the whole bottle. "I'm fine."

Gavin shoved a nervous hand through his hair. Yeah, he was pretty damn sure his girl was losing it. "How do you know you're fine?"

"Well, let's see. It's my body, and I've come to know it quite well over the last twenty-five years." She padded back over to him, a smile on her face as she once again slid her arms around his neck. "Want to know two things I bet you didn't know?"

Gavin released a sigh, attempting to go with the flow. "Sure."

Emily wiggled her brows. "One: you're very, very shmexy when you're worried."

Gavin chuckled. "Am I?"

"Mmm hmm."

"I've said it before"—Gavin smirked, loving her playfulness—"and I'll say it 'til the day they bury me. You're pretty shmexy yourself."

"Why thank you, sir." She pushed up on her tiptoes and kissed him. "Two: While losing yourself in all my dirty, kinky, Braxton Hicks-filled shmexyness, you failed to notice I'm wearing the sweatshirt you lent me one year ago tonight."

Gavin flicked his eyes down to the gray Zenga Sport sweatshirt he'd sworn disappeared into thin air. "No shit. Look at that." Grinning, he flipped the hood over Emily's head. "It definitely fits you better this year."

Emily's mouth dropped open, and Gavin laughed. Giggling, she swatted his arm. "You take that back right now."

"You know I'm kidding." Gavin kissed her pouting lips. "Do I need to make it up to you?"

"As a matter of fact, you do."

"Name it, sweets."

"Bottle caps."

Gavin popped a brow. "Bottle caps?"

Emily nodded. "Yep. A friendly game of toss the bottle caps."

"Is this some kind of wager for your forgiveness?" Gavin's eyes sparkled mischievously. "And *when* you lose, what happens then? Am I cast into one of the guest bedrooms for the night?"

Emily scoffed, heading for the French doors. "Why would you assume I'm going to lose, wiseass? And yes, you sleep solo if you don't let me win."

Chuckling, Gavin watched her stick out her tongue in true Emily fashion as she disappeared onto the balcony. In true Gavin fashion, he was about to test his girl's memory. Grabbing a remote and flicking on the surround sound, he hit repeat on one particular song. He tossed on a long-sleeved T-shirt and started for the doors. With the freezer bag filled with caps in hand, Gavin breathed in the salty smell of the ocean. Emily was leaning against the railing when he emerged into the cool night air. She smiled, sinking his heart the same way she'd sunk it a year ago. Hell, if there ever came a time she couldn't steal his breath, he'd know the world around him had gone crazy.

Dropping the bag of memories onto an Adirondack chair, he reached for her hand and gently pulled her to his body. "May I have this dance before we play our little game?"

"Looks like you've already decided that for me," she teased, resting her head against his chest as they swayed.

Gavin kissed the top of her hair. "Would you've been able to say no?"

"Never," she whispered.

"That's what I figured."

"You push your luck every chance you get, don't you?"

He chuckled lightly. "Always." With one hand splayed along the small of her back, he took the other, intertwined with her fingers, and pinned it to his chest. Staring at her, he smiled. "Do you know what song this is?"

"I do," she breathed, her gaze transfixed on his lips. Her muscles warmed as the memory of the first night they'd made love spilled through her. "Louis Armstrong's *La Vie en Rose*. I also remember the first time we danced to it."

"Very good, Miss Cooper. You continue to impress me."

He stopped moving, and Emily's heart sputtered as he bent his head, brushing his lips against hers. A tease of a kiss. Never enough. But Emily knew from the moment he'd first kissed her, she'd never get her fill of him.

"You know I'm going to dance with you to this song at our wedding one day. That is, if you'd have me?"

Emily swallowed, her breathing increasing. As her hair whipped around in the light summer breeze, a tear slipped down her cheek. One year. One full circle had been drawn around their lives, and although they'd been tested in every way possible, they were still together. "I could never not have you, Gavin. Never," she whispered, falling more in love with him than she'd ever thought possible.

As Louis Armstrong belted out soulful melodies about casting magic spells, Gavin cast his on Emily, as he always did. He pressed his lips to hers and kissed her slowly, deeply. Emily's heart dropped, knowing one year ago tonight on this very balcony, beers, memories, and tears were shared. Little did she know then, a stolen moment, a sweatshirt, many bottle caps, and few layers peeled back later, her life would never be the same.

And she thanked God for every minute it wasn't.

"How the heck did you talk him into going out on the boat?" Olivia smeared a heavy dose of suntan lotion across her chest. "You seriously have that man whipped. He adamantly declines the fishing trip every year."

Emily coated her legs with suntan lotion. "I didn't talk him into it. Colton did." She placed the bottle on the wrought-iron table and adjusted the umbrella above her. Sighing, she shook her head and lay back in her poolside chair. "I'm curious to see how sick he's going to be when he gets back. He insisted the water was calm enough. Now look at it."

Olivia nodded. "Oh, he'll be hugging the toilet, I guarantee it. He thinks because he stuck that stupid sea sick thing behind his ear, he's covered. Not a chance. I'm surprised he doesn't heave after swimming in the pool."

Both women laughed. Fallon returned from inside the house and handed Emily a glass of lemonade.

"Thank you," Emily said.

"You're welcome. What are you two laughing about?" Fallon questioned, getting comfortable in a chair.

"Gavin and the way he's, without a doubt, going to be making love to the many toilet bowls in his house when the guys get back." Olivia nodded knowingly, a wicked smirk twisting her lips. "Emily's definitely playing nurse tonight."

Emily's gaze drifted out to the choppy waters of the Atlantic. As she watched the waves crash against the shore, she wondered if Gavin was okay. She also wondered if he'd agreed to go on the trip in another attempt to keep his mind off the test results. Due any day, his nerves were becoming shot by the second. He and Emily weren't the only ones nervous, though. When his parents had arrived this morning for his Fourth of July party, Emily could see the worry in their eyes. She could see it in everyone. From Fallon, to Trevor, Olivia, Melanie, and Colton, everyone around them looked uneasy when she really paid attention.

"Olivia," Jude called from the pool. Slicking his sandy brown hair away from his forehead, he smirked. "If you don't get in with me, I'm getting out and coming to get ya."

Olivia shot him a look. "And if you do, your body will never feel the tip of my paint brush again." She kinked her head to the side. "*And* I'll never allow a certain *tip* of your body to feel mine ever again."

Emily watched as he pondered Olivia's threats. However, his deliberation didn't last too long. He climbed from the pool and darted toward Olivia. Within seconds, he had her hauled over his shoulder, dangling her kicking, screaming body over the pool. Emily took a laughing breath, and Olivia took an unwanted swim when Jude dropped her into the water. Loving that Olivia seemed to have met her match in Jude, Emily and Fallon giggled as they observed her spit water.

"Jude Hamilton!" Olivia sputtered as he jumped in with her. Pulling her into his arms, he hooted a laugh. "I'm so going to kick your fucking ass all over the place for this."

Jude swung his attention over to Emily and Fallon. "What do the two best friends think? I'm wondering if she needs a good dunk for that one."

"Do it!" Fallon chirped, tipping her wine cooler to her mouth.

"Crap off, Fallon," Olivia squealed, attempting to wiggle from Jude's hold.

Emily held her hands up in surrender. "I'm staying out of this one."

"Thank you, fr—"

Emily assumed Olivia's last word was going to be "friend" however, Jude dunked her, cutting her off. Emily tore her attention from the dunking battle when she saw Gavin and the gang of fishermen making their way across the yard. After tying her sarong around her unflattering waistline, Emily moved quickly but carefully across the water-soaked slate tiles. She couldn't help but frown when she saw Gavin's expression. Yeah, her man looked less than healthy.

Kissing his lips, she curled her arms around his waist. "No good?"

Gavin ran a tired hand over his sunburnt cheeks. "I've been better. But I need you to tell me why was it again I didn't listen to you about not going?"

Emily smiled. "That's because you wanted to look cool in front of the guys."

A hint of a grin appeared on Gavin's mouth. "Ah, yes. Me and my coolness. Do me a favor and chain me to the fence next year when they rib on me for not going."

"Deal." Emily ran her hands through his hair. "Shower?"

"Are you washing me?"

"Do you want me to?"

Gavin lifted a brow. "Is that a serious question?"

"I'm just making sure." She pouted. "You're looking pretty ill."

"Right," he agreed, sliding his hands through her hair. "But a little dose of Emily might cure my nausea."

"Come on, my sick man." She giggled and reached for his hand. "Emily will take care of you."

And she did. After a very long and very thorough shower, Gavin felt less... nauseated.

As the sizzling smell of burgers, hotdogs and chicken wings floated through the breeze, Gavin pulled out a chair and waited for Emily to finish up helping his mother inside the house. Everyone sat down to a hearty meal prepared by Gavin's father.

"Feeling better, man?" Trevor asked, chomping into a piece of corn on the cob. "Or do we need to be careful you might get sick all over the table?"

Fallon rolled her eyes. "Eew, Trevor, that's gross."

"It is, isn't it?" Gavin shook his head and chuckled. "Just for that, if I do feel sick, I'm aiming it at Trevor."

"Okay, seriously?" Olivia chirped, her forehead pinched in disgust. "We're trying to eat here."

"Why do women get freaked out over that?" Jude scooped a monster-sized portion of potato salad onto his plate. "There're nastier things out there other than throwing up."

"I agree." Gavin leaned back, folding his hands behind his head. A slow smirk lifted his mouth. "Like my nephew with his finger shoved in his nose right now. He's digging for something."

Everyone whipped their heads around to the table Melanie, Colton and the kids occupied. Sure enough, little Timothy had other plans for what he was going to enjoy for dessert.

An orchestra of revolted groans from Olivia and Fallon filtered through the air along with the sound of their chairs screeching back from the table as they plucked up their plates and walked away.

"Colton," Gavin called out, smiling, "bro, you might want to handle your kid."

Colton lifted his eyes from his plate. He flicked them between his two children, ultimately stopping on the guilty one. "Timmy, get your finger out of your nose."

Melanie sighed, reaching for the unoffending hand. She swept him up from his chair. "Come on. It's soap and water for you."

As the men laughed and joked about what'd just happened, Emily, Lillian, and Chad emerged from the house. They each took a seat at one of the two tables.

Emily placed her plate down, her expression curious. "Why did Fallon and Olivia just storm inside? Did one of you guys insult them?"

Another round of laughter went off, adding to Emily's confusion.

Jude stood and made his way inside. Gavin assumed he was attempting to go check on Olivia. Gavin draped his arm over Emily's chair. "No, we didn't insult them. They just have weak stomachs."

Emily started piling cucumber salad onto her plate. "Mmm hmm. I'm not even going to ask."

"Good. You're better off, Em." Trevor took a swig from his beer and pushed his empty plate away. "So what's the deal? You two have a name for the little one?"

Emily looked at Gavin. "We do."

"Noah," Gavin answered, trying to keep his mind from straying to unwanted thoughts of him not being his son. "Noah Alexander."

Trevor nodded. "Good name."

"Yeah, it is." Emily gave Gavin a weak smile, knowing his head was stuck in battle again. With a sigh, she turned to Trevor. "So, Fallon said you two are moving in together."

Trevor beamed. "Yep. She insisted."

Emily raised an incredulous brow. "I heard it was the other way around."

Gavin chuckled and shook his head. "She told us all about it the other day. The roses. The dinner with the nervous speech."

"Okay. You caught me." Trevor finished off the rest of his beer. "Like you're any better with Emily, you sap. Forget about speeches. Yours are infamous."

"Ah. They are, and I'm worse." Gavin smirked. "But you'll never catch me denying it, *and* my sappiness gains me swoon-worthy points."

Emily giggled.

"Dude. You're done for. Swoon worthy?"

"You got it, bro. I'm as swoon worthy as they come." Gavin massaged his fingers through Emily's hair. "Tell him, sweets."

Emily dropped her fork onto her plate and dropped herself into Gavin's lap. She curled her arms around his neck and smiled. "He's the king of swoon, Trevor. You really should take some pointers."

Trevor stood, stretching his long arms. "I'm out. You two are scaring me in more ways than one." He swiped his plate from the table and made his way into the house.

"Mmm, we scared him away," Gavin whispered, brushing his lightly stubbled jaw against Emily's cheek. "We're bad, huh?"

A sultry smile touched Emily's lips. "So very bad."

After indulging in a few stolen moments with the only woman he wanted to consider him swoon worthy, Gavin watched Emily disappear inside to help his mother prepare some desserts. It triggered an upsurge of relief. The past couple of weeks, the two had become close, and that's all Gavin wanted to see. As he enjoyed the sounds of his niece and nephew playing tag, Gavin was glad he'd cut this year's party down to close friends and family. With the sun getting ready to retire for the day, he took a seat around the fire pit alongside his father and Colton.

"Thanks, Pop," Gavin said, accepting a beer from his father. "Today turned out good."

"It sure did." Chad relaxed in his seat, his eyes landing on Gavin's. "The older you get, you'll start to notice the chaos of a big to-do party loses its glitz. This is what it's all about."

Gavin knew his father was correct. Somewhere between becoming successful with Blake Industries and playing the tiresome field with women, Gavin lost touch with what really mattered. Not that he hadn't held family close to his heart—it was impossible not to considering his parents raised him to treasure it—but the importance of what really counted in life became skewed.

"So how are you holding up?" Colton questioned. "Mom said you and Emily went for a blood paternity test a few days ago."

As Gavin swept his gaze to the house, where he could see Emily through the kitchen window, Gavin knew he wasn't doing well. Sure. He'd told Emily he wouldn't give up hope Noah was his son, but as the answer neared, he found it more difficult to hold onto optimism. Gavin shrugged, taking a gulp of beer. "I'm dealing."

"There's a reason behind everything, son," Chad sighed, clapping Gavin's shoulder. "Just remember that."

"Yeah, Pop? What would be the reason if it's not my kid?" Gavin hated questioning anything his father said, but Gavin couldn't find a string of sense if this outcome was about to mind-fuck him. The despondency in his father's eyes made Gavin feel like an asshole. "I'm sorry," Gavin somberly admitted, trying not to lose the faith his father had always attempted to instill in him. "I told Emily at the beginning of this we'd go through it scared together. I said that mostly to calm her down, but hell if this isn't killing me. The thought of having that asshole involved in her or the baby's life is fucking with me bad."

Gavin dragged a hand through his hair, his nerves kicking up with every evil whisper in his mind. Gavin shook his head. "He's calmed down a bit in the past couple of months, but I'm assuming that's because I've kept him in place. If he's this baby's father, it'll go right to his head, and he'll take it to a whole new level. The asshole let us know he's moving to Florida a few months after the baby's born. Emily's a mess over it. I'm going to fall in love with this kid and have to watch Dillon take him over the summer and holidays. It'll break us both."

With his hand still on Gavin's shoulder, Chad looked at Colton who was staring wordlessly at his brother. Bringing his eyes back to his son, Chad shook his head. His voice was soft but resolute. "Gavin, you're a strong man. You've always been. The first time I held you, you told me with your eyes you were going to make your mark in this world, and shit, son, you have. You've made your mother and me proud. I know you may feel that strength you were born with slipping from your grasp, but you have it in you to not let it go. Find it again. It's there. As a man and as a father to this child, whether yours biologically or not, you'll do whatever it takes to keep you and Emily from breaking. You're the man who's going to turn this child into a man. You and Emily need one another and you may need one another more than ever after this. But whatever you do, never question the decisions the heavens make for us. Again, there's a reason behind everything. All that matters is what you do with those decisions. You can let them break you or mold you."

With the words he needed to hear soaking through his mind, Gavin glanced toward the house. Watching his mother and Emily step from the porch, he tried to focus on what his father had said, but as the stars started to blanket the sky, he feared that until he had those results in hand, here and now, he wouldn't be able to find the strength he needed to walk them through this. As doubt plagued every muscle in his body,

Gavin stood and made his was over to Emily. Forcing a smile, he gently pulled her into his arms. He felt as if he was failing. A man who'd continue to fail if Noah wasn't his.

"Hey," she said, smiling. "Everyone's heading down to the beach to light off the fireworks. I didn't realize it'd gotten so chilly out here. I'm gonna run back inside and grab my jacket. Do you need anything?"

Gavin didn't answer. No. Instead, he bent his head, crushing his lips to hers. Ashamed and riddled with guilt for masking his feelings, he kissed her hard, burying his hands in her soft curls. He wondered if Emily could taste the fear on his tongue or if she could feel the uncertainty in his hold. He didn't know how long they stood wrapped in one another's arms, but in that moment, he wished he could stop time. Stop it from moving forward to a wicked place where he wouldn't be able to take care of her.

Emily slowly pulled back, her eyes searching Gavin's. "Are you okay?"

"Yes," Gavin lied smoothly. "I can go get your jacket."

"It's all right. I have to use the bathroom." She touched his cheek and smiled. "I'll meet you down by the beach."

Gavin nodded, and she made her way into the empty house. As she washed her hands after finishing up in the bathroom, Emily worried about the way Gavin looked. God, she just wanted their wait to be over. She wanted her carefree Yankees lover back. The waiting had stripped him of so much, and Emily couldn't help but hurt for him. On a sigh, she flipped off the light, praying the waiting would be over soon. In the bedroom, she yanked a light, spring jacket from her suitcase. She was glad she'd brought it with her. Emily pulled it on and started for the door, however, she came to a stop, her feet glued to the floor, when her gaze locked onto Gavin's laptop. A pang shot through her.

Curiosity leading her, Emily slowly sank onto the mattress. Staring at the laptop, she couldn't stop her fingers from tapping in Gavin's passcode. She knew the paternity test results weren't due for another couple of days, and she chided herself for even looking, yet something pushed her forward. She entered the URL into the proper space. With her heart starting to pound when the website popped up, Emily entered the case number she was given in order to check the results. Though she'd never been a mathematician or English major, this series of numbers and letters was burned into Emily's head. Her body tensed when the site started to load the information. It wasn't the same page that'd shown up the past couple of times she'd checked. Instead, a taunting hourglass popped up. Emily stared at it and it stared right back as she waited.

Breathe…

The wicked little hourglass disappeared…

Breathe…

A blue triangle representing the father showed up…

'Breathe…

A graph showing probable paternity said hello…

Breathe…

Emily's heart dropped, sinking right down to her feet. Unable to breathe, speak, or think, the only properly functioning body part Emily had left was her tear ducts. Those were working just fine because she broke out into hysterics, gulping for air as she tried to calm herself. In a daze over the results staring her right in the face, Emily slowly stood and made her way downstairs. How would she even begin to tell Gavin? She needed words for this moment and her mind was blank. Completely empty of coherent thoughts, her body trembling, Emily stepped onto the back porch. Her eyes landed on Gavin's. Sitting in one of the poolside chairs, he cocked his head to the side when he'd saw her. She was glad he didn't go down to the beach with everyone. She didn't want to tell him in front of anyone. She needed to tell him in private. She only wished she knew how.

She stopped in front of the pool, watching Gavin move toward. She could tell he knew she was a mess, and her heart bled from the look in his eyes. Standing before her, Gavin cupped her cheek and gently placed the other hand on her stomach.

"What's wrong?" he asked, his nervousness palpable.

Emily swallowed, her words stuttering between her deep breaths for air. "Did you know one year ago tonight you began saving my life?" Gavin went to speak, but Emily continued. "You did, Gavin. I didn't know it then, but you did. We've been through more in this past year than any two people in a new relationship should have to endure. We deserve a break." She looked at her watch and quickly back at him. "Kiss me right now. Kiss me the way you kissed me last year on this very night. I promise you I won't stop it, either."

Without thinking, Gavin pulled her to his mouth, sliding his tongue over hers. Though familiar, her kiss would always be new to him, something unexplored with each stroke of her touch. With blazing fireworks going off above them, Gavin kissed her the way he did the first time he was lucky enough to feel her lips, feel her in his arms. Emily didn't break the kiss this time; Gavin had to stop because of her sobbing. He went to speak, but she beat him to the punch.

"You said no matter who Noah's father is, you'd love and raise him as if he were your own."

Dropping his arms, Gavin felt the blood drain from his face, felt his heart hammer through his chest.

"When you told me that, I didn't know what to think," Emily cried, bringing her hands to his cheeks. "Do you know how many men would stay? Not many. You took me back after all the pain I caused you, and then you accepted the fact you might not be the father of the child I'm carrying. I would've loved you for an eternity before taking on that responsibility. After that, I knew I'd find you in my next life." She paused, brushing her lips over his. "Gavin Blake, fate fucked with us a little bit in the beginning… but it's done messing with us. It's giving us the break we deserved from the start. Noah's *your* son."

"What?" he breathed, feeling his shoulders sag from the lack of weight they'd been carrying. "I am?"

Emily nodded, tears falling in a torrent. "Yes, you are. I checked and—"

It was Gavin's turn to cut her off. He surged his hands through her hair, pulling her into his mouth again. Mind un-fucked, Gavin spoke between worshipping her lips. "Are you sure? Tell me you're sure, Emily."

"I'm positive," she cried, holding his face as she kissed him back as feverishly as he was kissing her. "He's yours, Gavin. He's yours."

"Jesus," Olivia quipped, making her way over to them. "There're plenty of bedrooms. I mean, it's a mansion, Blake. Take her inside." Emily giggled and wiped away her tears. Brows furrowed, Olivia looked confused as all hell. "Okay. Wait a minute. You're crying, but you're kissing him? Did I miss something?"

Gavin grinned, tossing his arm over Emily's shoulder. "Yeah. You missed the memo that says I'm Noah's father."

Olivia's eyes went wide. "Shut the cellar door!" She all but hopped into Gavin's arms, her squeals pitching above the blasting fireworks. "Are you guys for real? He's the baby daddy?"

"Yes," Emily laughed as Olivia bear hugged her. "He's the baby daddy."

Gavin smacked his smiling lips together. "The *swoon*-worthy baby daddy."

Clapping, Olivia started running toward the stairs to the beach. "I'm going to get everyone!"

"You go right ahead," Gavin called out. With his smile as wide as ever, he draped his arm over Emily's shoulder. Grazing his nose against hers, he pulled her bottom lip between his teeth. "Do you know how happy I'm going to make you?"

Emily smiled as her body let go of the last bit of tension curling through it. "I'm not sure you can make me any happier than you already have."

"Do you doubt my happy making skills?"

"I guess I just did," Emily giggled.

After celebrating the news with their friends and family, Gavin followed Emily upstairs. She had a doctor's appointment in the city tomorrow at four o'clock, and they planned on leaving relatively early to beat the holiday traffic. Before making the trip, Gavin planned on letting Dillon know not to bother showing up. He more than looked forward to making that call. Actually, he was pretty fucking sure he was going to record it. Still in shock he was no longer in purgatory, and feeling as if he were finally in heaven, Gavin couldn't help the smile molding his face when Emily crawled into bed next to him. As she lay back against the pillows, he also couldn't help but slide his body down the bed. He trailed kisses from her neck, down the graceful curve of her shoulder, and ultimately along the side of her stomach. Gavin slowly lifted her silk camisole, his smile widening as he settled his lips over the bare flesh of her belly holding *his* child. "Noah," Gavin whispered, kissing just below her navel. "Noah Alexander Blake."

Emily let out a satisfied sigh. "I like the way that sounds."

"I do too." Gavin kissed her stomach again and reached for her hand. Intertwining their fingers, he kissed each of hers, and looked at her. "Thank you."

Emily buried her free hand in his hair, stroking it away from his forehead. The look in his eyes, gentle tone of his voice, and the smile on his face had her heart bursting with love. "Thank *you*," she whispered, a single tear breaking loose. "Thank you so much."

Gavin rested his cheek on top of her stomach, chuckling when a little wave rolled across it. "Arm?" he questioned, enjoying the way it felt.

"Possibly." Smiling, Emily looked down at the movement. "Maybe his butt?"

Gavin shrugged, basking in the moment. "I wonder if he'll suck at bottle caps like his mother."

"I wonder if he'll be a wiseass like his father."

Gavin quirked a brow as he drew circles around her belly button. "A blue-eyed, sucky bottle cap playing wiseass. I like it."

Emily giggled. "Me, too."

Gavin kissed her stomach again, a devious smile tipping his lips. "I wonder if he'll hate your Birds as much as I do."

Emily groaned, tossing her head back onto the pillow. "I wonder if he'll be a *bigger* wiseass than his father."

"Lame comeback. You just used that one."

"It's fitting for the wiseass it was aimed at."

"Can't say I disagree." Gavin rained a slew of slow kisses along every inch of Emily's stomach, watching tiny goose bumps pop up over her flesh. "I wonder if he'll know just how beautiful his mother is, inside and out."

Emily touched Gavin's cheek, her soul warmed by his words. "I wonder if he'll be every bit of the man his father is."

Eyes softening, Gavin slithered up Emily's body, kissed the side of her ribs, the swell of her breast, and the slope of her collar bone. Hovering above her, he ran his hand through her silky hair. "I hope he falls in love with a selfless woman like his mother, who risks everything she has by taking a chance on his wiseass."

With vibrant flares of colors from fireworks spilling through the window into the darkened room, Emily's stared into Gavin's eyes, her breath catching as she tangled her fingers in his hair. "I hope he's as forgiving, gentle, and kind as his father is if that woman ever hurts him."

Gavin settled his lips over Emily's, whispering as he gently kissed her. "I wonder if he'll know how much I'm going to love him and his mother until the day I take my last, dying breath."

Although she wanted to, Gavin didn't let Emily speak again. Not only did he continue to leave a trail of sweet word prints in her ears, he entered her lifeblood, caressing her soul in ways he never had before. Heart racing with promise, Emily felt him become one with her and their child, his love unyielding with every delicate touch and sweet embrace through the night.

CHAPTER EIGHTEEN

Pulse

When Emily woke the next morning, the smell of bacon flared her senses as she climbed from the empty bed. Puffy clouds, gray as an old headstone, peppered the sky beyond the window. Clearly rain would haunt the day. With a lazy stretch and a yawn creeping up her throat, she scanned the bedroom. Poking her head from the door, she heard Gavin's and his father's voices coming from downstairs. She smiled at the way they joked and laughed. Deciding to get a quick shower before they left, Emily rummaged through her suitcase for a soft pair of capri pants and red tank top. Clothing in hand, she made her way into the bathroom and indulged in a long, hot shower. Once finished, she blew her hair dry, got dressed, and headed downstairs. Finding Chad alone in the kitchen, she glanced around, looking for Gavin.

"Good morning," Emily said, pulling out a chair. "Where's Gavin?"

Holding a spatula, Chad faced her. "Good morning to you too," he replied with a smile. "We ran out of milk. He took a quick ride up to the store." Chad poured her a tall glass of orange juice and slid it across the black granite counter. "Drink. It's good for you *and* my grandson."

Emily smiled, his proud tone warming her. "Thank you." She sipped the juice and glanced around again. "Is everyone still asleep?"

"Lillian's getting ready." Chad opened an egg over a sizzling frying pan. "Fallon and Trevor are awake. He came down and grabbed two cups of coffee. I haven't seen Olivia or Jude, yet." He gulped his orange juice. "Eggs and bacon?"

"Sure," Emily replied, her stomach growling from the tantalizing smell.

Chad scooped some eggs and a few slices of bacon onto a plate. Placing it in front of Emily, he smiled, the wrinkles around his blue eyes lifting. "Enjoy."

"Thank you." Emily picked up her fork and dug in. Over the next twenty minutes, she enjoyed listening to Chad talk about Gavin. She learned not only was her Yankees lover a *Mets* lover at one point, but he also pitched a no hitter in his senior year of high school. Afterward, he walked off the field, never to play again except for fun. Chad said they believed Gavin's decision to stop playing came from the pressure hounding scouts gave him about taking his talent all the way to the major league. This surprised Emily, considering Gavin's deep love for baseball. Nevertheless, she chalked it up to him wanting to become an architect. Either way, her curiosity was piqued, and she'd planned on picking his brain a little on the ride home. After she finished eating, Emily checked her watch. He'd been gone for over thirty minutes.

"Is Gavin milking the cow on a farm somewhere?" She pointed at the clock on the stainless steel stove. "He's been gone a while."

Chad squinted, his brow slowly rising. "Hmm. He has been gone for a while." He looked out the window at the fat drops of rain falling from the sky. "Maybe he's taking it slow. I know he mentioned he was riding his motorcycle up there."

"Oh," Emily said softly. A pang of unease settled over her limbs. Her mind rushed to a conversation she and Gavin had not long ago.

He'd gone into great, enthusiastic detail about how he loved opening up the bike to ungodly speeds while on the roads in East Hampton. "I'm going to call his cell and check on him."

Chad nodded, and Emily headed for the stairs. Taking two at a time, she reached the top in seconds. Rounding the corner, she collided into Olivia.

"Well, that woke me up," Olivia chirped. Towel drying her hair, she stared at Emily. "Why do you look all freaked out?"

Emily's eyes flew to an arched floor-to-ceiling window visible from the hallway. She held her breath as she took in the rain falling in thick, heavy sheets. Emily rushed past Olivia, her feeling of unease growing. With a quick hand, she dug her phone from her purse and hit the button for Gavin's number. By the fourth ring, she knew he wasn't picking up.

"Em, what the hell's wrong?" Olivia stood in doorway, her face edged with confusion.

Swallowing, Emily slid her phone closed. "Gavin went to go get milk, and he's not back yet. He took his damn bike, too."

Olivia shrugged. "Okay. It's raining. He's probably taking his time, chick. Calm down."

Emily nodded. Olivia was right. For whatever reason, she was overreacting. She knew Gavin would be smart enough to not drive like an animal, however, something was off, and she couldn't put her finger on it. Not quite a pull in her gut telling her something was wrong, but more of an emptiness slowly sneaking into her bones. As she tried to talk herself down from the cliff her mind was dangling over, the doorbell chimed through the air. Emily rushed to the bedroom window, and her heart stopped mid-beat as her eyes landed on a white and blue East Hampton patrol car. She flew past Olivia as she belted down the stairs. She came to a stop on the landing and brought her hand to her stomach as it cramped. Pain shot, ricocheting through her midsection. She curled her fingers around the railing and tried to slow her breathing, tried to slow her racing thoughts. Gavin was probably picked up for speeding. At least that's what Emily attempted to convince herself of as she watched Chad open the door. Gavin's full name…then the words. Although faint, they hit Emily's ears loudly, knocking her off balance.

Lost control…

Grave…

Air lifted…

Critical condition….

Emily tried to breathe as her body instinctively sank onto the steps, her hand gripping the cold metal baluster. A flurry of chaos ensued around her, but she didn't notice. She couldn't. She couldn't think or feel. Her mind slipped into a state of numbness, her ears blanking out Lillian's crying screams. She barely registered Trevor gently lifting her from the stairs and helping her out into the warm, humid air. A heavy raindrop hit her scalp. Another, her cheek. Before she knew it, she was soaked and seated in Trevor's car.

Green eyes staring blankly at the road flying past her, Emily's muscles froze with fear. Rain rioted the roof as her galloping heart shook her whole body. While her mind dragged through thorny yet beautiful memories of the last few months, the cold realization sank Emily deeper into her seat. Gavin was critically wounded. What the officer said rushed through floodgates, dowsing Emily with grief. A torrent of tears spilled as a brutal headache made a permanent nest in the darkest eaves of her skull.

By the time they pulled up to the hospital, the rain had grown louder, its rhythm as steady as an applause at a rock concert. Emily threw open her door and climbed out. Mind a scattered mess, she prayed as she made her way into the emergency room. Still unable to speak, Emily listened to Trevor and Fallon ask where Gavin was. After taking some information, the nurse behind the desk pointed toward the end of a hall. Eyes glistening with tears, Emily held onto Trevor's arm for balance as they stepped into an elevator.

"Emily, listen to me," Trevor whispered, his voice cracking. "He's going to be okay."

Fallon stroked Emily's rain-drenched hair. "He is, Em. You can't give up hope."

Lost control…

Grave…

Air lifted…

Critical condition….

Emily shook her head, her words stuttered. "You hea…heard what the off… officer said."

Fallon pulled her into her arms, holding her tight. When the elevator opened onto the ICU, Emily's blurry vision zeroed in on Gavin's parents, Colton, Olivia, and Jude talking with a doctor. Emily wanted to run to them to find out what was going on, but her body was frozen. Her feet wouldn't move. Her arms hung to her sides as cold as icicles hanging from gutters. With Trevor's aid, Emily stepped from the elevator. A deep sense of nothingness slithered through her chest as she slowly started for the group. The crisp, hospital air was loosely laced with the smells of ammonia and sickness. A chill shot down Emily's spine as her gaze drifted into several patients' rooms. Lying motionless with blankets drawn up to their necks, most were unconscious. As she approached the group, Emily could see the fear in Chad's eyes and it made her tremble. Her heart smashed, vibrating her body.

Lillian swept Emily into her arms, her tears soaking through Emily's top. "Oh, God. My baby. My baby boy. They're not sure if he's going to make it." Lillian's crying hammered though Emily's head, and her despair sliced right through Emily's heart.

"What happened?" Emily asked, barely getting the words out. With tears streaming down her face, she turned to the full-faced doctor. "There has to be something you can do. He's going to"—Emily choked back a sob—"he's going to be a father."

The doctor released a soft sigh, shoving his large hands into his pockets. "The motorcycle came out from beneath him in front of the Mill House Inn on Montauk Highway. He was thrown against on oncoming vehicle." He shook his head, his voice bleak. "We just finished up doing a CT scan on him. Though he was wearing a helmet, he's sustained severe injury to his brain, and he's non-responsive right now. We're trying to control the swelling, and we're going to do everything we can for him, but it doesn't look good. He has a punctured lung, three broken ribs, a broken femur, and internal bleeding in the abdomen. The surgeon will give you an update after he's out of surgery."

Emily felt her body go limp, felt her heart rip away from her chest. Sobbing uncontrollably, her legs slack beneath her, she leaned into the embrace of Trevor who was trying to hold her upright. However, his arms felt weak as he too struggled to keep himself together. Shaking, Emily made her way into a small waiting room. She sank into a chair, cradling her face as she rocked back and forth.

This couldn't be happening. It wasn't real. She refused to believe just hours before, her and Gavin's lives were complete, and now she could lose him. Their son could lose him. The thought of Noah never knowing the wonderful man his father was shook Emily's faith in all she'd ever believed in. With tear-soaked eyes, she slowly lifted her head and looked around the room. Faces pale with fear, not a single person in Gavin's life held a glimmer of hope in their expressions. Emily watched Chad hold Lillian, his grief burning a hole in Emily's mind. Seated next to a small coffee machine, Olivia rested her head against Jude's shoulder, her tears falling in streams down her cheeks. Emily swallowed as she dragged her gaze to Colton. Standing alone in the corner, arms crossed, he stared at the floor, crying silently.

Emily broke out into a cold sweat as images of what she and Gavin were supposed to be, the life they'd spoken about, slowly melted away. The clock on the wall ticked, its second hand sinister and ugly with each stroke of movement. Over the next few hours, everyone waited to hear a word. Light was fading from the damp sky by the time the surgeon entered the waiting room. Everyone jumped to their feet.

With eyes as empty as a dusty glass found forgotten on a windowsill, he began to speak. "We were able to stop the bleeding in his abdomen for now, and we'll keep an eye on it to make sure it doesn't start again." The surgeon paused, drawing in a slow, deep breath. "We had to perform an emergency craniotomy to relieve the pressure off the brain. The next forty-eight hours are critical. In the meantime"—he looked at each of them—"I feel its best you spend as much time with him as you can right now."

There was a moment of silence long enough for Emily to feel the quiet undertone of despair coating the room. But it broke as Lillian fell into Chad's arms, her cries screeching from her throat in puffed out heavy breaths. Emily's heart started throbbing in her chest so hard her fingers shook. As she watched the surgeon walk out, fog trapped Emily's mind. She sank into her chair, covering her face. She knew she couldn't see Gavin yet. She couldn't. The truth was, fear gutted her. It surrounded her, anchoring her frozen. She felt a gentle hand on her shoulder and looked up into Gavin's father's eyes. Dark shadows of grief painted his face.

"Come on," he mumbled, holding out a shaky hand. "We'll all go in together."

"I can't," Emily cried, unable to keep her voice from cracking. "I can't right now. You go ahead. I just need a few minutes."

Chad nodded pensively. Unshed tears clouded his eyes as he walked away, wrapping a supportive arm around Lillian's waist. Emily watched the grieving couple walk into the hall, her heart shredding with their departure. Head hung low and shoulders slumped, Colton followed them.

In seconds, Olivia was at Emily's side. She tenderly wiped tears from Emily's cheek. "Don't give up on him, Em," she whispered, her voice strained with fatigue. Blinking her bloodshot eyes, Olivia shook her head. "He needs you right now."

Longing filled Emily's chest. She didn't want to give up on Gavin; she knew she had to stay strong for him and their son. But somewhere in the back of her mind, hideous whispers told her otherwise. They screamed Noah would never see Gavin's warm, loving eyes. He'd never feel Gavin's spark, the way he lit up so many around him with a simple smile. Their poison warned of years dragging, one right into the next, with nothing but sorrow for the man she'd loved more than she loved herself. She silently begged them to stop their barrage on any hope she had left.

Trevor and Fallon stood, pulling Emily from the attack rumbling in her mind. Trevor cleared his throat and, with his arm over Fallon's shoulder, moved toward Emily and Olivia. Face splintered with grief, he shoved a hand through his hair. "I'm taking Fallon back to the house. She's going to keep an eye on Timothy and Teresa so Melanie can come up to visit." He paused, his eyes weary and broken. "Em, you need to eat. Let me pick you up something on my way back."

Emily shook her head. She couldn't wrap her mind around anything, not even eating. "I'm fine."

"Jude and I are going to grab something from the drink machine." Olivia kissed Emily's cheek and stood. "We'll be back in a few."

Emily nodded, able to tell everyone needed a minute to gather their thoughts. Mentally depleted and alone, Emily dropped her head into her hands, gasping against the pain. As she prayed to a God she was no longer sure existed, in that moment, a small flicker of hope shot through her. A flicker of what made her and Gavin one, what solidified them as two complete souls meant to be, washed over her.

Standing, she slid her trembling hands from her face, sucked in a deep breath, and started for the door. Upon emerging from the waiting room, her heart slammed as she slowly made her way down the hall. Stopping a few feet away from Gavin's room, Emily was nearly brought to her knees by Lillian's cries. Emily's stomach knotted, as a faint but noticeable contraction rippled through her, pulling the air from her lungs. Pushing through the pain, she entered the room.

With the view of the love of her life obstructed by the view of his family standing by his bedside, Emily watched silently, her hand over her mouth as she listened to Lillian speak to Gavin. She spoke of the first time he called her mommy and how that'd made her feel. Through tears, she trilled about his first day of school and how he'd clung to her legs, scared to get on the bus without her. She explained that though her heart had been crushed for him, she was proud when he let go and got on. Lillian broke down when she begged him to wake up so he could feel the same joy when his son let go of his hand on his first day into a very scary world.

A quiet sob ripped up Emily's throat, her body shaking from her fear of him missing so many beautiful memories. Countless seconds, hours, minutes, days, and years their son would need him. Sunrises and sunsets he had yet to share with Noah, explaining what it means to be a man, a real man. Little League, Boy Scouts, first date, prom, graduations, his first love, his wedding. Every morsel of life's precious gifts that he'd miss if he didn't pull through this.

A nurse walked into the room, breaking Emily away from dreams that may never happen. Dreams slipping away. She watched the middle-aged woman quietly check beeping monitors, replace clear, fluid-filled bags on Gavin's IV, and jot something onto a chart. Colton stepped back and caught Emily's gaze. As he approached her, she shivered at how much he'd looked like Gavin.

Hands in his pockets, he stared at her a beat before speaking. His voice was a shaky whisper. "He's so in love with you, Emily. I know the little bastard's trying to punch his way out of whatever he's in right now just to be with you." Lips trembling, Emily sucked in a shuddering breath as Colton gathered her in his arms. "He is. I know he's fighting. He's too stubborn not to."

"I hope he is," she choked out, clinging to him. "I can't lose him."

Lillian joined their embrace, her whimpers ringing through Emily's ears. Chad stood silently behind his wife, his eyes smothered with grief. Lillian held Emily's face. "You need time alone with him. We'll be in the waiting room if you need us."

Emily nodded, missing the gentleness of her touch as they walked out. With a shaky breath, she took a tentative step forward, her heart sinking immediately. Gavin's strong chest rose and fell in rhythm with the ventilator pumping oxygen into his lungs. Another step closer and her eyes dripped with tears as she observed his head wrapped in white gauze, a dapple of blood soaking through the material. His injured leg was hoisted up in some kind of sling. Breathing heavily, she reached the bed and touched his hand. There was warmth but no movement.

Not a twitch.

Not a flutter.

Nothing.

God. All Emily wanted to do was kiss him, but she couldn't. The tube in his mouth prevented her from doing so. She wanted to pull him from his pain, but she wasn't sure where to touch him. His body was covered in wires connected to the monitors flanking the bed. Unable to resist, she leaned over and placed a soft kiss on his black and blue bruised cheek. Letting her lips linger, a tear fell from her eye to his face. It slid down the side of his nose, almost as though it was his tear.

And that's when Emily really lost it.

"Please, Gavin, you can't do this to us." She brought a hand to his cheek, her body trembling as she sobbed. "You're the reason I'm breathing. I'm carrying the child our love created. Remember? The love they make movies about? That's us, Gavin. Our past is imperfect, but our future's breathtaking. You can't leave me. You can't. I need you. I need your bottle caps and twenty questions. I need your wiseass comments and that stupid look you give me when I try to cook for us. Please. God, Gavin, please fight. Fight for us. Fight for Noah. There're too many things I won't be able to teach him without you." Rain gurgled in a drainpipe outside the window as she waited for a sign. For a whisper of life. For anything that said he heard her, felt her.

Again… nothing.

"God, please. Please…" Her cries trailed off as she buried her face against his shoulder. The strong shoulder Gavin had so many times before tossed her over. She breathed in his musky scent that had made her dizzy for him the first time he was close to her. As she thought of every spoken and unspoken word they'd shared, her body jerked as an alarm suddenly sounded. Her eyes flew to one of the machines, its screen rapidly flashing red. Emily swallowed and stumbled back when a nurse ran into the room.

"I've got a Code Blue!" she yelled as she quickly unhooked the tube from Gavin's mouth. Screwing another in, she squeezed a bag over his mouth, manually pumping air into his lungs. "I need someone with a crash cart in here, stat!"

Eyes wide with horror, Emily heard the Code Blue called over the speakers as another nurse flew into the room. Frantically, the woman unsnapped Gavin's hospital gown and pulled it down. She pressed against his chest, hard and fast. Emily tried to breathe as another nurse tore in, dragging a cart with a machine on it behind her. Crying, Emily's vision blurred, voices muting, garbled in slow motion.

A male's voice hit the air. "What's his status?"

"V-fib," one of the nurses replied, continuing to press against Gavin's chest.

"Prepare to shock at two hundred joules."

After two large stickers were placed on his skin, another voice said, "Preparing to shock. All clear?"

Shaking uncontrollably, Emily watched the workers surrounding Gavin back away from the bed.

"All clear."

Thump... Gavin's body jerked...

Emily took a shuddering breath.

A second, a minute, an hour... Emily didn't know how long had passed. She couldn't think, couldn't move. Eyes glued to Gavin, her heart raced as she prayed his would continue to beat.

Thump… Gavin's body jerked once again…

The chaos around him continued as they proceeded to pump air into his lungs and press with vigor against his chest. Emily felt her back hit up against the wall, her mind a freight train of emotions as she cried out in hysterics, vaguely aware of Colton at her shoulder, trying to guide her frozen body out of the room.

"He's in astystole!" the nurse yelled.

The doctor looked at the monitor. "Push one milligram of epi."

Not a sound ushered through Emily's mind as she brought her eyes from Gavin's motionless body to the monitor, the mountainous waves on the screen, disappearing into a single flat line. There wasn't a long, drawn out beep, or if there was, Emily couldn't hear it. The only thing she could hear was Gavin's sweet words from the night before.

"I wonder if he'll know how much I'm going to love him and his mother until the day I take my last, dying breath."

"My last, dying breath…"

"Last…dying…breath…"

"Time of death: 10:28 p.m.," the doctor said somberly.

Emily's world skipped forward a few seconds, memories lost in a wicked lightning flash of pure darkness. She felt her throat twist and tighten. Her wide, green eyes stung. She willed her body to keep standing, but it couldn't. Backing away and hyperventilating, she landed painfully on all fours just outside the room. Words from others came and went in a fuzzy blur. Even Lillian's screams were distant. Far away cries from a mother who'd lost her youngest son.

Eyes soaked with tears, heart drenched with pain, and unknowing of whose hand was helping her from the floor, Emily tried to swallow. Tried to breathe. Trevor's trembling arms blanketed her body. He buried his weary face against her shoulder as he cried with her. Tonight, in the year her life was going to change in so many beautiful ways, fate had broken its promise and decided to fuck with everyone in Emily's life. In a haze, she watched a brother mourn his only sibling, a father cry out for his son, and friends gather in despair over the loss of someone they'd grown up with. Yet in all of the grief the hallway held, in that moment, Emily knew the largest loss belonged to the child she was carrying. His father was gone. Never to walk this earth again. Never to share a late night talk with his son. Never to hold his child in his arms for the first time.

He was gone...

No more stolen breaths before a kiss...

No more racing hearts from a simple look...

No more tingling skin without a touch...

He was... gone.

Breathe...

CHAPTER NINETEEN

Breathe

Breathe...

"Emily."

Breathe...

He's gone...

"Emily," the voice called louder.

With a gasp hurdling up her throat, Emily's eyes flew open, as she tried to adjust to the bright lights above her. Drenched in sweat and coughing, she sat up, kicking off the sheets. The sound of quickened footsteps grew nearer.

"Jesus, baby. Are you okay?"

Emily's eyes darted to the voice and her heart dropped when her gaze locked on Gavin. She rushed a hand to her mouth as she broke into hysterics. Body shaking like a leaf, and tears falling from her eyes in waves, Emily jumped from the bed and fell into Gavin's warm embrace.

"You were dead," she cried, smoothing her hands along his confused face. She needed to make sure he was real, make sure he was breathing, living. Her fingertips melted under the feel of his slight stubble as a painful contraction hit her, nearly knocking the breath from her lungs. She dragged her trembling hands along his bare chest as she feverishly kissed his lips, the words tumbling from her mouth between her panicked breaths. "Oh my God, Gavin. You died. You went for milk. The motorcycle."

Gavin cupped Emily's flushed cheeks and wiped her tears away with his thumbs. Staring into her eyes, a small smile touched his lips. "I'm here, sweets. Nothing happened. It was just a dream."

"It wasn't a dream," Emily cried, hunching over. Holding her midsection, another contraction zipped across her stomach. "Oh, God." She straightened, clinging to Gavin's shoulders as she kissed him repeatedly. Not wanting to close her eyes, she stared into his as her mouth moved over his soft lips. "It was a nightmare. You were dead." Another contraction followed by a kiss. "They shocked you. You wouldn't breathe. I begged you to keep fighting, and you couldn't. Your body gave up. Your mother's face. Your father. Your brother. Everyone was devastated."

Gavin gathered her tighter to his chest. Cradling her head, he ran his hands through her dampened hair. "Emily, calm down. I'm here, baby. I'm here."

Still frantic, she couldn't relax. Was he nuts? It was impossible. Visions of his lifeless body hung in her mind as clear as a cloudless sky. She pulled Gavin down to her lips as she continued to cry. "I love you. God, I love you so much, Gavin. I haven't told you enough." Another kiss, and another contraction. Zip. A deeper, shooting pain rippled through her stomach. These weren't Braxton Hicks contractions. Nope. Slowly backing away, Emily looked at Gavin, her voice a whisper. "I love you, Gavin Blake," she paused, wiping her hair from her forehead, "and we're about to have this baby."

Gavin swallowed and felt his eyes grow wide. "You're in labor?" he questioned, unable to keep his voice from cracking as if he was a teenage boy going through puberty. "You're not due for another three weeks."

She was the one in labor, but Emily could tell Gavin looked as though he was about to lose his shit. Pulling in a slow, cleansing breath, Emily nodded. "Yes, but I need you calm, okay?"

Gavin cocked his head back, convinced she had really lost her mind. Two seconds ago she was bugging about him dying, but now she was about to bring their child into the world and she'd become freakishly relaxed. "The bag!" he blurted out, turning toward the closet. He flung open the door and stopped. Spinning around, his eyes went wider. "Fuck, we didn't bring the bag. How are we supposed to do this without the bag?"

Though in slight physical discomfort, Emily felt mentally amazing. She stared at Gavin's scared face, wanting to drown in his eyes. It seemed so unreal he was standing in the room with her. She moved toward him, and touched his cheek, cradling it in her hand. "The baby's coming whether or not we have the maternity bag."

"Right," Gavin croaked, grabbing a pair of sweat pants and T-shirt. He slipped them on, trying his hardest to relax, but her calmness was making him nervous.

A subdued knock came at the door, followed by Olivia walking in. Sporting a pair of silk pajamas and furry bunny slippers, she squinted against the light. "You whackos do realize it's almost three in the morning, right?" She yawned and rubbed a tired hand over her face. "Considering Jude and I are right next door, is it possible you two could, I don't know, keep it down a little? You know I'm a light sleeper."

"Emily's in labor," Gavin answered, searching for his keys on top of the dresser.

Olivia's eyes went wide right about the same time another unwelcomed contraction started working its way through Emily's stomach. Hunched over, she tried to breathe through the pain.

Olivia and Gavin rushed to her side, each grabbing her arm. Olivia's mouth dropped open. "Holy shit, Em. We're all the way in the Hamptons. What the hell are you going to do? Drive back to the city? I mean, your doctor's there, not here."

Emily shook her head, her eyes drifting between Gavin and Olivia. "What's wrong with everyone?" she bit out, her voice not as sweet or calm as before. "I might be wrong, but women give birth all the time without maternity bags and without doctors they follow throughout their pregnancies. Right?"

"Right," Gavin and Olivia answered in unison.

"Thank you," Emily said, sinking onto the bed as she began to cry again. Between the pain and the nightmare, she was a mess.

Gavin glanced at Olivia, his voice feigning calm. "Can you get her out something to wear?"

Olivia nodded, and Gavin kneeled in front of Emily. Hands on her knees, he looked up into her eyes, thankful for everything she had and was about to give him. "I love you," he whispered. Emily ran her fingers through his hair, a weak smile touching her lips. "Scared together, sweets. Remember that. I'm here."

"Scared together," Emily softly repeated, accepting a shirt and maternity leggings from Olivia.

"I'm going to wake everyone up." Olivia popped a kiss on Emily's cheek and another on Gavin's head. "They need to know little Noah Olivia Alexander Blake will be here soon. Eek!" With that, she disappeared into the darkened hall.

Once again trying for the "I'm cool as a cat" act, when he was truly freaked the fuck out, Gavin helped Emily out of her pajamas and into her clothes. By the time they made it downstairs, the kitchen was awake with excited friends and family. Emily took a steeling breath as she stared at their smiling faces, her nightmare rushing back with full force. She couldn't help it; she broke down, tears exploding from her eyes.

Gavin wrapped his arm around her shoulder. He had a pretty good idea why she was crying.

Frowning, Lillian pulled Emily into her embrace. "You can get meds at the hospital for the pain, sweetie." She held her against her soft, black robe.

Taking in Lillian's concerned but happy demeanor, given she was about to meet her third grandchild, Emily pulled herself from the nightmare and stopped crying.

"How far apart are the contractions?" Lillian asked. "You've been timing them, right?"

Gavin shook his head, his throat suddenly dry. Damn. He was fucking this all up. He hadn't timed shit. He felt as if everything he'd learned in the many Lamaze classes he and Emily attended had flown right out the window.

"Just start timing them now," Fallon offered, pulling a chair from the table. She tossed her silver and green-streaked hair into a pony tail and sipped her coffee. "I read if they're closer than five minutes apart, the baby's coming soon."

Olivia shot her and Trevor a look. "You two *are* trying to have a kid, aren't you?"

Trevor smirked. "Sis, you are and will always be a nut." Olivia rolled her eyes and Trevor walked over to Gavin, shaking his hand. "Give us a few to wake up, and we'll meet you at the hospital. Born on the fifth of July. Cool birthday. Congratulations, bro."

"Thanks." Gavin smiled and walked Emily to the door. After hugging everyone goodbye, she stepped out into the dewy night air, making her way toward Gavin's car.

As Gavin went to rush after her, Colton caught his arm. "Just remember, little man, do whatever she asks. Don't take her threats or name calling personally. She still loves you. She just won't like you for the next few hours. *At all.*"

Chad chuckled, slapping Gavin's back. "I can't say I disagree with your brother. Linda Blair from *The Exorcist* comes to mind, but she'll calm back down."

Lillian swatted Chad's arm and pulled Gavin in for a hug. "Ignore your father and brother. Everything will be fine. Love you, baby boy. We'll be there soon."

Gavin kissed his mother goodbye and stepped from the house. Anticipating a full blown demon, he was surprised to find Emily casually leaning against his car. She still looked stressed, but he expected wicked. As if he had willed that demon into existence, he watched her face go from relaxed and loving to all-out pissed as she hunched over, grabbing her stomach.

"Jesus, Gavin, can you just open the door already?" she hissed, her fingers curling around the side mirror of his BMW.

Gavin nervously fumbled with his keys to unlock the door. He helped Emily into her seat, slammed the door, and shot around the vehicle. Once in, he looked at her, his heart sinking. "Breathe, baby. Remember the breathing techniques they taught you." He watched her toss her head back, and he heard some kind of grunt rumble up her throat.

She whipped her head around, glaring daggers at him. "I *know* how to breathe, Gavin. You just worry about getting me to the damn hospital so I don't give birth to your son on these leather seats. Got it?"

Yep, she was scaring Gavin. Throwing the car into reverse, he figured he'd speak only when spoken to for the remainder of the ride.

As lights along the darkened road came and went, so did the contraction possessing Emily's body. It left her feeling terrible, though. Sitting on her knees, she leaned over the console. Cupping Gavin's face as he stared at the road, she started raining kisses along his temple, hair, and jaw. Anywhere she could kiss, she did. "I'm so sorry." She kissed his nose, neck, ear, cheeks, and lips. She cried again. "You were dead. You were gone. I love you, Gavin. You're my Yankees-obsessed, bottle cap-giving wiseass. I'm so sorry. I love you so much."

Gavin's mouth twitched into a nervous smile. "This bottle cap-giving wiseass loves you, too." He paused and wiped a tear from her face, unsure whether or not he should say what he was about to. Her hands were tiny, but he knew his girl could throw a pretty powerful smack. "Um, sweets, you need to sit back down, okay? Get your seatbelt on for me."

Emily nodded. As she reached for the belt, her belly started to ball in pain. As it simmered, anchoring through her muscles, she felt a little pop. Still on her knees, warm liquid trickled down her leg. She pulled in a fast, harsh breath. "Oh... my... God," she cried out, her eyes wide with panic. "My water just broke. You need to drive faster, Gavin. *Now.*" She turned to him, her face twisted in pain as she held her stomach. "I'm not kidding. I know you know how *not* to drive like a grandfather. Get that big foot of yours to press harder on the gas. I. Am. Not. Kidding."

Gavin blinked, swallowed, and brought his eyes back to the road. With Linda Blair's twin sitting next to him, he didn't say a word as he gunned it. Though the love of his life was a bit scary, Gavin would never deny, when telling his grandchildren of this very night, he liked Emily giving him permission to drive like a bat out of hell.

In a matter of minutes, he had them screeching to a stop in front of the hospital. Jumping from the car, he fumbled for, well, he didn't quite know what he was fumbling for. But he was. Swiping a nervous hand through his hair, he swung open Emily's door and helped her out. By this time, she'd calmed down, exhibiting signs of severe bipolar disorder as she kissed him repeatedly. Breathing heavily, Emily cried her apologies as she clung to his arm while walking into the emergency room. He couldn't help it, but in that moment, Gavin wondered where she'd been all his life. God. He loved this woman, and she was about to give him the greatest gift ever, bipolar or not.

After a quick conversation with a nurse, Emily was seated in a wheelchair and whisked into an elevator. Destination: maternity floor. Emily shivered as she thought about the nightmare that'd plagued her sleep. Holding Gavin's hand, she looked at him, tears welling in her eyes. "I don't even want you here with me right now," she whispered, her body shaking. "I mean, I do. Of course I do. But I'm worried something's going to happen to you."

Gavin popped a brow, a grin smoothing across his mouth. "You know you're about to give birth to our child, right?" Emily nodded, and Gavin leaned down, brushing his lips along her forehead. "Emily Cooper, let me do all the worrying about *you* right now. Nothing's going to happen to me. Okay?"

She nodded again, gripping his hand tighter as another contraction slowly started to build. Its predecessors had nothing on this one. Breathing faster, Emily curled her fingers around the arm of the wheelchair. She swore her nails scraped the leather right off. "How many more floors?" she bit out, her eyes pinned on the nurse. From the look on Gavin's face, Emily swore she'd cut off circulation in his hand. "I'm not going to make it through this. I know I'm not."

The nurse patted her back, her twinkling eyes holding a wealth of knowledge. "I said the same thing with my first, second, and third. You'll be fine."

Hell no. Emily blew out a breath, completely, unequivocally, one hundred percent convinced she'd never let Gavin touch her again. When the elevator doors slid open, she was wheeled into a private room, her contraction easing its attack by the time she stood. The nurse handed her a hospital gown, and Emily made her way into the bathroom to get undressed. After changing and cleaning herself up, Emily stared at her reflection and her stomach.

Sighing, she started to relax. Gavin was fine. It was only a nightmare. Although what she was about to endure would be nothing short of torturous, at the end, not only would she have Noah, but Noah would have his father. A blizzard of emotions hit her when she heard agonized cries from a woman in the room next door. She swallowed, stared at herself for a long moment, and walked out of the bathroom praying she could handle this.

"Hey," Gavin said, helping her over to the bed. "You okay?"

She gazed into his baby blues, his love evident. "Right now I am." She pushed up on her tiptoes and kissed his soft lips. He held her, his embrace warm. "I'm apologizing now for the way I might act during…" Her voice trailed as another contraction started to erupt. Backing away, Emily held her stomach and sat on the bed. Eyes narrowed and breathing harsh, she stared at Gavin. "Oh God. Say something to keep my mind off the pain!"

Gavin's heart melted. Somewhat afraid to touch her, he gently ran his hand over Emily's stomach, praying she wouldn't take a swing at him. "I hope he looks like his mother." He kissed her forehead, pushing her hair away from her shoulder. "I hope he has your beautiful green eyes." He grinned and kissed each eyelid. "He'll have the ladies all over him if he does."

As the nurse adjusted a maternity belt over her stomach, Emily did her breathing exercises, convinced her back was slowly breaking. "*My eyes? I was hoping he'd have yours.*" She tossed her head against the pillow and rolled to her side. "Keep talking. God, keep talking, Gavin," she cried out. "Twenty questions, and don't you *dare* bring up anything sexual."

Gavin cleared his throat, grabbing her hand. "Pain killers or no pain killers?"

"Definitely pain killers," Emily grit out, her eyes locked on the nurse.

The nurse nodded with a sympathetic smile. "I'll get something for you as soon as I get this IV started."

Emily didn't notice the tiny pin prick as the contraction built in intensity. Continuing her breathing exercises, that she was pretty sure weren't going to help her for anything, Emily tried to concentrate on the baby's heartbeat whooshing through the air. "Another question. Something. Please, Gavin. Something."

Gavin held her hand tighter, wishing he could take away every bit of pain. "Crown molding or no crown molding?"

"Crown molding," Emily breathed, bracing against the side of the bed.

"Cake or ice cream?"

"Both. Oh God, both!" She rolled onto her back, the contraction making her feel as if she was about to lose her mind.

"You're peaking, sweetie," the nurse noted, pointing to a monstrous, angry green line on the monitor. "Watch. It'll start to come down."

Sure enough, it slowly dipped, allowing Emily to breathe in relief. The tension coiling in her shoulders deflated and her body sank into the bed as she released her death grip on Gavin's hand.

"I'll be right back," the nurse said, making her way toward the door. "Dr. Beck's on call this evening. He'll be in to talk with you and to check how much you've dilated."

Emily gave a weak nod and rushed a tired hand through her hair as she brought her gaze to Gavin's. She could tell he felt helpless. Emily managed a small smile. "Come lay down next to me. I promise I'll give fair warning when another starts."

"You think I'm scared of you?" he chuckled, lying as smooth as they come. He was afraid of her. Hell, she was pretty terrifying and this was only the beginning, but he'd never let her know that. He slid across the bed, gathered her in his arms, and stared into her eyes.

"I can tell I'm scaring you." Emily took a deep breath, losing herself in his embrace.

"Never," Gavin whispered. "You couldn't scare me if you tried."

Emily leaned her forehead against his chin and tried to relax. She had a few seconds of reprieve as Gavin caressed her spine, his touch soothing, before her belly balled viciously. Tensing, Emily could barely prepare herself for the foreign feeling taking hold.

"Breathe, baby," Gavin whispered. "Look at me and breathe through it."

Tears spiked in Emily's eyes as a slow, simmering twist knotted. Her back felt as though a bus was running over it. She gripped Gavin's shoulders, her finger nails digging into his T-shirt as she stared at him. "Oh, God. It hurts," she cried, her brows cinched. "Say something. Come on, Gavin. Twenty questions again."

"City or upstate?"

"Upstate," she answered, her stare leaving his as she looked over his shoulder at the monitor. Damn that line. It hadn't reached the plateau of agony yet. It wasn't even close.

"Wood or tile flooring?"

Squeezing his shoulders tighter, Emily brought her angry eyes back to Gavin's, the breath rushing from her mouth. "Wood. Jesus Christ, wood."

Gavin's heart clenched, watching the woman he loved suffer as her body prepared to bring his son into this world. "Pizza or pasta?"

"Neither," Emily hissed, tossing her head back. "Get the damn nurse, Gavin. No more twenty questions. I need something for this pain right now!"

Gavin shot up, nearly tripping over the bedside table. Before he could make it to the door, it opened. Easy smile in place, a young man in a white doctor's jacket, who didn't appear to be old enough to drive, strolled into the room. Behind him was the nurse from earlier armed with a vial of what Gavin assumed to be narcotics. With Emily screaming, Gavin couldn't help a few thoughts from filtering through his head.

The first: He didn't want this dude touching Emily. The second: Yeah, he still didn't want this dude touching Emily. "Are you a student?" Gavin brusquely questioned, his eyes wide.

The young man flashed a grin, his gaze transfixed on a clipboard. He jotted something down and looked at Gavin. "No, I'm not a student. I'm Doctor Martin Beck."

Gavin didn't acknowledge the hand the doctor extended. "*You're* delivering my son?"

"If your wife—"

"Girlfriend," Gavin corrected, his stomach twisting from the lack of facial hair on the guy's face. Gavin was pretty fucking sure the doctor was still a virgin.

"My apologies. If your *girlfriend* gives birth in the next twelve hours, yes, I'm delivering your son."

Speechless, Gavin watched him approach Emily. Her pain-filled face looked like she could care less if another species delivered their child. The doctor rolled a chair up in front of her and asked Emily to come down to the edge of the bed. He also asked Emily to open her legs for him. Oh Jesus. Gavin felt nauseated. Witnessing a doctor as old as his grandfather prod and poke at the part of Emily's body Gavin felt was created for him was bad enough, but now this? This was insane. Panic gripped Gavin, but before he could say a word, Emily, who now seemed to be in a blissful state of drugged up euphoria, did as the doctor asked, dropping her knees to the side. With his girlfriend spread wide for Doogie Howser, Gavin nervously swallowed, shoved a hand through his hair, and all but sprinted across the room. Depositing himself on the bed next to Emily, Gavin stared into her glassed over eyes, trying to concentrate on the fact she wasn't in pain at the moment.

"You're four centimeters dilated," the young buck announced, rolling away from Emily. Pulling gloves from his hands, he gave her a smile. "Being this is your first child, it's usually an hour or two a centimeter."

Gavin glanced at the clock on the wall. It was a quarter past four in the morning.

"Will you keep giving me whatever you just gave me?" Emily's lazy smile clearly showed she wasn't suffering much. "I like how I feel right now."

The doctor grinned. "That'll take the edge off the pain, but you'll still feel the contractions." He checked the monitor and scribbled something down on his clipboard. "If you want stronger relief, we can give you an epidural."

Eyes closing, Emily shook her head and yawned. "No. No epidural. I think I've scared myself from getting one. I read…" her voice trailed as she started falling asleep. She curled up on her side, her head nestled into the pillow.

With his grin still in place, the doctor looked at Gavin. "Like I said, the Demerol should clip some of the pain for her. She might wake up with each contraction, but it won't be as difficult for her now. In the meantime, you should also try to get some sleep. You both have a long few hours in front of you." On that note, the doctor left the room.

The nurse smiled at Gavin on her way to the door. "She's in good hands. Don't worry."

Gavin nodded pensively, trying to talk himself out of dragging Emily's sleeping body from the bed and off to another hospital to give birth. With that, he watched the nurse walk out. Sighing, he laid back against the pillow and stared at Emily, her breathing calm and peaceful. Though he was exhausted, sleep seemed oceans away. Instead, he gently positioned Emily's head on his chest, his mind reeling over the fact that in a few hours, they would be parents. Only a year ago, the woman in his arms was out of reach, yet here and now, she was about to spoil him with a son. She was about to make him a father. Feeling more than blessed,

Gavin knew he'd go through every second of pain all over again if he had to. He wouldn't think twice about it.

Emily stirred, a small whimper leaving her lips. Gavin's gaze fell to the monitor, his heart clenching, as he watched the line slowly start to climb. With tired eyes, he brushed his hand through Emily's hair. He hoped the pain killer was helping. It must've because she didn't fully wake. Over the next couple of hours, Emily tossed during the contractions, but somehow she managed to fall in and out of sleep. That was all that mattered to Gavin. As the horizon turned dusty orange with the waking sun, Gavin jumped when the monitor chimed. Within a few seconds, a nurse walked into the room.

Face pinched in concern, she gathered the long strip of paper from the machine and studied it. She turned to Gavin, her voice a whisper. "I need her to shift position. The baby's heart rate's dropped."

Gavin glanced at the monitor and back to the nurse, his adrenaline spiking. "Is he okay?"

"He should be," she answered calmly, but Gavin heard the worry in her voice. She made her way around the opposite side of the bed. "It usually helps if momma moves around a bit."

Gavin slid his arm out from beneath Emily. She moaned, clearly in pain. Gavin ran his hand through her hair and gazed into her sleepy eyes. "Emily," he whispered, stroking her cheek, "the nurse needs you to move around."

Nodding, Emily sat up. The pain killer was wearing off as a contraction started moving through her stomach. She blinked back tears, her muscles bracing with tension. "I think I need something more for the pain." She shifted onto her right side, grabbing at her lower back. "Please. I need something. They're getting worse."

The nurse stared at the monitor, her expression no less concerned. "Sweetie, I need you to get on all fours for me."

Heart jumping into his throat, Gavin could see the look on the woman's face. Emily let out another whimper as he helped her do as the nurse said. Trying to keep calm, he rubbed Emily's back and watched the nurse flick her eyes to the monitor again.

"Okay, Emily. Go ahead and lay on your back again while I get the doctor." The nurse rushed for the door.

"What's going on?" Gavin questioned, helping Emily lay back down. "You can't walk out of here without telling us if our son's okay."

The nurse whipped around. "The doctor will explain everything." She didn't give Gavin a chance to say another word as she fled from the room.

"Why isn't she telling us anything?" Emily looked at Gavin, her heart rate quickening with fear as the tremor from the contraction ebbed.

Gavin shook his head and tried to calm down for her sake. He cupped her face and brushed his lips against her forehead. "I'm sure it's nothing," he whispered, looking into her eyes. He could tell she didn't believe him. His heart sank. "Listen to me, okay?"

Voice groggy, she nodded. "Okay."

"Emily Cooper, you're about to give birth to the most healthy, amazing, sucky bottle cap playing, bouncing baby boy out there." Stroking her cheeks, he placed a gentle kiss on her trembling lips. "And he's about to love his amazing mother so much, he's going to make me jealous of you two. Please don't worry. Understand?"

"Yes," Emily whispered, wanting to believe him. She rested her hands over his and pulled in a deep breath. "A healthy baby boy."

A slow grin spread across Gavin's mouth. "Don't forget the sucky bottle cap playing part."

Emily smiled weakly. As she attempted to adjust the pillow behind her, the doctor and two nurses walked in. Eyes on the monitor, Dr. Beck watched it for a moment before bringing his attention to Emily. "The baby's in fetal distress. We're going to have to perform an emergency Cesarean." Gavin backed away when the nurses flanked the bed, yanking up the side rails.

"I'll see you in the O.R.," the doctor added as he left the room.

Emily swallowed and her throat felt as though sand was coating it. "Is the baby going to be okay?" she cried, her eyes darting between the two nurses. They didn't answer as they wheeled her bed toward the door. Emily's heart raced. "Wait, what about my boyfriend? He's allowed in the operating room, right?"

"They'd have to kill me to keep me out." Gavin followed her, his nerves zinging with fear.

A nurse turned around and rested a hand on Gavin's shoulder. "You can't go with her right now. You need to get suited up for the O.R. Give me a few minutes, and I'll be back with everything you'll need."

The woman's words were a blur to Gavin. He could barely think. Emily was the air he'd kill for, the carbon copy of his existence, and now he felt as though he was suffocating. With his heart climbing up his throat, he bent over the bed and focused on Emily's petrified face. Running his hands through her hair, he leaned down and gently kissed her lips. She held onto his shoulders, crying as she kissed him back. Gavin slowly pulled away, his mind telling him to stay strong.

"Remember what I said to you," he whispered. "An amazing, healthy baby boy."

Sniffling, Emily nodded as the nurses pushed the bed out of the room.

Standing in the hall, Gavin watched them rush Emily into an elevator. He swallowed as the doors closed. The world, his heart, time, and everything within it came to a screeching halt. Shoulders weak with fear, Gavin tried to contain the emotions sinking into his muscles. As he turned to walk into the room and wait for the nurse, his gaze snatched his parents making their way toward him. Their faces showed their excitement until they reached him.

"What's the matter?" Lillian asked, her smile fading.

Gavin shoved a hand through his hair, clearing a lump from his throat. "The baby's in fetal distress. They just took Emily into the operating room."

Lillian touched her mouth, the worry in her eyes mirroring Chad's. She pulled Gavin into her arms. "They're going to be fine. Don't you think otherwise."

Gavin nodded, trying hard to concentrate on his mother's words. He still couldn't believe what was happening. Down the hall, he could hear Olivia, Fallon, Trevor, and Colton. Their happiness was apparent too, until they saw Gavin and his parents. After a quick explanation, they all gathered in the room and waited for the nurse. Though small talk was attempted, tension hovered, its presence heavy as the minutes ticked by.

After what seemed like forever, Gavin surged from his chair when a nurse walked in. She handed him a heap of medical clothing, and he wasted no time hurrying into the bathroom to change. Once dressed, he said goodbye to his friends and family and followed the nurse into the elevator. He tried to hang on to hope, but as the elevator doors opened, Gavin couldn't help but feel as if he was walking into a nightmare of his own. He couldn't even begin to compute the death of a child, nor did he want to.

He felt his heart speed up, but he shoved the wicked thought to the back of his mind as he entered the operating room. Amongst the chaos, his frantic gaze landed on Emily, his breath evaporating through the chilled air when he saw her. Gavin's heart slowed, plummeting into his stomach as the nurse guided him over to Emily. Her delicate arms were flailed out to either side, her wrists secured with Velcro. She looked so helpless as she stared up at him, her watery eyes seeping with fear and uncertainty. It sank Gavin.

"I'm here with you, baby. Right here," he whispered through his surgical mask. His lips tingled to feel hers as he leaned over, his face inches from hers. "I'm not taking my eyes off of yours until I hear Noah cry."

The slight chill working over Emily's skin warmed as she stared into Gavin's eyes. She nodded, wanting nothing more than to touch him. She needed both her men safe in her arms. When the doctor announced he was about to begin, Emily squeezed her eyes closed. A tear slid down her cheek. Gavin intertwined his fingers in hers, and as promised, his gaze never left her eyes. As close as his face was to hers, Emily could feel the heat rolling from his body, felt his love pouring through her.

"I thank God for you every day, Emily Cooper," Gavin whispered. "You know that?"

Emily shook her head, her heart pounding from Gavin's words and the twinge of pressure curling through her stomach.

"I do," Gavin continued, his voice soft. "I also thank God the delivery boy quit the day you walked into my life. I thank God every time you burn a casserole and smoke the shit out of my house."

Emily gave a weak smile, holding his hand tighter. She couldn't see Gavin's mouth, but the shimmer in his eyes told Emily he was also smiling.

"I thank God for every minute you've ever given me. Even the bad minutes." He paused, bringing his face closer. "You told me once you thought you'd broken us. You didn't break us, doll. You fixed us. Those bad minutes shaped us into what we are. They molded us into what we're going to be together. We were written for one another, and I wouldn't change one line in our romance novel. The good, the bad, the in between. It's ours. We own it."

The room was filled with loud chatter and frenzied movement, but the only thing Emily could see or hear was Gavin's eyes and voice. Breathless, she swallowed. The need to hold him skyrocketed through her chest. "I love you," she softly choked out, feeling a tug in her stomach. "And it's me who'll love you until the day *I* take my last, dying breath." And she would. The man standing above her had saved her in so many ways, she was sure he'd never fully understand what he meant to her. It was impossible.

As she stared into Gavin's eyes, a second of haunting white noise rocked the air, followed by Noah's beautiful, screaming entrance into the world. Pressure lifted from Emily's stomach, and she felt a warm tear from Gavin's eyes hit her cheek. As she listened to Noah's hearty wails and watched the man she loved shed his first tears in front of her, Emily felt whole. Her heart throbbed with completeness when Gavin tore his nervous gaze from hers. It also throbbed when she heard him let out a proud, soft chuckle.

Her man was a father. Her Yankees-loving, bottle cap-giving life saver was a father. And she, a mother. In that moment, Emily cried for her own mother, realizing that every mistake she'd made with Emily, she made because she was human. Though Emily hadn't laid eyes on him yet, she felt her love for Noah soak her soul, the same way she knew her mother's love for her must've soaked hers.

Not knowing if he was allowed to but not giving a shit, Gavin yanked the surgical mask from his face. Between laughing and trying to catch his breath, Gavin spoke against Emily's lips as he kissed her, his heart jumping in his throat. "You're amazing. Thank you so much. Jesus Christ, he's beautiful, Emily. He has a full head of brown hair like yours." Gavin looked over the sheet hung in front of Emily, his smile wide. "Hey, Doogie Howser!" With a raised brow, the doctor glanced up. "Ten fingers? Ten toes? Healthy?" Gavin probed.

"Yes to all of the above. Congratulations to you both." Smiling inquisitively, he tilted his head. "Though I must admit, I'm not sure who Doogie Howser is."

Gavin chuckled. "Of course you don't. You're too young. Thank you for delivering my son. Now, can I hold him?"

Still appearing quite confused, the doctor nodded.

As one of the beaming nurses carried a tightly swaddled Noah over, a once unruffled Gavin suddenly felt nervous. He didn't know where this was coming from, considering he'd held Teresa and Timothy when they were infants. He licked his dry lips and tried to compose himself as the woman placed Noah into his arms. As if that nervousness never existed, Gavin instantly calmed as Emily's reflection stared back at him when he looked into the dark blue eyes of his son. In complete awe, Gavin's eyes traced Noah's face, his mind imprinting every second into his memory. Gavin swallowed and gently brought his fingers to Noah's tiny button of a nose, chuckling when his son yawned.

"You think *you're* tired, little guy?" Gavin asked, kissing his soft cheek. "Tell that to your mother. You made her turn a little psychotic there for a while. She scared me, and I'm a tough one to get going."

Emily's heart swelled at Gavin's easiness and instant love. She wasn't surprised though. Smiling, she watched Gavin proudly dote over their son. With Noah cradled tightly in his arms, Gavin brought him over to Emily. Leaning over her exhausted body, he held Noah to her lips, allowing her to inch up and kiss his forehead. His satiny skin felt like heaven. No longer drowning in a nightmare, he was a waking dream for Emily. She sighed as contentment bloomed wildly in her soul.

"He's beautiful," she whispered, tears creeping from her eyes. Aching to hold him, her fingertips tingled with the need to touch him. "My God. He's so beautiful, Gavin."

Gavin placed a soft, lingering kiss on her lips. "Just like his mother." He stared into her watery eyes, his breath stolen by the pure happiness smoothing across her face. "Thank you. You've given me the greatest gift a woman can ever give a man. Ever. Nothing trumps it." Gavin kissed her again, his voice a sweet caress. "I didn't think it was possible, but I'm more in love with you now than before. You've rocked my entire world, Emily Cooper."

With tears of happiness streaming down her face, Emily stared at the two men who'd stolen her breath, heart, and soul the second she laid eyes on them. Though good, bad, and ugly had plagued the path she and Gavin walked along the way, she'd never take any of it back because each step brought them closer to this beautiful moment. In those minutes, during the beautiful summer the year her life changed forever, the year her future began, Emily knew she was the one that'd been given the greatest gift ever.

Now... she could finally breathe.

CHAPTER TWENTY

Welcomed Endings and New Beginnings

The morning sunlight danced over Noah's face as Emily stared into his sleepy eyes. After a feeding and a good hearty burping, he looked blissfully content. Lying on her side with him curled next to her in bed, Emily gently ran her fingertips across his cotton candy-soft hair. Giggling when he stirred lightly at her touch, warmth traveled up Emily's spine and settled in her heart as she continued to visually inhale her precious angel.

Lowering her face to his plump cheek, Emily breathed him in, wanting to burn his glorious scent into her memory. He smelled sweet like flowers but carried something uniquely his own. Emily smiled against his skin, cradling him closer. She held her pinky against his tiny hand, her soul blooming with amazement as he wrapped his fingers around hers. The first few days home with him were simultaneously the most exhausting and beautiful of her life. Needless to say, she fell head over heels in love with Noah, and she also fell fast into the role of a mother easier than expected. Not only had she not dropped him, and was pretty confident she never would, she hadn't encountered any problems with ointment control, either. As Emily watched her first blessing drift off into a peaceful sleep, her second blessing strolled into the bedroom, his smile as bright as ever.

"He's out cold," Gavin whispered. He slipped under the sheets with Noah and Emily, sandwiching their little man between them. Lifting a brow, Gavin's smile widened. "He needs to get a job soon. I'm tired of his laziness."

Emily beamed and traced gentle circles along Noah's tiny bow of a mouth. "I know, right? I figured he'd have a good work ethic. But this? This is just ridiculous."

Chuckling, Gavin brought his hand up to Emily's cheek. "How are you feeling?"

Emily leaned into his palm, her body soaking in his warmth. "Amazing." And she did. Though still sore from the staples lining her belly, she hadn't felt this good physically or emotionally in what seemed like forever. "How do you feel?"

"Like a king," Gavin whispered, cautiously leaning over Noah. He placed a soft kiss on Emily's lips, his heart filled with joy beyond comprehension. "I'm in my castle with my queen and prince. I honestly have everything." Gavin stared into her eyes, his breath hijacked as always. "Thank you."

From something that'd started off so confusing, so tortuously wrong in countless ways, Emily couldn't believe where she and Gavin were. Her stomach dipped, overflowing with love for the two men in her life. Her two saviors. "Thank *you*." She kissed him again, drowning in the feel of the lips she'd forever love. "And thank you for breakfast. I'll eventually master cooking something beyond burnt casseroles and frozen microwave dinners."

A wiseass smirk appeared across Gavin's face, and Emily prepared herself for the wiseass remark she knew she'd opened herself up to. "No need. We'll do fine surviving on nothing but sodium and crisped up meatloaf." Emily rolled her eyes, and Gavin chuckled. "And how can I forget your specialty boxed mac and cheese?"

"Watch, you'll see," she countered, playfully smacking his arm. "I'm going to take cooking lessons and knock your mother's *mediocre* lasagna from your memory."

Gavin lifted an incredulous brow, his smirk turning full-blown megawatt. "Mediocre? I'd love to see you try to beat it."

Emily carefully slid from the bed. Hands on her hips, she tilted her head. "Is this a challenge, Blake?"

"The biggest of your life, sweets." Gavin picked up a stirring Noah, positioning him against his chest. He looked down at his little bundle. "Your mother's seriously lost it, kid. She thinks she's going to learn how to feed you and me better than your grandmother can."

Eyes wide, Emily huffed. "Oh my God. Just for that, all you'll see is my mac and cheese." Smiling, she wagged a finger at Gavin. "Noah will eat well, but you? Nope, not you. Burnt meatloaves for life. Hope you're happy." Gavin let out a full, throaty laugh as Emily flipped her wavy hair, spitefully puckered her lips, and blew him a less than loving kiss. Gavin was just happy she didn't flip him the finger. "I need to get ready before everyone gets here. There's cold, crisp, burnt meatloaf in the fridge if you get hungry." On that note, she disappeared into the bathroom.

"You know what an angry Emily does to me," Gavin called out, laughing and patting Noah's back.

Though muffled from behind the closed door, her words rang loud as the doorbell chimed. "Good. I hope your *stone* turns blue."

"Ouch." Holding a semi-awake Noah, Gavin stood and made his way down the hall. "She's certifiable, buddy." Before he opened the door,

Gavin kissed his son. "But she has magical powers. Somehow, she'll get you to act like a complete fool around her."

"Give him to me," Olivia squeaked when Gavin opened the door. Arms held wide, the smile on her face showed her excitement.

"What?" Gavin questioned. Grinning, he shook his head. "Am I no longer worth anything?"

Trevor clapped Gavin's shoulder. "You've officially turned into Al Bundy from *Married with Children*. Get used to it, bro."

Colton barked out a laugh and shuffled into the penthouse. "I have to agree with him."

With an equally excited expression melting across her face, Lillian popped a quick kiss on Gavin's cheek and snatched Noah out of his arms. "Of course you're still worth something, sweetie." She cradled her grandson and dowsed him with kisses. Eyes filled with joy, she looked at Olivia. "Grandma gets first dibs, Livy. Sorry."

Gavin laughed as Olivia frowned, watching his mother dance over to the couch. She continued to rain unrelenting, grandmotherly kisses over the family's newest addition.

Olivia sighed, but that didn't stop her from reaching for Timothy and Teresa's little hands and sinking onto the couch right next to Lillian. Under normal circumstances, Gavin figured his mother would've considered Olivia's closeness an invasion of her personal space. However, both women were too busy fawning over Noah to complain.

After setting a large silver tray of food down on the counter, Melanie pulled Gavin into her arms. "Aww. I still love you."

"Thanks, Mel," Gavin replied as she joined the group of baby excited oohing and ahhing family members on the couch. With curiosity getting the better of him, Gavin peeled the lid away from the tray. His eyes took in his mother's lasagna.

There was no doubt Emily would get a kick out of that one.

"Mom's lasagna." Chad sniffed thoughtfully, hovering over the tray. "She made it for me on our third date, and that's when I fell in love with her."

Gavin chuckled, running his hand through his hair. "You're kidding me?"

"Well, I should say it sealed the deal." Chad smiled proudly. "I'm going to go do the grandpop thing with my lasagna-making lover."

Gavin grinned and watched his father take off toward the couch. Arms crossed, Gavin leaned against the island, admiring everyone drooling over Noah. With warmth spiraling through him, Gavin soaked it in. His father was right. Family was what it was all about.

"Where's your other half?" Colton probed, pulling up a stool with Trevor. "And how's she feeling?"

"She's in the shower," Gavin answered. "She seems to be doing well."

"So how do you feel about her making me go with you today?" Trevor popped a smirk and yanked his glasses from his face. Staring at Gavin, he cleaned them with the hem of his shirt. "I'm kind of your bodyguard in case shit goes down."

Gavin drew up a brow, finding the situation comical. "Don't get high on yourself, bro. I'm taking you because Emily insisted. I don't need you there. If anything, Dillon's lucky you're coming with me." Gavin moved to the refrigerator and plucked out a bottle of water. After taking a sip, he shook his head. "If he gets out of line, neither you nor anyone else will be able to stop me from finishing what I started months ago."

"Be careful, little man," Colton warned, jerking his head toward Noah. "Keep him in mind if Asshole pushes the wrong buttons. Dillon will never be worth going to jail over."

Gavin's gaze fell on Noah. There was no denying Colton's statement was correct. Gavin began to think Emily's desire to have their lawyers send a letter on their behalf, notifying Dillon that Gavin was the father, was a good idea. He'd originally planned on a simple phone call. Although he did call Dillon, it was only to lie about Emily's next doctor's appointment. But something deep inside Gavin wanted, no, needed to see Dillon's face when he heard the news. It screamed out in revenge for all Dillon had put them through. It was payback time, and Gavin wanted to cut the fucking check.

With that, he headed for the bedroom to see if Emily was finished. When he entered, he found her in the bathroom blow drying her hair. He stared at her a long moment, almost regretting his decision to go against her wishes, but it only lasted a second. Visions of the hell she'd suffered with Dillon hit Gavin's thoughts, relinquishing him of every bit of guilt he felt about doing things his way.

On a deep breath, Gavin stepped into the bathroom and came up behind Emily. Staring at her beautiful reflection, he slid his hands around her waist, resting his chin on her shoulder. "I'm getting ready to go," Gavin whispered, hating the look in her eyes. Emily stared back at him in the mirror, her unspoken words ripping him apart, but he couldn't stop himself if he wanted. "Everything's going to be fine, Emily. I have to do this. For me. As a man. I have to."

Emily wasn't about to argue the issue any further. She'd spent the last several days trying to convince him that seeing Dillon in the flesh to deliver the news wouldn't do anything but make an already insane situation worse. Though she'd never fully understand his reasoning, Emily knew she had to stand by Gavin's decision. She nodded, closing her eyes when Gavin buried his face in the crook of her neck. Without another word, she watched him walk out of the bathroom. Now Emily just needed to convince herself what she was allowing him to do was going to be okay.

"How come I feel like this is the calm before the storm?"

Gavin flicked his gaze from the red glowing numbers on the elevator display to Trevor. "What makes you say that?"

Trevor shrugged. "You're too calm. It's kind of freaking me the fuck out. I've never seen you like this."

"I can't be relaxed?" Gavin asked, lifting a brow. "Is this a new rule?"

"Not this relaxed, dude." Trevor rushed a hand through his hair. "Look at yourself."

With his hands tucked in his pockets, leaning casually against the wall, Gavin smirked. He found Trevor's nervousness amusing. "You think I'm going to hurt him?"

"I think you're going to do some kind of number on him, yeah."

"Right," Gavin chuckled. "It's called the 'Dillon, go fuck yourself. I'm the father' number."

Before Trevor could blink, the elevator doors slid open. Smirk holding steady, Gavin strolled out, his eyes scanning the chaotic scene of brokers pacing. Not only did Gavin ignore the stares from Dillon's coworkers, he ignored Dillon's secretary. When her jaw dropped open, Gavin found himself amused for the second time in less than two minutes.

"Gavin!" she yelped, shooting up from her chair. Fumbling in her mountainous stiletto heels, her breath was a ragged mess when she caught up with him. "You can't go in there."

Gavin placed his hand on her shoulder, a grin softening his face. "Hi, Kimberly. How've you been?"

"I've been good, Gavin." She sighed, her tone nothing short of begging. "Please don't do this to me. I was told to call the cops if you ever show up here."

It was Trevor's turn to place his hand on her shoulder. "Hi, Kimberly. How've you been?"

She rolled her eyes. "Hi, Trevor. I'm fine."

"You're not going to call the cops on Gavin." She rolled her eyes again, and Trevor smiled. "You know how I know you're *not* going to do that?"

She dug her hands into her hips. "How do you know I'm not going to call the cops on Gavin, Trevor?"

"Because a little birdie from this very office called me the other day and let me know that not only is Dillon… sweetening you up in his bed, but he's also sweetening up Pricilla Harry from Sheller Investments on the seventeenth floor. They also mentioned he really isn't digging the little mermaid outfit you wear for him as much as he makes you think he is. " As Kimberly's eyes narrowed, lighting up like searing coals, Trevor gave a leisurely shrug. "Am I wrong when I say you probably *want* Gavin to go into Dillon's office right about now?"

Kimberly whipped her head in Gavin's direction, her voice seething. "You have five minutes."

"Not a minute longer," Gavin replied as smooth as silk, feeling somewhat bad for the girl. He swung his blue eyes in Trevor's direction. "Why don't you keep Kimberly busy while I tend to business? She looks like she needs some comforting."

Trevor nodded and Gavin turned, heading right for Dillon's office. Not even bothering to see where the asshole was positioned, Gavin reached for the handle and swung open the door. There was one thing he did the same as last time. Yeah. He made sure to lock the door.

Let the *second* motherfucking game begin.

With widened eyes, Dillon surged to his feet.

The shock and nervousness on his face forced a barking laugh from Gavin. "Whoa, whoa." Gavin held up his hands in mock surrender. "Caught you a little off guard, I see."

"Fuck off, Blake. You can't just walk in here like that," Dillon pointed out, his body language showing he was braced for a fight. "You were supposed to call with Emily's next doctor's appointment. That was the fucking agreement when you left the message saying she wouldn't make her last one."

Slight tension crackled through Gavin's nerves as he stepped toward Dillon. "Calm the fuck down." Gavin held up a small, blue envelope and tossed it onto Dillon's desk. With a slow grin twisting his lips, Gavin stared at Dillon's hand resting on the phone. No doubt he was getting ready to pick it up. "I didn't come here to physically hurt you, Dillon," Gavin continued, attempting to hold in a chuckle. "Today, I'm the bearer of… *good* news. Emily no longer has any more doctors' appointments." Gavin paused, his grin widening. "Well, not prenatal appointments."

Still appearing as if he was about to yell for help, Dillon's eyes piqued with curiosity as he reached for and tore open the birth announcement. Gavin wasn't sure how long Dillon took to scan over the teddy bear-riddled card highlighting Noah's July 5th entrance into his life, but somehow, Gavin wasn't filled with the joy at witnessing any of this the way he thought he'd be.

"Emily had the baby?" Dillon questioned, his face bleeding confusion. "This was over a fucking week ago. How come I'm just finding out?" After crumpling up the announcement, Dillon chucked it into the garbage pail. With a smirk, he rounded the corner of his desk and walked up to Gavin. Their bodies were less than a foot apart when Dillon spoke up again, his voice as cold as a snowy winter morning. "It's all good. Just tell me where I have to go and what I have to do to prove I'm this kid's father."

Remaining silent, Gavin didn't know how long he stared into Dillon's lifeless, dark eyes. The eyes of a man he'd once considered a friend, a buddy. The eyes of a man who hit the woman Gavin loved, adored, and couldn't live without. The other half of his soul. It was then Gavin realized not only was he wasting oxygen, he was also wasting precious time away from two people that no piece of shit in the world should ever come before. The battle was over, and Gavin knew he'd won in more ways than Dillon would ever be lucky enough to experience. Sword down, no longer needing to see Dillon's reaction and feeling like an asshole for leaving Emily and Noah, Gavin handed him the envelope holding the paternity test results. Dillon's confused expression was the last thing Gavin saw before he turned and walked out of the office. The sound of Dillon opening the envelope was the last thing Gavin heard as he walked out of Dillon's life for good.

CHAPTER TWENTY-ONE

Past, Present, and Breathless Futures

Time. Emily never looked at it the same way after her mother died. Her perception of what life should mean and how it could be taken at any second was forever changed the day she watched her mother's cherry wood coffin slowly descend into the rain-soaked earth. With her mother gone, vanished like a swirling vapor, time held new meaning for Emily.

As she closed the penthouse door behind her, Emily found herself wondering where the last seven months had gone. Time slipped through itself, a black hole sucking in memories, leaving behind Noah's beautiful fingerprints. Like shooting stars in her sky, Noah left his beautiful mark on Emily's life in so many magical ways. Emily's loving gaze fell on Noah, sitting up like the big boy he was turning into, as he reached out his tiny hand to Gavin's. After smothering a block with his sweet saliva, Noah chucked the block at Gavin's head. Laying on the floor next to Noah, a chuckle belting from his mouth, Gavin mocked sadness as he looked at his son.

Giggling, a few thoughts flew around Emily's mind. One: Gavin was lucky he was wearing his Yankees hat. Two: Gavin was even luckier the alphabet-speckled block was made of cotton. Three: Surrounded by an array of toys from one end of the living room to the next, Gavin looked completely edible, wearing nothing but that Yankees hat and pajama pants on this fine, Sunday afternoon. Yeah. Though time was disappearing faster than Emily could blink, faster than she could catch her next breath, each second was nothing short of magnificent.

"Look who's home, Noah," Gavin announced, sliding from the floor to the couch. He grinned at Emily and adjusted his baseball cap. "And she came bearing gifts for us. Will we be fed, Mommy?"

Smiling at Gavin and Noah, Emily plopped two paper bags of groceries onto the counter. "That depends." She pulled out a loaf of rye bread. "Is the laundry folded?"

Gavin quirked a brow. "My brother was right. You've domesticated me beyond belief."

"I take that as a yes." After shoving a head of lettuce into the refrigerator, Emily dug her hands into her hips. "And don't lie. You love being domesticated."

Gavin chuckled, reaching for the newspaper on the end table. "Yes, boss. To be honest, Noah folded the whole pile." He flipped open the paper, his teasing blue eyes peeking out from the sports section. "But we took a man vote. We're in agreement we're both tired of folding laundry. We want the housekeeper back." Beaming a dimpled smile, Gavin looked at Noah. "Right, buddy?"

With one hand wrapped around a musical clown rattle and the other shoved in his mouth, Noah gave a single nod.

"That's my boy," Gavin laughed, swinging his eyes to Emily. "See? You're outnumbered, doll. We win. I'm calling Leslie and hiring her back on fulltime. It's a done deal."

Jaw dropped open, Emily giggled. "This is obviously a conspiracy. It's bad enough you have my son decked out in a Yankees onesie. Now you have him turning on me? Evil. Pure evil."

Gavin cackled like a ghoul and flipped to the business section. He grinned that very same mouthwatering grin that'd snared her the first time she'd met him. "Hey. You've known this for a while," he reminded her with a shrug and a wink. "And you love every evil inch of me."

Shaking her head, Emily continued to unpack the groceries. Every fiber in her being agreed. Without a doubt, she'd forever love every evil and un-evil inch of him.

"Emily," Gavin called, pulling her attention from a cooking magazine. In the checkout line, a recipe for creamy baked chicken had caught her eye. Unlike the last two times, she was determined to make this evening's dinner work out without giving her or Gavin food poisoning. "What does Noah have in his hands?"

Emily squinted, trying to see across the room. "I don't know. A block?"

"Can you get it from him?" Gavin stared over his newspaper. "He has it in his mouth."

Emily furrowed her brows. "Gavin, he's teething. He'd chew on my shoe if I gave it to him."

"I know," Gavin replied after clearing his throat, "but I don't want him chewing on *that* block." He smirked, his eyes lighting up with amusement. "Or your shoe for that matter. Can you just take it from him? It might be… dirty."

Tilting her head, Emily dropped her shoulders and rolled her eyes. "One: You're a clean freak. Two: I'd rather him chew on *my* shoes than yours. Three: You're right there. You take it from him, nutter."

"Nutter?" Gavin questioned, chuckling. He paused for a second, quite impressed at his new name. "My back hurts. You get it."

"Yes, nutter," Emily sighed with a smile, placing the magazine on top of the table. "You're just trying to get another massage out of me."

She rounded the island, completely convinced her OCD, massage-conniving boyfriend was losing it. Shoeless, she stepped onto the down comforter Noah was playing on.

Though square, it wasn't a block he was chewing on. Nope. Not even close. Emily flicked her gaze to Gavin, who was sporting a full, megawatt smile, and back to the black velvet box Noah was thoughtfully sinking his newly rooted tooth into. Before Emily could blink or take a much needed breath, Gavin slipped from the couch, depositing himself cross-legged onto the comforter. Scooping Noah into his lap, Gavin flipped his Yankees cap backward, eased the box from Noah's hand, replaced it with a tiny book, and stared up into Emily's unblinking green eyes.

"Come sit with us," Gavin said, his voice soft. "We have something for you."

Emily swallowed, her throat suddenly parched. Trembling, she slowly sank down onto the comforter, sitting cross-legged in front of Gavin. Knees touching his, she stared at his lazy grin, her heart racing as he leaned in to kiss her. He let the kiss linger until Noah started to fuss his displeasure about being smashed in between them. Pulling back, Emily let out a nervous giggle and swept her hand through Noah's wavy hair.

"He's just jealous," Gavin whispered, placing a kiss on Noah's head. Bringing his gaze back to Emily's, it was Gavin's turn to swallow. For the second time in his life, he was about to propose to a woman. However, for the first time, not a shred of reservation ran through his body. Gavin knew she was the one created for him. With a shaky hand, he cupped Emily's face, his heart pouncing.

"I love you, Emily. You'll always be my best friend. You'll always be my... Molly." Eyes wide, staring into hers, Gavin leaned in and brushed a gentle kiss upon her quivering lips. "You're the mother of my child. You and Noah have brought color to *my* empty canvas, light into *my* darkened life." With the pad of his thumb, he wiped a warm tear from Emily's cheek and pulled in a deep breath. "Let's paint the full picture together and light up the sky, sweets. I love you both more than anything." He drew up a brow, his sexy smirk showing off his chiseled features. "Remember? You trump Valentine's Day chocolates." Sniffling, Emily giggled.

Gavin smiled, but his face sobered quickly, his voice a gentle whisper. "I believe in forever, and that's what you and I are. We define eternity. This may sound cheesy, but you make me go there. You give me butterflies, Emily Cooper. I've never had that before, and I don't want to let that go for anything. Ever. I asked you once to crash with me, and you did. Now... I'm asking you to take the full ride. Walk with me the rest of the way until we're old, sitting in our rocking chairs and watching our sugar-high grandchildren play in our yard. I've seen this world a million times over, but I've never seen it with you by my side. I want you, no, I *need* you to be my wife. I need to wake up every morning knowing you're Mrs. Emily Michelle *Blake*." He paused, and Emily could see his eyes misting over. "Please. Take this last step with me." He cracked open both sides of the box. Cushioned in the middle of Harry Winston's classic signature lay a round, brilliant diamond set in platinum with smaller diamonds encircling its base.

Emily found her breath evaporating from her lungs. She froze under the gravity of his words, but her heart, filled with a riot of emotions, took off excitedly. Gavin's declaration sang in her ears, musical notes of love reverberating through her. "I love you," she choked out, her eyes stinging with happy tears. She wrapped her hand around the back of Gavin's neck and pulled his smiling lips into her mouth. "And, yes, I'll take every last step with you, Gavin."

"Yeah?" he questioned with a chuckle between kisses. Once again, Noah squealed in displeasure, trying to squirm from Gavin's hold by kicking his chunky legs in frustration. "You're going to be my wife?"

"Yes. I'm going to be your wife," Emily cried, lifting Noah onto her lap. He settled down when she handed him a bottle, his little body relaxing with instant gratification. Emily's limbs went weak as Gavin reached for her hand and slipped the engagement ring onto her finger. Her soul warmed from everything it represented.

"Thank you," she whispered, staring into Gavin's eyes. "I have no words that could possibly describe what you do to me every day." And she didn't. He'd found her broken, withering away into nothing. He'd mended her heart, bandaging her soul with his presence. Through it all, he showed her what true love was. He *was* a dream. The only thing she could do was pray she never awoke from this bliss. His bliss. Gavin dowsed her lips with more intoxicating kisses as she ran her hand down his bare chest. Time was of the essence, but now time would always be filled with everything Emily could've ever imagined, everything she could've ever hoped for.

"You already gave me the only word I needed to hear," Gavin said softly. He kissed her again, massaging his fingers into her hair. "Now, you need to get up, and go get ready. There's a gift for you on the bed."

"Get ready?" she asked. She laid Noah, out cold, onto the comforter. Smiling, she stared at him a moment and soaked in his tiny, exhausted body. "Where are we going?"

Standing and bringing Emily along with him, Gavin stretched, his hard, rigid physique catching Emily's attention in an instant. She bit her lip, her gaze roaming over his golden skin, needing to follow the glorious

388

dragon's descent below Gavin's pajama pants. It was all good, though. Every inch of her had a lifetime to worship the beautiful work of art on her fiancé's extraordinary body.

"I'm taking you out to celebrate." He leaned into her ear, his tongue stroking the lobe. Chills shot, prickling over Emily's flesh. He kissed her lips one, last glorious time, soft and gentle. Gavin stepped back, leaving her body aching from his absence. "Olivia will be here in fifteen to watch Noah for us. I'm spoiling my lady tonight." Eyes locked on hers, Gavin jerked his head toward their bedroom. "Go ahead. I'll see you soon, future Mrs. Blake."

Gavin always came up with the sweetest things to say, but those particular words rolled from his tongue like chocolate. Breathless, Emily nodded and made her way down the hall, her head fuzzy with joy, excitement, and love.

Upon entering their suite, Emily's eyes fell upon a large rectangular box lying on the bed with a red bow crisscrossing around it. Emily wondered what the certified-wiseass love of her life had in store for her. A horrid, pink Yankees sweat suit came to mind, but since he'd said they were celebrating, she figured he probably skipped that idea. On second thought, she wouldn't put it past him. He loved putting his *stamp* on things. She sank onto the bed reaching for the box, her curiosity more than piqued. After sliding off the bow, she lifted the top. A laugh escaped her lips when she spotted silver, blue, and white Yankees tissue paper hugging whatever gift was hiding inside. She shook her head, praying he wasn't going to make her endure a night out on the town swathed in his favorite team's gear. Hands itching to find out, she tore the paper away with the velocity of a rocket shooting into the air. On a gasp, mixed with a sigh of relief, she was thrilled to find her man wasn't going there.

No. Instead, the attire he'd chosen for her was a single shoulder, glossy black silk wrap dress with elegant ruching above and under the bust. Standing, Emily held the breathtaking cocktail dress against her chest as she stared at her full-length mirror. Hitting just above the knee, with a stunning jewel appliqué cinching the waist, there was no doubt the dress would accentuate her newfound mommy curves. To top off her surprise, Gavin had picked out a pair of the season's newest black, strappy Manolo Blahnik's. With giddiness flowing through her, Emily turned to get ready for the evening and spotted Gavin leaned casually against the doorframe.

"Have you been watching me the whole time?" Emily asked, feeling a flush run up her cheeks.

"I have, and I've enjoyed every minute of it." Arms crossed, he gave her a lazy smile. "Did I do well?"

Emily strolled across the bedroom, her eyes feasting on his chiseled face. She tangled her fingers in his soft, dark hair and brought him down for a kiss. "Do you ever not do well?"

"Mmm"—he smirked, running his lips across her jaw—"now that you mention it, I guess I'm pretty on point all the time."

Emily giggled, nuzzling against his bare chest. "So confident."

"I am."

"Well, Mr. Confident, where's our child then?"

"Asleep in his crib." He popped a brow, looking at her. "Now kiss me for the good daddy deed."

Without hesitation, Emily did as he asked. Before she could devour his lips with the intensity her body screamed for, the doorbell sounded. "Olivia," Emily breathed, attempting to regain her bearings as she backed away.

"Perfect but imperfect timing," Gavin sighed as he turned toward the hall. "You get ready, and I'll get the door. Right after I calm myself… down." Semi-hard, Gavin tried to think of something, anything that would take his mind off Emily's luscious lips. However, nothing was working. As he opened the door, he hoped Olivia wouldn't notice his very awake, very enthusiastic response to Emily's touch.

"Eeek!" Olivia all but yelled as she darted into the penthouse. "Where's my godson?"

Running his hand through his hair, Gavin smiled and closed the door. "He's asleep."

"Oh, come on already." Olivia frowned and chucked her purse onto the foyer table. Continuing to pout, she marched into the living room and sank onto the couch with a huff. "Every time I come over he's sleeping."

With a look of confusion laced with amusement, Gavin shook his head. "Liv, that's what babies do best. They sleep." She rolled her eyes as dramatically as Sarah Bernhardt. Gavin lounged into a soft, leather wingback chair. "Aren't you curious if Emily accepted my proposal? I'm surprised that wasn't your first question."

Olivia rolled her eyes again. "Pfft. I don't ask questions I already know the answer to. There was no way she would've not accepted, and had she, I would've beat her ass down, ran off and eloped with you, and legally adopted that precious baby who seems to be in a permanent state of sleep. Are you two drugging him?"

Gavin's mouth dropped open, though he wasn't quite sure why. The things Olivia said would shock a serial killer before entering a gas chamber to his death.

Rising to her feet, Olivia tapped her cheek, her expression showing she was deep in thought. "Speaking of drugged-up, sleeping babies, I'm going to wake him up. Aunty Liv needs some Noah lovin'."

Gavin shrugged. "That's on you. I'm warning you now, no matter how much he likes you, you'll become his worst enemy if you fuck with his nap."

"I'll take my chances," Olivia quipped, hurrying toward Noah's room.

Before long, Gavin heard Noah wailing along with Olivia attempting to calm him down. Gavin chuckled and decided that was the perfect time to get himself ready for the evening. Yeah, Olivia had it coming to her, and Gavin was pretty sure Noah would deliver a clean, solid blow.

"So where exactly are you taking me?" Emily took in the scenery as Gavin eased onto the Taconic Parkway. Even though the cold skies of March anchored the air, and trees had yet to bloom, it never ceased to amaze Emily at the way the city seemed to melt away into a spectacular pallet of nature. With Manhattan's skyline long vanished from view, the harshness bled into nothing but peace. Mountainous boulders hugging the road were a glorious difference from the chaotic jungle they lived in. In a way, this part of New York reminded Emily of Colorado. Different in many ways, yet it held the same warmth home always would.

"It's a surprise," Gavin answered, flipping on his right blinker. He glanced in the rearview mirror before he pulled off onto the side of the road. He popped the vehicle into park, grinned, and leaned over, placing a soft kiss on Emily's lips. "One you need to be blindfolded for." Without another word, he opened his door and stepped from the car.

Curiosity coiled deep in Emily's belly as she watched his lean, toned frame gracefully move around to her side of the car. God, he looked amazing decked out in a tailored black Armani suit, a crisp, white button-down peeking out from underneath, and his effortlessly sexy "just fucked" hair. He opened her door and pulled said blindfold from the back pocket of his pants. Reaching for her hand, he helped Emily out, his smile playfully dotted with mischievousness. He gathered her in his strong arms, shielding her from the cold, as Boyce Avenue's live acoustic version of "Find Me" spilled from the speakers. For a moment, Gavin stared into her eyes and swayed with the music.

"Déjà vu," Emily said dreamily. She recalled the last time they'd danced like this on the side of the road in Mexico. "You're very smooth, Mr. Blake." Gavin shot her a lazy smile, and Emily drew up a brow, her curiosity growing by the second. "What are you up to?"

Before she could blink, Gavin slipped the silk blindfold over Emily's eyes. He pressed his lips to her ear. A small gasp left Emily as Gavin lightly traced his fingers along her jaw, his voice soft, causing heat to slither over her skin. "We're about to play a game. And, no, it's not twenty questions, doll."

"No?" Emily breathed. The sounds of cars rushing by, along with Boyce Avenue's beautiful love song disappeared as Gavin's fingers continued a trail against the slope of her neck.

"No," he answered. "This game will stimulate each and every single one of your five senses beyond human comprehension. Sight..." He pulled her closer, and Emily could feel his growing arousal hard against her stomach. "I'm going to show you things you've never seen before." Brushing her gray wool pea coat slightly away from her shoulder, he feathered his lips against her collar bone. Emily shivered, goose bumps popping up all over her body. Every hair stood on end. After a moment, he brought his lips back to her ear and lightly nibbled on her lobe. As he swirled his warm tongue around diamond earrings he'd bought for her for Valentine's Day, Emily swore she was about to melt into the gravel on the side of the road.

"Sound..." He teased his fingers into her hair, her body screaming for release. "Do you like it when you feel my breath on your ear?" Emily swallowed and nodded. Words were a thing of the past as she sank, plummeting into his touch.

"Taste..." Oh, he was really getting her riled up as he slowly, so achingly slowly, ran his soft tongue along her parted bottom lip. "I'm addicted to the way you taste, Emily. I always have been, and I always will be. But I want you addicted to me in the exact same way." Was he nuts? He'd already turned her into a fiend for all his flavors, yet she had a feeling he was about to make her a full-blown addict, praying for her next hit.

"Smell..." He ran his nose against her hair, down her neck, and back up her flushed cheek. The sound of him inhaling her scent rushed a feeling of need straight to her dampened panties. "Mmm, the way every part of your sweet body smells would lead me to kill for it if it ever disappeared from my possession. It's... *mine.*" Emily puffed out a breath, the dominance bleeding through his tone awakened nerve endings she never knew existed.

"And last, but certainly not least, touch..." Emily heard him step back. Her body felt deprived in the wake of his warmth. It needed more. Wanted more. Craved more. What was he doing? Surely he should be touching her. "Well, that, Miss Cooper," he continued, "shouldn't be hard to figure out. We're going to touch, smell, taste, hear, and see everything one another has to offer in ways we never have before."

Breath stripped from his words, and sight gone, hidden beneath the blindfold, Emily felt as though she was a mad woman about to attack. Thankfully, Gavin brought her back down and saved himself from an embarrassing display of her ripping the blindfold off and sexually mauling him to death. Though she was pretty sure he wouldn't mind. She felt his fingers intertwine with hers as he carefully guided her back to the car and helped her into the seat. The sound of the door closing made Emily's already nerve-shot body jump in anticipation. His feet crunching over the gravel made her already heightened senses acutely alert. Once he got in the car, the humming of his breath made her racing heart beat faster.

He started the engine, pulled the strap of her seatbelt over her waist, and clicked it. Barely grazing her skin, he drew circles around her newly engaged ring finger. Oh, yes, he was teasing her, and he was doing it very well. A brush of his hand on her neck, a slight touch on her thigh, and a light stroke through her hair every now and then made the remainder of the intensely quiet ride torturous. By the time she heard and felt car come to a complete stop, Emily was so sexually charged, she was convinced she was about to lose her mind.

Parked in the circular driveway of a two-story Mediterranean-style home he had built for them, complete with every feature Emily unknowingly gave him over the last several months, a reverent smile broke out across Gavin's mouth as he watched Emily's chest rise and fall with her shallow breaths. The sight of her next to him, unaware of what he was about to show her, made him high. His little game wasn't over just yet. No. He was going to savor the moment for as long as he could. With the flick of a button, the ornate wrought-iron gates swung closed. Gavin stepped from the car, his smile growing as he opened the passenger side door, and helped his blindfolded future bride to her feet.

"Where are we?" Feeling his arms slip around her waist from behind, Emily's lips puckered into a smile. "I'm a little afraid right now."

Gavin pulled her body flush against his chest as he steered her across the multicolored, sandstone driveway. His heart rate escalated the closer they got to the front door. "Take a step up," he whispered. Emily did as he said. "Another." Again, she complied. "And, guess what?"

"Another step?" she asked, giggling.

"You got it," he answered.

Once on the porch, Leslie, Gavin's housekeeper—who he'd already hired back on fulltime—quietly greeted them when she opened the front door. Gavin nodded, mouthed "thank you," and watched her skirt down the driveway to her car.

Stepping into the marbled foyer, Gavin closed and locked the door, slipped Emily's coat off her shoulders, and softly kissed her lips. "Stay here. I don't want anything happening to you."

Crossing her arms, Emily tilted her head. "You can't see my eyes right now, but I'm rolling them, wiseass."

"I bet you are," Gavin laughed. He strolled over to the cascading staircase and hung his suit jacket and Emily's coat on the intricate, hand-carved cherry railing.

"Come here," he called, grinning. "My voice will lead you."

"Are you kidding me?" Emily heard her words echo in whatever space she was in. "I'm about to take off this damn blindfold." Before she could, the sound of Gavin's quick, solid footsteps hit the air, followed by the feel of his hand pressing against the small of her back.

"No," Gavin said, leading her into the spacious, open living room. As requested, Leslie had everything he'd asked for ready and waiting. "The blindfold stays on. I have another game we're about to play. After that, and only *if* I see fit, I'll remove it." Gavin loved the small, sexy pout forming across Emily's lips. He kneeled in front of her and grazed his hands down her calves. "Hold on to my shoulders for support."

Considering she couldn't see a thing and her body was hyperaware of his touch, Emily was more than happy when her hands found his hair. She buried her fingers through his silky strands, a smile curling her mouth. "No shoulders, but this will do. Should I pull on it?"

"The same way you beg me to pull on yours when I'm behind you?"

"Mmm hmm," Emily hummed as she did just that. Tugging his hair, she felt him kiss her stomach. An involuntary shiver moved up her spine.

Gavin slipped her heels from her feet, smoothing his hands up her thighs. Emily's body starting to shake had him wanting to skip his little game and get straight to business, but he would wait. His next step was the biggest part of his surprise. Gavin stood, took Emily's hands, and guided her onto a large, cream-colored Alpaca rug circling the entire living room.

"Where are we?" Emily whispered, feeling the soft material under her feet. "And what are you doing to me?"

Hands still wrapped around hers, Gavin sat down on the rug and slowly brought Emily down onto his lap. Positioning her legs around his waist, Gavin was definitely fighting for control as his eyes scanned the luscious black straps of her garter belt peeking out from beneath her dress. Emily emitted a small gasp as Gavin lazily dragged his fingers around her waist, pulling her flush against him.

"We're about to take a stroll down memory lane." Gavin gently kissed her, sucking her bottom lips between his teeth. "And when we're finished, we'll be in our future." Gavin reached for a canvas bag holding an assortment of their past. The first piece was a conch shell he'd brought back from Mexico. Holding it to her ear, he was about to stimulate her sense of sound. "Do you hear that?"

"Yes," Emily breathed, hearing the distant ocean. "Is it a shell?"

"It is. What does it remind you of?" he asked, touching his lips to hers.

Emily tried to breathe as his other hand caressed her back. "It reminds of the Hamptons."

"Close," Gavin whispered, pulling the shell away. "It's from our time spent in Mexico. A time that started off bad but ended very good. Wouldn't you agree?"

Emily smiled, memories of the bittersweet time dowsing her heart. Seeking his lips, she leaned forward, coming close to hitting her mark as she placed a kiss against Gavin's nose. "Yes." She wrapped her arms around his shoulders. "Thank you for that memory."

"Thank you for coming after me," he replied softly. He reached back into the bag. Pulling out a peanut shell, he figured this memory might be a little bit harder for her to figure out. He held it under her nose to tap her sense of smell. "Sniff."

Emily breathed in the peanut aroma. "Peanut butter?" she questioned, her forehead wrinkled. "Hmm, I know we like to use whipped cream, but I don't recall peanut butter, Blake. Are you confusing me with another woman?"

Gavin smirked, bringing his free hand up to the nape of her neck. He drew her face within inches of his. "Never. But you're close, Miss Cooper, soon to be Mrs. Blake. I'd eat anything off your body that you know. You have my permission to consider yourself my own personal peanut butter and jelly sandwich."

Emily smiled. "What's it from?"

"Damn you, woman," Gavin laughed. "Maybe this will help." He chucked the shell in her hair.

Emily reared back. "Did you just throw something into my hair?"

"Yeah. What are you gonna do about it?" Wishing Emily could see his monstrous smirk, Gavin leisurely rested his hands behind him on the rug. "My game. My rules. Deal with it."

"You've lost it," Emily pointed out with a giggle. After finding the spot where the peanut shell was buried, Emily plucked it from her hair and blindly shot it in the direction she hoped his face was in. It went rocketing over Gavin's head and landed on the stone hearth of the fireplace. "The baseball game." Emily beamed. Seeking his shoulders, she grabbed hold and yanked him back against her chest. "Though the game sucked because your Yankees beat my Birds, it's a memory I'll never forget."

"They whipped their asses," Gavin reminded her, pulling yet another memory from the bag. Emily sighed and shook her head. Smiling, Gavin figured this next memory would rouse her sense of touch, and he was pretty damn sure she'd know what it was the second she felt it. Reaching for her hand, he placed a bottle cap in her palm and watched her face immediately lit up.

"My favorite," Emily whispered, kissing the cap. She leaned in to kiss whatever part of him her lips could find. Hitting just above his jaw, she smiled. "Bottle caps for life?"

"Always," Gavin replied, guiding her lips to his. He kissed her tenderly, soaking in the fact his girl found such a small gesture so grand.

"Can I take the blindfold off now?" Emily nearly begged.

"Be patient, little one," Gavin replied, retrieving the final two memories from the bag. Taste would be the next sense he'd spark. Gavin wondered if Emily would remember the conversation that sparked it all. "Open your mouth," Gavin whispered, watching soberly as she parted her glorious, full lips. After peeling away the lid from a small container of creamer and tearing open a packet of sugar, Gavin poured both delicious contents onto her pink tongue. Before Gavin could take a breath, Emily somehow found his mouth. Their lips moved desperately over one another's in a cream and sugar flavored kiss. Their tongues danced as one.

"I know what this is," Emily purred.

"Do you?" He kissed her deeper as he maneuvered them up off the floor. Swooping her into his arms like a groom carrying his bride, he continued his delicious onslaught against her lips.

"I do, Mr. Cream and Sugar. Now I demand this blindfold comes off." Her voice was husky, riddled with need, want, and desire as a result of the sweet torture he'd put her through.

Gavin did as she asked, slowly pulling away the blindfold. He watched her blink open her beautiful green eyes, the surprise in them immediately sending prickles of satisfaction over his skin. Her glorious gasp throttled his ears. "Welcome to our future."

Feet dangling over Gavin's forearms, Emily couldn't decide which way to look as she took in her surroundings. Wood floors, polished to a shine, spanned the spacious living room. Its size made Gavin's penthouse seem like a college dorm. Her gaze landed on the marble staircase, which split at the landing, situated in the middle of the foyer. Ceilings marked by exquisite crown molding soared over panoramic windows that showcased an in-ground pool in the backyard. Arched entryways dappled every direction.

Gavin carried her into a kitchen harvesting endless amounts of cream-colored granite. Stainless steel appliances fit for a master chef stood out among sleek cherry cabinets. Though unfurnished, the grandeur of the home spilled from one room into the next as Gavin whisked Emily in and out of a library, billiard room, and an office. It hit her, and Emily's heart swelled. Gavin's infamous twenty questions game, always including some odd bit of information concerning either a color, texture, or a design, was what made up their home. Their future. Pieces of her answers were scattered everywhere.

"I love you," she whispered against his lips. "I love every single sneaky, conniving inch of you." She kissed him harder, deeper, needing to show him how thankful she was for him, for all he'd given her. "Take me back into the living room so I can make love to my shmexy fiancé."

Gavin ignored her words with his decadent grin, carrying her up the stairs. "You think I'd make love to you on a bare floor?"

Kissing his neck, the tantalizing aroma of his musky cologne tickling her nose, Emily couldn't care less about the location in that moment. She needed him. "We've had sex in a dressing room at Neiman Marcus." She brought her mouth up to his and nibbled at his lip. "We've had sex on the beach in the Hamptons." Smoothing her hands down his broad shoulders, she started unbuttoning his shirt. "We've even had sex in a utility closet at my school. All of a sudden you're worried about a bare floor? Since when did you become selective as to where you inhale me?"

A devious gleam struck Gavin's eyes as the memories of each and every encounter Emily mentioned rippled through his mind. She was correct, but today was different. He had other things planned for the way he'd inhale her. Ignoring her words, he continued to carry her into what would be their master suite.

Emily's breath caught as her eyes roamed over an elegant four-poster canopy bed. King in size, deep mahogany in color, and draped in white sheer netting, the lone piece of furniture gave the room an ethereal, romantic feel. Gavin gently set her down with her back pressed to his chest. Moving her wavy hair away from her neck, he leaned into her ear and slowly unzipped her dress. "I plan on inhaling every inch of your body on that bed," he whispered, easing the single strap off her shoulder. "Is that okay with you, Miss Cooper?"

Emily couldn't think, breathe, or move as her dress hit the cool wood floor, leaving her heated body close to bare in a black, strapless corset and garter. "Yes," she breathed, feeling Gavin's hands ghost over her chest. In seconds, he had her corset unhooked, freeing her breasts from their confinements. The silk lingerie joined the discarded dress. The sensation of his touch was beyond delicious as Gavin palmed her breasts, kneading them softly. He skimmed his greedy mouth up and down Emily's neck and her head fell back against his strong shoulder. A soft moan filtered past her lips.

Reaching behind her, she started unfastening his belt, her hands working feverishly over the leather. Dear God, she couldn't get it undone fast enough. With one hand making love to her breast, Gavin slid the other into her panties, his fingers massaging her clit in soft, slow circles. Soaked in desire and needing to hold on to something, Emily's hands stopped unfastening his belt. She dragged them up his neck, curled them in his hair, her quick, panting breaths echoing through the sparsely furnished room as Gavin slowly finger-fucked her into oblivion.

"Jesus, you're always so wet for me," Gavin said, his voice ripe with erotic sweetness. Sucking on her neck, his fingers dipping in and out of her, he gently bit her flesh. "You're mine, Emily."

She moaned, a corresponding tug of heat building deep within her pussy with each stroke. "Forever," she breathed as hot pleasure tore through her. Her body melted, throbbing to have him inside her. No longer able to wait, she faced him.

His eyes, the color of blazing blue fire, stared intently into hers, the emotions swirling behind them raw, fierce with passion as she finished unbuttoning his shirt and pants. She stripped him of his clothing, and

Gavin's mouth caught hers, his beautifully etched lips soft, warm. Melded together, he backed her toward the bed. The heat radiating from his skin nearly set Emily aflame. In one slow, torturous motion, Gavin knelt before Emily, pulling her panties, garter, and thigh highs down to her ankles.

"Lay down," he said, his expression laced with hot, carnal promise.

Staring at him, Emily slid across the massive bed. The cool Egyptian cotton sheets further awakened her senses. With her head nestled against feather pillows, her body trembled in anticipation as Gavin crawled between her shaky legs. Like a hawk stalking its prey, he hovered, his eyes pinned to hers for a beat before his mouth found hers again. He pressed his lips to hers with scorching possession and tasted her with unrushed, deep licks.

With their kiss building in intensity, Emily intertwined her fingers through his hair, her lips parting in a gasp when she felt the thick crown of his cock barely ease into her. It flared open her entrance. Another gasp left her lips when he slowly pulled it out, leaving her quivering for more. Sinking his mouth to one of her breasts, his eyes locked onto hers, holding her in place. Growling, Gavin swirled his hot tongue around her hardened nipple. As if the air had been sucked out of the room, Emily tried to breathe, but she couldn't. She was drunk with pleasure, drunk with need, as Gavin continued to lick slow, languorous circles around her swollen breast, his fingers flexing restlessly against the other.

"Do you know how beautiful your body is?" Gavin asked, his voice throbbing with emotion, his eyes glazed over with desire as he hitched his arm under Emily's back. She shook her head, staring at him. "This beautiful body gave life to our son. I'll worship it forever. Treasure it like the gift it is. Like the gift it gave to me."

His words so powerful, so intense, sent a tremor through Emily's limbs. Breathless, she licked her lips and watched Gavin slowly kiss his way down her ribs, his biceps, thick and sculpted, flexing as he moved. He stroked his tongue across the middle of her stomach, letting it linger before dipping it over the rigid scar left behind from her Cesarean. Gavin looked up at Emily, her eyes showing a flicker of self-consciousness as he moved his tongue over the gorgeous imprint representing Noah's life. He trailed his fingers along the raised, pink flesh.

"Thank you for *this* permanent scar," he whispered, cupping her bottom. He lifted the lower half of her body to his face, gently kissing each inch of her stomach. "Thank you."

Not only did Emily's entire body tremble from his touch, but so did her heart. She was overwhelmed by the intense emotions rocking through her. Pleasure radiated, and heavenly zips of electricity curled around every muscle, fiber, and cell as Gavin settled his mouth between her legs. His tongue flicked softly against her swollen clit. Goose bumps raced and tingled across her skin, each stroke sending a ferocious wave of ecstasy tumbling deep within her stomach. It balled, simmering hot like lava. Her hips lurched up, pressing her wet warmth against his devouring mouth.

Squeezing her ass tighter, Gavin licked through her tender flesh, his tongue feasting in her sweetness. Her moans propelled his senses higher; her trembling legs wrapped tight around his head sent him reeling. Desire needled him as Emily's long, drawn out cries dissolved into whimpers. Emily clutched his hair, tugging his face into her harder, and hell if it didn't make Gavin go nuts. She was close. So fucking close. He could feel it, taste it. Pushing two fingers through her slick opening, the excruciating need to bury himself inside her burrowed thick in his balls. Amped up and feeling as though he was about to lose it, Gavin sucked faster and harder at Emily's swollen bud, her body mind-fucking him for his own release. Her calves and thighs, resting on his back, started to quake as her clenching pussy drew his fingers in.

"Come for me, baby," Gavin roughed out, tripping his thumb over her clit. "I need to taste all of you. Give it to me."

Emily's belly dipped in response to the silkiness of his voice, the heated rasp of it melting her to the bones as she let go. Falling, her skin tingled and glistened with sweat. Her nipples hardened like gemstones. Her sex throbbed violently as her orgasm hit, crashing over her body like an angry wave. Before the world could settle back down around her, Gavin slithered up her body and pushed the wide crest of his cock inside her. Emily gasped and spread her legs wide to take all of him. Tangling his hands in her hair, Gavin closed his mouth over hers in a lust-fueled kiss, groaning as he licked into her deeper, harder. Tasting her tanginess on his tongue, Emily moaned, the thick, burning of him spreading her open, nearly hurtled her into another orgasm. But she welcomed the aching soreness, ate it up in all its deliciousness, knowing she'd never get enough. God help her, she knew she'd never be whole without him. He was vital to her being. Her shelter from a storm.

Losing herself in the sensations and sounds of their bodies becoming one, Emily stared into Gavin's eyes as his lips abandoned hers. He gazed at her with an intensity she'd never seen, his eyes showing another level of love. A heightened level of passion. Under his siege and under his spell, Emily caught his mouth with hers, their kiss flavored with the saltiness of their sweat. Trembling, Emily gripped his shoulders and her nails left flaming red streaks across his caging biceps as she clutched him tighter. His glorious flesh was taut everywhere, layered with slabs of hard muscle. He was nothing but primal, perfect male. Gavin slowly slid over her, and Emily could feel their bodies slickened with their mingling need for one another.

With a shaky hand, Gavin brushed an errant piece of damp hair away from her forehead. "I love you, Emily," he groaned as he circled his thumbs along her temples. "You're my world. My life. The air I fucking breathe. I can't believe you're going to be mine forever."

Emily felt his hand drop away from her face, as he brought his mouth down to her breasts, layering his tongue over each swollen, taut peak. With their heartbeats quickening together, Emily was so entranced, so mesmerized, and overcome, tears born of her love for Gavin spilled from her eyes. She sank, melting into him with each slow lick, searing touch, and passionate kiss he worshipped her body with. As Gavin pushed harder, pure fire burned inside her, making the sweltering gash of need grow. With her lips melded to his, licking into his mouth and thrusting her hips in rhythm with his, Emily felt Gavin start to tremble, felt his body stiffening. His muscles tightened, and the tension built in his body. Ecstasy breathed hard against her skin as Gavin's deep, smooth, guttural groans danced through her ears.

Clawing at his back, she sucked in rapid breaths as a rising tide of orgasm overtook her, sending her soaring over a cliff. "Don't stop," she begged, her body hot, her eyes on his. Her pussy twitched, clamping down around his cock as he thrust into her harder, faster. "Oh my God, Gavin, keep going."

Muscles tensing, Gavin tried to breathe through each stroke in an attempt to prolong her pleasure, but hell if he wasn't making it hard on himself as his gaze fastened on the heavy sway of Emily's lush breasts. Determination firmed his jaw as he watched Emily fall into a fray of bliss. He pumped deeper into her as her orgasm became another, then a third, until she screamed out in a final rush of release.

Mentally unraveled, physically turned inside out, and raw from head to toe, Emily clutched at Gavin's damp hair. She dragged his beautiful mouth down to hers. Kissing her hard and slow, Gavin let out a long, low growl. Emily felt his silky jet of semen spill into her, his warmth filling her again and again. His rigid body jerked above hers, his fingers knotting in her hair. With their hearts thundering, breath mingling, and souls intertwining, for Emily, it felt as if their bodies knew what they meant to one another.

Spent, Gavin burrowed his face into Emily's neck, breathing in, and drowning under the scent of their combined mixture. His mouth floated across her cheek, his fingers massaging her hair. "I need to hold and make love to you all night."

And, God, he did. Showing her over and over again how much he needed her, Gavin wiped away Emily's memories of a ruthless past, closing the door to what never should've been. As he held her through the night, her breathless future was contained in the expanse of his warm, strong arms, and she knew this magnificent start to what lie ahead would be forever ingrained in her heart.

MOLLY AND MR. TALL, DARK, AND FUCKABLE HANDSOME'S EPILOGUE

One. Glorious. Year. Later.

Gavin slid his key in the lock and walked into the savory smell of a home-cooked meal. He was impressed by how far Emily had come over the past year with her culinary skills. She'd said she would master cooking, and hell if she didn't. Though he'd never admit it to his mother, Gavin thought Emily's lasagna made hers taste like the frozen kind. Without Emily's knowledge, Gavin stepped into the kitchen and watched with adoration as she pulled a roast from the oven.

Placing his briefcase on the table, Gavin's eyes roamed over her black heels, up her shapely legs beneath a skirt that stopped a few inches above her knees, to the gracious contour of her jaw. She was Gavin's angel. His walking, breathing, amazing for life, mind-blowing, all-consuming angel. Emily stabbed a meat thermometer into the sizzling roast. She must've burned herself because Gavin heard her gasp. It was possible his angel's cooking skills weren't as great as he thought, but that didn't matter. She still blew his mind.

Coming up behind her, he snaked his arms around her waist and buried his face in the crook of her neck. Emily jumped, and Gavin chuckled. "Did I scare you?" he whispered, running his lips along her neck. "And did the roast attack you? If so, I'll kill him."

"Yes, you scared me," Emily answered, facing him. With a smile, she slowly shoved her index finger in Gavin's mouth. He sucked it lightly, his swirling tongue bringing her burn instant comfort. "And yes, he attacked me. But I'd rather you not kill anything today." She pulled her finger from his mouth, her brow drawn up seductively.

Gavin pressed her back against the counter, his hungry blue eyes zeroed in on her plump lips. He untied the Betty Crocker-looking apron from her waist and dropped it to the floor. "Where's Noah?"

Emily looped her arms around his neck. "I had your parents pick him up for the night so I can show you a good time on your birthday, old man."

Armed with a lazy grin, Gavin bent his head and crushed his mouth to hers. Emily moaned, and Gavin grabbed her thigh, hiking it up around his waist. "Old man?" he questioned between kisses. "I'm thirty. And let's not forget all the swoon worthy"—he kissed her harder—"intense… satisfying"—he nipped her neck—"mind numbing… hot as hell"—he licked her earlobe—"'Gavin give it to me harder now, please don't stop, oh my God, keep going' moments this old man's shown you."

"Mmm hmm. You have given me quite a few of those," Emily purred. Sexual need balled low in her belly. Kissing her deeper, Gavin started unbuttoning her blouse. Emily's eyes fluttered closed as he dragged his lips down her jaw, across her neck, settling them on the swell of her breast. She tangled her fingers in his hair. "Gavin, wait, I want you to open your gift first."

He didn't stop. Hell. No. He slowly pulled the scalloped edge of her black lace bra just below her nipple. With a devious smile, he looked at her as he flicked his tongue across the hardened bud. Emily gasped and bit her lip. "I thought it was obvious I *was* opening my gift, Mrs. Blake." He lifted her onto the cool granite counter, pulled her tiny apple ass to the very edge, and shimmied between her legs. Licking into her mouth, he groaned, his body riveted by her tantalizing taste. "I'm the birthday boy, which means I get to call the shots. Sex. Lots of it. Here and now. With my hot wife on the counter."

Tilting her head to allow Gavin to devour her neck, Emily released another moan and hooked her legs around his waist. Over her increased breathing, she heard her heels hit the wood floor. Gavin kissed her harder, making it difficult for her to stop. But she knew how to get him. "How about your hot wife incorporates wild sex into the gift she got for you? Sound good?"

Gavin caught her lip between his teeth and stared into her eyes for a long moment. Eventually, he released it and backed away slightly, his grin wide. "Incorporating wild sex into a gift you've already gotten me? Mmm, I can't say you haven't piqued my curiosity. Does it require batteries?"

Emily nodded, her smile salacious. "Oh, yes. It requires a very *large* battery." Gavin lifted a curious brow, his grin widening. She hopped off the counter, grabbed Gavin's hand, and started leading him toward the garage door. "Close your eyes," she whispered.

"What are you doing?" Gavin probed, a devilish smirk curling his mouth.

With a quick hand, Emily pulled him by his necktie down to her mouth. Running her tongue along his irresistible lips, she swung her arm around his waist and squeezed his ass. Tight. "It may be your birthday, Mr. Blake, but I'm the one running the show. No questions. Got it?"

Yep, his wicked angel knew how to make Gavin's stone harder. "I'm nothing but a peasant to your demands, sweets." Smiling, Emily watched him close his eyes, proud of the authority she held. "But I'm definitely pulling the alpha caveman card on your pretty little ass during our sexcapade."

Severely loving the authority he stripped from her, she ran over to her discarded apron. Picking it up, she shoved her hand into the pocket and whipped out the very blindfold he'd teased her with when he showed her Noah's nursery and the house. Oh yes, payback was about to become Gavin's bitch. Coming up behind him, she slid it over his face, making sure his intoxicating baby blues were covered.

Gavin tossed his head back, laughing. "Very sneaky. I like."

Emily intertwined her fingers in his as she led him through the mudroom and into the garage. "I've learned from the best of them."

"Can't say I'd disagree with that statement." Gavin crossed his arms, a grin lighting up his face. "I've taught you every single naughty thing you know."

Shaking her head, Emily hit the garage door opener and smiled at not only Gavin's over-confident remark, but her carefully thought out birthday gift. Sleek, as silver as a shiny bullet, and wrapped in a larger than life Yankees bow, Emily's eyes scanned Gavin's new… minivan. She couldn't bring herself to purchase a forest green one. Nope. And being it wasn't in the same class as the insanely priced sports cars Gavin was accustomed to driving, the Chrysler Town and Country would be something that would take some getting used to. However, considering the lower end vehicle held more meaning than she could ever imagine, Emily was pretty positive this color and model might fit the bill.

"Okay. Are you ready?" Emily draped her arms around Gavin's neck, breathing in his cologne. Kissing his chin, she felt excitement rushing through her veins. "This is a… few gifts wrapped into one. I just want to make sure you're prepared. I don't need your old ass having a heart attack on me."

Gavin shook his head, his dimpled smile as contagious as ever. "You're turning into a certified—"

"Wiseass like you." Emily ran her hands across his chest and pushed up on her tiptoes. Lips grazing Gavin's ear, she closed her eyes and huskily dropped her voice. "I have a couple hot, delicious, naughty things to teach you, Mr. Blake." She slowly slid the blindfold from his eyes. "Class starts in five." She nipped his ear and backed away. Watching him blink open his eyes, his dimple deepening with his growing smile, Emily clapped as Gavin's mouth dropped open.

"You didn't," he said, chuckling.

"Oh yes I did." Emily wasted no time making her way over to the passenger side. Before opening the door, she reached into a utility closet and snatched the keys to the new ride. She chucked them over the roof and giggled when Gavin caught them. "Get in. We're taking this bad boy for a spin. Oh, and check out your customized plates. They fit you to a T."

Brow drawn up in curiosity, Gavin padded to the front of the vehicle, his eyes landing on the plate his certified wiseass wife had made for him. With a Baltimore Orioles emblem winking at him, Gavin scanned the letters BRDLVR. Belting out a laugh, Gavin tossed the keys in the air and caught them before he hopped into the driver's seat.

"Am I good or what?" Emily questioned, a proud smile toying at her mouth. "I mean, you know you had it coming, right?"

Gavin shook his head and slid the keys into the ignition. "Yes. I had it coming." Engine started, he leaned over the console and reached for Emily's seatbelt. He clicked it in place and brought his lips to her ear. "So when does this class begin? I'm an eager student, more than willing to learn new tricks from the teacher."

Goose bumps popped over Emily's flesh as she stared into Gavin's eyes. "I'm glad you're an eager student," she breathed, her body caught in his easy vortex of seduction. Damn. She swore he'd be able to pull this shit on her when they were well into their golden years. Wrinkled, barely able to walk, and sucking on an inhaler, she was convinced he'd never need Viagra. Ever. "But I'm not done giving you your gifts."

A smirk formed at the corner of his lips. "I know. I'm trying to coax the others out of you right now." Emily's blood coursed violently through her veins as Gavin's hand crept behind her head, his fingers melting through her hair. He teased his lips to hers, his voice a low whisper. "Am I doing a good job?" He didn't let her answer. He probed her mouth with his tongue, seeking the sweet taste he could never get enough of, the sweet taste that would forever belong to him.

Emily's limbs went pliant, her pulse racing as she gasped into their kiss. Lips locked in wanton indulgence, she breathed in everything that made Gavin. His touch, taste, and the spark of life that continued to light her world on fire time and time again. His presence soothed her. His arms protected her. His soul loved her. He was a cleansing, a purification, and a fresh start at a life she never believed she'd hold. He'd always know how to carefully stalk the fringes of her heart, how to steal her breath, and how to make her worries seep into the nothingness where they belonged. In a blink, he was there. In a flash, she'd almost lost him. But here, and now, he was hers. Leaving behind what once was, and no longer holding visual remnants of chaotic past that'd almost broken them, Emily slowly drew her lips away from his, her need to fill their present with continued happiness growing by the second.

"I love you, Gavin," she whispered, her mind burning every precious second, minute, and hour they'd spent together into her memory. "You've given me everything I could've ever imagined and more. I hope I've done the same for you." She paused and cupped his cheek, her pulse racing. "Your other gift's waiting for you in the back seat."

Gavin dragged his gaze from Emily's, which had suddenly become teary, his eyes flicking from Noah's car seat over to a smaller infant seat. The difference in size was so overwhelming, yet the two fit together like pieces to a puzzle. Side by side, an older brother and a younger sibling. Swallowing, Gavin felt his heart start to hammer in his chest, bursting with a mixture of fear, excitement, love, and joy. Each a delicious, vivid component of what it felt like to be a father. A father to a first, and now a second child.

Gavin's trembling hand immediately flew to Emily's stomach, his voice nearly trapped in his throat. "You're pregnant?" The words rushed from his smiling lips.

Emily giggled, tears slipping from her eyes. "No. I usually make it a habit of buying a few spares just in case." She unclicked her seat belt, climbed over the console, and deposited herself onto Gavin's lap. He chuckled as she wrapped her arms around his neck and peppered kisses against his lips, nose, and cheeks. "Yes, I'm pregnant, Blake. It's not funky forest green, but we're filling this minivan with bucketloads of kids."

Gavin cradled the back of her head and slanted his mouth over hers as he spoke. "Simply amazing. This girl named Molly—you might know her—but yeah, she stormed into my life and hasn't stopped rocking my world ever since."

And in the year following the season that'd changed Emily and Gavin Blake's lives forever, fate finally played fair. It stopped its wicked games and decided to let up... just a lil' bit. From beautiful do-overs on a long stretch of highway in Mexico, to many layers of life peeled away, filled with bottle caps and another car seat in the back of a minivan, time had tick-tocked its way to where it belonged.

Fate... such a funny little thing.

ACKNOWLEDGEMENTS

Joe, Joseph, Matthew, and Ava. I love you all. Mom's back. I promise. I missed you more than you'll ever know. Thank you for dealing with not having me around. Nothing can ever bring back the time we lost, this I know, but I swear from here on out, the little memories we build together will last us when I slip back off into another world.

Wow. Where to begin? That's the proverbial question. This ride—writing *Pulse*—was insanely different than that of when I wrote *Collide*. Both in glorious and wicked ways. Both amazing and scary. Both... very opposite. I published *Collide* thinking I'd sell a few copies, gain a few readers, and get my work out there to some people who might enjoy the story well enough. Boy, was I wrong. Overnight, I was thrust into a spotlight I could've never prepared myself for. No matter how many times I might've dreamt for what I've experienced, nothing, and I mean nothing, could've have readied me for the road I walked. Wait. I take that back. I didn't walk anything. The road I ungracefully stumbled, tripped, skidded down, and fell face first onto. I learned quite a few things. Most of which were very hard to swallow—razors down my throat hard to swallow—but nonetheless, I've been more than blessed.

The red, velvet curtain is sliding open right about now. Please take a bow when I call your name, and most of all, thank you for not casting judgment, changing on me, or ridiculing my every move while you tripped with me down this road.

Cary Bruce, Brooke Hunter, Angie McKeon, Lisa Maurer, Stephanie Johnson, and Teri Bland. Almost the original BCBW's with Angie being a great addition. Thank you for always keeping it real. The brutal honesty kept me where I needed to be while writing. I don't need to say much to you ladies, as we speak regularly for the most part, and you know how much I severely adore you all. So, I'm giving you each a few words you'll understand. Cary: You got your monkey. Happy? Brooke: Readers will now know it was YOUR idea to kill Gavin. I may have written the devastating words, but you thought it up. Pure. Genius. Lisa: The world is my people. I will never forget that ride! Angie: My evil teaser queen! Stephanie: Diaper. Ha! Great catch and yuck at the same time! Teri: Asystole and Craniotomies!!!!! I could thank you each to the moon and back, and it'd never be enough.

Melinda Atkinson-Medina- Thank you for catching me, friend. There will never be a time in my life I couldn't count on you.

Lisa Kates- We split a bit during this, but we're not broken.

Ashley Hartigan Tkachyk, Joanne Arcarese Schwehm, Becca Manuel, Laura Babcock Dunaway, Kim Rinaldi, and Jennifer Pikul Gass. My second round of betas. Thank you all for accepting the split second notice before Pulse went into editing. Your willingness to jump right into it amazed me.

Tina Reber- Thank you for the much needed chat sessions. You've anchored me in so many ways and every piece of advice you've ever given is tucked in my head.

To my cover artist Regina Wamba from Mai I Design and Photography- You're simply amazing. Many indie authors in this industry said you were wonderful to work with, and they weren't kidding. Every book I write will have your stamp on it.

To my formatter Angela McLaurin from Fictional Formats- Again, thank you. Your wonderful design and little surprises for me in *Pulse* were astounding. I look forward to many years of working together.

To my editor Cassie Cox- Thank you for kicking my ass. No, really. I am being serious. Thank you. You scared me at first, but you cut my 'shit' where needed.

To the sick, twisted, amazeballs women in TFC- Madeline Sheehan, Emmy Montes, Claribel Contreras, Syreeta Jennings, Trevlyn Tuitt, Karina Halle, and Cindy Brown. You ladies have seen me on my worst and best days. You witnessed many times when I wanted to throw in the towel, but your words pushed me forward. Either way, you listened. You gave me an ear to rant to, a shoulder to cry on, and a stage to express my fears. Our fears. I got nothing but love for each of you.

To my blog tour: True Story Book Blog, Angie's Dreamy Reads, 'Ssh Mom's Reading, Fiction and Fashion, Vilma's Book Blog, Book Boyfriend Reviews, Flirty and Dirty, Books Babes and Cheap Cabernet, Sinfully Sexy, The Little Black Book Blog, Whirlwind Books, Swoon Worthy Books, Three Chicks and Their Books, Bridger Book Bitches, Romantic Book Affairs, Becca the Bibliophile, The Rock Stars of Romance, Mommy's Reads and Treats, The Boyfriend Bookmark, First Class Books, Book Crush, I Love Indie Books, Sugar and Spice, Ménage a Book Blog, Up all Night Book Blog, Morning After a Good Book, Kindlehooked, TheSubClubBooks, Smitten, A Book Whore's Obsessions, The Book List Reviews, and Smut Book Club. Thank you all for participating. Your blogs, among every other blog out there, whether people realize it or not, are the veins of our reading community. The blood pumping books out to readers. I said it in my acknowledgements in Collide, and I'll say it again. Each blog amazes me. Simply... amazes me. No matter how chaotic blogger's lives get, they still put time aside to reach out to their readers and promote books from authors they love. Authors they believe in. Authors they've never heard of. Some of you take a chances on unknown authors, and that says a ton. Your reviews, be them bad or good to writers, are passionate. It takes a lot to put your review out there the world, and I admire you ladies for doing so each and every day. In the grand scheme of things, blogs are overlooked. Just know most authors realize how much time and dedication goes into running one. I thank you, all listed here—and not listed here—for getting the word out about Collide and Pulse.

Last, and so not even close to the least… my readers. Hot damn, you loved my characters! What??? Let me say that again… what? Shocked doesn't even begin to skim the surface here. Not. One. Bit. I've mentioned a ton of wonderful ladies above, and let me just say, on days I wanted to pull out of this ride and promptly get a refund, slip off the rollercoaster and go home, not only did they stop me, but so did you. Thousands upon thousands of emails kept me writing. Thousands upon thousands of comments on my author wall, posts, and online delivered to me what I needed the most: the drive to push on. The courage to move forward on this glorious, scary, humbling, and blessed ride that was set forth in my life. Thank you for loving my characters as much as I do. Thank you for believing in me as a writer. Thank you for telling your mothers, sisters, aunts, cousins, nieces, and friends about *Collide*. Though I left your mouths agape at the end of *Collide*, thank you cheering for me while I wrote *Pulse*. Not kidding when I say this, but you all have mentioned fan-girling when you've spoken to me, well, there's not a time I haven't fan-girled over you. No joke. I hope I've done well by you all. I hope I continue to do well. Just know, I'll always try.

Turn the page for a sneak preview of *Fear of Falling*
by S.L. Jennings coming July 2013

FEAR

of

FALLING

S.L. Jennings

Coming July 2013

Shit happens.

I never really understood that saying. Yeah, there were certain situations in life that were shitty, but they were just that; they were *life*. So it really wasn't the shit in life that was, well, so shitty. It was life itself.

Life happens. That was much more appropriate.

Unfortunately, many of us found that out earlier than some. We found out just how awful life could really be. We found out that monsters were, indeed, real. They walked among us. They looked just like you and me. They came in the form of the people that we loved and trusted the most. The people whose only job was to love and protect us.

Funny thing about life is that it never turns out the way you want it to. It's never fair. It's harsh and brutal. It kicks you when you're down. It makes you wish you could give up and part with it just to have a semblance of peace.

I almost felt that peace unintentionally. And if I had known exactly what I was fighting against, I would have succumbed to it. I would have traded my young, shitty life for the peace that came with death.

I should have. I would have been free.

Chapter One

I needed a drink. A strong one.

One that could possibly knock me on my ass and make me forget what I had done just 20 minutes ago. This was always the hard part. The guilt, the self-loathing. Sometimes it strangled me. I hated what I did. I hated the pain I inflicted but it was part of the process, part of what came with being me.

I hurt people, and it wasn't something I was proud of.

Pulling into the parking lot of the first bar I spotted after leaving the scene of the crime, I punched in a number on my cell phone, speed-dialing Angel. "It's done," I announced, not even bothering with a cordial greeting. Those were reserved for days when I didn't feel like locking myself away from everyone and everything. For days when I didn't feel myself breaking into a million pieces.

Angel sighed on the other end, feeling my pain through the receiver. "You okay, baby?"

"Yeah. I will be. Down to get shit-faced?" I chuckled though I truly couldn't find the humor in my own request.

"I'm always down. Where are you?"

After giving Angel the address, I fixed my smeared mascara in the visor mirror. I could have just stopped at a liquor store and gone home to drown my troubles, but I needed an excuse to hold it together. A distraction. In public, I'd have no choice but to plaster on a phony smile and ignore the immense guilt I felt. I'd be forced to pretend.

10...9...8...7...

I started the mental countdown ritual. I could do 10. Twenty was reserved for extra shitty days. Fifty was for all-out hellish catastrophes. Today felt more like a 10: a craptastic situation.

"You can do this," I whispered to the reflection staring back at me. "It's ok. You're ok. It had to be done. You have to keep going. You can do this, Kami Duvall. You will not break. Not today."

The bar's marquee stated Dive, though it only slightly resembled the traditional, hole-in-the-wall dive bars I was accustomed to. As I scurried into the air-conditioned building, seeking refuge from the relentless Charlotte summer sun, I could tell it had been recently upgraded with modern furniture and a fresh coat of paint. I liked it already though ambiance was not a requirement for what I had planned for the rest of my evening.

I settled in at the bar and ordered a shot of tequila along with a Long Island Iced Tea chaser. When the bearded bartender raised a questioning brow at my request, I diverted my eyes to a bowl of peanuts a few seats down. I didn't need his misguided judgment.

"Damn, baby. Sure a pretty little thing like you can handle a drink like that?" a voice laced with a southern drawl called out to me. I looked up to spot a smiling onlooker across the bar. Great. Judgment *and* an asshat with my beverages.

I smiled sweetly before grabbing my shot of tequila, downing it, tossing the slice of lime to the side, and slamming the glass on the bar. When I looked back up, Asshat was already making his way towards me, obviously intrigued with my shot-pounding capabilities. Unfortunately for him, that'd be the only thing getting pounded tonight.

"Hey there, honey. I've never seen you 'round here. You must be new. I'm Craig," he smiled, extending his hand. I looked at it, scanned the length of his body and turned my attention back to my drink. It was much more exciting. Craig took the hint and pulled his hand back but still settled in the seat beside me. I rolled my eyes; he was a persistent little prick. Normally the southern charm was endearing to a California girl like me, but after what I had just been through, it was annoying as hell.

"Craig, right?" I asked after a long pull from my Long Island. He nodded and flashed a hopeful smile. I couldn't wait to wipe that dumb look right off his face. "First off, calling the wrong person 'honey' could very well get you cut. And second of all, how would you know if I was new? Do you hang out here on a regular basis?"

"Easy there, darlin'," he chuckled, holding his hands up in defense. "Just making friendly chit-chat. And yes, actually, I do come 'round here often. This happens to be my family's place."

I eyed Craig disapprovingly. With his wavy, chin-length brown hair, light brown eyes, and the bit of scruff on his chin, he wasn't exactly bad to look at. He was actually pretty cute in that young southern gentleman kinda way, but I was too far gone on the self-depreciation train to even fall for his charm.

"So what? That gives you a right to harass all the paying patrons?" I replied with a raised brow before downing the last of my drink. It was strong, but not strong enough to stow my bitchiness.

"You are an exotic little thing, aren't ya? Yes, in-deed," Craig appraised, ignoring my jab. He finished his beer just as our empty glasses were quickly swiped from the bar. "Let me guess- you're one of those *moo-lot-toe* girls."

I nearly choked, and probably would have spit my drink right in his face just for shits and giggles if I'd had a mouthful. "Excuse me? Are you trying to say *mulatto?*"

"Yeah! That chocolate and vanilla swirl! I'm right, aren't I?"

Wow. Craig was a bigger asshat than I initially assumed. I had played this game with guys before. The whole, *What are you? Let me guess…* " bit was not new to me. Usually I shut it down, but since I had nothing else better to do than stew about my predicament, I thought I'd humor Craig and eventually make a fool of him. I didn't think it would take long anyway.

"No, I'm not *moo-lot-toe*, jackass. Chocolate and vanilla? Do I look like an ice cream cone to you?" I snickered. Craig's eyes widened with glee at my choice of words, instantly making me regret them. Thankfully, the bartender returned with our drinks, so I could get back to the task at hand: getting stupid drunk.

I looked up to say thank you and was met with a hooded pair of chocolate brown eyes and a boyish grin. His hair was covered in a worn baseball cap, and he had just the right amount of scruff on his chin and upper lip to give his baby face an edge. His hands and arms were covered with intricate, colorful tattoos. He was different from what usually attracted me and absolutely beautiful. So beautiful, in fact, that I had to tear my eyes away before I used Jedi mind tricks to undress him. I wanted to see what else those tattoos covered. Badly.

"CJ, I hope you're not botherin' this young lady," the younger, much more enticing bartender smiled, his deep voice laced with a touch of southern drawl. His large hand (yeah, I noticed) clapped Craig on the back as he shook his head, a lock of brown hair escaping his cap and falling into his eyes. His gaze came back to me, and he winked.

Under normal circumstances, the move would have probably made me blush, and/or flash a flirty smile, but my mind and heart were still heavy with grief. I returned the sentiment with a nod and a nervous half-grin. Sure, he was attractive, painfully so, but that thought would be all I could allow myself to enjoy.

"Aw, you know me, Blaine. Always makin' friends," Craig snickered before taking a sip of his fresh beer.

Blaine.

Even his name was sexy as hell, and I resisted the urge to try it out on my tongue. He placed his palms against the bar, and leaned in, looking at me expectantly. Shit, I really didn't want the attention. But he looked at me intently, his head cocked to one side, with his mouth curled up, and I couldn't think of anything witty or even rude to say to make the guys go away.

It made me nervous. Like, *really* nervous. So I tore my eyes away from his and nodded towards a HELP WANTED sign propped up on a high shelf. "You guys hiring?"

Blaine turned and looked at the sign before bringing those brown eyes back to me. "Yeah. Waitresses, line cooks. A bartender. Looking for work?"

"Maybe," I shrugged before taking a sip of my drink while I surveyed the room. It was a good-sized place, and it was centrally located. But, it was virtually empty aside from a few bar patrons. "Did this place just open or something?"

"Nah," he responded with a little shake of his head. The lock of hair fell farther into his line of vision, and much to my dismay, he swept it to the side, tucking it back into his cap. "Just got new management."

Craig snorted and rolled his eyes before taking a chug of his beer. He turned his attention back to me and waggled his eyebrows. "So darlin', where were we? Oh right…how about Puerto Rican? Mexican? I have to be close. Did I get it right? Or are you just gonna keep me guessing all day?"

Ignoring Craig completely, my gaze fell to Blaine's hands. They rested on the bar, just inches from mine. On one hand, he had a letter written in some type of old script on each finger. The other had a design on the back that fused into the piece crawling up his arm. My eyes followed the vibrantly detailed pattern slowly, studying every line and curl. Even shrouded in ink, I could tell his arms were magnificently cut and defined with muscle. Muscles that flexed and quivered as he leaned against the bar, causing his biceps and shoulders to strain against his fitted, plain white t-shirt.

"So are ya?" Craig asked, intruding on my thoughts and pulling me away from the splendor of Blaine's arms.

"Huh?" I sputtered, looking up with a doe-eyed expression and praying that neither of them had noticed my shameless gawking. They both chuckled, making me believe that my prayers had gone unanswered.

"Are ya a spicy Latina?" Craig asked as he leaned in closer, hoping to steer my attention to him.

I could feel my lips curve into a grimace, and I swallowed down the disgust I felt at that very moment. Without knowing what to do or say next, I looked up at Blaine, whose eyes were still trained on me, an amused grin on his face. Initially, my eyes widened as if to plead for help then settled into a dreamy stare. They wanted to continue their study of Blaine's physique and I really couldn't blame them. And who was I to deprive my peepers of the sexiest piece of man-candy they had seen in years?

Noticing the flash of desperation in my expression, his smile broadened, and he turned to Craig, releasing me from his compelling gaze. "As always, you're way off, CJ," he said, as he turned his body sideways to rest on an elbow. The move allowed me a better inspection of his torso, and revealed a chest and abs under the thin fabric that just begged for a tongue to trace each defined cut. The weight of his body supported by his elbow caused his bicep to stretch his shirt even more. I envied that damn t-shirt.

"How so, cuz?" Craig asked, pausing before bringing his beer bottle to his lips.

Blaine looked away from Craig to meet my eyes again, however, his gaze was different this time. Less playful and curious, and more... intense. Almost lustful. It held me on my barstool and refused to let me look away or even blink. It burned right into me, marking me in an uncanny way. His expression both disturbed and aroused me, and I couldn't decide which I was more upset about.

"Well, first off," he finally said, "she isn't mulatto or even Hispanic. Look at her eyes...perfectly slanted and sexy. Soulful. And her hair... so dark and thick, slightly curled. Hair that beckons you to run your fingers through it from root to tip. Maybe even pull a little," he smiled crookedly. "And then there's the shape of her lips...how they dip and curve into a full pout. Lips that you can't resist staring at for hours. Lips that beg to be kissed."

Blaine chewed his bottom lip and narrowed his eyes, as they continued to scan every part of me that he had just so eloquently described. I was nearly dizzy from the breath I didn't even realize I was holding.

"Asian. You're part Asian, right?" he asked simply, no trace of seduction in his voice. His eyes no longer smoldered or emitted the fiery passion he had displayed just seconds before.

The switch in gears nearly made me fall flat on my face. Luckily, my roommate/girlfriend/savior strolled in and successfully diverted the attention from me. Every eye turned to witness the grand arrival of Angel Cassidy, dressed in too short cut-offs, a red tank that was suggestively torn and cut to reveal her plump breasts and lace-up black platform heels. She was the quintessential blonde bombshell that filled every guy's fantasies. With her heart-shaped cherry lips, milky white skin and curves for days, she easily resembled a younger, edgier Marilyn Monroe.

I masked the disappointment of losing Blaine's attention and gave Angel a wink. She strutted over to me, a hand on her hip, and gave me a wicked smile. She clutched the back of my head, tangled her fingers in my dark brown hair, and crushed her glossed lips to mine. A moan rumbled her chest as I pulled her body into mine.

It was the kiss heard 'round the world. Well, 'round the bar, anyway.

Other than a few audible gasps at seeing Angel's pink tongue dart out of her mouth, Dive was completely silent as she flicked my upper lip before pulling away. The two guys before us each wore amused grins that screamed of lustful possibilities.

"Oh, hell yeah!" Craig exclaimed, breaking the deafening silence and smacking Blaine's chest with the back of his hand. "Lesbians! Now *that* explains it!"

"How are you, baby?" Angel cooed, tucking a lock of hair behind my ear while gazing at me adoringly.

I matched her soft smile and placed my hands on her narrow waist. "Better now that you're here."

"Wow! Can you believe this, B?" Craig still rambled excitedly.

I turned back around on my barstool to assess Blaine's reaction, which was unreadable if not indifferent. Good. Better for him, and everyone else, to see that there's no chance with me. Not that I thought he was thinking that.

"Can I ask you ladies a question?" Craig chimed in. For once since meeting him twenty minutes before, I was glad for his intrusion. I had to stop looking at Blaine. I had to stop giving him the impression that I was interested. Because I wasn't. I couldn't be.

"Sure!" Angel piped up, sliding her arm around my shoulders and leaning into me.

Craig took a hefty gulp of beer and cleared his throat before leaning closer. "Ok. I know you gals are gay, and all, but *lez-be-honest*...you gotta miss that full, thrusting feeling," he snickered in a mock whisper.

"CJ, dude!" Blaine scoffed, smacking him upside the head.

"Ever been with a guy?" Craig continued, ignoring Blaine's pleas to knock it off. "Because I'd love to be the meat in your sandwich."

With that, Angel and I rolled our eyes before making our way to an empty table. Blaine was still scolding Craig for his comments, and I honestly had to refrain from laughing. Craig was certainly an asshat, but I had to give it to him- he was a funny asshat.

"So what happened?" Angel asked once we were settled.

I shrugged and looked down at the table, digging my fingernail into a nick in the tabletop. "Same thing that always happens. I hurt him, he cried, then I came here."

"He cried?" Angel grasped my hand, her sparkly black fingernails a drastic contrast to her pale complexion. "You wanna talk about it, babe?"

"No," I replied, shaking my head. I hated that part of the game. Each time, I told myself I wouldn't get involved- that I would be better off without the trouble. Yet, each time, I somehow let myself break the rules. Then came the pain.

Before I could delve deeper into my own self-inflicted misery, Blaine strolled up, giving me a clear view of the rest of his body. Worn blue jeans hung from his hips in that way that showed off his chiseled frame without being too tight. His plain white tee clung to his torso and, if I looked closely, I could see the outline of eight perfectly hard mounds, comprising his midsection. And, I could tell that there was more ink, arousing my interest even more. I forced my eyes back up to his, silently cursing myself.

"Hey ladies, sorry about my cousin. He was dropped a lot as a baby," he said with a smile before crossing his arms in front of him and leaning against a nearby table. The movement caused those luscious biceps to bulge and, once again, that lucky-ass t-shirt stretched.

"Oh wow, you're related to that tool?" Angel snickered. "My sincere apologies."

"He's an ass, but he's harmless," Blaine replied with a one-shouldered shrug and a crooked grin. The combination was incredibly adorable, and I had to squelch a rising swoony sigh. "So is there anything else I can get you ladies?"

As always, Angel commanded attention. "Well, handsome, we will have two shots of tequila to start." She peered at my melancholy expression through dramatically long eyelashes. "Actually, make that four shots. Maybe I'll get lucky," she winked.

Blaine smirked knowingly before scraping his bottom lip with his teeth. Something inside me clenched. "Was I right?" he asked, suddenly directing his attention to me.

I frowned, completely caught off guard. "Huh?"

He uncrossed his arms and took a step forward, causing me to take in a sharp breath. "About your nationality. I was right, wasn't I?"

"Um uh…" I stammered. I wasn't entirely sure why I had suddenly lost my train of thought, but all I could focus on was that pesky lock of hair that was slowly easing its way from outside of his ball cap once more.

"Oh, Kami's nationality?" Angel piped up, her eyes darting between Blaine and me questioningly. "Her mom's from the Philippines."

With his eyes never straying from mine, Blaine smiled crookedly and nodded. Then he turned away from the table, stealing my breath and taking it with him back to the bar to retrieve our shots.

"What the fuck was that about?" Angel squeaked in her high-pitched soprano. The crude comment was a direct contrast to her bell-chime tone.

After regaining the usage of limbs and brain function, I turned to Angel. "Nothing. He and his cousin were trying to figure out what I was."

"Yeah, yeah, I get that... I'm talking about the obvious *Take me, take me now* stares. I mean, seriously, did it just get hot in here or what? I thought he was about to ask you to grab your ankles!"

I shook my head and looked down at my peeling nail polish. "No, you're seeing things. Besides, I'm not going down that road again. I'm done."

"Sure, sure, sweetheart. Whatever you say. I love you anyway," she grinned, blowing me a kiss and eliciting a chuckle from me. "There's that smile!"

Just as I was beginning to unwind, Blaine returned with a tray of shots, lime slices, and salt. With one extra. He distributed our four, then picked one up for himself, raising it in a toast. Angel looked to me with a wicked gleam and picked up the saltshaker. She leaned over, then seductively licked my neck and sprinkled a little salt on it. Feeling satisfied with my compliancy, she eased a lime wedge between my lips and picked up her shot glass. My eyes fluttered closed when her small hands cradled my face and sucked the salt from my neck, licking and nuzzling as if we were alone in the room. Then she pulled back, clinked her glass against Blaine's, and downed her poison. For the second time today, her lips pressed against mine, as they sucked the wedge of lime.

Blaine didn't even bother with his own slice; he was too busy staring at the girls practically making out in front of him. From a few yards away, I could hear Craig catcalling and cheering, yet Blaine was silent, a small smile playing on his perfect lips. It made me wonder if he was just being respectful or was gay himself.

"Ok, your turn, Kami!" Angel exclaimed. With a sigh, I nodded and began to make my way towards her neck when she grasped my shoulders, halting my approach. "Not me, silly! *Him*. He doesn't have another shot, and I want to take the next one with you. Don't worry, I won't get jealous."

My eyes instantly whipped to his furrowed brow, both our expressions full of surprise. "Um, Angel, honey, I think that is highly inappropriate. There's no way I could do something like that to him. He works here."

Blaine licked his lips and cleared his throat. Somehow it sounded more like a groan. "I don't mind if *you* don't, Kami," he said. My name sounded different on his tongue, almost dirty. The delicious kind of dirty.

I bit my bottom lip, and glared at Angel, knowing exactly what she was up to. She made everything into a game and was always looking for ways to be entertained. That attitude was embedded in her poor-little-rich-girl persona. She returned my evil eye with a wink and waved her hand towards Blaine.

Not feeling nearly drunk enough, yet warm from my previous drinks, I rolled my eyes and returned my attention back to the deliciously tattooed bartender before me. "Um, ok. I guess."

Blaine smiled sheepishly before pulling up a chair and straddling it backwards. Now he was closer to me, so close that I could smell him. And I'll be damned if he didn't smell amazing. It was a mix of mint and spicy cologne that paired with his body's natural scent in a way that made my mouth water. I silently cursed again, but directed it at Angel this time. I should have never smelled that man. It was wrong. So, so wrong. Yet so, so good.

I mustered up my courage and inched towards him slowly. Blaine kept his eyes on mine, refusing to even blink in my pursuit. I knew he had to hear my heart nearly pounding through my chest; hell, it was all I could hear. His gaze never wavered. When I was only inches from the smooth, tanned skin of his neck, he sucked his bottom lip into his mouth and tilted his head, giving me full access to the known erogenous zone. By this point, my heart was hammering double time, and I thought I might go into cardiac arrest at any second. I had to keep going. I couldn't let him see just how much he affected me. Angel and I had done this plenty of times with guys way less good-looking. This man should be no exception.

The taste of his skin caused a tiny moan to escape my throat as the tip of my warm tongue licked a trail toward his earlobe. He tasted exactly how he smelled- of mint and spice. It made me want to keep licking and suck that earlobe right into my mouth, to nibble it gently between my teeth. Aware of the spike in his breathing at the feel of my wet tongue, I pulled back to gauge his reaction. Blaine's eyes were hooded, low, and smoldering, and I knew that they matched my own. His teeth released his bottom lip and his tongue rested on it, ready for... I don't know what. But I noticed. I noticed everything about him in that moment. With the taste of him still lingering on my tongue, it was damn near impossible not to.

Angel cleared her throat and nudged me with the saltshaker, bringing me back to the here and now. I took it from her, not even bothering to acknowledge her presence, and sprinkled a bit on the moistness drying on his neck. With another nudge, she passed me a lime wedge. Tentatively, I advanced towards him again, my eyes trained on that tongue. With just an inch separating my fingertips and his lips, Blaine opened his mouth just a fraction, and I saw it. A barbell. His freakin' tongue was pierced.

I knew I should have stopped there. I was getting in way over my head. Really? Body shots with a complete stranger? Not only that, but a tattooed, pierced stranger that screamed recklessness? But I couldn't stop myself from leaning forward. I couldn't keep my tongue from darting out and licking that salty trail, sucking his skin gently into my mouth, and causing him to groan. After I downed the shot of tequila, his flavor still hadn't left my mouth. It coaxed me to cradle his face and crush my lips to his. The wedge of lime may have separated our mouths, but I distinctly felt Blaine's soft lips and the warmth of his breath. I didn't even bother to suck the lime at first. I just let my eyes close for a split second and enjoyed the intimate feeling. It was... incredible. Stupid and dangerous, yet incredible.

Remembering the task at hand, I gave the slice of citrus a suck, eliciting another groan from Blaine. Then I realized I was actually sucking his lip. His bottom lip, so soft and sweet, was in my mouth, and I had been running my tongue along it. I pulled away quickly, abandoning the lime and letting it fall to the floor between us. Neither one of us made a move to pick it up. There was too much...there. I don't know what it was that crackled between us, but it was there. And it was confusing the hell out of me.

Blaine's expression was still full of desire and question, making me believe that he was just as confused about what transpired. My lips burned and I wanted to feel that fire again immediately. The way he licked his lips signaled that he wanted the same.

"Woo hoo, cuz!" Craig sidled up, clapping Blaine on the back and breaking our trance. "Looks like you wanna be the meat in the sandwich tonight! You lucky sonofabitch!"

Blaine looked up at his cousin and blinked rapidly, as if he had been entranced for the past five minutes. Jumping from his chair with enough force to make it screech against the hardwood, his eyes darted between Angel and me before settling on my face. Then he…frowned. He frowned like I had just manipulated him and forced my tongue down his throat. Like he regretted the semi-kiss we just shared. I looked down at my last shot and threw it back, not even bothering with salt and lime. I don't think I could ever use those accompaniments again.

"Um, uh, if there's nothing else…" he stuttered, chewing that lip again. The very same lip that I had just sucked lime juice from. "Yeah, I'll be at the bar if you need anything." Then he turned and retreated back to safety, leaving us with his dim-witted cousin.

Plopping down in the chair that Blaine abandoned, Craig smiled brightly at us as if he were next in line. I rolled my eyes at him and looked to Angel who was wearing a devilish grin. I was beginning to think those were the only kinds of smiles she possessed.

"So, it's CJ, right? Hi, I'm Angel Cassidy," she announced with an air of arrogance that only Angel could pull off gracefully. She extended her hand to him and he received it eagerly.

"Yeah. Well, the name is Craig, but people been callin' me CJ since I was a kid. Real good to meet ya, Angel. Real good. The name certainly fits."

Angel held up her hands in warning before CJ could go any further. "Ugh, do not ask me if it hurt when I fell from heaven, or if I have wings, or any other dumb ass pick-up lines."

Tuning them out as they made small talk, I looked towards the bar, instantly locking eyes with Blaine who was staring intently. Several seconds ticked by before either of us could do anything but breathe. Finally, a bar patron grabbed his attention and stole his gaze from me. I was thankful and highly irritated, all wrapped into one.

"So CJ, what's your cousin's deal? Is he seeing anyone?" Angel asked, provoking me to whirl around and narrow my eyes at her.

Craig looked back towards the bar where Blaine was still helping a customer. "Who, B? Nah. He doesn't have a girl. Not anymore. Why?"

"Oh, no reason," Angel replied, darting her eyes to me. She was up to no good, which was usually the case. Before she could inquire if Blaine was a boxer or briefs guy, the older, bearded guy that served me earlier poked his head from behind a door a few yards away and summoned Craig to the back.

"I think it's time to go," I said, forcing myself not to look towards the bar.

"What? I haven't had nearly enough to drink!" And with that, Angel waved directly towards the area I was trying to avoid.

Seconds later, Blaine was in front of us, his tattooed hands grasping the edge of the table. His presence brought it all back to me...his scent, his taste, the way his body was a work of art that I wanted to paint with my tongue. All the reasons why I most definitely should not speak to him again.

"Hey Blaine, can we get a couple more? And don't forget to grab a shot for you too," Angel winked.

"He can have mine," I mumbled, refusing to look at him.

I felt a lone finger brush against my forehead, pushing a lock of hair behind my ear. Then it traced the curve of my earlobe, making me shiver. His touch resumed the pesky pounding in my chest.

"Are you sure, Kami?" he asked with a husky voice. The same voice he used with me before as he described my eyes, my hair, my lips…and what should be done to them.

Unable to string a sentence together, I simply nodded. Blaine made no move to leave. He kept touching me, like feeling my skin was the most natural thing in the world to him. Slowly, he leaned down to me, coming in so close that his scent of mint and spice filled my nostrils. We were almost eye-level, and I couldn't do more than hold my breath with anticipation. I should have been scared by his touch. I should have stopped him before he moved any closer into my personal space. But I just…couldn't.

"Hey, you don't have to pretend anymore," he said just above a whisper.

"Pretend?" I exhaled, the word coming out in a rush. What does he know of my pretending? There's no way I could be that transparent. I'd had years of practice.

"Yeah," he grinned crookedly. "CJ's gone. You can stop pretending…that you girls are together. That you're gay."

"Excuse me?" Angel piped up, her voice laced with annoyance. "What makes you think that we're pretending to be gay?"

Blaine's eyes darted to Angel for a split second, and he shook his head lightly. "Not you." Then his chocolate brown gaze was back on me, sweeping over every inch of my face. It was like he was studying every feature, trying to unveil some big mystery. "Her. She's pretending."

"How do you know I'm not a lesbian too?" I asked. The question was meant to come out with a trace of attitude, but it ended up being breathy and light.

As if the sound of my betraying voice amused him, Blaine flashed that boyish grin. My tenacity was going…going….gone.

"Because I'm pretty sure you're feeling the same thing I'm feeling right now."

Then he did something that had me yanking my purse open, throwing down a twenty, and high-tailing it out of there in 3.5 seconds.

He took off his worn cap and ran a hand through his hair, the light brown locks settling into perfectly messy "just-fucked" hair. Hair I wanted to grab and tug while his tongue slid against mine. Hair that I wanted to feel tickling my sensitive areas while he worked me over with that metal-studded tongue.

I was in my car and flying out of the parking lot before Angel even made it outside.

24497438R00239

Made in the USA
Lexington, KY
20 July 2013